PERFECTLY Wild

LEESA BOW

Copyright © 2022 by Leesa Bow

All rights reserved.

This book is a work of fiction. Any references to real events, real people, and real places are used fictitiously. Other names, characters, places, and incidents are products of the author's imagination, and any resemblance to persons, living or dead, actual events, organizations, or places is entirely coincidental. The use of psychedelic drugs is illegal in many countries. The author does not advocate the use of these substances. It is mentioned for fictional purposes only.

All rights are reserved. This book is intended for the purchaser of this e-book ONLY. No part of this book may be reproduced or transmitted in any form or by any means, graphic, electronic, or mechanical, including photocopying, recording, taping, or by any information storage retrieval system, without the express written permission of the author, except for the use of brief quotations in a book review. All songs, song titles, and lyrics contained in this book are the property of the respective songwriters and copyright holders.

ISBN: 978-0-6456871-2-5

Editing by <u>Swish Design & Editing</u>
Proofing by <u>Swish Design & Editing</u>
Cover design by Letitia at <u>RBA Designs</u>
Cover Image Copyright 2022

Please join my <u>mailing list</u> to be notified of Leesa's latest releases.

You can learn more about me on my <u>website</u>.

If you're on Facebook, I haver a reader group where I chat about books, offer giveaways, and sneak peeks of upcoming books.

You can join here.

To Vickie,
An adventurer and inspiration for my characters.
Thank you for sharing your travelling stories, and for your love and
strength as a sister by my side.
A sister and a best friend.

PROLOGUE
EDEN

The energy of waves flows through the ocean from one side of the globe to the other.

Wind whips over the surface, carrying droplets in the icy atmosphere. The blustery force encircles my body with the power of a tsunami crushing ribs and forbidding air to my lungs. A usual winter's day, only it's exacerbated after Samuel bursts through the office door.

The door slams closed.

I suck air into my lungs, needing a moment before taking the stairs to my parents' penthouse.

Samuel tightens his hold on my hand. "Hey, are you okay?"

I stare deeply into those blue eyes for the first time now we're alone. The hues of his eyes remind me of the sea in summer, unlike the stormy, gray Southern Indian Ocean mere feet from the back door. There are many questions loaded on my tongue, only I need to focus on breathing, and all I want to do is feel *him*.

"Not really," I murmur. "You're so calm, and I feel electrified from the shock." I shake my head still in disbelief.

"I'm not calm, Eden," he says gently. "My heart is racing, and I'm trembling internally not knowing how this would go down."

He tilts his head, and for a second, I see sadness in his eyes. Just as quick, his expression changes, distracted by Rose touching his shaven head. His face lights up, and he kisses Rose's cheek, then leans in, and his lips crush mine. I touch him, taste him, and inhale his forest scent. He may have escaped the jungle, yet the aroma surrounds him as though ingrained into his skin.

Our lips part, he leans his forehead to mine, his eyes close, and I sense this is painful as is the overwhelming joy of us being together after what has passed.

"Let's get upstairs," I whisper. "I need to feel you."

He spins, not letting go of my hand. Each step feels like twenty when all I want to do is fall into his arms and never let him go. I let go of his hand to unlock the door and shove it open, the impatience building. I make a beeline for the couch before my shaky legs give way. Samuel balances Rose on his hip and slides next to me, kissing my neck and cheek. Tiny kisses and then his mouth is on mine, reminding me how much I have missed him.

Rose slaps our cheeks as though it's a game, and I laugh, breaking the kiss.

As much as he wants me, he's not letting go of his daughter. She stands on his thighs, and he balances her with the other arm that's not curled around my shoulders.

"Dad-da needs to kiss Mommy," he coos at her.

Resting my forehead on his shoulder, I can't hold it in any longer.

I burst into tears.

Tears of happiness.

Tears of relief.

My stomach clenches.

The happiness I have longed for hurts, an ache deep in my chest. A surge of emotions streams through me. "Why didn't you tell me you were coming?" I croak. "At least I could have prepared to not be a mess."

"I'm sorry." He pulls me closer and kisses my forehead. "But I'd still be a mess."

I reach for his shaky hand draped over my shoulder. His body trembles against mine. Silent tears stream down his cheeks. He rests his forehead against mine while we take a moment to simply breathe and allow our bodies to calm some.

Mum walks into the room and finger-combs her windswept hair. "Here, let me take Rose."

"I don't want to let her go," Samuel rasps.

"You both need time together," Mum insists. "Get some rest. Rose isn't going anywhere."

I squeeze his thigh, the boniness prominent beneath the material of his trousers. His face is gaunt. The reality of him fighting to survive the past eight months hits me with the force of a wrecking ball.

"I think that's a good idea." My thoughts scramble. A long road of healing—physically and mentally—lie ahead of us. I stand and hold out my hands for Rose and kiss her cheek before giving her to Mum. "Thanks. We appreciate it."

I lead Samuel to my room and pull him onto the bed with me. For a few seconds, we simply stare. For me, I'm still somewhat in disbelief.

"So, this is where you spent your nights," he whispers. Rolling onto his back, Samuel looks around the room and then stares at the ceiling. "Every night I tried to imagine you sleeping. What you saw from your bed. Your room. You…" He kisses me again, and his hands roam, lightly scratching my skin.

"My room is basic. I'm not one for clutter." I follow his gaze to an oil painting on my wall—a palm tree and the ocean. A snapshot of serenity. On my bedside table is a framed photograph of us taken while we were in Brazil.

Taking his hand between mine, I study his fingers. Scaly skin peels around his nails. Every nail is short and cracked. His palm has a callous beneath every joint.

"How long were you home before coming here?" I whisper.

His gaze darts over my face then his lip quivers, and his demeanor cracks. His body shakes, and as much as I want to hold him, heal him, he's scaring me. "Hey, you're here, and we're all safe and together," I say gently. He's never cried like this. Not even when I was in the hospital, those were tears of a man stricken with worry. Before me is a broken man, and I can't let go of the feeling *I did this to him*.

I cry with him. Our bodies are entangled together. The physical bond is not enough to stop the pain of our broken hearts.

He needs time to heal.

Inesa's tragedy broke Samuel. He abandoned society, hid in the jungle, and denied himself love. His mission was to be a better man by helping others, a physician working for free. His promise to prove he's a good man. That promise transformed into a commitment to the people he called family.

His loyalty is second to none.

He vowed to come home to me.

It almost killed him.

I make a silent promise to help him pick up the pieces and show him he's worthy.

Prove my love for him is everything he'll ever need.

For right now, I feel unworthy of this man's love.

1

EDEN

Two weeks later…

Happiness.

Many define it as the emotion of feeling extreme joy.

I'm now wiser in understanding I had to go through a period of complete sadness to experience the bliss, and I'm now riding the happiness wave every single day. From the moment I open my eyes, I feel only contentment waking up beside Samuel.

For months, I worried he might not come out of the jungle alive. If he survived the arduous trek through the jungle, finding seclusion for the Ularans' safety came with a cost—the impossibility of finding his way out.

It's been two weeks since he surprised me and burst through the office door, returning to me. A week where I cried, overwhelmed with many emotions. We've made love every single day, hugged each other, and sobbed or sat in silence simply to be together.

He's still not ready to talk, only mentioning how the journey took every fiber of his being to find his way out.

Instead, he asked for time.

Time to heal.

Time to forget.

The thought of him traumatized by a dark memory fills me with terror—a silent scream slicing through my brain. The pain is an unforgotten memory of how I suffered when he was unconscious and almost lost to an unexplainable entity. In the dark of night, my anxiety heightens, reminding me of what I could lose.

For now, he's content to be with Rose and me, and already his spirit has been lifted by being reunited as a family.

To help him focus on each day and not the past, I undertook a personal role as his tour host and showed Samuel around Adelaide. I was so relieved to see him smile and enjoy the coastal city I call my home, even if it's significantly colder than what he's used to.

The cracks are there.

Even in the way he holds Rose or takes her hand while she sleeps. His love for her warms my heart, yet something isn't right, and it shows in his eyes. Beyond love is a flicker of uncertainty and fear. Here, he's not the powerful man I knew in Ulara. Considering the trauma he has suffered, he needs to heal, and Rose and I may not be enough.

It's why *I need* to see his smile and hear his laughter. Even now, while lying on his side on the beige carpet of the living room helping Rose build a tower with her blocks, the joy on his face is comforting. After taking him on a winery tour and a weekend away to a secluded beach house, it turns out he's happiest here, playing with Rose. By focusing on activities so he'd fall in love with my city as much as me, I didn't consider the toll on Samuel's body during those initial weeks at home. He's still awfully thin, and given he has not consumed alcohol for years, the two glasses of wine made him sick and drunk.

It was my first fail.

The second was buying clothes too big. He told me not to take them back as he'd fit into a medium size soon.

Soon.

Time to Samuel differs to the rest of us.

For years, he lived by morning time, noon time, night time, and moon phases. Not by the clock or calendar days of the year.

For the past two weeks, he has managed small healthy meals mainly of fruits and raw vegetables with some fish for protein. If he overeats, he vomits.

He refuses medical help and says he'll be fine in a matter of time.

It's hard to argue with a doctor.

When he first arrived, exhausted and gaunt, I went through a checklist, including private health and insurance options. In the few weeks he stayed in Los Angeles, his parents arranged the initial medical assessments and then helped him set up a financial plan to come to us. Even though I have not met his father, I understand good deeds come at a price, and Samuel has promised him to do the *right thing*. Working and supporting us doesn't sound like a bad deal, only I know it holds more than meets the eye.

Rose knocks the blocks, the castle tumbles, and the pieces scatter across the carpet. She bursts into laughter, and I can't help but chuckle at the sound.

Samuel notices me. His eyes flick over my face and then travel down to where I'm wearing an olive-green jumpsuit. "You look lovely. Are you going somewhere?"

"Lunch, I hoped. It's the last weekend of freedom,"

I emphasize the last word as my holiday is over. "My friends are hanging out to see you again, and Faith is coming over tomorrow. So, I was thinking lunch today, just you and me."

My phone buzzes, and seeing my sister's name, I read the message.

<blockquote>Can we come over today and meet Samuel? We're all out of quarantine, and I can't wait another day.</blockquote>

"Faith wants to come over today."

Samuel looks up from where he's playing with Rose. "I'm looking forward to meeting her." He smiles at me. "And since you're dressed, I could take you out to dinner tonight?" He glances at Mum. "If you don't mind watching Rose for us, Grace?"

"Of course, it's fine. Knowing you two are moving out upsets me that I won't see our angel all the time."

"You can see her whenever you want, Mum." I kneel beside Samuel. "Ready for the thousand and one questions?" His gaze meets mine. I sense his nervousness and pat his back. "I got you, and I'm only telling you this because I know Faith, and it's her thing. She drags information out of you like a suction tube."

His eyes round as though he's pondering the situation. "Fine. I better shower and prepare myself for the onslaught." His gaze meets mine in warning. "I'm not ready for hard questions, Eden. You know that. I'm happy to discuss minor things, especially about your aunt." He then pushes up and heads to the bathroom.

I send a reply as I stride into the kitchen.

<blockquote>Samuel is looking forward to meeting you too!</blockquote>

"What do you want me to get for lunch?"

"All good, honey. I have a lasagna in the freezer."

"How about salads? I can pop out and grab some fresh stuff?" Lasagna is Faith's favorite meal. Samuel will struggle.

Mum gives me one of her trademark frowns. "I have it covered, Eden."

"Thank you." I don't have the same confidence in my sister, so I send her another text.

Eden: *Please go easy on Samuel today. He's not ready to discuss his journey with anyone.*

Faith and I have different ideas about the meaning of easy.

An hour later, Faith and her boys burst through the door. The boys call "Nanna" with excited screams. "Eden," Seb yells as soon as the front door closes. His tiny feet pound the floor, sounding more like an elephant as he sprints toward me. "I got pox," he says excitedly.

We break into laughter.

Seb sprints to the kitchen and leaps into Mum's arms to kiss her. "Nanna, I got pox."

"I know, darling," she says with an empathetic expression. "Mummy told us all about it." He wiggles to get down. Sometimes I wish I possessed the energy of Faith's boys. James crawls after Seb. He uses the cupboards to rise to wobbly feet, peers up at Mum, and touches his chest. "You too, darling," she says and lifts him to plant a loud kiss on his cheek. "Are you better now?" James lifts his top to show Mum the few spots on his belly.

Rose turns on hearing her cousins' voices, and she babbles, not to be left out. I love she recognizes them.

Faith drops her bags inside the door and hangs her coat on the wall hook before pulling me into a tight hug. "Where is he?" she asks and steps back to peruse the room.

"In the bathroom."

"That jumpsuit is gorgeous on you. Are you heading out?" She pushes unruly strands of hair out of her eyes. Only now do I notice the dark rings around Faith's eyes.

"Thank you. We were heading out to lunch. It's now a dinner date." I wink.

"God, I'm sorry. I've been dying to meet him and can't believe I've had to wait because of isolation. Some blisters have scabbed. James didn't have many spots. Seb's stomach was covered in them. There's even one on his penis, and it was a challenge to stop him from scratching. He wouldn't stop crying," she moans.

The way Faith is rambling, it's evident the isolation has affected her. "I can remember having chicken pox as a kid. It's horrid."

Samuel walks into the room, looking as handsome as ever wearing denim jeans and a blue T-shirt. The sky-blue shirt highlights his eyes, larger and more beautiful with his buzz cut. It's all I see as those eyes tell a story. Right now, he's deep in thought. "Did you try the oatmeal and chamomile baths?"

Faith's face lights up. I understand because although he's handsome in pictures, his presence demands attention in the room in a good way, as he'll enlighten us with knowledge while being mesmerized by his good looks. "I did, and thanks for the tip because it eased the scratching in his sleep."

"Did you apply coconut oil and a drop of lavender

and tea tree oil?" She nods, staring at him. Faith is lost for words. "If you have an aloe vera plant, you should continue rubbing it on their skin." He beams his beautiful smile, and his big, blue eyes hold her captive. "It's nice to finally meet you, Faith."

"Oh, the pleasure's all mine," she says, shaking his hand and reaching in for a hug. "I've waited years to meet you, and I have to say my sister didn't exaggerate your good looks." He pats three gentle taps on her back before breaking apart.

"You're taller than I imagined."

"I'll take it as a compliment." He grins at Faith, and I now assume he spent time in the shower mentally preparing himself.

"Shall we?" I tilt my head toward the kitchen where Seb is running in circles around the dining table in a game of chase with himself.

"Enough," Faith demands. "Find a chair and sit on it or get a toy and play quietly in the lounge room."

Rose screams with no attention on her and crawls after us. Faith scoops her up before her son crashes into her. "And no toys with small parts. Only Duplo blocks or your cars, okay?" She turns to Samuel. "One day I'd like some quiet time with you because I'm not the crazy woman I am now."

Seb stops running and notices Samuel. "Eden, I got pox," he says as he leans into my thigh, staring at Samuel.

"Are you better now?" I lift him into my arms and rub his little back.

He exaggerates a nod. "Mummy said you have a boyfriend." He's still eyeing Samuel curiously.

Samuel's brow pulls together as he mouths, *boyfriend*.

A giggle erupts from me.

"Thanks for throwing me under the bus." Faith huffs. She rounds the table and takes James from me. She lowers him to the floor to stand. He immediately plops onto his bottom before crawling back to the chair, pulling himself up.

"Ugh, I swear this kid hates walking. At this rate, Rose is going to be running around before him."

"Give him time," Mum cuts in. "Your father walked late. At eighteen months, actually."

When Mum tells us things about Dad's childhood, I often wonder if it's because Gran wasn't there to help Pop raise him."

"At thirteen months, he could be walking. He chooses not to and would rather crawl." She blows dark strands of hair from her eyes and then adjusts her long ponytail off her shoulders.

I place the salad and serving utensils in the middle of the table.

"Is there anything I can do to help?" Samuel asks in his polite American accent.

Faith beams the biggest smile. "I love your accent." She turns to me and winks, then takes a seat beside Samuel. She coughs to clear her voice. "I'm sorry for your loss."

He eyes me momentarily before turning to Faith. "I appreciate your kindness."

I warned him.

"Take a seat." Mum slips on her oven gloves. "The lasagna is ready." James crawls up onto Faith's lap, and I place Rose in the highchair beside me. Seb slides onto a chair between Mum and Samuel.

The aroma of Italian herbs and the strong lasagna sauce fill the room. Out of the corner of my eye, I notice how Samuel's hand casually covers his mouth and nose until he adjusts to the strong scent. I'm not sure what does or doesn't make him nauseous, and currently, everything is a trial.

"Eden told us how much you loved the jungle. To be honest, when you were trekking toward Colombia and the notion of you being close to the Brazilian border, well, I was freaking out with her. You had us worried for months." She places her hand on his shoulder. "We're glad you're back here with Eden and Rose, yet understand how hard it must have been to leave the people you love. And when she told us about the shaman…" She shakes her head. "I'm so sorry. It must have been traumatic for all of you."

Samuel lowers his gaze to his hands. "Yes, it was extremely sad."

She waits a while, only he doesn't say another word.

"Please pass the salad," Mum says to Faith.

Faith scoops out some for herself and then passes the bowl to Samuel.

"Eden falling in love with you has been a blessing. She has never been happier, and you have also given us the gift of an aunty we never knew. So, thank you."

My sister could seriously speak underwater.

Mum points her knife at the lasagna. "Faith, could you please serve since you're closest." One by one, we pass Faith our plates. She holds her hand out for Samuel's plate.

He waves a hand. "I'm fine with salad, thank you."

Faith looks at me, then at Mum, and I know she's bursting with more questions, especially because she hugged him and would've felt his skeletal frame.

"Faith, please eat," Mum says casually without giving her a second glance.

2

EDEN

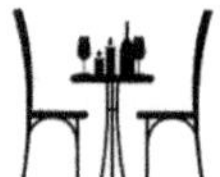

Later that night, I read the menu out loud.

I stop speaking when Samuel looks around the restaurant. His brow has a slight dent.

Something concerns him so I reach out and take his hand. "Relax, babe."

His beautiful eyes meet mine.

"What is it?"

He shakes his head. "Nothing. I'm merely assessing the situation."

"We don't have a situation. Tonight is our alone time to simply be together and enjoy a meal." I squeeze his hand, and when he squeezes mine back, it offers hope he'll lower his guard.

"Technically, we're not alone. There's always potential for a situation, especially in a crowded space with people moving about." His gaze roams over the crowd. "It's ingrained into me to assess."

He's not talking as a doctor. It's about his time in Ulara and being mindful of transmitting disease when they have no immunity to certain diseases. Except he doesn't have to be concerned for the Ularan community in this Italian restaurant.

I watch him for a while before I speak again, "What are you not telling me?" I whisper.

His eyes meet mine, and we hold each other's gaze for a few seconds. His brow softens. It's something I've noticed since he's returned like he's composing what he's going to say before he speaks to me.

"I haven't told you many things. I will, in time. It's taking a bit to adapt to the people and the noise." He picks up the menu and reads it for several seconds before placing it aside.

"Have you decided already?"

"There are few salads to choose from." He smiles at me. "What's your favorite dish?"

It didn't click before, probably because I focused on showing him the best places around the city. Samuel is concerned for his own immunity, and it's why he evaluates every place we visit.

"Well, I'm also full, so I'm happy to go with a salad." I place the menu aside and try to snag the server's attention to order our food.

I thought a date night would be fun, but now I know I need to stop pushing him into doing normal couple things. He's not ready even though he agrees to do whatever I suggest.

It's taken me until tonight to see through him, and a wave of disappointment hits me that I didn't see it before.

He'll say yes to everything I ask to make *me* happy, even at a cost to him.

And now his charade is over.

🌴

The following afternoon, Samuel and I make our way from the front of our apartment to the green grass of the esplanade. There's barely a cloud in the sky.

I collapse onto the lawn, laying my forearm over my eyes to block the sun's glare. Samuel lowers to sit beside me, legs bent to his chest and arms wrapped around his knees. He still moves in stealth mode and if I weren't peeking, I wouldn't know he was there.

"I'm exhausted," I whine.

"Last night too much for you, princess?"

I take his arm and slightly pull until his face is close to mine. "Making love to you is never too much."

His lips find mine, and in seconds, his kiss turns passionate yet still gentle. He licks over the contour of my lips. "You're sweet and addictive." He stretches out alongside me and kisses me again. "*I can never get enough of you,*" he whispers against my mouth.

Caught in the moment of a deep kiss, children laughing in the distance remind us we're not alone. Other couples and families enjoy the early spring weather and take in the beach view.

I push up onto my elbows. The blue-green ocean meets a baby-blue sky. The scent of salt fills the air, and I catch a hint of lavender wafting from a nearby garden. We remain silent, taking in the scenery or closing our eyes and simply being.

His words play over in my head.

I can never get enough of you.

"Samuel," I whisper and wait to get his attention. "I've never felt the relief and happiness I did when you waltzed through the door holding Rose. The journey out of the jungle," I shake my head. "I won't pretend to understand how hard it was or the suffering to help the Ularans and then to find your way out to be with us." I let out a long sigh. "I get you need time to process everything. And I'm sorry if I'm pushing you to show you my favorite places to visit, only I'm scared you're going to change your mind. So if I show you the best places—" I stall.

"I appreciate what you're doing, Eden. Admittedly, I did the same in Ulara by wanting you to fall in love with the place I loved and called home. I wanted you to stay and tried to convince you it was paradise before realizing my selfishness and the danger I placed you in when you weren't equipped to survive in the jungle."

"Yet I did."

He smiles. Samuel lies back, his elbows supporting his weight. "Yes, you did. I knew you couldn't stay. It was for a short time. I could protect and teach you, yet I'd never ask you to live out your life in the jungle like I'd chosen."

I knew you couldn't stay, I replay his words and brace myself for what he's about to say.

His eyes rise to meet mine. "There's much to tell you —" His voice cuts out, and he coughs to clear his throat. "All I can do is focus on each day as it comes. When good days become good weeks, we can talk about the future." He takes a piece of hair and tucks it into my ponytail. "Be assured I can never leave you as I can't suffer like that again." He kisses my forehead. "My heart is bound to yours, and I'm only whole when I'm with you. So, you don't need to impress me with your pretty city. I'll go wherever if I'm with you. One day at a time."

Glancing down at our linked fingers, I squeeze his hand.

"We're a little closer to nature by the beach, and it does something to my heartbeat and blood pressure, and everything around us slows." He takes me in his arms, and I place my head on his chest. Closing my eyes, I concentrate on his heartbeat. It's a steady rhythm, yet I understand he's not at peace even though he has found Rose and me.

3

EDEN

Waves roll in over the white sand, the sound hypnotic. At dawn, the ocean is a dark gray, and for a few minutes, the stillness of life surrounds us—a calm presence until the seagulls squawk, alerted to the break of light.

"I enjoy this time of the morning," I say to Samuel as we meander along the esplanade. Rose woke early to feed, so she came with us in the stroller, enjoying the first minutes of a new day. Samuel is at peace here though I'd rather stay in bed and cuddle up close to him. Only today is my first day back at work.

"What's on your agenda today?" Samuel steers the stroller, ready to cross the road to home. We wait for several dedicated cyclists to pass before stepping onto the narrow street.

"I'm following up on the construction dates for a pool on the northern garden bed. We have a garden storage structure that must be removed first."

"A pool, yet you have an amazing body of water a mere fifty feet from your door." He gives me a sideways glance as we step onto the path.

"Not all our guests like the ocean," I remind him. "And the pool will be heated so visitors can swim in the colder months as well. The sea is damn freezing in winter with the wind blowing up from Antarctica."

He grins at me and tilts his head toward the ocean. "Yet swimmers are braving it now."

I chuckle. "The Icebergs. They're a dedicated group. Only the thought of drying off in the icy wind isn't for me."

He grins at me. "The Icebergs. Does everything have a nickname in Australia?"

"Almost." My phone beeps with a message.

"Are you on the clock already?"

"Not yet." It's a message from Dana. "I'm following up on something since Dana has resigned." I let out a sigh. "She has been part of our business and family since I was a teenager, and I can't believe she's leaving."

"Has something happened for her to want to leave?" He sits on one of the outdoor cane chairs and signals for me to sit beside him.

"Her husband has a new position in Queensland. They have always wanted to retire up north, so they're setting themselves up for a few years before they do."

He nods slowly. "Is your father replacing her?"

"Eventually. I'll take over her work until he creates a new role."

His eyes meet mine. "Is this what you want? In Ulara, you spoke about returning to university to study nursing."

"Circumstances have changed, Samuel. I now have Rose to consider."

"*We* have Rose to consider," he emphasizes. "I'm not questioning your decision. I only want you to be happy."

Me to be happy. What about him?

"I'll care for Rose while you work the extra hours until your father finds a new employee." He drops an arm over my shoulder. "Although, anytime now, the paperwork will be approved for me to work."

Samuel sat for an exam the first week he arrived in Adelaide and passed. My man has a photographic memory, not forgetting his former training.

"Until then, I'm free." He kisses the side of my head, his lips lingering longer than a normal kiss.

I want to ask him if this makes *him* happy, except I can't because I know it doesn't, and it scares me, especially since he must begin his specialist training from scratch. He's here for us, and in this society, we all need to work.

Later in the morning, I get off the phone from the construction company and toss it across my desk. "Why do we have to jump through hoops to get something done?" I moan into my hands. "Seriously." I stand and meet Dana's gaze.

She stops tapping on her keyboard. "Anything I can help with?"

I shake my head and glance at Ethan, who's typing away, unaffected by my outburst. With pods in his ears, I assume the music is cranked.

"Yes. Do you want to get coffee?"

"Thought you'd never ask." Dana stands and signs out of her computer. She picks up her handbag and wraps her signature hot pink silk scarf around her neck. It's bright like Dana, and I need people like her in my life.

We move past Ethan's desk.

He glances up, taking out one pod from his ear. "Everything okay?"

"We'll be back in five," Dana says quickly before I invite him.

He's barely talked to me since Samuel burst into the office a few weeks ago. Today, I need time to chat with Dana.

When we're out on the footpath, the salt-infused air hits us, and I inhale a deep breath and let out a sigh.

"Is it that bad?" she asks.

"It'll work out. The resort pool would never be smooth sailing past all the fine print." I shrug.

"Not what I meant." She bumps my elbow. "You don't want to be here. I can see it. You're only staying to please your father, and it's… easy. Not easy work. It's what you know, so it's comfortable."

Dana has always understood me.

We turn the next corner and head straight to the café.

Deanne greets us with a wide grin. "Morning, ladies. A table for two?"

"Yes, please. How are you, Dee?"

"Awesome," she sings and leads us to my favorite table by a window. "I hear your man is back."

"He is." The mere mention of Samuel's name radiates heat through my chest. I take a seat. "I want to introduce you, and perhaps you could talk to him about your time in Brazil."

She pauses. "Be happy to, since it's one of the best times of my life."

We order coffee, and moments later, Dana stares out the window as though she's deep in thought.

"I'm going to miss you," I whisper.

Her gaze falls to the table as if she's aligned her

thoughts before she looks up. She fiddles with her short ponytail before her brown eyes meet mine. She swipes at the tears, leaving a smear of mascara beneath her lashes.

"Not going to lie, it's gonna be tough. I've been part of your family for as long as I can remember."

"I know." My mouth dries thinking about the time when Dana leaves us.

She picks up a glass of water from the table and guzzles a few mouthfuls. Then she lets out a long audible sigh. "For years, we've dreamed of retiring somewhere warmer. Escape these damn winters." She laughs once as if the idea is silly. She wipes her nose, then picks up the glass of water and drinks more. "When Kerry requested an interstate transfer, it excited us about the next phase of our lives. The grass is always greener on the other side, right?"

I sense regret, yet say nothing.

"You. Well, you were making plans to leave. You have this new incredible life." She frowns. "Please remember those plans because it's a whole other can of worms I want to discuss with you."

"O-kay."

"Ethan—" she shakes her head. "I'm not sure what he's up to. But I won't stick around while he walks all over me when he's only been at Monte for seventeen months. The Montefords are *my* family."

I reach across and squeeze her hand. "You are family. I've always considered you to be more, so I was surprised when…" My throat tightens on the last word, and I also need to take a few sips of water. "You've always been there through the good times and the bad," I croak.

Dana makes a strangled noise. "The bad times." She

shakes her head. "The absolute worst time wasn't business related, and my heart ripped open for you like you were my own daughter. I remember everything he did to you. And yet you have easily forgiven him."

I swipe tears before they fall. "Forgiven but not forgotten." I hold her gaze. "There's a difference, and it was easier to do after I found happiness. It cleared my head, and I realized…" I remember my time in Ulara, especially my first holiday, when I discovered more about myself in a couple of months than in the past ten years. "It took more energy to resent him." I glance down. "Trust." I meet her eyes. "I have a new team, and you're my main gal."

She smiles and shakes her head, and I laugh once through my tears. "Where's the damn coffee?"

"No matter what, you're only a phone call away," I murmur.

"And a short flight," she adds. "So please come and visit me in Brisbane."

"I promise I will."

When I leave the office to find Samuel sitting on a deck chair with Rose asleep in his arms. He's wearing his jeans and a black tee, and to me, he looks as hot as he did in Ulara half-naked.

"Hey, you." I lean over and kiss him, one that lingers. His tongue finds mine, and I groan when he deepens the kiss.

He chuckles lightly. "How was your day?"

"Better now I'm with you," I gush.

"Are you ready to resign yet?" he murmurs.

"What?" I straighten.

With his free hand, he runs it over the snug material of my skirt along the contour of my hip. "Let's take a walk." He pushes up with Rose in his arms.

"Here, let me." I take Rose and kiss her cheek. "How long has she been asleep because we'll never get her to sleep tonight?"

He runs a gentle hand over her fair hair. "Only ten minutes. After half an hour, I'll wake her. It's why I want a quick chat while we can."

Samuel places a hand on my lower back as we head toward the beach. The sun is low on the horizon. Twilight on the foreshore is nature's gift to enjoy. I have Samuel and my time in the rainforest to thank for my gratitude, including the strength to weather the storms.

"How was your day?" he murmurs.

"You already asked me."

"And you didn't answer. I have approximately half an hour to make it better."

"You already did," I say. "Just by being here fixes everything."

We take a seat on a boulder by the sand. "I'd like to believe it, only I don't have the power to wield happiness."

"No." I stare down at Rose. "You both do."

"Eden, as reassuring your words are to me, we should discuss our future."

I assume it's the promise he made to his father and how being a workaholic is his foreseeable future. It's what his father believes taking care of us and his responsibility entails.

"I bought a house. It's nearby. You could walk to work."

"Like a block away? Wait. You bought one without me?"

"I wanted to wait, only it happened so fast. After lunch, I was perusing the real estate app and found this house. It was open for inspection within the hour and before the auction. I thought, why not?"

"You bought a house," I repeat more in surprise, not anger. In fact, I'm delighted he wants to take the next step to stay here with us and build a life in a family home.

"It ticked all the boxes. On the esplanade and with a modern Scandinavian interior design. It reflected your style."

"My style? I didn't know I had a certain style since I haven't designed a place of my own yet."

"When the bidding commenced, something came over me, and I had to have this house for you. For us."

I nod, slowly taking it all in.

"It's only three blocks away on the beach." He points in the house's direction, the opposite way we usually walk.

"I'm familiar with the house." I shake my head. "I can't believe you bought it.

"The cost is not what concerns me. I received a phone call and email to say I can start working in a week."

I shake my head again to find sense in all the news he's sharing with me. "Are you concerned about Rose? Because Mum is happy to mind her until I find a childcare facility."

"Our life together will be nothing like the one we had in Ulara. I'll be on a rotating roster and—"

"Hey, I understand," I murmur, knowing it's inevitable.

"If we're planning for our future, I want you to consider what you want. Do you want to continue working for your father's business?"

I let out a sigh. "Dana mentioned the same thing today."

"I want you to reflect on what it is you want for yourself at this time of your life?"

I shake my head, unsure of what he's asking me. "Do you want me to stop working and care for Rose?"

"Is that what you want?"

I stare out to the golden horizon, searching for answers. The breeze has picked up. Loose strands of hair blow around my face, and I don't brush them away. Instead, I hide my face behind a curtain of hair. "I want to spend more time with my daughter. I also want to focus on something for me. I enjoy working, not every day, as I want time with Rose."

"So don't work. Study part-time," he says to the sunset as though it offers new hope. "You can spend some time studying at home as well. Simply choose something that interests you and you'll enjoy because it's an ideal time to change. Life may only get harder to make a big career change."

"Is it how you feel? Do you believe it's too late for you to change?"

He frowns before meeting my gaze. "The promise I made to my parents before coming here was I'd do the right thing by Rose and you… continue with my medical studies, support you both, and be responsible. This all translates to resuming my residency at a hospital."

"I understood oncology wasn't the right path for you. I recall you saying how finding a cure made you happy. Patients dying and sick children tore your heart out."

He looks to the sand, where the waves crash close to the rocks. His eyes glaze over, deep in thought. I know he misses Ulara, the people, his friends, and his adopted family.

The shaman.

"I assumed you'd continue in medical research. You enjoyed working—" I stop myself from saying more. He puts his hand in mine and squeezes it. I'm thankful he's discussing our future and wish he'd talk about what happened on his journey with the Ularans because until he does, he's not really here with me. Only physically while he silently mourns.

"Honestly, I'm happy to continue working at Monte for a while longer. I have plans and renovations I want to see come to fruition. You should find a new career or work that makes you happy since money isn't a problem." This deal he has made with his father seems to be tied up with a monetary bow. "You're an intelligent man, so study something of interest to you. You're in a new country, a new city, appreciating a different ocean. Tomorrow is a new day. Make it yours."

He turns and kisses me. "I wish it was that easy. I made a promise, and I need to honor it."

Are you bloody kidding me?

We barely finished discussing how he's free to choose his own path.

His parents aren't here.

We're in control of our future.

He thinks my father has a hold over me. Well, his parents are next level. I study his face, only he is wearing his unreadable professional expression.

Twenty months ago, I fell in love with this beautiful,

honorable man. His morals impressed me, and I knew he was someone I could trust. I have faith in us, only we have a long way to go before *he* is happy.

All I can do is keep chipping away at his armor and hope I don't break him in doing so.

4

SAMUEL

On Friday, Samuel waits outside Eden's office. Sitting on a cane chair, he takes in the ocean view. The ocean offers him a sense of peace. He closes his eyes and simply listens to the waves breaking, the gulls squawking, and distant laughter.

A door slams and he snaps out of it when the king of douchebags walks out of the office.

"Ethan." Jaw clenched, Samuel gives a curt nod of his head. He despises Ethan for breaking Eden's heart, yet he should be thankful as it led her directly to him.

Ethan gives Samuel a sideways glance, throws his key ring in the air, and catches it while whistling to himself as he walks over to his sports car.

His gaze lingers momentarily, weighing him up.

If he owns the latest dang BMW, why is he working for Eden's small family business? And why is she driving around in an at least ten-year old beat-up Holden?

Ethan revs the motor, a sound demanding attention.

Samuel looks away and focuses on the ocean.

"Hey." He turns in the direction of the voice to the woman who's his world.

"Evening." He stands and kisses Eden. The loud motor beside them has her pulling away for the attention-seeking douchebag.

"Hey, Edes. We're heading to The Shores for Friday night drinks. After the week we've had, I thought you might want to come along?"

Samuel glares at the asshole. It doesn't have any impact because Ethan only has eyes for Eden.

"Sorry. We have plans. Please say hello for me." She waves and then turns to Samuel. "Where's Rose?"

Glancing over Eden's shoulder, Samuel waits until the black car disappears from his sight.

Ethan's words sink in.

He takes her hand and links his fingers between her delicate ones. "You haven't mentioned having a terrible week."

"It hasn't been all bad," Eden says in her sweet voice. "Especially since I came up with the brilliant idea to get away for the weekend. Just the three of us, then Sunday night the girls have asked to catch up."

"With you."

"No. With us." She smiles. "Where did you say Rose is?"

"With your mother, shopping." For the past six months, his emotions have been in turmoil, and everything he learned in Ulara about shutting down emotions, being a better man, is lost in a matter of months. Even more so with men like Ethan who have no respect. A part of Samuel's past from when he was at college finds its way back into his thoughts, wanting to teach the asshole a lesson. Then Eden kisses him, and the bitterness evaporates. She makes everything better, and he understands Ethan wanting her back in his life because Eden makes us all better men.

Only Ethan blew his chance. Big time.

He may understand the need to want Eden, yet there's no changing Samuel's opinion of the douchebag.

"Only the three of us?" He pulls her into a hug. "Where did you have in mind?"

She smiles as if he doesn't understand her. Her eyes widen playfully. "It's a surprise."

"Now, I'm afraid."

"You should be," she says and laughs.

"Do I need to buy more clothes? I haven't really been shopping—"

"No." She reaches up on her tiptoes to whisper close to his ear, "When Rose is sleeping, we'll be naked."

Samuel's grin broadens. "Now, you should be afraid."

🌴

"We come here every winter to watch the whales," Eden says, standing on the sandy beach in front of their holiday house at Victor Harbor. They have built sandcastles with Rose for the past hour. It may be springtime, but Victor Harbor is south of Adelaide, and the wind is considerably colder.

"The sharks don't bother them?" Samuel asks and wraps his arms over his chest, thankful for the sweater Eden suggested he pack. He feels the cold even more after living in the rainforest for almost a decade. His thoughts wander to the fact he has minimal fat on his frame, but he pushes it out of his mind.

"Does the ocean scare you?"

He wants to say no and be the man Eden knew in Ulara, only his anxiety has attributed to fearing things that normally wouldn't concern him. "Everything in

34

your sea has the potential to kill." He knows as he did extensive research before boarding his flight.

Eden's eyebrows arch above her beautiful eyes. "You find the ocean more of a threat than living in the jungle?"

"Hmm… sharks, bluebottles, blue-ringed octopus, box jellyfish, white stinging sea ferns, flower urchins, stonefish, and let's not forget stingrays. Then if I avoid the ocean for safety sake, I'm met with some of the most poisonous snakes in the world… the redback spider, funnel web spider, crocodiles, cassowaries, which I've recently learned about, and…" he emphasizes, "… a sunburned country with one of the highest rates of skin cancer in the world." He shakes his head. "I must have been delusional to leave the safety of the jungle."

"The jungle is hardly safe, Samuel."

Samuel widens his eyes. "Will you protect me?"

"Please, most of those creatures are on the East Coast or up north. I squish redback spiders all the time, and I never swim deep enough to be shark bait."

"Shark bait," he mumbles. "God, please don't tell me you stomp redback spiders with your bare feet?"

"No. At least they're not hairy like tarantulas, and we don't *eat* them." She cups his cheek with her hand. "You have nothing to fear." She winks at him. "I've got your back."

"I wish it to be true," he murmurs.

She gives him a puzzled look.

How can he be honest with Eden when he's not being truthful with himself?

"Come on, let's go up and shower before dinner. I hope Rose goes to sleep early so you and I can have some fun."

"Fun is why I came to Australia. The country of fun."

Eden chuckles at his response.

They both take Rose's hands and give her a chance to walk aided before he scoops her up in his arms.

"Dad-da." She taps his chin, and he pretends to bite her fingers. Rose giggles, and the sound warms his heart.

"How long have you been searching for poisonous animals on the internet?" she whispers.

"Too long," he mutters. "I was looking for something to amuse myself while you were at work."

"You surprise me, considering how fearless you were in Ulara." Samuel gives her a sideways glance, and her face drops. "Sorry. I know you're not yourself since..."

"I'm orientating myself to the surroundings as I did in the rainforest. And I'll need to treat patients if they're bitten by one of the hundred thousand killer creatures lurking," he adds quickly.

"So, you're being proactive in your research."

"Right."

Eden jumps in front of him before he can respond. "Tonight, I'll remind you why you're here."

🌴

Eden gently closes the door to where Rose sleeps. A quiet click is the only noise he hears. Closing the magazine where he was blindly flipping pages, he moves so Eden can sit beside him on the couch. Only she straddles him, her mouth covers his, and the kiss escalates quickly. "Let's take this to the bedroom," she murmurs against his lips.

He should carry her.

One of the many things he finds himself incapable of performing in his current condition.

His failures disappear from his mind when they're on the bed, clothes stripped, and under the covers. He fists her hair, giving her neck the perfect angle, kissing every inch of her neckline down to her perfect breasts. Sucking and flicking her nipple with his tongue, her moans of pleasure guide him, tracing his fingers along her stomach, lower, and between her legs. She arches her back and whispers his name, a desperate plea from her lips. She takes his shoulders and encourages his lips to meet hers once more. Her hands wrap around his body, running her fingers over a thin frame. Lining himself, he eases inside her, takes both of her hands, and holds them beside her head. Eden's pleasure is all he wants to see without her eyes portraying worrying thoughts as fingertips trace over every rib.

"I love you," she whispers.

Samuel thrusts harder and faster, and Eden cries out, her legs wrapping around his thighs, her heels pressing into his muscles. Every skin cell tingled, every neuron fired, he's lost to her. Every right or wrong decision has led to this moment, to this joy he feels with Eden, all concern evaporating from his thoughts.

The discipline he learned in Ulara is lost to animal instinct, even from the moment he saw her on the beach in Salvador. For months, he ignored the pull she created like the moon's gravitational force on the ocean. With the certainty of the tide rolling onto the shore every day, Eden wasn't going away. She affected his life.

She's his weakness and heart source in one. She terrified and excited him equally. There's no getting the upper hand. Eden rules his heart, and he'd do anything to be with her, the one constant in his life.

She calls out, and he smothers her mouth with his, kissing her as he thrusts until the high of his orgasm blinds him. A shudder rips through him, his muscles burn with pain, and he collapses over her. Easing his grasp on her hands, she pulls away, wrapping her arms tightly around his body.

After a few minutes, his breathing slows. "I love you," he finally responds when the fatigue fades. "More than anything." It sounds lame, only he's unable to focus, and all he wants to feel is her. Like most nights, exhaustion sets in quickly. Like a drain, energy gushes out of him. He positions himself beside her, wraps an arm around her waist, and closes his eyes. He drifts into sleep, aware of her hands moving over his skin as though she's making an invisible map, touching his hips and every rib before coming to rest on his chest over his heart.

Naturally, she's concerned about his weight loss. If it were her, he'd also be worried. He can't afford to be vulnerable. He needs the upper hand, and proving he's fine helps him to believe it to be true.

Masking the truth isn't a lie.

His throat tightens when he cries out.

A strangled noise.

He can't breathe.

Lifting blood-stained hands, he looks around, terrified. What happened? His heart pounds hard against his ribs. "Eden," he yells again, only she's lying on the ground lifeless.

The shaman beside her.

"Nooo," he wails. "Please, no."

"Samuel."

Gentle shaking.

"Samuel," a beautiful voice calls to him. "It's okay, honey."

His chest weighs heavy as though a crate of lead is on top of him, and he can't take a breath.

"You're safe."

His eyes flutter open and search the darkness. His vision adjusts to her silhouette leaning over him.

"It's just a bad dream. You're fine."

He attempts to swallow and moisten his dry throat. "Sorry." He blinks several times. What time is it? "Did I wake you?"

Soft fingers stroke his forehead. "You were having a nightmare."

Samuel closes his eyes to allow his head to clear.

"Do you have them often?" she whispers.

"No." The first here in Australia. Every second night when he was in the jungle—lost—afraid he'd never see her again.

"Here." She takes his hand so it touches a glass. "Have a drink."

His shaky hand takes it. "Thank you." The water cools his throat. "Did I wake Rose?"

"No." She places her hand on his forehead.

"I'm not sick, Eden. I need a moment." He places the glass on the table and slides down the bed. Eden rests her head on his shoulder and wraps an arm around his body, holding him tight.

"I worry about you." She kisses his chest.

Weak and vulnerable. It's not how Samuel wants her to see him. She has enough to worry about, and he doesn't want to be another thing added to her list.

Running his fingers over her soft hair calms him, lying this close more so. "It can happen when you've suffered a shock," he tells her. "It's nothing for you to be concerned about." He kisses the top of her head. "I'll be fine."

In the dark, Samuel stares at the ceiling, afraid to close his eyes again. He senses her awake, not moving or making a sound, simply listening while holding him close. Neither of them speaks, yet his mind is far from quiet.

Closing his eyes, he focuses on the steps to calm his mind and eliminate the thoughts that cripple every part of him—thoughts of how his world has stopped making sense.

🌴

A bright light burns Samuel's eyelids. He remembers watching the sun rise and the gentle warmth shining through the blinds. He intended to get up and attend to Rose. The comfort of daylight must have lulled him into sleep.

A soft melody comes from the other room where Eden is singing. He rolls over to check the time on his cell—half the morning is lost. He leaps out of bed and strides to the kitchen. "I overslept." He runs his fingers over his head.

She chuckles as her eyes wander to his boxers. "Good morning to you, Mr. McMahon."

He glances down at what has her amused.

"Dad-da." Rose holds out her arms for him.

"Give Daddy a moment." Eden grins at him.

After changing into jeans, he walks back into the kitchen. "Have you both eaten?"

"Almost ready for lunch. I didn't wake you, not when you looked so peaceful."

Samuel appreciates the gesture. "I had full intentions of getting up to Rose while you slept."

"I'm fine, Samuel. Please don't worry about me." She wraps her arms around his waist and leans back to look him in the eye. "If you don't want to work as a doctor, then don't. We make our own rules, and the last thing I want is for it to exacerbate anxiety."

"I don't have anxiety," he murmurs.

"Samuel." She lets out a sigh. "Don't pretend with me. I'm here to help you through it. You have experienced some horrific things and lost someone you loved. Grieve. Don't hold it in, and stop trying to be so damn brave."

"Brave is the last thing I feel," he mutters under his breath.

"And stop googling the shit out of this country." She rests her cheek on his chest. "You need time to adjust to a new life with me."

His woman is so wise.

"You're working in the wrong field." He kisses the top of her head and tightens his arms around her back.

"And so are you if you settle for anything less than what your heart wants you to do."

5

EDEN

"You finally made it here, my favorite monkey man." Amy hugs Samuel. It's his first time at The Shores cocktail bar. "You had us worried."

"Monkey man?"

"Tarzan. King of the Apes," she continues. "Lives in the jungle."

Samuel's brow tightens.

"He gets it, Ames." God, she's blonde. I shake my head. *Not helping.*

"We've missed him, that's all." She hugs him again, and by Samuel's expression, he doesn't know how much my friends adore him because they have listened to me for months. They know what it means to have him *home.*

We find a table by the window overlooking the ocean.

"It's good to see you again," Yasmine chimes. "How are you enjoying Adelaide so far?"

He glances at me. "It's a pretty city… only I asked Eden to slow down. She was adamant about showing me every sight in a single week."

My friends chuckle.

"It's not the jungle, but it's nice." Yasmine smiles at Samuel and tucks a dark ringlet behind her ear. "Have you heard from Michael recently?"

Oh shit. They're diving straight into questions.

I signal to the server and ask for a bottle of rosé. "No, not for many months."

He glances at me.

I give a subtle nod to go on.

"I know he was an asshole in Peru…" She turns in her seat so she's facing Samuel. "We've been chatting again. I'm going to meet up with him in a few months."

Samuel's eyes widen. "To do what?"

The server returns and fills our glasses. Samuel refills his glass with water.

"Ayahuasca. You know I've always wanted to try it," she says more to me.

My eyes meet Samuel's, and I signal for him to intervene.

"Then you need to prepare in the long term. For a start…" he inclines his head to her glass of wine, "…can you give up alcohol?"

Yasmine slides her glass toward me. "Done."

Samuel folds his arms over his chest and straightens his back. "If you're serious, I have a diet to follow. You need to adhere to it to give your body a chance to prepare. It's like a detox and promotes the benefits of the tea because you've already cleansed."

"You were going to advise her not to take it," I whisper.

"Yasmine is a strong woman. No matter what we say, her heart desires this. Her spirit calls to her. I can offer the best advice to keep her safe. With or without our approval, she'll do this."

"With Michael," Amy mumbles.

Yasmine's eyes sparkle. "You know he's apologized to me several times. He's back to the same guy I met in Rio."

Samuel's expression remains reserved. "Michael… has a big heart. Occasionally, a selfish side of him surfaces. Unfortunately, poor decisions highlight that side."

"I surprised him when I mentioned you were here. I didn't give him details of what had happened," she says gently. "Only how you reconsidered and decided to give Australia a go."

Samuel stares at Yasmine, and no one speaks for a few seconds, which feels like minutes.

"What did he say?" Samuel's legs move beside mine. I don't want him to feel uncomfortable, especially when we haven't discussed what happened in any detail.

Yasmine removes the scarf from around her neck. She rolls it up and stuffs it in her handbag. "He said he'd like to visit here, but it depends on how *we* get on in Peru."

Amy rolls her eyes.

She still hasn't forgiven Michael. I remember how distraught she was when alone, and Michael took a sick Yasmine into the jungle.

This was supposed to be a fun night of simple conversation, yet tension weighs heavy in the air around us.

The patrons on the opposite table have ordered food, and an herbal aroma wafts toward me.

"Do you want to order?" I ask Samuel. "Some bread?" I change the subject. "Samuel hasn't tried Lombardi's yet."

Samuel smiles at me. "Is your social life all about where to go for the best food?"

"Abso-bloody-lutely," Amy sings.

🌴

Cuddling into his side, Samuel pulls the bedsheet over my shoulder and my eyes flicker closed. An uneasiness surrounds me, but I focus on the positives, the wonder of Samuel being with us until my thoughts slow.

Then a light is bright enough to disturb me so I pry open one eye.

Samuel is awake and reading his phone in the dark.

"Is everything all right?" I murmur.

"It's an email from my parents."

I haven't expressed my frustration to him about how they wouldn't listen to me when he was lost and in danger.

"Are they okay?"

"It's an update on the position Dad secured for me. He knows a professor and is asking about my working visa." He continues to stare at the screen. "They want to come out here for Christmas," he says in a lower tone. "Meet you and Rose. And then tour some."

"That's great. Rose needs to know her grandparents." He says nothing, so I rub his chest in small circles. "I can do an itinerary for Adelaide and the wineries. It will keep them busy for weeks."

Samuel chuckles and places his phone on the table before turning to face me. He strokes my face, pushing strands of hair away from my eyes.

"How desperate are you for money? I mean, is it why he's hurrying your visa?"

A grin creeps along Samuel's lips. Then it drops away. "Eden, don't ever feel afraid about money. Ever. Rose and you will always be looked after."

I push up onto one elbow. "How so?"

Samuel pulls me so I'm lying on top of him. He kisses me hard. "I've told you before that money isn't an issue, and if you want to quit work, you can."

"Then why are you hurrying back to work? Why are you proceeding in a career that makes you miserable?"

Even in the dim light, I make out his furrowed expression. "My father has expectations. My grandfather also possessed expectations, and to continue receiving his inheritance each year, I need to adhere to some rules elaborated in his will."

"What? If you don't, are you cut off?" He remains quiet, and I take it as a yes. "Why haven't we spoken about this before? Anyways, we don't need the extra money. We have what we need, and I want you to be happy. Do anything as long as you're happy."

He kisses my forehead. "Touché."

"I don't need a flashy house or the best car and clothes. I only need you." And all this news of his family and inheritance doesn't make me secure knowing I'm cared for. My stomach churns, understanding there's someone else controlling our decisions and happiness.

Warm fingers stroke my back. "It's not that I don't enjoy my work. It's more where I work."

I open my mouth to say you don't have to work in a hospital and then realize he's talking about society. The city.

My thoughts race.

"Why don't you convert to naturopathy, and we could buy a property in the hills away from everyone, and clients could drive to you? We could have a room out the back and—"

His kiss silences me. "It sounds wonderful. Only I

need to uphold a promise, and I'll continue to work as my father sees fit."

I let out a long sigh.

"This week I need to find a car for us."

"I have a car." I attempt to roll off him, and he stops me, adjusting my legs. His mouth comes within my breathing space. His face hovers, his eyes caress my face, and God, I feel it like fingertips tracing over every contour. His lips skim along my cheek to my mouth. I'm lost to his kiss, his touch, and his passion as Samuel shows me his perfect love.

The following morning, Rose is having breakfast and talking gibberish to Mum while eating her scrambled egg. I have minutes before I dash out the door. Samuel is still asleep. "He had a restless night," I tell Mum. I recall periods of his phone light disturbing me.

"I'll watch Rose until he wakes." She has maintained a distance, allowing us to be a couple while we're all living together.

"Dana has been asking to see Rose, so I'll take her down with me for a while. I'll bring her back in an hour. Samuel should be awake then."

"If not, I'll watch over her." Mum smiles at me. "I miss our special time together."

"Well, you'll get plenty of it when Samuel begins work." I lift Rose from her highchair. "Let's get you cleaned up."

After changing her into a cute lemon-colored dress, we walk down the stairs to the office. The space is quiet. Ethan's head lowers as he reads over something on his desk while Dana focuses on her computer screen.

"Morning," I chime.

"Morning," they both murmur back and then do a doubletake.

"And a fine morning it is." Dana pushes out of her chair and is by my side in a flash, regardless of her tight pencil skirt and pointy two-inch heels. "Come to Aunty Dana." She holds her hands out, and Rose goes to her, all timidness lost. Rose has the sweetest smile, and then she touches Dana's red lips. "Do you like the color red?" she asks against her finger, making Rose giggle. The sound has us all grinning. Dana takes her to her desk and sits Rose on her knee. She gets out her phone and plays something to keep her entertained while she continues to read her screen. It gives me a moment to start up my computer and begin reading the long list of emails. A particular email has my attention. "Construction is starting tomorrow?" I stare at Ethan wide-eyed.

Ethan smiles as though he was waiting for me to see the email. "We'll finish it within a month. Then it's the landscaping, and the pool will be ready at the end of spring."

"Oh wow. Our summer guests are going to be thrilled." Most come to enjoy the beach and swim in the ocean, yet there are always some who dislike the ocean and prefer a pool.

My thoughts race to Samuel and what he said to me. This is the one project I wanted to see through. And it's going to be complete in a matter of months. I spoke to him about the freedom of choosing his own career, and I'm struck with the reality of freedom for myself.

Rose whimpers, and I turn to check on her.

"Oh, honey, Aunty Dana is almost done."

"Let me take her for five," Ethan offers. He stands

and goes to Dana. "I'll hold her until you finish, and Eden can respond to the email." He takes Rose, then turns and smiles at me. "I purposely didn't respond as I assumed you'd like the honors."

"Thank you." I immediately tap out a response on the keyboard, my lips taut with a smile.

I'm vaguely aware of Ethan walking around the office pointing out things to Rose. He says each word to her as though teaching her to talk. *How cute.* I don't have time to dwell as I'm attaching the last of the files to my email when the office door swings open. Samuel is standing there in his board shorts. My eyes wander over his bare tanned chest and broad shoulders. He remains thin, yet every muscle is visible, and when he lifts his arms, his biceps contract. He mesmerizes me until I see his pinched brow and realize what's irritating him.

He strides over to Ethan. "I apologize. My alarm failed this morning."

Ethan looks at me, then back to Samuel. "It's fine, man. Rose is a delight to babysit." He hands Rose to Samuel and watches as he walks away with her.

"Honey, it's fine," I tell him. "I was going to bring her to you soon." I move around the table to walk him to the door. "Are you doing anything today?" His brow pulls tight. I wasn't implying laziness. "I thought maybe I could bring Rose down on my lunch break so Dana could spend time with her."

Samuel dips his head slightly, leans in, and kisses my cheek. "I'll see you then."

I close the door behind him, and the click of the switch is like a finger snap in my brain. He didn't have a good night, and I can only imagine what he's thinking.

6

SAMUEL

Samuel arrives in the city by mid-morning.

After tipping the cab driver, he folds Rose's stroller and secures her straps. He stands on the footpath and takes a deep breath, preparing his mind to be the man he used to be when he negotiated business in LA.

In a mere thirty seconds, the Porsche salesperson is beside him. "Are you looking for any style in particular, sir?"

Samuel stares down at him momentarily before perusing the room. "Sporty, classy, and also family-friendly."

"I see." He holds out a hand. "I'm Gerard, and can definitely help you."

Samuel shakes a hand. "I'm Samuel. If you have what I want, then I'll make it worth your while to process the paperwork quickly as my daughter's patience won't last all day."

Samuel loosens the top button of his white shirt.

"Come this way, sir."

Gerard and Samuel weave around several cars and stop by the glass window beside a sparkling black 911.

"We offer our own child seats to fit." Gerard smirks as though he has won the lotto. Maybe he has as it piques Samuel's interest. "Take it for a drive, and you won't need any more convincing."

"Can you fit a child seat now?"

Gerard's hands go to his hips. "You seem like a man who knows what you want. And I'm the man who can make it happen."

"Stop boasting, Gerard, and show me how good you are."

Gerard scratches his jaw. "So, you want to take it now?"

"Do I appear the type to mess you around?" They eye each other momentarily.

Samuel slips into the driver's seat and wraps his fingers around the sporty steering wheel. He closes his eyes and imagines the smooth sound of the turbo engine and how it easily slips up a gear with his fingers controlling every move. A powerful and intelligent car. He remembers it well when driving his father's car mere weeks ago. He remembers how a small part of him could easily slip back into the past where wealth and power had defined him.

Gerard appears by the open door, standing beside Rose's stroller. She looks up at him and smiles. "My assistant will fit the child seat now."

"Perfect. Lead the way to your office, and we'll settle the paperwork."

Gerard's brow pulls tight. "I understood you wanted to take a test drive?"

"No need. I drove the car a few weeks ago."

Gerard's smile is almost ear to ear. "All right then. Do you have a color preference?"

"Gerard." Samuel steps from the car and stands over

him. "You must have misunderstood. I want you to fit the child seat immediately so we can tick off the paperwork, and I can take my daughter somewhere fun."

"I'm sorry, sir, but this car…"

"… will be mine in a matter of hours. I told you I'd make it worth your time. If it's not done by the time my daughter is bored, then I walk."

7

EDEN

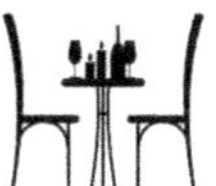

A notification flashes across my screen with a text message from Samuel.

What time are you finishing work?

I glance up. It's already five o'clock.

I booked a table at a Greek restaurant
for 6:30 p.m. Is that okay?

It sounds wonderful.

Although an early night sounds good right now because I could fall asleep sitting upright. I scan through my emails for any late replies. We're ready for tomorrow's demolition of the old buildings and the commencement of new foundations.

"I'll see you in the morning." Ethan tucks his satchel under his arm.

"Yeah, I'm signing off now as well." Everything else can wait for the morning. Dana clocked off an hour ago, and Dad's been in Sydney and Melbourne for the past two weeks on business. He visited my brother, Will, in Melbourne, and seeing Will always cheers Dad up.

After logging off, I follow Ethan out of the office. A horn sounds while I'm locking the door. A black sports car cruises into the soon-to-be-demolished parking lot. I'm about to warn them not to park here overnight. We forewarned guests to park on the street until construction is complete. The expensive car stops beside me, and it's not any car, it's a Porsche. The tinted window slowly lowers.

"Samuel?"

"Jump in, beautiful."

Rose squeals, and I peer in to see her excited face in the car's rear. "Did you buy this?"

I close the door and note his attire. Navy pants and a white button-up shirt. "Cars are significantly more expensive in Australia."

"Is this your idea of a *family* car?"

He steers to where Ethan has parked, quickly reversing the car. "No, this is my car."

My window remains lowered, and I give Ethan a quick wave. His eyes round, and then he gives a curt nod before Samuel reverses quickly.

"The family car that's yours arrives next month."

I gasp. "Which is?"

"A Range Rover. If you want to show me this beautiful country, we'll need a four-wheel drive."

Material things have never appealed to him, so why is he spending a hell of a lot of money on things we don't need?

"Is this a work car?"

He gives me a sideways glance and grins. "Do you like it?"

Cars are meh to me, and why I didn't care about

driving an old car. Yet, I take in the dark, sleek interior with touch-screen prompts. How can I not? "I do. Dad has always driven a BMW, and—"

"So does Ethan," he finishes. He's smiling smugly.

"Are you showing off?"

"Me?" he asks incredulously.

"It's not your style to be flashy, and I don't want you to change from who you are because you're here."

"Here, as in Adelaide?"

I don't want to say 'society' because he told me many times about how he didn't want to return, and it's played on my mind ever since. "You know what I mean."

He veers onto the street and my thoughts race to why he needs these expensive cars. Is he trying to impress me? "Is it rude of me to ask how much you have spent on cars today even though it's your money and none of my business?"

"Our money," he adds. He gives me another sideways glance. "It's *our* money, Eden." Taking my hand, he raises my fingers to his lips. "And we need to go shopping for a ring."

I pull my hand away and stare out the window to gather the right words, then shake my head. "What the hell is going on? It's like I'm talking to another man. And where the hell is all this money coming from?"

"I told you about the inheritance. It was on hold while I was in Ulara. A sizable sum of money is sitting in my bank that really needs to be spent so the government doesn't take it. So please, don't feel guilty. And I haven't changed. I need to spend the money on whatever makes life comfortable for us. I've never told you before because I didn't want it to define who I am. I'm still the same man, and I don't need these material things in my life." He places a hand on my leg in an attempt to soothe me. "I have the money, and it needs to be spent. That's all. I'll be investing in other areas. I'll always take care of Rose and you."

"You're missing the point. We don't need all this to be cared for. We only need you, and, more than anything, for *you* to be happy. And while I can see you're enjoying the car and spoiling me, it's not you and not us. And if it means giving up work and doing what your heart craves, and yes, losing your inheritance and upsetting your father, so be it. We only answer to each other."

"For me to come to Australia and get a working visa quickly after being out of the workforce for some time, my father managed to pull a few strings. And I made him a promise. In two years, we can reassess our lives to where we want to be."

There's my answer.

He has given himself two years in society.

I have two years to help him be happy living in my hometown. If not, I'm not sure where we'd go because even his ultimate home in Ulara is no longer possible. And it concerns me as to how it's affecting his mindset.

He steers into the restaurant parking lot.

I take his hand and squeeze it as I know he's trying. Restaurant dates are a big thing for him since he still can't eat much, and certain smells make him nauseous. "Have you ever been to Greece?"

"I have in my teens. What do you call spring break here… schoolies?"

"You went to Greece for schoolies?" I shake my head. "Where we stayed last weekend in Victor, well, that tiny coastal town is where we go, and I thought we were cool."

Samuel chuckles. "I only went to Mykonos to party and would gladly go on a family holiday to see the sights."

"All this talk has me starving and craving Greek food."

🌴

We arrive home, and Samuel places Rose in her crib. I can hear him telling her a story. I open my bottom drawer and retrieve Gran's journal she wrote while in Ulara. Untying the string around it, I carefully flick a few pages. A small puff of dust blows up in my face. It all appears intact. Rubbing my nose to stop a sneeze, I then lift the journal and inhale. I envisage her scent, only I'm hit with a pungent, musky aroma.

The door clicks behind Samuel. "Why the frown?"

I hold up the journal. "Remember my gran's journal? Well, this is the one she wrote while in Ulara. I'm ready to read it and revisit Ulara with her."

His eyes widen as he lowers himself onto the bed beside me. "I realize it's private, except I'd like to read it as well. Imagine what it was like around fifty-plus years ago."

I offer a brief nod, thinking if I should keep it private for Gran. "Okay, but there might be parts I'll screen in case, you know."

"It was smart to document her journey, her thoughts, and life in the village." He removes his shirt. He's unbuttoning his trousers, and I'm distracted by him *and* the dusty book in my hands. "All her experiences aren't lost. I should do the same."

Samuel agrees.

Wow! I moan as he slides his boxers down his thighs.

I want to toss the book aside when he strips down and slips under the covers. He kisses my neck, and I close my eyes, my stomach fluttering as he dots kisses over my skin. "Maybe you could write what happened to you. It might help you…" I fail to find the right words for *heal*.

"You're the only help I need," he says all breathy. He takes the journal out of my hands and places it on the bedside table. "Now, come here, and I'll show you why."

🌴

The following morning, I wake early to a quiet house.

Samuel's breaths are steady and deep before I climb out of bed and check on Rose in the other room. In the cot, her head is down, and her bottom is up in the air. I have no idea how it's even comfortable to sleep in this position. Turning the door handle and holding it tight to minimize the click, I wander back to my room, take Gran's journal, head out to the living room, and curl up on the couch, ready to embrace the first chapter of her journey.

8

IVY

November 2, 1962

After walking the corridors of the ship for the last time, I was glad to leave the stench of vomit behind and embrace the extreme humidity introduced a few hours before docking. Passing the mess deck, where several broken chairs remained scattered across the floor, I remembered the fights that broke out each night due to the restless, bored, and drunk men. With every step, I gripped the handrail, unsure if my wobbly sea legs would carry me down the stairs to where land awaited.

Considering I only had a small case, most of my clothes needed a good wash, as did I.

Like sheep, they herded us off the ship in almost perfect lines. From here, I observed lovers hugging, kissing, and sobbing. The ship was far from full. Some were volunteers like me, and others were immigrants seeking work of promised treasure. The ship will be at capacity on the return trip with immigrants hoping for a better life in Australia. Almost three months at sea, and I don't want to think about the journey home while my stomach is unsettled. Some days were so bad I imagined the moment I'd sight land and considered disembarking regardless of where. I didn't care where I lived my life if I could get off the ship to stop the endless puking.

When I did, I'll never forget those first few hours of dealing with the heat.

Never had I dealt with humidity so extreme my rigid lace bra stuck to my skin within minutes of stepping outside. A shuffle on the wharf alerted me to the large number of military present. It wasn't the guns that spooked me. More, the shouting in another language, and I couldn't understand their demands. If I didn't understand, how would I know if I was doing something wrong or even illegal? How could I reason with anyone? Not learning Spanish added to my long list of regrets as I stepped into a foreign world that will be my home for at least the next twelve months.

When I reached the wooden deck of the port, a woman, Maria Pérez, greeted me. She took me aside and after confirming my identity, led me past the military, shouting something in Spanish as we walked.

It took all my energy to keep up with her, especially since my sea legs were not cooperating. I asked her why people were shouting. In her thick Spanish accent, she explained they were calling out Yankee interference about the Americans coming to work as they have a better tax system and can return with more money than if they stayed in the US.

Politics. I was clueless, so I asked her about our itinerary, and she spoke so quickly I could barely make out what flight we were to take to Venezuela. I caught her words 'visa' and 'passport,' and I already packed them in my small case. The plan was to then continue onto another flight to Canaima come morning. Diego will meet us for orientation for my medical role in the camp.

After months at sea, the four-hour flight didn't bother me, nor did the never-ending questions Maria had to translate at customs. The following morning, we were ready to board another flight to Canaima, a tiny, beat-up aircraft that barely appeared capable of leaving the ground. Only then I wanted to stomp my foot and say enough.

Until I remembered what I had given up on coming here to live my dream — Albert and Winston were back home, surviving without a mother and a wife. If I were to give up now…

No, I was stronger than that.

So, I boarded the plane and prayed we landed safely. And we did so in an hour of flight time.

As Maria promised, Diego was there to meet us at the flight strip and would drive us to the camp. He told me how appreciative they were to have someone like me with my expertise. They have volunteers only, and more are needed as most head to Africa or Europe. They would pay me well in gold, even as a volunteer.

If I were to reread this entry, I'm to remind myself of the ride in the jeep as the bumpiest I've ever experienced. Hence, the bad handwriting.

Only my thoughts are fresh, and I intend to document every part of my journey.

I'm about to be overwhelmed with emotion when we arrive at the base camp.

I hope to write about the most amazing adventure while helping those unable to receive the benefits of modern medicine like many of us in the modern world.

9

SAMUEL

Samuel's dream seemed real as it's almost a recount of the past. With his people, they trudged against stems of thick leaves to forge their own path—a path into the unknown. Yet they trusted and relied on him to get them to safety wherever it may be.

He tosses and turns in the covers, his dream broken by the roar of modern heavy machinery that sounds like it's coming through his window.

Rubbing his face, he then clambers out of bed. Construction work has begun on the resort pool—the project Eden is determined to see through. Rose screams from the other room, so he dashes to her and swings open the door.

"Dad-da." She lifts her arms for him.

"Come here, my beautiful girl." Lifting her into his arms, he presses her head against his chest. "Dad-da is here. You're safe with me." A promise he'll uphold her entire life. He takes her to his bedroom and points down to the trucks.

Eden is standing nearby wearing an industrial yellow

hard hat, looking every bit as sexy as the day they first met. "Mama," she coos.

"Yes, Mommy is down there," he says in his American accent to influence his daughter. He's curious about what accent she'll take when she learns to talk.

He turns and checks the time.

"It's breakfast time, cupcake." He heads toward the kitchen and notes Ivy's journal on the couch. He places Rose on the carpeted floor and examines the cover. The weight of the memories between the covers makes the book seem heavier than what it is. Memories of a place he still dreams of, a place he longs for but not without the two loves of his life.

A suffocating weight tightens his chest.

He closes his eyes and takes a moment to reel in his thoughts. Pressing the journal to his chest, he then places it on the table. Yesterday showed glimpses of the old Samuel. Money held power, and he remembered it as he stepped into the car dealership with the salesperson almost falling at his feet after realizing the commission he would receive.

He hated the man he was.

Hated his life of wealth and fake people.

He promised Rose a different life, yet he has fallen back into society and his old ways in a blink of an eye. Samuel draws his energy from the ocean, and being close to nature is his one requirement to stay.

The dreams have left him exhausted. He's mindful of eating healthy, yet it will take time for his body to adjust. The walks along the esplanade with Rose are therapeutic, although he's mindful not to burn energy and lose more weight.

Sitting on the couch, he takes Rose's hands, and she

pushes up to her feet. She takes a few supported steps toward him then bounces up and down on her toes.

"You want to jump?" He lifts her, and the sound of her giggles is something he'd love to bottle. Rose is a needed distraction helping him get through each day. She melts away his dark thoughts, thoughts he knows he needs to explain to Eden. She wants to know what happened, only he's not ready to unleash his memories. Every night snippets creep out of the locked cupboard in his brain to terrorize him. Retelling his ordeal like a story to Eden will require more strength with the mountain of emotions unleashed from his memory.

His phone pings in the other room, and he leaves Rose on the floor to find it. When he returns, he finds Rose standing up alongside the couch, using it to balance and get around the room. Rose then reaches for the coffee table, and holding onto the furniture has expanded her walking space.

He sits on the couch to monitor her and opens his email. The hospital has received his paperwork, and orientation is arranged for the afternoon.

"There go our plans, baby girl," Samuel murmurs.

🌴

Before leaving the house, stomach cramps almost crippled him into postponing the appointment—a combination of nerves and stress exacerbated by his current health ailments. He felt numb like the clock had wound back, and he was no longer in control of his life. His life mapped out in a similar way before he escaped to Ulara.

The interview went smoothly.

He stayed for a tour and then was introduced to the

staff. Thankfully, he slipped into a work mindset of familiarity.

On the drive home from the hospital, Samuel's nausea eases somewhat.

One day at a time.

When he walks into the apartment, Eden is on the couch with a glass of red wine. She turns and smiles at him.

"Did I tell you how sexy you look in a suit?" Her devilish grin has him thinking the suit isn't an entirely a bad thing.

He sits beside her. "Mum and Dad are out to dinner and staying the night in a fancy hotel in the city, so I thought we could get takeout?" She places her red wine on the table and plants a kiss on his cheek. "How was your interview?"

"I begin on Monday. I met some of the staff." He shrugs. "Everyone was pleasant."

"Okay, great." She takes his hand and squeezes.

"Not for Rose. I don't want your mother to care for her five days a week. She has her own life."

"I know. She said she doesn't mind in the interim." She lowers her gaze and smiles like she has a secret. "When the pool project ends, I'm going to resign. I'll be home with Rose until I work out what I want to do. Either study or a change of work or both."

He brings her in for a hug. "I'm proud of you. I'm sure this wasn't a simple decision to make."

"No, it wasn't. I'm confident Dad will understand." She lays her head on his shoulder and lets out a sigh.

"Maybe I should have a glass of wine with you to celebrate?"

Her eyebrows arch. "Is that wise?"

He understands her concern. His nausea comes and

goes, yet he's learning to live with it for now. "Only a small one as it seems we have much to celebrate. To add another thing to the list, the cooling-off period ended, and we're now the proud owners of a new home."

She smiles at him and takes his hand. "The one you bought *without* me."

He strokes her face. "You'll love it, I promise."

"I'm sure I will." She kisses his cheek. "In the future, big decisions are something we make together." Eden opens her mouth and closes it, and he senses her holding back in not wanting to offend him. She desperately wants him to be happy living in her city. If only she knew he'd be happy anywhere if he's with her. Spontaneity is unusual for him—only the house felt right. "You're right. And if our home isn't what you dreamed of, then we'll sell and find something together."

"Samuel, I trust you." She curls into his side and wraps an arm around his waist.

Samuel rubs a hand over his heart. Her words weigh heavy on his chest, along with the other people in his life relying on him to 'do the right thing,' especially after what happened to the Ularan people.

He can't fail again.

10

EDEN

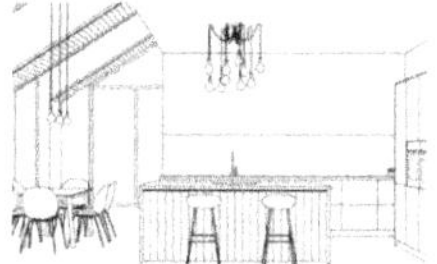

"You were talking in your sleep last night."

Samuel stills. "Was I coherent?"

Pulling the bedcovers over my shoulder, I curl into Samuel. "Not really. I stroked you until you settled."

Samuel stares at the ceiling, and it frustrates me I can't help him. "It might help to talk about it."

He remains quiet. I wrap my arm around his waist and kiss his shoulder. I don't want to push, only he needs a gentle nudge. It's Saturday morning, and I'm grateful to have this time with him in the morning to lie with Samuel and hold him, even if it's in silence.

The quiet doesn't last as Rose calls out and continues to talk gibberish. At least she wakes happy.

I bring Rose into the bed with us, positioning her in the middle.

"Morning, princess." Samuel turns on his side to admire our daughter.

"Her little feet are weapons, so protect your balls." I laugh at Samuel's expression.

My phone vibrates with a text, and I read the message from Faith.

"Did you make plans for this morning?"

He frowns. "Should I have?"

I chuckle. "Maybe because Faith and her family are coming over for morning coffee."

"We better put a helmet on you, princess," he says to Rose.

I laugh. "Jake wants to meet you. It seems you're the flavor of the month."

"And you wonder why I went into hiding."

🌴

"Na-na. Na-na," James yells.

"Okay, buddy, you can have a banana." Faith stands and chops a banana and places it on a plate. She plops James in a seat beside Samuel and opposite me and puts the plate on the table before taking a seat.

"I do too," Seb yells out.

"Come and get it, Seb. You know how to peel and eat it."

Five minutes after formalities, Samuel's head is moving side to side like at a game of tennis, watching Faith's energetic boys.

Seb races in and jumps onto a chair to reach the fruit bowl on the counter. Then he runs back to the television.

"I'm usually monitoring their screen time, but since they were all sick, I allowed it for my sanity." Faith turns to Seb. "Half an hour, mate, then it's off."

I'm watching Samuel's expression and doing my best to withhold the flicker of a smile. He looks exhausted just sitting next to Faith. Beside me, Jake is also grinning.

"When are you both trying for a second baby?" Jake teases. "Eden said you have the patience of a priest."

Samuel's eyes widen at me, then he kicks his chair out from the table and stares down at his crotch.

"Oh, I'm sorry," Faith says quickly. "James, you can't squish banana onto people." Faith stands and wets paper towel.

"It's fine." Samuel takes the paper towel and wipes the mashed banana from his board shorts.

Rose passes wind, and it's so loud it even surprises me. "Oh, that doesn't smell good." I wave my hand in front of my face at the rotten egg odor coming from my daughter amid the giggles from around the table.

"Allow me." Samuel drops the paper towel and mashed banana in the trash before lifting Rose from her highchair. "We won't be long." He carries Rose out of the room.

Samuel calls my name.

I stare at Faith and tilt my head. *Weird because he's capable of changing a nappy.*

"Eden," Samuel shouts again.

I dash to the bedroom, believing something is wrong with Rose. Samuel is standing over the change table, Rose is kicking excitedly, and poop covers his outstretched hands all the way to his elbows.

"Oh my…" I step tentatively toward the table, poop covering it. When I meet his gaze, his eyes beg for help. I can't help it and burst out laughing. "I'm going for backup," I say and rush out of the room, laughing way too hard.

"Don't leave me," he calls out. "I can't touch anything."

"What's going on?" Faith asks with a coffee now in front of her.

"Samuel has poop to his elbows. Can someone help us?" I ask, trying to be serious.

"Jake, watch the kids." Faith jumps up to follow me.

"Gladly," he chimes.

"There has to be something wrong with her. It was like a projectile of feces," Samuel moans. His arms are stiff, and he's afraid to move.

Faith chuckles while pushing up the sleeves of her navy sweater. "We've all experienced days like this. It's funny when it's someone else."

He ignores Faith and stares at me. "Someone will have to turn on the faucets for me."

"Faith, take Samuel to the laundry room," I instruct. "I'll finish cleaning up Rose in the bathroom."

11

SAMUEL

Rose is the devil in disguise. Her pretty face was distorted as fecal matter blasted from her tiny sphincter covering everything in a one-foot radius. Immediately after emptying her gut to what appeared as the last week of stomach contents, she smiled at Samuel and kicked her legs in relief.

"Okay, doc, stick your hands under here," Faith says as she stands by the sink with one hand on the faucet. She turns the water on and stands back to avoid the splash. Matter washes away, and she squirts soap onto his hands.

"Thank you. I appreciate the help."

She makes a strangled noise. "Surely, you have experienced this in your day, doc? You're acting a little precious." She grins at him.

"Obviously, yes. In a hospital environment, there are vinyl floors and faucets I can turn on with either my foot or an elbow, not in someone's luxurious home. More soap, please."

"What about in the jungle? You didn't even have running water to wash your hands."

"It was different." A memory flashes into his head—excretory products landed on dirt and were covered quickly to absorb into the earth.

"Okay, you're good to go. I'll splash disinfectant around the basin to be sure."

"Don't bother," Eden says from the doorway. "Can you please take Rose, and I'll clean up after I'm finished."

"Allow me to wash my hands one more time," Samuel says.

Faith snorts and then grins at Eden. "He won't feel any cleaner for a while even if he scrubs the skin off the bone."

"You better take off your clothes so I can soak your T-shirt and shorts as well."

Samuel heads to the bedroom and changes his clothes. Faith is right. When did he become precious? His first reaction was to assess her condition because he's still not convinced this is normal.

"Are you okay?" Eden asks when he hands her his soiled clothing.

"I feel foolish. Thank you for helping me and for cleaning up the mess."

"It's fine, it happens. She has only done it once to me before, and thankfully, Mum was there to help." She offers him a warm smile. "Join the family. I won't be a minute."

"After I wash my hands one more time."

He hates to admit it, but Faith is right. No amount of soap, water, and meticulous scrubbing made him feel any cleaner.

He heads into the kitchen and takes his seat at the table. "I'm sorry for upsetting morning tea."

"You didn't upset me," Jake says and smiles.

"Sam, do you have photos or anything since I missed everything while in quarantine? I was so out of it."

"I do, but—"

"Faith gets to call you Sam?" Eden looks at me wide-eyed.

"And doc." He rolls his eyes. "She's not someone I'd correct."

His comment causes laughter around the table.

"Sam's a quick learner." Eden winks at me.

"Guys, I suffer from FOMO, and knowing you've been here for three weeks and I'm not sitting at the table hearing your stories and learning about my aunty has tortured me." She looks past Samuel to the lounge room. "Seb, turn the TV down. I'll not ask you again," she warns.

"I told you Samuel has barely discussed it yet." Eden reaches under the table and squeezes his hand.

"There were photographs, right?"

"It's fine," he murmurs. "I can get the photos and show Faith and Jake."

"I'd like to see them again," Eden adds.

Eden had promised her family to make extra copies, only it completely slipped her mind while showing Samuel around the city.

"He bought a house?" The surprise in Faith's voice projects to the bedroom, where Samuel is searching for the pictures. He heads back into the room and hands Faith the images.

"I hear congratulations are in order."

"Thank you."

"Eden is a better woman than me. No way would I allow Jake to buy a house without me checking first."

"Eden trusts my judgment, and I base my decisions on what's best for them."

Faith's gaze lowers to the first image. "Well, we know she trusts you after running away from home to live in the jungle while *pregnant*." She lifts her gaze to meet Samuel's momentarily before concentrating on the pictures.

"Faith," Eden says gently.

"I'm sorry. I know she trusts you." She turns the image around. "Can you tell me who this is?"

Samuel's throat tightens. "The shaman."

"I started reading Gran's journal," Eden says quickly, and he knows it's for his benefit. "Only the first entry, and it's when she gets off the ship. The way she describes the voyage, she must have endured some hardship for three months on a boat with everyone puking around her and feeling sick herself would have been horrid."

Faith meets Eden's gaze. "I'd like to hear about her travels. Can you tell me what happened after you read each entry *if* it's something she'd want us all to know? I'm still getting used to the notion you were supposed to find Samuel and find out about Dawn, and it's eerie, yet I want to know about Gran. She was so brave, and it helps us to understand her. I'm putting pieces together when I think about some memories."

Eden nods. "It does. I believe she'd want us *all* to know the truth and what she experienced so we can understand some of her past."

"And your father," Jake says and smiles. "We have Samuel to thank for leading you all closer to Ivy."

"Ah-hmm," Eden clears her throat. "Pretty sure I helped."

"This is true." Samuel pats Eden's back. He admires

his beautiful partner in life. He pushes blonde hair away from her blue eyes, reminding him of the ocean mere yards from where they sit. "You and Faith are similar." He runs his fingers along her long ponytail. "You persuaded me to ask questions and bent every rule in Ulara."

"Oh, I don't bend rules, and I'm not a risk-taker," Faith says without looking up. "I may ask questions, but I follow protocol. Eden is more like our grandmother." Faith lifts her head and smiles warmly at her sister. "You have softened Dad in the last eighteen months. And I'm sure he'd like to know what's in the journal. That reminds me, when did you last visit Brenda?"

"Not for a while. My plan is to read more of the journal so I can talk to her about it because I'm sure she'd have read it or listened when Gran vented to her. And I know what you're thinking," Eden adds. "Her Alzheimer's prevents her from understanding, yet I hope talking about Gran might trigger some happy memories, even if it's only for a few seconds."

Faith agrees. "When are Mum and Dad due back?"

"Around lunch, I assume."

Faith's gaze homes in on Samuel. "Is it okay to ask you some questions, and then we'll put the photos away? I know Dad's accepting of all this, but it's still raw, and he needs time to process everything."

Don't we all?

After Faith, Jake, and her children leave, Samuel and Eden take a stroll past their new house. It's a spring day in September and not one to be indoors. They come to the three-story house on the esplanade and pause on the pavement to admire the frontage—a white-rendered home with floor-to-ceiling windows to capture the panoramic view.

From her stroller, Rose watches the seagulls fly overhead and looks everywhere except at her new home.

He points to a covered veranda on the second level. "I picture a telescope there for us to view the night sky. It's been some time since I've had the privilege of stargazing."

Eden wraps an arm around Samuel's waist and leans her head on his shoulder. "I picture us as a family, enjoying everything a seaside home offers."

Samuel kisses the top of her head. "Thank you for trusting me."

Rose whimpers and kicks her legs. "It's time for an afternoon nap. We should get back."

"I'm thinking I'll take a nap with her," he says.

"It's been quite a morning already."

After walking back and a half-hour later, Rose is asleep, and Samuel is drifting off on the bed, exhausted. He's aware it will take time for his body to heal.

Long days working will take a further toll on his body. With no other choice, he'll find other means to manage his health.

He has to, for her.

The dense canopy blocks out the last of the light before darkness falls. A thick, pungent aroma fills his nostrils—decaying leaves, moist air, and a never-ending buzz around his head. It has never felt more like home. Only there's no familiarity, and his breath is laced with fear, a scent predators seek.

He has lost sight of the river, treading deeper into the

unknown and further from any known points on his map. His satellite phone, an emergency source, was lost weeks ago in the Negro River. Survival weighs heavily on instinct, knowledge to avoid danger, and his awareness of the location of Colombian guerrillas.

The men spark a fire. The children string hammocks to trees and secure palm throngs overhead to protect them from the rain.

Some nights the downpour drenches the camp.

Come morning, everyone is tired, sick, and exhausted before they begin their trek south toward Peru.

Life has changed for the entire village.

Safety is compromised every step of the way.

In the months passed, they have lost souls—elderly and the young, depending on the disease and their fight to live.

Another four weeks before they stop walking.

Another four weeks will mean more loss of life.

Yet, they can't stop. They'll be safer in a denser part of the Colombian jungle with nearby waterways and mountains. From there, if threatened, they can travel south toward Peru.

Kaikare informs Samuel they must rest. They need time to heal. The men have agreed to build sturdier structures and set up a hunt for food.

The Ularans are unhappy, and if undermined, it could lead to them losing trust in his judgment. So, he agrees to resting for a week.

A decision he regrets as on the third night, gunshots wake them.

"Timenneng," he screams, hoping the warriors secured the boundary.

A gentle stroke to his forehead calms him.

The fire flickers, yet he's blinded beyond the trees.

Another gunshot.

"Nooo," he yells, only his voice chokes, and no one can hear him.

"Samuel, you're okay. I'm with you," a gentle, familiar voice reminds him. "I got you."

The safety in her voice pulls him out of his dream.

"It's okay, honey. It's only a bad dream."

Only a bad dream…

He wishes it were true because he'll never forget what happened next.

12

IVY

November 30, 1962
Venezuela

The days and nights have blurred from exhaustion.
My initial welcome was less than favorable from a corrupt group
even though this country recognizes the Peace Corps.
The company I'm working for is somewhat smaller and less
influential when bargaining with criminals. This particular group
highjacked us the moment we pulled up in the jeep as though they
were expecting my arrival. The moment I jumped out of the car,
they grabbed and dragged me away, regardless of Maria screaming
at them in Spanish. Looking back, I should have heeded the
warning and got on the first ship back to Australia.
"They think you're a spy," Maria had yelled after me and not at
all reassuring. "I'll have you released in no time."
Communication between the channels was poor, and for two days
and nights, they kept me in a locked room, awaiting their decision
on my fate. Each night seemed like an eternity when begging for the
bathroom in a cockroach-infested derelict building.
It turned out these gang-like groups are everywhere and are not
government-run. Regardless of any importance my visa and

passport held, they were deciding if I could be of financial benefit to them.

Thankfully, Maria returned with the police before they decided my worth.

She told me I was lucky not to be kidnapped, taken away, and held for ransom. I think the constant prayers to the universe helped with my fate, not so-called luck. And any investigation may have led them to believe I was a nobody.

Ever since, my nerves have been on edge after learning these raids happen at any time, and some villages live in terror.

It has taken a month for me to write about it.

On a positive note, it's been four weeks of doing what I came here to do.

There are no creature comforts in the indigenous village, and it has taken a while to adapt to sleeping in a hammock. Alongside the American and Brit volunteers, we spend nights by the fire discussing medical treatment if it's not raining. Apparently, the daily inch of rain is mild compared to what May will bring.

It has opened my mind and eyes as we practice without sterilization procedures or any hospital standards.

We sleep in thatched grass or mud structures. Every hammock is sheathed with mosquito netting, and along with a daily chloroquine tablet, I hope it's enough to ward off malaria.

After day one with Maria and the doctor, I realized there was no job description. I'm not sure of Diego's role, but he has done little to help me. If I can do something even if by Western standards it's considered doctor's work, then I attend to the patient as best I can. In a matter of weeks, I have learned to suture a wound. It's more of a problem keeping the wound dry and clean so it can heal. Bandages are washed and boiled over a fire then laid over twine made into a makeshift line to dry before being reused. Resources are scarce, and if something can be reused, then its value is like mining gold.

Today, I have cared for babies with a fever. Measles broke out in the village, and although I contracted the disease as a child and have antibodies, I'm even more fortunate not to suffer from any serious side effects. Here, the treatment is difficult, and I'm relieved to learn about a vaccine. It's not available yet, however there are shipments going to major cities.

Our community isn't high on the list for distribution, and it angers me how the value of human life holds more importance in certain locations as can the color of your skin.

Racism is everywhere. I witnessed it in Australia with our own indigenous. Racism is one thing I'd love to see eradicated along with life-threatening diseases.

Over the years, I have watched the young and the old die. Another thing I hope to accomplish is to see vaccines offered to all, regardless of demography or social status. If supplies of the new measles vaccine were given to the indigenous, it could have a massive impact on survival rates and the spread, especially when it's often carried into communities by outsiders.

My time here is short, a year, maybe two. If I make it my mission to fight for this, then it's something I could be proud of when I return home to Albert.

For now, it's back to helping with basic hygiene, even assisting the dentist with oral care since no one even owns a toothbrush.

While we might be helping, Maria explained how many deaths in the community have occurred from respiratory infections. We're providing the care, yet the indigenous label us for bringing 'cough' diseases into their community, and the balance between remaining isolated or receiving help from the outside world swings on a pendulum.

Part of my duty is recording name, gender, date of birth, and estimated age in a registrar for our records. Not the work I signed up for, but at least I'm learning the names of some locals.

Once a fortnight, we get two days off, and Maria has already planned where she's taking me. Heading to one of the official holiday resorts in Canaima for a cold beer sounds good to me.

. . .

December 5, 1962
Camp Canaima

No experience or knowledge prepared me for tonight.
It's no surprise babies decide to come of their own accord. When a
young girl who appeared no older than fifteen went into labor close
to midnight, it's commonly perceived as a natural occurrence.
Maria translated the doctor's orders since most of the local
volunteers communicated in Spanish or their native tongue.
Only the baby was breach and couldn't be turned.
With no definitive gestation date, the staff went by her size, and
her stomach wasn't big. A rough estimation assessed her to be thirty
weeks.
Regardless, she went into labor. We were concerned not only by the
size of the baby but at thirty weeks implicated the probability of
survival and multiple complications of the girl delivering a breach
baby were highly likely.
For the next two hours, my stomach sat in my throat, and I wanted
to puke with nerves. Extra help or emergency care wasn't available,
as there's no nearby hospital and no roads lead to Canaima. By the
time we got her on the canoe, then a plane, and to a city, it would
be too late. And she owned no health insurance.
I'll never forget her screams as long as I live.
Never forget the way her eyes pleaded with mine.
Maria explained we were out of time to perform the ways of their
labor rituals. The labor came on hard and fast.
She tried to squat, then the staff assisted her in lying down.
When dilated, the baby's bottom came into view. The doctor tried
to maneuver the baby with his fingers, only the young mother's heart
gave out first.
Maria and I performed CPR for half an hour.

The doctor delivered the baby, yet they pronounced him dead at birth.

It was the most heartbreaking and traumatic day of my life, and I experienced it in my first month of volunteering.

I wanted to mourn their deaths with her family.

So, I sat with them and cried and cried.

Me, the woman who had left her own child to be here to help them.

I need to make it all worth it after this devastation.

13

EDEN

Placing Gran's journal on the side table, I swipe a tear from my eye. Samuel stirs beside me so I give him a moment to wake.

"Morning," I whisper. "Are you okay?"

He rolls onto his side and kisses me. "I am now."

"These dreams," I begin. "You're having them regularly. You need to talk to someone, if not me."

I stroke his face and wait for his eyes to open then he meets my gaze. "I'm not ready."

"Samuel."

"I'll talk to you eventually. It's not something I'm comfortable sharing, especially if questioned why I was there. I'm protecting the Ularans' location."

"I want you to talk to me. I'll listen to you any time, but I hate seeing you suffer." He doesn't respond. "Can you tell me what happened last night?"

He shakes his head. "It's not where I want to start. I'll tell you about Kaikare and her bravery during the hardest days. It's a positive memory, and it's best I start there."

I smile at my beautiful man. "Did she mention me?"

He kisses my lips. "Every day. She misses you, and said she tries to find your spirit when she takes the tea. She has connected with your Gran and hopes to connect with you too."

I gasp. "She visualizes Gran?"

He smiles reassuringly.

"Can she connect with me even though I'm not dead?"

"I've been thinking about this. If there's a time you could take ayahuasca safely, and if you connect with your Gran, which you already have, you could connect with Kaikare through your Gran's spirit."

This isn't the conversation I thought I'd be having with Samuel, yet it has offered some hope.

"Wow." I shake my head. "It's like in the movie *Ghost* when he's in Whoopi's body. She's a host or medium or something."

He chuckles lightly. "Or something."

I wanted to ask him more questions, except Rose has awakened, and he jumps out of bed to get her. He puts her in the middle for our morning time together, and I roll onto my side. I do love this part of the day when the three of us relax in bed as though there isn't a care in the world.

Tomorrow will be a different story.

This upcoming job could change him, and it scares me.

The following night I'm sitting out front watching the golden orb sink slowly into the ocean. The crashing waves then the fizz of foam hypnotizes Rose and me until a noisy seagull squawks overhead and kills the moment. Rose screams in delight and reaches up to the bird.

"Don't, honey." I nuzzle her arm down. "It will think you're feeding it." I gaze out to the ocean to catch the last of the sunset along with walkers lining the foreshore, many with dogs on a leash.

I hear his car before I see it. It has a cacophony of sounds and is rocketlike when his foot is on the pedal. Even at a safe speed, as I know he's mindful of pedestrians, the sound is its essence. He pulls up beside me, and the window's dark glass lowers.

Rose's excited screams demand his attention. "Hey, baby girl. Daddy missed you." He stares at me. "How was your day?"

"Fine. Everything went according to plan. Mum said it was noisy, and we needed to apologize to the current guests." I shrug as we can't avoid it. "How was your day?"

"Different. Interesting. And yet the same." He glances down at the steering wheel. "Anything planned for dinner?"

Asking me this, I realize how food still consumes his thoughts, how it stresses his mind whether it makes him sick, and more so, why he isn't putting on weight.

"Mum has prepared a beef stir-fry."

A few hours later, I'm surprised when he finishes his meal.

Maybe he has turned a corner?

Later, when Rose is asleep and we're ready for bed, he stoops over and grabs his stomach.

I go to him and place a tentative hand on his back. "What is it?"

"My stomach." He winces.

"You don't have to eat everything Mum offers." I rub his back. "You're not used to rich sauces."

"It's not it." A muscle ticks in his cheek.

I hate seeing him in pain.

"Something is wrong. Excuse me a moment." He rushes to the bathroom and closes the door. The distinct sound of puking comes from the other side.

I open it a little. "Are you okay? Do you want me to stay with you?"

"No, Eden. It's unpleasant," he moans.

I ignore him and burst in. "I can handle unpleasant." Kneeling beside him, I rub his back, unroll toilet paper, and give it to him to wipe his mouth. "Do you want me to wet a towel?"

He shakes his head and then lies on his side on the cool tiles.

"Honey, come to bed."

"I can't. I need to stay here a while," he whispers.

I leave him to fetch a pillow and then position the pillow under his head. I lay beside him and rub his back. "I'm not leaving you."

At two in the morning, we crawl back into bed, my back aching from spending hours on the cold bathroom floor. "Please get checked out," I murmur as I snuggle in beside him and he drifts off.

Only I can't sleep with my stomach in knots, so I research potential causes on my phone. Apart from food poisoning, indigestion, migraines, and gastroenteritis, other causes were from medication, excessive alcohol, motion sickness, or chemotherapy. God, I hope my mother hasn't poisoned him. No one else is sick, and he said it was more than indigestion.

I research some more and find encephalitis, appendicitis, meningitis, intestinal blockage, and brain tumors as likely causes. He had his appendix out as a child. I know he'll rule out everything I mention and shrug it off in the morning.

Researching on the internet makes me even more concerned for him.

And doctors can be the worst patients.

🌴

Come morning, I roll over to a space. Samuel is up and gone without disturbing me. I let out a long sigh. I hope he's okay for work today. Yesterday, he talked a little about his position and how he's still working his way around a new building.

My day was uneventful, and I sent a text to Samuel every hour, asking for an update. I received one reply at lunch saying he was fine.

We've barely seen Dad the last few weeks with business trips and a dinner in the city with clients last night, but tonight he hopes to chat with Samuel. When Faith called in for a quick visit and offered to take Rose for a sleepover, I said yes far too quickly, hoping for some alone time with Samuel.

I'm in the kitchen preparing fish and a leafy green salad for our dinner when Samuel walks in.

"Hey, you're just in time."

He comes to me and plants a kiss on my lips. "Sorry I'm late. Where's Rose?"

"Having a sleepover at Faith's."

His brow creases.

"She's fine," I murmur.

"Samuel, come and sit, and have a drink with us," Mum calls from the living room.

"Evening, Grace." He nods at Dad. "Sir." He shakes his hand.

"Please sit, son. How was your day?" Dad asks with his feet elevated in a recliner chair.

"Busy. Most of the day is at a computer reading material relative to the residency and reorientating myself, and then I'm on a ward with my supervisor."

"Dinner is ready," I call out. "You can have a drink after dinner."

I place Samuel's meal in front of him.

"Thank you. It looks delicious." He turns to my father. "How was Sydney?"

"Too busy for me." He chuckles. "Beach-side real estate is five to ten times more than what you pay here. We're blessed with one of the best sunset views in the world."

"This is true," Mum adds. "It's why our guests keep coming back."

The simple conversation continues until we finish cleaning the dishes. I'm distracted and hurrying to clear the table so I can get some quality time with Samuel.

"Samuel has some studying to finish, so I'll see you both tomorrow," I say to my parents.

"Eden," he says to me as we head to our bedroom. "I wanted time with your father."

"Not tonight." I take his hand. "You need to rest, and we need to talk."

After showering, I climb into bed, and before I say anything to Samuel, his face changes color. "Are you okay?"

He closes his eyes and winces. "No, not again." He

races out the door toward the bathroom. I'm right behind him, sitting on the white tiles, stroking his back.

"It's not food related. The fish was grilled, and the salad contained nothing to upset your stomach. What's going on, honey?"

"I'm not sure," he mutters and wipes his mouth.

"Is it stress? Because you don't need to continue along this path?"

He leans over the toilet and bows his head. "It's not stress. I'm enjoying the work."

I shake my head. "Then you need to get checked."

He pukes again. "Go back to bed, Eden. I'll be fine."

"You're not fine. This isn't normal."

He closes his eyes and hunches his shoulders. "It's the next stage of grief. I'll be fine. It's simply a bodily response."

Grief?

What have I made him do?

The following day I can't stop thinking about Samuel, so I call Yasmine for a chat. "Can grief cause disease? Because Samuel is vomiting, and it's the first symptom to come to the surface besides his nightmares. I'm wondering what else he's not telling me."

"He asked for time, right?"

"Yes."

"He knows he should talk about it, only I'm not sure his mind or body is ready. He's with you, and he's loved. Show him he's in a safe place," she says in a gentle tone.

"All he wants to do is give Rose and me financial security. New cars. A new house. He's talking about enrolling her in the best private school. This isn't him.

It's not us. I'm not sure why he's doing it." I close my eyes and imagine the worst as if he is setting us up for when he's no longer around.

"He's lost. He's acting like he did back in LA. You need to put your foot down and stop him from spiraling downward. Tell him you don't need material things and find a balance between city life and his life in the rainforest."

"You're right." I pause for a moment. "I need a plan. Can you meet us this weekend?'

🌴

On Saturday night, Samuel and I park in front of Yasmine's.

"I'm not staying." He kills the engine. "I need sleep, but you should stay and hang out with your friends."

I pat his leg. "It's a quick visit." My intention is for him to talk, have some fun, and maybe reminisce about Ulara with Yasmine for positive reasons.

"Deanne and Amy are on the front balcony," she says after letting us inside. "Do you mind if I steal Samuel for a moment?"

"Sure." I release his hand so he can follow Yasmine."

"Bubbles is in the fridge door," she shoots over her shoulder.

As I fill a crystal glass with sparkling wine, I overhear Yasmine from the bedroom.

"Lie on the yoga blocks for a few minutes. It will open your heart space."

"And why do I need to do this?" he asks. I imagine him with his arms crossed over his chest and a defiant expression.

"We've all had a broken heart, Samuel. This exercise will help."

I choke on the first mouthful. *God, I love my friend. She knew how to help him without my asking.* Trusting my man in her care, I head out to the balcony.

"Eden." Amy jumps up and gives a tight hug. "I've missed you."

Deanne stands and gives a lighter hug. "You've had a haircut."

Deanne shakes her head, and her brown tresses jiggle with the movement. "I wanted short and manageable since I'm thinking of traveling to Peru with Yasmine until she meets up with Michael. Then I'll do my thing. When she's ready to come home, I'll accompany her back."

We clink our drinks. "She'll appreciate that."

It's reassuring to know Yasmine will have a friend if she needs one.

"How's your week been?" I ask Amy.

The girls tell me about their week, and then finally Samuel emerges from the bedroom with Yasmine.

"Good evening, ladies." He sits down and looks west toward the ocean.

From Yasmine's apartment, we can see a sliver of ocean between the tall buildings, a perfect slice of heaven at sunset. Splashes of orange and pink line the horizon on a cloudless night.

"What are your plans for the evening? I assume you're not dressed like this for Eden's and my sake."

Amy points a finger and makes a clicking sound. "Very observant of you. We're heading to The Shores." She shrugs. "A standard Saturday night."

He turns to me. His brow pinches. "Did you do this every weekend?"

"Not always, but at least once a month."

He nods slowly as understanding crosses his face. "Why?"

"Do you want to go out?"

"No. Why?"

He shakes his head. "Because I don't want to stop you from having fun with your friends."

"You're not."

"Samuel," Amy says, demanding his attention. She runs her hands along her long blonde ponytail to sit it over her shoulder. "If we had a man like you, then we wouldn't be heading out either."

"That's not completely true," Yasmine murmurs. "We'd be more selective on where we'd hang out."

Amy points to Yasmine. "Right, girlfriend." She turns back to Samuel. "Guys hang out at The Shores. Most we know and…" she rolls her eyes, "… we won't go there, but we hope to meet someone *nice*."

"Nice?" Samuel tightens his brow. "You mean perfect for you."

"Exactly."

"Never settle for anything less, Amy."

Amy sighs. "Eden, can we please take Samuel out with us? I need him to say, *not that guy*."

I laugh. "One day, Ames." I rub his leg and tilt my head toward my friends. "Deanne is heading to Peru with Yasmine. I told you she lived in Brazil for a year, right?"

Samuel asks Deanne some questions, and before long, Yasmine joins the conversation as it swings to Ayahuasca and its purpose. I overhear a few pointers and let out a long breath when he tells my friends it's not a 'fix-all tonic,' and you need to prepare. He explains how everyone reacts differently, and then he asks why they want to take it.

"Need a refill?" I ask Amy. She stands, and we head inside.

"I feel excluded, not wanting to drink the tea," she whispers once we're out of earshot. "You and Samuel… after seeing what Yasmine went through, it scared me. I don't understand her fascination with it?"

I hand Amy her glass of bubbles, and we sit on the couch to give the others some privacy. "She's heard stories. It's why I wanted Samuel to speak to her. He had a terrible experience and wants Yasmine to be aware because, like he said, it doesn't fix everything, especially only once. I was lucky." I shrug. "Although I was also in a different headspace. I don't want to do it again, but…" I shrug because after what Samuel told me about connecting with the spiritual world, I understand our world is more dimensional than what most of us believe. "I never say never to anything now."

She clinks my drink with hers. "Never say never to finding a perfect man at The Shores nightclub." She raises her glass before taking a swig.

I smile at my gorgeous friend. "You'll find someone when the universe says so. For now, the stars might want you to find yourself first."

14

IVY

December 8, 1962

We sat around the fire tonight, all the volunteers sitting on fallen tree stumps. Each stump seated three or four people, and it's the time of night when we discussed our day. A long day, to say the least.

I haven't recovered from the young girl dying. My heart feels like it's been ripped out of my chest, stomped on, then thrown on the fire before being transplanted back into my body. My throat burns, and my mouth is dry. There never seems to be enough water, and although they have some sort of treatment for the well-water before boiling it in pots over the campfire, my stomach hasn't adjusted. And the drop hole of a toilet isn't ideal.

Only our discussions are important to brainstorm what we feel is problematic in the village. Felix sat next to me and assumed he could educate me on infectious diseases. He's in his late twenties and from London. I like him, although his tone often sounds like he is talking down to me.

He alleged some symptoms could be from worms entering through your feet. He reflected on how he read up on it in the Australian indigenous community.

I informed him it's Strongyloidiasis, a parasitic worm. Although I didn't believe it to be the cause here, I know not to rule anything out.

Not to take any chances, I adjusted the strap on my dusty sandals since the parasite enters through the feet. The symptoms of the parasite—cough and a wheeze, body rash, and abdominal cramps—are signs of many potential causes and diseases.

Our deliberation was interrupted when Jennifer, the American nurse, mentioned one child presented with symptoms of yellow fever, although it could be malaria. She asked me to assess him in the morning. Jennifer is twenty-one and came here as soon as she completed her nursing certificate. Her mother had also volunteered, and Jennifer wanted to do the same in her honor. Since I'm older than Jennifer, she valued my opinion in the few weeks we worked together.

Although Felix is older than me, he hadn't studied infectious diseases and seemed put out when Jennifer asked for my advice. As much as it honored me that she valued my opinion, I suggested speaking to Dr. Leon and Maria, as they held more experience and authority than me.

Despite my exhaustion, I'm fulfilled by doing good deeds in my life. My dream to volunteer centered around helping those with poor medical supplies and caring for the sick. Beneath the positive reinforcement, I struggled with the truth. It didn't prepare me for the heartache or the suffering, especially the children. Late at night, I second-guess my decision, especially when I have my child and husband at home without me.

Exhaustion plays a significant part in my mindset, yet I must do more than simply help with the symptoms or make people comfortable before they die. How can I prevent the diseases? An impossible feat with limited finances and supplies.

Everyone deserted the fire for an early night, allowing me to write entries in my journal in private.

Maria strolled by and suggested we go on a tour to Angel Falls on our day off. She told me I'd love it, and it would help me forget about the humidity, something I'm still not coping with, but it's the least of my worries.

Earlier tonight, Jennifer had complained about the rain. She said it's nothing like the rain in Minnesota because it's freezing and more likely to snow. She described it here as hot rain saturating us to our bones.

She made me laugh, and I enjoyed listening to her American accent. Diego said we're due for a heavy wet season.

Few of the huts here are on stilts. Some are barely raised.

Do they frequently rebuild since these huts aren't built to last? The rainy season…

What the hell was I thinking coming here?

December 14, 1962

Every letter I send to Albert, I finish it with the same words.

Miss you and love you both very much.
All my love,
Ivy xxx

I don't expect any letters in return. Although, in this letter I have given the Canaima Lodge address. I have wished for them to have a wonderful Christmas and asked for them to not miss me but make this Christmas one to celebrate together. Make happy memories with my son as I'll soon be home and have many more Christmas with them, and my time away will be forgotten.

I posted the letter at the main lodge in Canaima.

Tomorrow, we will travel by motorized canoe to Angel Falls.

December 15, 1962

*It was a little after dawn when I met Maria, and we boarded
what she called a curiara to travel along the river—a wooden canoe
with planks for seats and nothing but a motorcycle motor to propel
it along the river.*

*I held onto the edge of my seat as we sailed along the river for five
hours, only stopping when we ladies needed to find a shrub to pee
behind. And it had to be strategic as the rainforest walled most of
the river in. The guides knew where to stop, and I was amazed by
the abundance of flowers and bird life surrounding us. In these
pockets, the bird songs overpowered the screech of the monkeys, and
it was refreshing to hear. Maria told me the rapids were okay to
ride through as it's outside the wet season. It's why she urged me to
take this trip sooner rather than later, as the waterfall slows to a
drizzle soon and is not so impressive.*

*Nearer to the falls, we disembarked the canoes and trekked uphill
through the rainforest. My fitness is shocking, and I struggled to
keep up with the guides' pace. Thankfully, they stopped to show us
macaws and a toucan in nearby trees. I was sure the monkeys were
laughing at me.*

*I find them to be cute animals and also a menace when they steal
our hats and bottles from the campsite.*

*I don't know how long we walked, yet it was worth it to see the
majestic waterfall. I had to cover my eyes from looking up directly
into the sun to see the beauty of the waterfall in its entirety. Maria
mentioned it's the tallest in the world, and I simply stared for
minutes at the rocky formation of the mountains surpassing the
clouds in the sky. Thankfully, I snapped plenty of photographs on
my camera.*

The lagoon below the falls is one of the cleanest water pools I have ever swam in, and even here in the tropics, the cool water temperature surprised me. It was a much-needed dip before the return hike down the hill, only to stop to admire the various plants, orchids, and animal life.

On our trek back, Maria told me she had spotted a puma. I quickly caught up to the guide and remained by his side until we reached the river. She laughed at me and said it was a puma, not a jaguar. I told her wild cats don't roam freely where I'm from, well, not the kind that eats humans.

On the trip home in the curiara, we discussed the myths of Angel Falls and the surrounding flat-top mountains.

Tepui is the indigenous term. I believed the mythology to be all fairy tales until we came to a fork in the river, and the mood in the canoe changed. We sailed past the confluence in silence. Beyond the overhanging branches almost blocking the river opening, I could see a short distance ahead. There were children swimming in the river.

I pointed them out to Maria, she shook her head, and covered her lips with one finger. The silence piqued my interest, especially when I sensed happy children. After studying science and nursing for years, surely, she'd understand I didn't believe in hoodoo.

So, I waited many hours until we arrived safely at Canaima Lagoon, and I asked her why she couldn't talk about the people living along the secret river.

She spoke about tribes that missionaries haven't touched. These tribes refused to have contact with the outside world. Not influenced by modern man, they live solely off the land and use the jungle as their pantry. It's not unlike the community at our camp. It's not like we have a shop to buy groceries. The men hunt and fish and the women work the fields and cook the meals. In the few weeks I've been here, I've lost any excess weight I may have carried by comfort eating chocolate. Even on the boat trip over, I packed enough blocks of chocolate to ration over the months at sea. It helped with the nausea and gave me some energy when I couldn't stomach the ship's food.

When I asked more questions, she said a powerful shaman lived there, and the Pemón community respected their privacy. Many years ago, Caucasian religious missionaries breached the river opening and were shot at with poison arrows, so she emphasized we must not travel there. Ever.

It should have been a red flag.

A clear warning, yet it has sparked curiosity to see these people living in their native life. I don't want to interfere or make contact, simply observe. I'm not a religious missionary trying to convert their way of life to follow my god or behave a certain way in a modern world.

I merely want to sit on the bank on the opposite side of the river and observe from behind the trees.

No one will even see me.

Maria doesn't have to come with me.

I know the way and could borrow a canoe and be back by dinnertime in one day.

December 20, 1962

After giving another letter to the lovely man at reception, I walked the trail back to our camp. It was a five-mile walk each way, and it gave me time to reflect and understand the overwhelming emotion that keeps hitting me like a freight train from the moment I open my eyes.

Overnight, we lost three children to measles, a disease that spreads like wildfire. It could decimate this community as the people have no immunity. One child suffered respiratory complications, and sadly, I assumed pneumonia killed him in the end. The other two were from encephalitis. I believed both girls were recovering. One day, they were sitting up talking and eating. Their fevers had broken. Then their brains stopped communicating with the muscles. In a short time, they couldn't move, fell into a coma, and died. I'd seen it before and should have known not to be complacent in the recovery window. Measles fools us all.

Measles didn't distinguish between the rich or the poor or the color of your skin.

We have developed some immunity from our society, yet I still fear for the young children back home. Here, the indigenous have no immunity from a disease transported to their community from Europe, America, and Australia.

Microbiologists in the United States are trialing the vaccine. It can't come quickly enough.

15

SAMUEL

Dr. Tolley appears in the doorway of where Samuel is sitting at a desk finishing the notes of a patient he reviewed.

"Dr. McMahon, please come with me." She turns and heads out of the room, and he catches up to her in the long hallway. "Dr. Edwards is performing a lower leg amputation on an osteosarcoma patient. They cleared us to watch from the observation windows." She gives him a curious look, one questioning why Samuel has special status when he's only been at the hospital a few weeks.

He offers no explanation and instead walks in silence.

Dr. Tolley is a tall, dark-haired woman in her late thirties, he presumes. She has more clinical experience than him, yet she's only a few years older. He senses a drive in her that can't be taught, and he ponders if he could open her eyes to the wonder of treatment beyond these walls. Modern medicine saves lives, except Samuel believes there's a place for modern and natural medicine to work together side by side to complement and strengthen the other.

They scan their ID cards, and thick double doors open to another long hallway with multiple side doors. They pass radiology and the nuclear medicine departments before scanning their cards once more, and the large doors open to a smaller room void of any furniture. Dr. Tolley is required to scan her card and then punch in a pin to enter the next door.

"The pin changes daily…" she tells him, "…depending on the surgery and the surgeon."

Samuel follows her along a wide passage with windows beginning from his hip and extending to the ceiling where seats are positioned behind the glass. It reminds him of his residency training in California, viewing surgeries from an upper level.

The staff, including his supervisor, Dr. Tolley, aren't privy to Samuel's background or his training in California. As far as they know, he has no experience in a specialty except for Professor Roxby, his father's contact who could pull all the strings, including his clearance for today's procedure. The professor passed Samuel to work as an intern for a year and then return to his oncology specialty training. Before his time in Ulara, Samuel was two years into his specialty training in California before deciding to quit and volunteer abroad, a decision that brought him a mountain of happiness and an equal amount of distress to his father.

Samuel has never been interested in performing surgery, only specializing as a physician. Only his past decisions landed him two steps backward in his training. And if he never went to South America, he'd never have changed and, more importantly, never met Eden.

Eden has led him on a path to finding genuine

happiness. Hence, he has taken a full circle in his medical training. At the very least, he's thankful he didn't need to train from scratch.

Dr. Tolley brings up her iPad and opens the screen. "X-rays before and after chemotherapy are available to view. The patient insisted on the chemotherapy although amputation was inevitable."

Samuel has seen a similar surgery performed many years ago. Yet he remains tight-lipped and listens to Dr. Tolley, awaiting new findings in modern technology to be mentioned. When she discusses the remaining muscles and skin form a cuff around the bone to fit in the end of a prosthesis and the new prosthetics available—all a vast improvement from what he remembers—she has his full attention.

He returns to the ward many hours later and is to work alongside Dr. Tolley for the rest of the day. Her stiff manner softens as the day progresses, and when in a room with a man in his forties and his two children are playing nosily by his bedside, Dr. Tolley surprises Samuel with her gentle approach.

"Dr. McMahon, this is Mr. O'Toole." She turns to Samuel. "A MVA patient with multiple fractures, and after further blood tests and x-rays, they diagnosed Mr. O'Toole with leukemia," she says softly. "His wife is in labor in the maternity ward."

"Afternoon, Mr. O'Toole," Samuel introduces himself. He picks up the chart and assesses his medication. "Are you in any pain?"

"No pain," Mr. O'Toole grunts.

Dr. Tolley leans closer to Samuel to speak. "The problem we have…" she whispers, "… is he doesn't trust us. Believes we're creating more illness by having him here."

One boy plays with a car on the floor, and the older one has picture cards spread out on the floor. Dr. Tolley smiles at the boys. "Are we having fun?"

"Vroom, vroom," the child roars, and Dr. Tolley chuckles. "Their aunt should be here soon to collect them." She turns to Mr. O'Toole. "We'll keep you updated on your wife when we hear more."

"I should be there with her," he snaps. He turns to the tubes coming out of his arm. "If you could disconnect me, I could *walk there myself*," he roars. His head flops back onto the pillow, and his face pales as though he realizes he's incapable of walking the distance.

"As soon as your sister arrives to take the boys, we'll set you up in a wheelchair so you can be with her. She's only in the early stages," she reassures, then turns to Samuel. "It happened quickly. His wife went into labor while visiting him this morning and went to the labor ward from here. We're waiting for her sister to finish work to pick up the children."

A nurse joins them in the room. "Excuse me, I was just talking to your sister on the phone. She apologizes for being held up and will be here in five minutes." She places the call button closer to the patient. "Please call us if you need anything."

"A cuppa tea would be good, love." His voice softer for the nurse.

Dr. Tolley's phone buzzes.

"Attention, code blue in room 203. Code blue in 203," comes over the speaker.

"Follow me," Dr. Tolley instructs.

Samuel quickly matches her pace. His thoughts are racing quickly as he prepares himself for an emergency.

By the time Samuel arrives home, Eden and her family have finished dinner.

"I'm sorry I'm late," he says to Eden. He pulls her close and holds her for a few moments longer than usual.

"Are you okay?" She pats his back. "I just put Rose to sleep."

"Fine." He pulls away and kisses her lips. "Exhausted, that's all."

"Samuel." Mr. Monteford stands from the lounge and shakes his hand. "How was your day?"

Samuel does his best not to allow the exhaustion to surface. Mr. Monteford has wanted quality time with him when Samuel first arrived in Adelaide, only his busy schedule interfered with moments for meaningful conversation. Since Samuel began working, his thoughts have been associated around the hospital, and fatigue prevented him from spending time with Eden's family.

"Interesting and exhausting, yet I'm enjoying the work. I've missed the patient contact."

Eden frowns at him as though she doubts his words.

He enjoys the work, always the patient contact. It was the demands on his life, other aspects of how he was perceived, and the arrogance of his peers that wore him down. Along with Inesa's words, he viewed modern medicine in a whole different light. It's why he wanted to volunteer as a doctor and care for those who couldn't afford private insurance or more, to the point, they were not privy to any medical care beyond their community.

He bows his head with the memory.

"Are you hungry," Eden asks gently and takes his

hand to lead him to the kitchen. "Are the long hours too much? You should wait until you're stronger."

"I'm fine," he murmurs. "Exhausted but fine." For the entire day, not once did a memory of Ulara come to mind, and he feels as though it's the perfect distraction.

Eden places a gentle hand on his back. "I'll warm up your dinner."

He sits at the table, and her father comes and takes a seat beside him. "I believe congratulations are in order with your new home and two new cars. If you need any help—"

"I'm fine, sir. It's the least I can do for Eden and Rose." Samuel is aware of table manners, yet he leans his elbow on the table to support some weight from his aching back.

"The least? This is extraordinarily generous of you, and please don't call me sir. You are my family."

Samuel stares at Mr. Monteford. He's not sure if it's a gentle prompt to make his relationship with Eden official or if he's being friendly. His blue eyes home in on Samuel, the intense color reminding him of his daughter's. "Thank you, I appreciate you saying that."

"Dad, do you mind if I have a quiet word with Samuel? You'll have time to chat when he's not so tired."

"I'm sorry if I imposed." He stands from his chair.

"Not at all, sir… I mean, Winston." Winston chuckles lightly. "I promise I'll be bubblier in a few days."

Winston presses a firm hand to Samuel's shoulder. "Of course."

Eden places a plate of roasted vegetables and a small piece of chicken in front of Samuel.

He grabs her hand. "Thank you. I know I haven't

made our relationship official or set a date for a wedding, but I promise it's something we can discuss later."

She leans in and kisses the top of his head. "To be honest, it was the furthest thing from my mind. We both have a lot going on."

"Thank you for understanding. I really am the luckiest guy." Taking her face in his hands, he kisses her lips with the need to taste Eden more than any food. He dips his tongue and finds hers. God, she tastes good. If he had the strength, he'd carry her to their bedroom right now and lose himself inside her. His imagination shows, and his kiss turns into a wildfire burning on their lips.

"Samuel," she moans. "Eat first, okay?"

"I'd rather eat you," he whispers in her ear.

"When did you say we can move into our new home?" She bites his ear playfully. "I have so many plans for when we're in a bedroom with solid walls, and you can make me scream."

Her eyes drive him wild, weariness leaving his body with thoughts of tonight.

If only the happiness from Eden came in a tablet form Samuel could take every day. In the back of his mind, he knows even Eden can only heal him so much.

Now that the nightmares have returned, he's fighting something not even Eden can cure.

16

EDEN

In the dark, I reach out to silence my phone on the bedside table. The high-pitch ringing sound brings me out of my sleep. Before I tap any buttons, I squint at the name on the screen.

Michael FaceTime Video

"Samuel," I whisper. "Michael is trying to FaceTime us?"

"What?" he murmurs. "How does he have your number?"

"Yasmine gave it to me a long time ago just in case. He's never tried to FaceTime. Something could be wrong. Is he trying to reach you?"

"What time is it?"

"Almost midnight." I sit up, flick on the light, adjust the covers, then swipe the screen. "Michael, is everything okay?"

"Morning," he says, all chirpy. In the background, the branches on the trees are swaying and a rustling noise comes through the speaker. Michael's face zooms closer as he takes a sip of coffee in a takeout cup. "I have no clue when an ideal time is to call." He hesitates. "Sorry if I've woken you."

Samuel pushes up and leans into me so his face appears on the screen. "Michael."

"Christ, you look like shit."

"It's the middle of the night, and I have work tomorrow, so what's up?" Samuel runs his hands up and down his face to wake himself.

"I know you're not in contact with anyone. Last night Brant was killed in a car accident."

I inhale a sharp breath. "Brant, who attended college with you both?"

On the screen, our faces are minimized in the corner. A dark shadow falls over his face, yet his expression is unreadable. It's how he processes emotion.

In Ulara, Samuel told me how Brant was not kind to Inesa, yet it doesn't make it any less sad.

"Right." Michael wipes an eye. "He'd reached out to me only a few weeks ago to say he got his shit together, and we planned to catch up. I put him off until next week." He looks into the phone and directly at Samuel. "We're not supposed to die at our age. And I've been waiting to tell you the same thing, that I have my shit together and finally working in a great accounting firm. Been promoted in less than a year."

This is what Yasmine has been trying to tell us.

"Michael, while I appreciate the call, I'm sorry about Brant, but I can't chat now. I have work in the morning, and so does Eden. We can do this on the weekend."

Samuel hits the end button and rolls onto his side. "Brant wouldn't have cared if I died in the middle of the fucking jungle." He pulls up the covers to his neck as

I rest a gentle hand on his shoulder. "And I don't want to talk about it tonight."

I let out a sigh and switch off the light. The Samuel I know is compassionate and caring and, under the circumstances, would have given Michael the time to chat. I understand Samuel is stressed and exhausted. Only this isn't him. He was abrupt. Brant had changed. Michael is trying. The way Samuel is handling his stress concerns me. It's why he can't manage more emotion and sadness because his sanity is hanging on by a thread and could snap at any moment.

I slide down the bed and spoon him. Wrapping my arm around his waist, I simply hold him.

"I love you," I whisper.

For now, all he needs is love.

The following morning, I don't recall Samuel kissing me, something he does before he leaves for work. I don't want to sound needy, yet I feel as though I've missed a step in my morning routine by not being woken by his lips.

My day is the same as the last few days with only a few hiccups in the pool construction. It's running smoothly, and I wish I could say that about Samuel's work. I can't stop thinking about last night and why he was terse, yet I know better than to bring it up with him again because I'm choosing my battles, and the bigger fight is for his health.

During my lunch break, I head down to Glenelg shopping district and wander through the bookstore. I stop perusing when I stroll past a table full of journals. One cover catches my eye. It has green vines and palm leaves in a jungle theme. I tuck it under my arm and notice another vivid white cover with the word GRATEFUL embellished in gold.

These past months, and after being inspired by Gran's journals, I decided to write anything that comes from my heart. And being grateful is a positive step. I purchase both journals before heading back to the office.

Ethan and Dana have other commitments after lunch, so I'm working alone in the office since Dad is at a meeting in the city.

Around three o'clock, I call it a day and head upstairs to see Mum and Rose.

After a quick cup of coffee with Mum, I set Rose in the stroller, and we head along the foreshore to inhale the fresh salted air. Steering the stroller down a path and onto the sand, I lift Rose out of the straps and let her feet touch the sand while I hold her hands. She smiles at me and stomps her little feet, giggling with the sensation. "This summer you'll be a little beach baby," I tell her.

She giggles again and looks up toward Monte's white building. "Dad-da?"

"No, honey. Dad-da won't be home early today."

It turns out Samuel hasn't made it home early all week and has not seen Rose since Sunday. *TGIF is all I'm thinking.* When Dad headed into the city for a meeting, he mentioned it would end up as dinner, and Mum would join them. With no idea what time Samuel will arrive home, I assume he won't get time with Rose until tomorrow morning.

After Rose tires of the sand play, we head back. With Rose on my hip, we walk past Mum's bedroom. The door is open, and she's sitting at the dresser applying the finishing touches of makeup.

"You look beautiful," I tell her.

She glances up at my reflection in the mirror. "Thank you, Eden." Her gaze moves to Rose. "Did you have fun at the beach?"

Rose squeals, wanting to play with Mum's makeup thinking it's paint.

"Not a chance." I reposition her on my hip to stop her squirming. "After I bathe Rose, I can drive you into the city. Then you'll only have one car, and if Dad has a few extra drinks…" I smile at her, "… it's one less car to worry about."

"Oh, honey, thank you, but it's unnecessary." Mum stares back at the mirror and smacks her red lips together. "I can catch a cab."

"Rose and I are visiting Aunty Yasmine anyway, so it's halfway there. It's the least I can do after what you have done for us. You deserve a fun night out."

Mum smiles at me. "I appreciate it. I assumed you'd be wanting some alone time with Samuel?"

"I do, although I doubt he'll be home early, so I've already messaged Yasmine to meet up with her."

As a teenager, Amy always had my back. If I worried and struggled with decisions, Yasmine was the one we both spoke to. Yasmine has a worldly instinct—she simply knows things, and she can see problems from multiple angles and help work out a puzzle.

Mum meets my gaze in the mirror. "It will do you good to chat with Yasmine."

She glances down at her nails. "Shoot. If your father gave me notice, I'd have had a manicure."

"You know what Dad's like with communicating his work schedule. I should have forewarned you."

🌴

Just before sundown, I arrive at Yasmine's apartment.

Yasmine answers the door in a pink and green boho maxi dress. It looks great on her. She takes Rose from my hip, and I follow her to the lounge area. A lemongrass scent fills the air, and as we pass through her small kitchen, I spy a candle burning on the counter. She dots kisses on Rose's cheek, then places her on the beige carpet and empties a small box of toys in front of Rose. Toys she's bought especially for my daughter.

"Thank you for letting us hang out here. I'm not sure when we'll hear from Samuel. He'll be relieved to find an empty house so he can go straight to bed." I place my bag on the counter and turn at the sound of a pop. "Have I missed a celebration?"

"No." She hands me a glass of sparkling wine. "You can have only one since you're driving. I can have more, although as we get closer to the flight date, I'll be abstaining from all alcohol."

"The date?" I take the crystal flute and have a long sip. I'm still scared for my friend.

Yasmine and I sit cross-legged on the carpet alongside Rose while she plays. She takes a sip of her sparkling wine before placing the glass on the coffee table. She picks up a toy and puts it in front of Rose.

Yasmine meets my gaze. Her brown eyes hold warmth, and her expression tells me she's not about to argue with me. "Michael and I will see a shaman, and then we'll meet with Deanne again. He's changed—"

"I know. He called Samuel the other night."

"I heard. He realized the timing was off, but he wanted to set up another time. He'd only just heard the news, and he rang Samuel before anyone else because he wasn't thinking straight."

"It was nice of him to reach out to Samuel, only his

work…" I pause and take another sip of wine to cool my throat. "It's too early. He's exhausted from work. At this rate, in a couple of weeks, he'll be losing weight again from the stress." I meet Yasmine's gaze before saying what worries me most. "He hasn't given himself time to grieve."

"He could end up with PTSD," Yasmine whispers.

"At the very least." Pulling my phone from my jacket pocket, I check the screen for missed calls before dropping it back in my pocket. "I've bought him a journal and hope he'll make entries to ease the emotion he has inside. Of all the people, he knows how to handle grief, yet he continues to suffer and not share the burden with anyone."

Yasmine rests a hand on my arm. "You're waiting for him to break?"

An image of a waif-like Samuel flashes into my mind. He's withdrawn from society, and I feel his pain in a dark cave where he refuses to come out. "I keep seeing this image," I whisper.

"It's not real, Edes. That's *your* fear."

"I know. I can't even tell what stage of grief he's suffering. For the months after the shaman's death, I can't imagine him being in denial or anger as he bore a tremendous responsibility, and they were all close to dying. I sense guilt, and he's not going through the stages like other people, and it's a problem."

"How we cope is a personal journey. In Ulara, Samuel learned to view the world and deal with emotion differently than the rest of us. He needs time to process and adjust to his new life."

I sniff and wipe my eyes. I'm not crying, yet the tears fall on their own. Talking helps release the tension and the fear building inside me every day. "Part of his new life, going back to work in a hospital, is what will be his downfall. You know Samuel… he made a promise, and he'll never break it."

"Edes." She rubs my back. "Let it go. I know you want to protect him, but you have a battle on your hands that might end unfavorably for you. Give him the journal. Give him time. He'll find his way home." She offers a warm smile that reaches her brown eyes, knowing it's supposed to comfort me, yet I can't rid the gut feeling he won't be fine. "Find something to distract you."

"I've been reading Gran's journal, and it helps."

"Good. Go home and read some more but please stop stressing."

Rose stands and walks to the television then points to the screen. "Dogga. Dogga."

"Did you see that?" Yasmine's eyes widen.

"You walked by yourself," I sing. "She has taken a few steps, although she's all wobbly. To stand and walk, what a clever girl." I clap my hands, and Rose turns around. "You walked, Rose."

"And Aunty Yas got to see it first," Yasmine cheers.

I laugh at Yasmine. "She wants to watch *Bluey*."

"Anything for our angel." Yasmine turns on the television.

"You never told me the date of your flight?"

Yasmine pulls a throw blanket over her knees. "First weekend in November. I can't wait. It's the beginning of the wet season, but I hope it's not too heavy to visit Iquitos and do the ceremony straight up. We can tour later."

"Except you'll stay and prepare for a week?"

"Aha. I really can't wait, Edes. It's all I think about."

I reach for her hand. "Please listen to Samuel and

follow his guidelines. You might see a vision, you might not. It's unpredictable. Whatever you choose, please stay safe."

"Of course." She brushes off my concern.

"When will you be home?"

"A few days before Christmas."

Christmas.

"You'll get to meet Samuel's parents. They intend on visiting."

"So, they'll stay with you in your new house?"

I hadn't thought that far ahead. "Now I know why Samuel is rushing into everything. He has an internal ticking time bomb to get his ducks in a line within the next three months to please his parents."

17

EDEN

Last night I didn't hear Samuel come to bed.

Rose coos in the other room, so I creep out of bed, grab some clothes, and take them into Rose's room to dress. He needs rest, so I close all the doors in an endeavor not to wake him. After attending to Rose and changing out of my pajamas, I find Mum and Dad in the kitchen eating breakfast.

"Morning."

Rose holds her hands out for Dad. Like Samuel, she hadn't seen him for a few days.

"Good morning, our little angel. Do you want a banana?"

"Na-na," she repeats. Dad peels the banana, and Rose holds it while taking a little bite.

"How was your dinner last night?" I sit beside Dad and peel a banana for myself.

"Good. Dana and Kerry joined us. They're now moving before Christmas."

"What?" My heart sinks. "She said six months."

Dad inclines his head. "Circumstances have changed. Faith will work two days a week."

"Faith?" I choke. "At Monte?"

Mum chuckles. "I had the same reaction. It seems she now cares about what happens to the family business, and she'll be an asset in HR." Mum is smiling as though it was all her idea. "We discussed one day of child care, and I'll look after her boys for the other."

"It's time for Rose to be in child care, mingling with children her own age." Here I was thinking about writing a resignation letter.

"Winston and I wanted to discuss this with you, especially about you working part-time."

"Really?" A weight lifts from my shoulders.

"Eden," Dad begins. "It's time. We'll hire a junior receptionist. If you and Faith work the same two days, it would be better for your mother and the business."

I'm smiling hard.

"I'll mind the three kids because they enjoy spending time together. I understand my limitations, and two days is reasonable," Mum adds. "Faith is insisting on one as she said childcare would be good for the boys."

"Finally, I get to work alongside Faith." I wink at Dad. "Could be dangerous."

He chuckles, and Mum laughs along with him.

Then I think about Dana. "I'll miss her," I whisper.

"We all will," Dad murmurs.

Are his eyes watering?

Mum pats his back. "Dana is excited for a new adventure but sad to leave Monte and us. They were notified yesterday Kerry's position is now in Cairns, not Brisbane as they assumed."

"It's a thousand-mile difference." I gasp.

Mum's nod seemed heavy. Final. "They're happy about it since Dana always wanted to live in the tropics."

"Morning." Samuel stumbles into the kitchen while rubbing a hand over his face. "I'm sorry I slept in."

"You didn't. It's only eight, and you had a late night."

"Emergency needed extra hands. Friday night is when everything turns nuts."

"Go back to bed." I offer an understanding smile. "You need the rest."

"Dad-da." Rose holds out her hands, and his face softens.

"Hello, beautiful girl." He takes her from Dad and swings her into the air. "Dad-da has missed you." He plants an exaggerated kiss on her cheek. "Do you want to go shopping?" He turns to me. "Have you found any furniture online?"

Furniture has been the furthest thought in my brain. At this point, I don't care if we sit on the floor. Can't he see his health is our main priority, not furniture shopping? "I thought we'd have a quiet day."

"We have a matter of weeks to organize furniture, and some can take months to be delivered."

"This is true," Mum adds.

The start of… getting his ducks in a row.

At least the three of us will be together.

🌴

We arrive home mid-afternoon, exhausted. While Samuel and Rose take an afternoon nap, I open Gran's journal.

Following Yasmine's advice, I'm distracting myself from worrying about Samuel. I understand he's on a path of recovery and finding a new purpose, and it's giving him a new direction and consistency. In consistency, he's finding security despite what he's doing to his health.

We are his responsibility.

His words, not mine.

He's stubborn in doing the right thing by us. The problem is his idea of doing right by us and working himself to the ground isn't what I want. It's his father's belief, and when we meet, I'll be giving Dr. McMahon, Sr. a piece of my mind.

Samuel mumbles in his sleep. I don't wake him, only listen. He sounds distressed. Anxious. Nothing he murmurs is comprehendible.

"Nooo." He gasps then rolls on his side.

For now, the nightmares may be the only way for him to deal with the trauma.

I don't wake him.

Instead, I distract myself as Yasmine suggested, and read the next page of Gran's journal.

18

IVY

January 5, 1963

Christmas came and went with minimal celebration.
I have received no letters from home, yet I'm unsure of the time a letter would take to find me, or it may even be confiscated somewhere between the Venezuelan shore and our camp. Every night, I hope and pray my husband and son are healthy and happy. Are they missing me as much as I'm missing them?
Some of us celebrated in the new year when Jennifer brought bottles of alcohol from the Canaima resort. I'm not game to try the traditional alcoholic beverage after witnessing the women chewing yuca roots and spitting into a bowl. An enzyme in the saliva turns the starch into sugars, and it begins the fermentation process. No thanks!
The volunteers love it. Jennifer and I prefer our beer in bottles, which is harder to come by, depending on who travels back to Canaima.
Today is my first day off in what feels like weeks.
One should be excited, yet considering I've seen nothing but death over the past seven days, I'd rather be working to distract my thoughts. I'm sinking into a mood pool of dark, murky quicksand.

It doesn't feel like enjoyable work when watching life drain away in a child's eyes. It's bloody torture, nothing less, and I'm not sure how much more I can take. And I can't spend my nights drinking beer to forget because there isn't enough pure water here to cure dehydration and hangovers. It's rained for ten days without a break, and I'm convinced it harbored the microbes which made saving the children more difficult. Maria told me it was unusual for this time of year. I'm thankful it's nothing but blue skies today, although the air still reeks of musty, rotten, decaying wet wood.

I need time on my own to reflect and recharge, so I asked to borrow the curiara and cruise the waters for a couple of hours. Dr. Leon was reluctant, especially with the lack of fuel for the motor. I reassured him I'd also use the paddles and not go far. He had listened to me cry night after night, and possibly it's the only reason he agreed.

My snacks are packed in my bag, and I'm ready for a few hours of peace.

How I feel in the jungle, the true essence of Mother Nature's heart…

After traveling the river for hours, I came to the river fork, killed the motor, and sailed beyond the long overhanging branches concealing the entrance. I paddled quietly, taking in the beautiful rainforest, untouched and full of animal life. I drifted closer to the shore and stopped to sketch the beautiful landscape before me. An eerie silence surrounded me. Today there was no laughter from children frolicking in the water. I sighted a sandy riverbank only a couple of hundred yards from the river fork, so I paddled to the bank, climbed out, and tied the canoe to a nearby tree trunk.

Sitting here, I'm surrounded by a sense of serenity. Apart from the mosquitoes continually buzzing above my head and the monkeys screeching in the treetops, there's no other life besides the plants, birds, and insects. Sitting in the sand watching the river current gives me a sense of contentment. Butterflies flutter past, and their

beauty catches my eye. Their flight path is toward the trees where it lands on some berries, opening and shutting pretty blue wings.
Beyond the calm, I feel like I'm being watched. Only when I check, there's nothing. I can't ignore the tingles along my spine.
I'm rushing to write this last entry because I know I am being watched. I'm sure I saw a dark-haired man with equally dark eyes beyond the trees.
Now he's gone.
I should return to the curiara and leave.

I'm back at our camp and writing this quickly before nightfall with no light in my hut.
My heart is still racing.
I want to write every little detail as I remember it.
When I turned back to the river, he was there, coming out of the water like a god rising from the river. Long, dark hair fell past his shoulders. He wore nothing except a twine skirt that didn't cover much, especially when wet. I dragged my eyes up his muscled, lean stomach and chest to those dark eyes that held me to a point I was incapable of moving. I stood so stiffly, if he touched me, I'd have fallen like a log to the ground. He stalked slowly toward me, and beyond his curiosity, he didn't look threatening. Because up close, he appeared to be a teenager, nineteen maybe. Only he had the body of a man, not a boy. Beautifully handsome for a wild man. For a few seconds, he stood there, staring. Then he reached out and caressed a strand of my hair, and I realized the source of his fascination. He didn't see me as a threat. Instead, my white hair confused him. And maybe my blue eyes because the way he stared sent shivers through my entire body. Voices sounded beyond the trees. He held up a hand and pointed to the river.
I didn't need words to comprehend what he was telling me. I fled in the curiara and paddled as fast as I could before any arrows reached me.

I keep telling myself I must never go back there again.
Yet, all I can think about is what would have happened next?
This place is messing with my sanity because what would have
happened is his people would see me as a threat, and they wouldn't
want an intruder observing them.

19

SAMUEL

The gray hallway of the hospital matches Samuel's mood. He has fallen into a routine like a robot.

Walking stiffly toward the meeting room, his life is no longer his own. He's back in society for her, for them both—acting responsibly, providing for his family, and doing the right thing. He'll do it for as long as he can, yet there are cracks in his façade.

Eden warned him it was too early.

He refuses to break a promise to his father.

In society, material things provide for more than love alone. And Eden deserves a luxurious house and car after what he put her through in Ulara. With the rest of his savings and inheritance now frozen, his wage is what will support them.

Yesterday he dreamed of Ulara.

Until it reminded him of his intrusion being the beginning of the end. How he failed half the people by the time they discovered a haven.

"Did you have a restful weekend, Dr. McMahon?" Dr. Tolley greets him and has already changed into scrubs.

"I did. Although we lost Saturday to shopping for furniture for our new house." He smiles because furniture was the furthest thing from his mind. In a small jewelry store, he found a perfect ring for Eden. A rose-colored diamond surrounded by smaller diamonds, the smaller diamonds embedded into the band.

Samuel went to hide it in the drawer as there was no ideal spot. They shared a space where Eden stashed scarves and gloves, and a drawer she wasn't using at this time of year. When he reached to the back, he found another box containing a ring with diamonds in the band. He considered it to be a gift, only the modern design wasn't an heirloom, and his thoughts drifted to one other person. The thought of how she came to be with it filled him with nausea.

"Dr. McMahon." Dr. Tolley's stern voice pulled him back into the room. "Are you okay?"

"Yes, I'm fine."

A lie.

He wasn't fine.

Not physically.

Not mentally.

Yet skilled enough to hide the truth from everyone.

20

EDEN

Six Weeks Later…

On Saturday morning, I'm standing at the International terminal gate, and part of me wants to go on an adventure with my friends. With so many fond memories of our travels, I'm happy how Yasmine's following her dream and creating more memories.

People rush past making a dash for their gate. A buzz of excitement surrounds us with nervous and happy chatter. Looking around, there are mainly smiles and only the occasional wipe of an eye with loved ones saying goodbye. It opens a sad part of my heart, like a wound that hasn't healed completely when I remember saying goodbye to Samuel.

The second time was harder than the first. In hindsight, I'd have never gotten on the private jet without him if I knew what the future held for him.

"I'm going to miss you." I hug Yasmine one last time. "Please keep in contact."

"I will." Yasmine's eyes flick across my face. "Don't worry about me."

I feel happier knowing Michael and Samuel are talking again, chatting at least once a week. If Yasmine needed anything, I'm comforted knowing Michael would reach out to Samuel.

However, her expression hints at something else.

She hugs me again, only this time she leans in close and whispers, "Samuel is having tests for his abdominal pain. He doesn't want to concern you." She leans back and looks me in the eye before her lips are close to my ear again. "You have known for a long time something isn't right. It's time you intervene."

"Ready, chickee?" Deanne comes in for a group hug. "See you at Christmas time, peeps."

Yasmine gives me one of her concerned looks then smiles at Deanne. I'm not about to rain on their happiness. "See you soon," I call out.

Wrapping my arms around my middle, I feel so alone watching my friends walk away and soon be in another country. Amy accepted a teaching contract in a country town for the rest of the year, and Dana leaves in a couple of weeks.

And now I find out Samuel is keeping a secret from me.

My chest is tight in an anxious way. Bit by bit I can feel my world crumbling around me. I need fresh air so I dash toward the exit.

After keeping my shit together on the drive home, I pull up in Monte's new undercover parking lot.

The pool is complete, and the accomplishment sends warmth through my chest. The car beeps with the security lock, and I stroll over to admire our design. The landscaping looks great with established palm trees and subtropical plants. It has the appeal of a resort along with covered street parking.

So much has happened in six weeks.

My brother, Will, came for a whirlwind weekend visit, and I'm glad he got to meet Samuel.

Samuel *is* making a life with us.

I need to focus on positives.

I'm working two days a week and spending more time with Rose.

We have moved into our new house. *Our* home, and I love it.

Life should be good.

Yet I feel dread in the pit of my stomach. And it's eating me up. Every time I try to speak to Samuel, he brushes me off.

And now I learn he has kept a secret from me regarding his health.

I head up the stairs slower than usual. Rose slept here last night as I stayed the night with Yasmine, her last night. I don't know if Samuel worked late. When Michael called Yasmine early this morning to confirm he had arrived in Iquitos, she went quiet on the phone.

It all makes sense now.

I swing open the door to Samuel playing on the carpet with Rose. "Oh, you're here?"

"Yes, I missed my girls, so I came for a stroll."

"He came for breakfast." Mum laughs. "Both have eaten blueberry pancakes."

"And now we have full tummies." Samuel tickles Rose's stomach, and she waddles away laughing.

Samuel jumps to his feet and comes to me. "I missed you last night." He pulls me in for a hug. "Are you okay?"

"Yeah. I just worry about her." I place a hand over his lower abdomen, glance at my hand and then look at him straight in the eye. "Like I worry about you."

His gaze flicks over my face. "She'll be home soon, and Michael has promised to watch out for both girls."

I decide not to quiz him further until we're alone.

"Did she sleep well last night?" I ask Mum.

"From seven to seven." Mum smiles. She packs up the last of Rose's toys and zips up her bag. "How was your night with Yasmine?"

"Fun. I'm happy for her, although I'm going to miss her."

"Perhaps you should make a trip to see Amy?" She hands me Rose's bag and smiles.

"You read my mind. I was going to call her tomorrow. Anyway, we'll get out of your hair as I'm sure you and Dad have plans."

"It's always a pleasure to have Rose. Dad popped out right before you got here, and when he returns, we're looking at some furniture stores. The couch is giving me a sore back so we're going shopping for a new one."

"Good luck. It took me weeks to decide." I grin at Samuel then pick up Rose and position her on my hip.

"Thank you for sharing your story of Dawn with Winston," Mum says to Samuel.

I look between Mum and Samuel. "Kaikare? What story?"

Mum places a hand on my arm as her eyes soften. "Samuel told us a few things about Kaikare… well, we like to think of her as Dawn."

"Nothing you don't already know, honey."

I bite my lip. He's finally opening to us, even if it's from years ago. It's a start.

Samuel walks Rose home, and I take the car. I drive into our underground garage and wait out front on our esplanade fence. In the distance, Samuel walks with

Rose, holding her little hand. Then he lifts her onto his shoulders because at her snail's pace, it's going to take all day.

I pad the half-dozen steps to our double glass doors and press the code to unlock the doors. Rose takes each step by herself, screaming if Samuel tries to help her.

"Someone is quite independent." He laughs. "Shall we head to the beach for a picnic today?"

"You two go. I have washing to finish."

"No, Eden." He lifts my chin until I meet his beautiful blue eyes. "We're a family today. Everything else can wait." He kisses my lips, and I want to fall into his arms and beg him to tell me the truth.

On the kitchen island is a cane basket. Beside it is a large picnic blanket. "I have everything ready. All we have to do is apply sunscreen."

🌴

The waves roll in one after the other and break along the foreshore. It's not hot enough to swim, and the water is cold on my feet. Rose jumps in the shallows then runs away as though playing with the waves in a game of chase.

"She loves the ocean, like you."

"Not as much as I love you." His gaze locks with mine, and there's a seriousness behind them, reminding me of our days in Ulara. "Rose, come here." She chases a seagull and attempts to waddle past Samuel. He scoops her up and swings her around in the air. He kneels and places her on one bent knee. Samuel whispers in her ear, and she giggles.

"Mum, Mum wing." She giggles again, and then he

dips a hand into his pocket and gives Rose a box. Rose looks at me and holds it up.

"Not so quick." He laughs, taking the box and opening it. She screams, and he hands it back to her.

"Samuel." I gasp, realizing what's happening.

"I originally planned a candlelight dinner for the two of us. Only I wanted to include Rose as it really is the three of us, and I imagined no better place than here at our beach." He stands with Rose on his hip and her still holding the box in front of me.

With his free hand, he guides my hands away from my shocked face and takes my left hand in his. "All my life I have waited for you, and I never want to lose you again. I love you with all my heart and want to spend the rest of my life with you. Eden, will you marry me?"

I burst into happy tears as he slides the ring on my finger. "I said yes many months ago. A hundred times yes." There were times Samuel and I didn't need a ring to define our love. Nothing has changed, and yet my heart is full. It's a step forward to a future together.

"God, I'm glad it fits. When we went furniture shopping, I hid one of your other rings in my pocket and hoped I grabbed the right one."

"You're lucky I don't wear jewelry every day." I swipe the tears from my cheeks so I can admire my beautiful ring—a rose diamond. The significance to our daughter makes me choke out a sob. "I love you," I rasp. "You kept it a secret."

"A wonderful secret." He kisses me, holding my face to his. Rose giggles at our feet. He stoops to lift Rose and include her in our hug.

We continue playing along the shoreline until Rose whimpers so we pack up the picnic basket and cross the road to our home.

I wait until we are inside the house before I speak again, "Earlier, I was talking about *all* secrets." I hold his gaze and wait.

"Do you mean other rings as secrets?"

I freeze.

"I wasn't prying." His hand rests on my cheek. "When I was searching for a place to hide this box, I stumbled across another box. The only reason it concerned me is because it appeared new, and if you'd bought it, then I imagine it would be with your other jewelry."

Lowering his hand from my face, I take both his hands in mine. "You know I'm referring to you." I bow my head, knowing I should have told him about the ring Ethan gave me when he first came home, only it was the least of my concerns. "Yes, I should have told you." My eyes plead with his. "And I'll explain it, but first, I need to know about these tests you're having for abdominal pain."

"It's nothing to be concerned about." He lifts my hand, admires the new sparkly diamond, and kisses the palm of my hand. "I anticipated a parasite, which is of no surprise, or something else I contracted in the jungle. I'm having multiple tests for elimination's sake. I'm fine, so please don't be concerned."

"Easier said than done." I spring up onto the white marble counter and pull Samuel to stand between my legs.

His brow furrows. "Should I be concerned about the other ring?"

Oh, we're back to that. I let out a sigh. "You're changing the subject."

"Am I?" He leans in and kisses my neck. "And you're distracting me."

He nips my skin.

"You also said to give you time," I murmur. He leans back, and his blue eyes turn dark, the same color when his mood becomes serious. "It's been ten weeks. Are you ready to tell me what happened?"

Samuel steps away and runs his fingers through his short hair. "I'm dealing with it in my own way," he mutters.

"By working yourself to the bone?" I croak out the last word as it holds more truth than anything. I reach for him so I can wrap my hands around his neck and stare into those beautiful eyes of his. "At least write in the journal. It helps. And then when you're ready for me to read it, it will be easier than you having to live it over again."

Samuel stares at me for several seconds. He nods, it's subtle, but I don't miss it. "Now, the other ring…"

"Dad-da," Rose trips and hits her head on the corner of the coffee table. She screams hysterically. Samuel grabs a clean dish towel and applies it to the cut while I hold her in my arms.

Blood is on her cheek and hands. "It's okay, baby," I whisper to soothe myself as much as her.

"Come here, munchkin." He takes her to the bathroom and sits her next to the basin. I help hold her hands while he cleans the blood away. She's still sobbing, and all I want to do is cuddle her.

"It's okay, Rose." I take her in my arms so she's at eye level for Samuel.

"It's close to her eye." He shakes his head. "She is lucky. I'll grab a surgical pack to clean it and then dress it."

"Does she need stitches?" I shout after him.

"No, I have special glue I can use."

I play games with Rose in the mirror to distract her until Samuel returns.

"I also have Moo-moo." He hands Rose her special pink fluffy toy she sleeps with or cuddles when she's upset.

Rose takes Moo-moo and squeezes it close to her chest. I lift her chin, and she watches Samuel's face closely as he assesses her. She stares at the glue as he applies it, and when it dries, he covers it with a tiny piece of dressing.

"How long will this last?" He winks at Rose.

"Were you seriously asking Rose?" I laugh.

He lifts her down and ruffles her hair. "Go slow, kiddo."

"I bought a round coffee table so we wouldn't have accidents like this." I follow behind Rose.

"It was impact, Eden. Her skin just split. Happens to kids all the time."

I settle on the lounge next to Rose and switch on the television for her to watch her favorite program. "Do you see a lot of kids at the hospital?"

"Some." Samuel comes and sits beside us. "You were about to tell me something before Rose fell."

I take his hand and envelop it in mine. "Before you came back, I felt lost. Afraid. Ethan was there for me and as a *friend*," I emphasize the friend part. "He was trying, and over eight months, I knew he'd changed." Samuel says nothing, yet I sense his contempt for Ethan. "On my birthday, he gave me a gift, a friendship ring."

"Eight diamonds as a friendship ring and no strings attached?" The lines on his forehead deepen. "Bullshit," he states. "He hoped for more."

"True," I say quickly, not wanting to lie. "He knew I wasn't ready. Two days later, you came home. I tried to give it back, but he said to keep it. A gift and nothing else."

"Did you ever wear it?"

"Twice. Before you…" I swallow hard.

Samuel gazes at the television, and I can't read his face. "You realize by keeping it he'll always think there's hope for you two."

"I told him there's not. You're the love of my life."

His brow furrows, and his gaze lowers but not to me.

"They're simply words to guys like Ethan." He turns and looks me in the eye. "It's best for both of you if you give it back. It's not just a friendship ring. Otherwise, he would've gifted you a candle or something less committal."

I let out a long sigh. "You're right. I didn't want to rock the boat. He's still a friend."

"And a friend would understand you'll never wear the ring. Please give it back."

Samuel's right. My concern isn't what he'll do with it. Because I'll never wear it. It's sitting there, a waste of money. If it's mine to do whatever, then I could sell it, except we don't need the money. He's never given Bree a ring like this, and he's closer to her as a *friend* than me.

It's true.

Keeping it gives Ethan hope.

"I'll take it to work on Monday."

21

SAMUEL

Samuel never told Eden the truth.

Not a lie as he has had every test, including those for parasites, and still no findings to indicate a reason for his extreme abdominal pain. He doesn't believe stress or grief is the cause. The nightmares are happening less. Yet his health isn't improving. The lethargy remains, and he's struggling by the end of the day, barely placing one foot in front of the other.

Sundays with his family are special. Soon, he'll be working weekends. Eden will be alone for longer periods, and after what she said about Ethan, he knows the douchebag will take every opportunity to win her back. He hated himself for insisting she gives the ring back. It's not in his makeup to be jealous, but when it came to *him*, Samuel isn't taking any risks.

He rolls over on the couch and stares at his beautiful fiancée. In his heart, they're already married, sealing their love in Ulara. Except society measures a couple in other ways. Family and friends have expectations. A shaman's ceremonial word will hardly convince Eden's father that Samuel is here for the long ride.

Eden's eyebrows pinch. He checks the book she's reading—her grandmother's journal. The words inside have opened a new world of understanding of her grandmother, and Eden wants Samuel to do the same. The journal she bought him is on the coffee table, a pen beside it.

He picks it up, and Eden's eyes meet his. No words, only understanding. Her gaze lowers to her grandmother's words of the past.

Samuel opens the first page of his journal.

His mind refuses to cooperate, so he acts as if he's at work and making initial notes.

December 2018

- *Eden is safely on a plane, and when I return to Ulara, everything has turned to crap.*
- *The shaman is shot.*
- *I make a promise to protect Kaikare and lead the Ularans to safety. The promise includes continuing Kaikare's training to be a healer. I deliberately avoid the word 'shaman' as I have taught her to incorporate some modern medicine practices.*
- *Convincing the elders to leave immediately didn't happen quickly enough. Kaikare stepped in, and I realized I had to earn their trust in my role as a leader.*
- *Many of the elderly knew they wouldn't make the journey, which is why they refused to leave and preferred to die in the only home they have known.*
- *When I couldn't convince them otherwise, it again divided the people as they knew I deserted them to their own fate. When I asked Asoo if he could*

investigate their well-being, he told me he already heard the miners had taken over the area, and the elders were gone. What or how he doesn't know, but it was too risky for him to ask further questions. I didn't want to implicate him in any way.

- *For several weeks we walked and slept in makeshift camps, pacing ourselves for the elderly who attempted the journey. If I knew what I did now, I'd never have made them leave. They may have suffered less if death came by way of a bullet in Ulara.*
- *For months, my endeavors to save them led many to their fate. Some of them were aware and yet trusted me with their lives. The burden became heavier every passing week, especially when my survival looked bleak.*
- *Kaikare is the strongest person I know.*
- *People died because of me.*

22

IVY

January 6, 1963

I'm sitting by the river, trying to organize my thoughts.
I haven't been able to stop thinking about my encounter with the
long, dark-haired man.
Had he seen people outside the village?
I saw nervousness in his brown eyes, but curiosity overruled any
fear. He didn't see me as a threat.

Maria came and sat by my side and spoke quietly in case anyone
overheard. A gang, or soldiers as she calls them, came to the camp
yesterday. They were looking for me. They aren't military, more-
independent military gangs. She used another word, only I struggle
with the Spanish terms.
They held Dr. Leon and her at gunpoint in their hut and demanded
to know about me. She thinks they're looking for ransom money and
unsure when they'll come again. She told them I'm no one of
importance and only want to help the sick. They told her I could be
of use to them.
God, why me?
So now we must be cautious.

She told me I should go home.

Wise words.

I should listen.

Only I have a gut feeling my work here isn't done. I have some sort of purpose beyond helping the sick. And more importantly, I want to be here for the measles vaccine and give this community hope. Safety measures have changed, and we require an escape plan if I need it. Maria is organizing a shelter for Jennifer and me in a nearby camp. So, if we need to leave fast, we can take the boat and go there, then she'll come back and get us when it's safe to do so. She said they won't be back for a while as Dr. Leon threatened them, so we should have a plan just in case.

I then told her about the young man I saw.

Maria became angry.

She told me not only did I place myself in danger as the Ularans forbid any contact beyond their village boundary, they also have a powerful shaman. She reminded me of the young man who was shot at with poison arrows. Her mood changed when she explained the Ularans have occupied the land before we created any government, and they have a right of ownership in her eyes. Their neighboring communities have welcomed outsiders to help, but they're survivors and wish to remain hidden from the rest of the world. To do this, they must resort to more forceful ways and only use weapons they make with their own hands. Guns and steel blades are foreign to them, and if we reveal their existence, they could be wiped out in seconds.

I now understand the need to protect their home, their land. The Europeans have converted some indigenous communities to the Catholic religion and a white person's way of life.

Promises of a better life…

It wasn't until she chastised my irresponsible actions of possibly transmitting diseases, even the common cold to them, I realized the result could be dire even though, in my mind, I was being careful. My selfishness surfaced to satisfy my curiosity. I could have created

*the very thing I'm doing my utmost to prevent here—a viral
outbreak with the potential to kill.
I apologized to Maria and promised not to return.
She went on to tell me why.
Some authorities believe there are no isolated indigenous
communities in Venezuela. Only relative isolation and have been in
contact with missionaries. Few people are aware of the Ularans,
and we need to keep it that way and respect their community's
rights. The more they're spoken of, and if other missionaries
believe they need outside help, it becomes known, and logging and
oil companies will believe they have the right to the land and
invade the boundary. Currently, it's certified we care for that part
of the river, even though we never go there. We do all we can to
protect the people. Maria then said she's impressed how I came out
of it unscathed. Blonde hair is fascinating to the Indians, although
she really doesn't know how I returned without an arrow in my
back.*

January 30, 1963

*When Brenda told me she was excited to study midwifery, I felt
sorry for her. At the end of our training, there were many other
courses and pathways I wanted to follow, and midwifery wasn't
one of them. My subconscious may have considered babies and
marriage a doom for my career, and staring at vaginas every day
and listening to screaming babies was unappealing, at least to me.
After giving birth to Winston, I understand it's much more. And
now here, in an isolated community, I'm grateful to have some
experience. A total of thirteen babies have been delivered since my
arrival. Brenda would be proud.
Five newborns and three mothers have died. I understand why they
breed quickly because a child's future is uncertain. Many deaths*

*come from the children not surviving viral and bacterial infections,
and most fatalities are from pneumonia.*

We need more antibiotics.

*Maria continues to tell us supplies are coming. She also told me in
confidence how the gangs were intercepting and stealing supplies for
their own. I don't blame them for wanting our supplies to help their
community, so why can't we order more so there's stock for
everyone? It may create more peace. Then Maria reminded me of
our lack of funds and barely enough for the community here.*

*I suggested we call the police, only she told me the policía would
not intervene. I asked more questions, then she insisted I stop
talking and accept the ways while I'm here. Focus more on
surviving.*

*She suggested we spend the next weekend in Canaima and hang out
at the local bar and relax.*

*I'm not sure if she meant relax and forget or relax and get off her
back?*

*Either way, I'm happy to have a night to ourselves with a few
bottles of beer.*

23

EDEN

I close Gran's journal.

Samuel has placed his journal on the side table.

We stare at each other for a long minute before he speaks, "It's difficult." An indent deepens between his brows. "I don't know where to begin and what to write. Nothing will ease the p-pain." His voice cracks on the last word. I glance at Rose. The Disney movie is more than halfway in, and she's sitting quietly on the carpet.

Grabbing the soft cushion from my back, I place it on my stomach and hug it. "How about you start at the beginning?"

He shakes his head, and I'm not sure if it's a no or whether he's trying to clear his thoughts. "You know what happened in the beginning. The shaman was shot, and it forced us to immediately evacuate before someone came to inspect the explosion."

"And what happened once you began your trek into the jungle?"

He drags a hand down his cheek, closes his eyes, and slowly opens them. Those eyes convey emotion and deep sadness. "When we were away from Ulara, we gained a sense of security. Most of the people were accustomed to walking and hiking. Yet I held onto guilt for leaving several elders behind. The ones too old to hike long distances. Everyone transported their belongings on their backs. The women carried baskets of food on their heads. Young warriors offered to carry those elders on their backs, but they were adamant they would die in their birthplace. These elders had no family, their sons and daughters having died before them. Ulara is a sacred place, and they believed their loved ones' spirit remained." He glances up with tears welling in his eyes then he blinks and closes his eyes tightly, and I can see him fighting the pain. "It killed me to leave them to die."

I pull Samuel into my arms and hold him tight. "Did you hear any more about them?"

He shakes his head. "When I reached LA, I called Asoo. There's no way he could investigate without bringing attention to himself. Illegal miners had overrun the area, and if he approached, they became hostile."

"And you believe you could have saved them if they came with you?"

His arms wrap around my waist, and he clings to me before speaking. "No."

"So, it was beyond your power?"

"Remove me from the equation as though I was never a presence, and they would still be living in peace."

"And we wouldn't be together," I whisper. "I believe it's fate, Samuel. Even my grandmother being drawn to Ulara was fate. She risked her life to find destiny." I massage his back in slow, gentle strokes but his muscles tense beneath my fingertips. "And during your time in Ulara you saved many lives and formed wonderful friendships. The people were lucky to have you, and the shaman and you learned from each other. In doing this, you passed on modern medical knowledge to Kaikare. As the new shaman, Kaikare is wiser for knowing you."

He breaks into a sob. I offer silence for him to deal with the emotion bubbling out of him like a hot spring, small therapeutic bubbles releasing from deep inside his mind.

"In the beginning… were you able to hunt for plenty of food?"

Samuel swipes his eyes. "We'd ventured deeper into the rainforest, and wild pigs and fruits were plentiful, thanks to the Ularans knowing where to search for food. We stayed a few days at cach site with makeshift beds in hammocks and secured palm leaves overhead to protect us. Everyone packed mosquito nets. We were near a river with a good water source, and fires burned day and night, depending on where we stayed. We'd walk solidly for one day, then rest for two." Samuel blows out air between his lips as though talking exhausts him.

"I imagine it to be difficult, although it sounded like it was going to plan."

He nods slowly. "For about a month, it's what I expected."

He remains silent for a few minutes. Even if he doesn't tell me more, we've made more progress in the last hour than in the past two months.

"The rain came early."

I let out a sigh. Already I know of the hardship in the rainy season without being lost in the jungle.

"It was difficult to see more than a few feet in front and blinded to a ravine with raging flood water. Four men tripped and slipped down the muddy slope with water gushing like a waterfall into a newly formed river.

Two young men we never saw again. The other two, Mari' Iwoi and Wayara, followed our path from the other side. If we became separated, they had a chance with Wayara's swift survival skills. A small sense of hope, but among the people, I sensed their loss of faith in me after losing the other two men. Even though the Ularans were exceptional at hiding emotion, the cracks were showing, and Kapeá Tapire sobbed, cuddling her child." He stops talking, and his blue eyes meet mine. "She reminded me of you. And at that point, knowing you were probably feeling the same loss and fear as her, I had to do everything in my power to get back to you."

I squeezed his hand then patted the pillow, so he settled his head on my lap. I stroked his forehead, hoping to relax him enough to keep talking. "You had everyone else to consider as well as me."

He closes his eyes as though he's visualizing the memory. "We continued to hike for half the day, only we needed to get up high off the ground. Everyone's feet were suffering, so we couldn't walk as far each day. We needed to dry out before fungus infections took hold." He blows out a long breath. "Maybe the spirits helped us, for after a few days, we discovered a tree had fallen across the ravine, and Wayara and Mari' Iwoi crossed back to us."

"Kapeá Tapire would have been relieved," I whisper.

His eyes open. "It wasn't that simple. The log was unstable, and it took some time for one of them to cross. It was slippery, and they crossed on their hands and knees. Wayara went first to assess the log. When it came to Mari' Iwoi's turn, he slipped and went upside down, clinging onto the log, but his fingers were losing their grip. Thankfully, the men found a vine and secured it to a tree. Wayara tied it around his waist and ran and jumped, grabbing hold of Mari' Iwoi, and they both slammed into the mud slope. The men then pulled them to safety."

"How scary. What were you doing?" My choice of words insinuated he watched and did nothing which wasn't my intention.

"I carried the chief's wife on my back."

"Oh, Samuel." I stroked his head again. "How long did you carry her?"

"Until she died."

We remain silent for a few long seconds.

"I'm sorry," I whisper.

"Sore Dad-da," Rose says and points to the cut above her eye.

Samuel stands and scoops her up into his arms. "I'll get her some pain relief and check her pupils again."

Samuel had already told me she didn't have a concussion, although lately, he's second-guessing everything. It all adds to his stress, his choices, and not coping with his grief.

I keep asking myself what else I can do to help?

This week I spent with Mum and Faith, either shopping for new items and furniture for our house or with our children building sandcastles on the beach. Every day is a cloudless sky, and the warm temperature indicates summer is almost here. It's a step closer to Christmas, and Samuel's family coming to stay. Last night, we chatted briefly about what tourist places we'll visit. Samuel hinted most responsibility will fall on me with his work commitments.

The conversation didn't please me, and it ended with him suggesting I use the days to better acquaint myself with his parents and allow them time to get to know their granddaughter. I'm not sure if he's avoiding them or proving to his father by working long hours, he is living up to his father's expectations and Samuel's part of the deal. He said his hours had increased at the hospital due to staff shortages on leave, so he couldn't possibly take leave.

He's always trying to prove his worth.

At least it's Friday afternoon, and he'll be mine for the weekend after barely seeing him all week.

It's the same thing every night.

After twelve-hour days, he eats dinner and heads to bed.

Rose has missed him and keeps asking for *Dad-da*.

Tonight is a date of sorts. Not the two of us. We're attending the Building Awards, and our builder invited Dad, Ethan, and me to attend the formal function. Dad couldn't attend as he's in Sydney on business until tomorrow. Dana is busy packing up her house so Dad suggested I take Samuel.

Mum arrives around three to pick up Rose.

"Thank you for looking after her tonight," I say while packing her pajamas into the bag.

"It's fine, love. Do you have her stroller?"

"It's in the garage. I'll grab it for you on your way out."

"I'll head home and wait for Faith and the boys to come for dinner." She says it as though it's the highlight of her week, having her three grandchildren together.

"Rose will enjoy that."

"It's easier if she sleeps at ours, and I'll bring her back in the morning." She glances at the lilac dress I borrowed from Faith hanging on the door. "What time will Samuel finish work?"

I shrug. "Hopefully, with enough time to catch a cab to the Convention Center, I'm going to take my time getting ready."

My phone beeps with a message from Samuel. "He must have heard us." I laugh.

> Working late again. I'm so sorry. Enjoy
> your evening x

I toss my phone on the table and can't help feeling annoyed with his work taking this night away from us. "Samuel can't make it." I tilt my head back and sigh.

"He mustn't be happy working late, knowing you'll be alongside Ethan."

"You've worked it out as well." Mum's blank expression has me wondering if I'm looking into it more than I should. "Although he also didn't want to be at the same table as him."

I pick up Rose from the floor and kiss her.

"There's a spare seat paid for by the company. I said I confirmed a plus one."

"Count Faith and me out." Mum takes Rose from my arms. "We have the night planned for the kids, and I can't disappoint them."

"You're a wonderful grandmother," I say warmly.

"I learned from an amazing lady." Mum smiles, and immediately Gran's smiling face flashes before me. "She was so good with us when we were young."

"I know. I believe she tried harder with Faith and you, even as toddlers, to make up for time lost with your father. It's a shame Will didn't get to know her like you girls did." She takes my left hand and looks admiringly at my rose diamond ring. "It's exquisite, Eden. He really loves you. Try to relax and enjoy the night."

"I know." I let out a sigh because I have never doubted his love. Yet the disappointment inside me stays.

My phone beeps with another message.

"Let's hope Samuel's situation has changed, and he can now make it. I was looking forward to having a night with him."

"Honestly, darling, he'll probably fall asleep during those mundane speeches."

I giggle at Mum because she used to love formal evenings and boring speeches.

"Nope, it's Amy," I say, reading the message. "She's back for the weekend and wants to catch up."

"And there's your plus one," Mum says and beams a smile at me.

24

EDEN

Fifteen building awards were presented before the renovation awards began. Amy and I have finished our second bottle of champagne. Admittedly, many images projected onto the large screen motivated my creativity to do more to our apartment complex, which I believe is the reason our builder invited us to the awards. He believes we could add more specifics and be in the running for next year's award in a category of renovations up to one million dollars.

"Gee-sus," Amy moans from beside me. "I can see myself waking up next to him."

"Amy," I chastise under my breath. But she's right. The guy on stage is remarkably good-looking—dark hair and tanned skin. Even from here, he has a face you can't help but admire and a voice that demands attention. A voice like Samuel's. One that has you stopping whatever you're doing and listening.

Samuel's voice still does this to me, and Amy is equally mesmerized by Mr. Builder on stage in the navy tuxedo.

"He's engaged," Ethan says from Amy's other side.

"Didn't stop you," she hisses.

"Amy," I repeat in a firm voice.

Oh God. It was Ethan who suggested we place Amy between us because he remembers all too well some of Amy's antics at parties after drinking too much. And the alcohol is free, so it acted as a double precaution rather than have her seated near any members of Spurlo Constructions. Except Anthony Spurlo is seated next to me and overhears, and laughs at Amy.

"Please don't encourage her," I whisper.

He gives me a playful nudge. "It's fine. I agree with her."

My eyes widen. "You want to sleep with him too?"

"No." He chuckles under his breath. "I've been to enough of these shows to know it can quickly get boring. And we also appreciate the free beer. All the awards complimenting your renovations are over, so if you want to slip out the door, do so now while dessert is served.

"Edes, I don't feel so good." Amy grabs her stomach.

"Thank you, Anthony. We'll be in contact, and I'll speak to Dad about your ideas." He shakes my hand, and then I place a hand under Amy's arm to help her to her feet.

On her other side, Ethan helps her to balance. "Okay, okay." She pulls away from us. "I can stand on my own." She pokes Ethan in the chest. "And I don't need help, especially from you."

Amy attempts her first step and her ankle buckles. Her ability to walk in her heels when sober is remarkable. However, being intoxicated could lead to her falling down the staircase. We assist her beyond the oversized wooden doors opening to a vast foyer.

"Stop." She stares at us incredulously. "Where are you taking me?" She stumbles to a long table where pre-dinner drinks were served, and thankfully, most of the crystal has been cleared away. "Oh no," she moans and leans over the table and heaves. A small amount of puke ends up on the table.

"A fast-track way to get us kicked out," Ethan says and chuckles lightly. It surprises me as I assumed he'd be repulsed.

"I'll grab a towel or something." I spin, and before I move, Ethan stops me. He rips off his designer suit jacket and mops it up.

I'm equally grossed out and impressed by his action.

"I'm sorry." Amy rests her head on her hands.

I place a hand on her forehead for support. "I love you, Ames, but dear god, please don't do this here."

"Why do I do this?" She moans. "Because I get overexcited thinking about the good times, and champagne is the common denominator."

Ethan glances over his shoulder. "Is she talking math?"

"And answering her own question." I rub her back.

With her head down, Amy's hand reaches out and touches mine. Her fingers rub over my engagement ring. "Did I ruin your diamonds?"

"No, Ames."

She lifts her head. "Did you see Eden's diamond ring, Ethan?" she says sarcastically.

"Yes, Amy." He glances at me and grins.

I shake my head. There's no knowing what she'll say next. "We need to keep her moving." I spin around and pray we can get her down the stairs.

"Is everything okay here?" The waitress' gaze flicks from Amy to Ethan, who is holding a soiled jacket, and she steps back. When he speaks, she meets his gaze and smiles. "Ethan, I'm Sienna's younger sister, Chloe."

Sienna.

Sienna, who I found pressed up against my bedroom wall with a butt-naked Ethan. Chloe's red hair should have given it away. Ethan didn't even blink an eye.

"Hey, Chloe. Good to see you. I need some help here. My friend is unwell. I hope it's not food poisoning. Could you dispose of this jacket for me?"

Chloe takes the soiled jacket without flinching. "It's good to see you," she calls after us before her eyes slowly lower to her hands.

Turning, I steal one last glance because she obviously didn't recognize me or maybe, like her sister, I'm invisible and insignificant when they see something they like. "Thanks, Chloe," I call back. "I'm Eden. Make sure you say hi to Sienna for me." Recognition dawns and her smile falls away.

"Was that necessary?" Ethan shoots me a sideways look, although he's more focused on holding Amy on both legs while her other hand swings loosely over his shoulder.

"Did someone say Sienna?" Amy mumbles.

"Come on the other side, Eden." Ethan gets a better hold on Amy while I press the button on the elevator and place Amy's other arm around my neck.

The doors slide open, and we stumble in.

"I'm the worst friend," Amy murmurs. Her head droops forward though her eyes remain closed. "After countless drunk times, you think I'd be a little more mature."

"You're our fun friend, honey. We love you for it." *I wish this elevator would hurry and the doors open.*

"The loser friend," she adds. "I'm sorry to be a pain."

"You're not." I tighten my hold around her waist.

"You've had my back countless times, and I thank every day for having a friend like you."

"You know I can vouch for you," Ethan quips. "You're the friend everyone needs."

I'm taken aback by his kind words. Only I don't have time to dwell as the elevator door slides open, and we stumble out to the ground foyer and toward the exit.

With his spare hand, Ethan pulls his phone from his pocket.

"I'll take Amy to mine," I tell him. "She's only home for the weekend, and her mum gets funny when she's this intoxicated. It sets a poor example for her younger sisters."

"You can't stay when you have a baby, and with Sam's work hours, he wouldn't want to be disturbed."

I stare at Ethan. For months I have witnessed him become a better person. "Where do you suggest?"

"Mine, of course. I live alone, and sleep hasn't been my friend for months. It's overrated." He smiles, and it reminds me of the playful Ethan I knew back in high school.

"Is it why you're at work at the crack of dawn?"

"Nothing else to do."

The doors to the event center open, and we assist Amy outside. There's a slight breeze in the cool night air. Music, cheering, and the familiar sound of revelry come from further along Hindley Street.

"An Uber is five minutes away." He drops his phone into his trousers pocket.

"I can't let you watch over Amy alone. God knows what will happen when she wakes. Frankly, she'll probably assault you."

Ethan chuckles. "Nothing I don't deserve."

"We all make mistakes."

"Yet I don't sleep, reliving the times I messed up my life."

"Hey, you have a pretty good life now. A secure job and your own place to live. And—"

"Here it is."

We help Amy into the car first.

"If you vomit, you pay," the driver snaps.

"All good," Ethan replies. "I'll pay extra when we arrive because you're a good sport."

Amy is snoring by the time the Uber pulls up in the street behind Monte and not far from my home. *Why didn't I know this?*

"When did you move here?"

"Three weeks before you moved out of Monte."

"You didn't mention it."

He shrugs. "I had to move on with my life. And it's personal and nothing to do with business. Who knew I'd love the beach as much as you?" An amused expression quirks up the side of his mouth. "And I can walk to work. Beats driving in peak-hour traffic."

The streetlight shines bright enough to see Ethan has a relatively new gray-rendered brick townhouse on a small block of land yet close to the beach, which makes it prime real estate.

"This would have set you back," I remark.

While I'm balancing Amy, he scoops her into his arms and carries her as though she weighs nothing. His football days are beyond him, but it's obvious even in clothes covering his muscles, he still works out.

"Let's get her inside before she pukes in my new garden."

He punches a code into the door keypad, and I wait for him to step inside, then he says a command, and the lights turn on.

Fancy.

I head to the lounge, only he turns down a hallway.

"There's a spare room on this level where she can sleep. The laundry is the second door on the right. Grab me a bucket, and the towels are in the cupboard."

The laundry has black tiles from the floor to the ceiling and a white marble counter. Black cupboards line one wall, and a pot of green pothos vine cascades over the counter. It suits Ethan. All class. I grab the bucket and towels and dampen a washcloth. By the time I arrive in the bedroom, Ethan is fluffing the pillow under Amy's head.

He places her heels in the corner of the room along with her clutch purse. He moves to the other side of the bed and climbs on the bed on all fours. "I'll lift her head, and you place the towel underneath it." I do it so some of the towel hangs over the side to protect the bedding in case she pukes again.

Positioning the bucket on the side of the bed near her head, I watch Ethan position Amy on her side.

I admire his efforts.

He moves off the bed and stands, hands on his hips. "We should get her some water."

"You know she's going to be pissed to wake up here in your house, right?" I try to say it gently.

His gaze remains on Amy. "Yeah. She saw straight through me when I was an ass." His gaze flicks to mine. "Figure I could prove I'm not that guy anymore."

I snort. "By risking your life with Amy's wrath?"

He grins at me. "You monitor her, and I'll fetch some filtered water."

I sit on the bed and place the folded wet towel over Amy's forehead. "I'm apologizing now because you're going to be pissed off when you wake up." I use the other damp cloth to wipe makeup from her eyes and face. "Don't be too hard on him, okay? He really is trying to be a better guy."

"Okay," Ethan says as he enters the room. "I'll leave this here beside her." He places a glass and a jug by her bed. "Go. I'll keep a watch."

"All night?"

He shrugs, sits on the bed, then he stands again.

"Why are you really doing this?"

"I told you." He rests a knee on the edge of the bed. "Okay, I haven't forgotten that look."

"What look?"

"When you don't believe me." He pats Amy's leg. "A guy in my football team died after aspirating his vomit after a big night out with the boys." He shakes his head. "You didn't know him, and it happened while you were on your holiday."

"I'm sorry, I didn't know." God, I've never seen Ethan so anxious. He swipes his dark hair out of his eyes —his dark eyes convey his emotion, and I can't turn away.

"If one of us looked out for him, even kept him off his back, he might've lived. Ever since, I promised myself I'd never leave a mate if he was intoxicated and out of it."

"Shit, Ethan. Amy will be impressed you consider her your mate." I say it to lighten the conversation, but it doesn't work.

"We all used to be mates." His eyes meet mine, a pained look marring his face.

"You've gone through quite the transformation."

He smiles. "A little too late, yet I'm grateful we can still be friends."

"We will always be friends. Shit." I spring off the

bed when Amy raises her head and heaves. I grab the bucket and secure her hair from falling forward. "And she better be grateful tomorrow," I joke.

Ethan wipes drool from her lips then offers the glass of water with a bamboo straw. "Have a drink, Amy." She does so without asking questions then her head falls back on the pillow, and she's out like a light.

"I'll go empty it." He's gone, returning a few minutes later with a clean bucket. "Do you mind waiting while I grab a few things?"

"Sure." I wipe Amy's mouth again.

Ethan walks through the door wearing a T-shirt and boxers. If I were into him, I'd be mush—I'm not blind to respect a beautiful male body when I see one. He places his water bottle on the other side table along with a book and slides onto the bed near Amy. "Go. I promise I won't fall asleep. If I need you, I'll let you know."

"I think she'll be fine. Honestly, she had bigger nights in Brazil," I murmur, not wanting to tone down his generosity. "But talking of friends…" I open my clutch and retrieve a tiny velvet box. "I've been carrying this with me trying to find the right moment."

Ethan sighs. His shoulders rise and fall. "There's never a right time."

"No," I murmur.

"If it makes it easier, I've been waiting for you to give it back even though I insisted you keep it as a friend."

"You weren't waiting in hope?"

He shrugs. "A guy always has a slither of hope. I knew you were happy, and it's all I wanted. If you weren't, then I'd be letting you know he wasn't the right guy for you."

My eyes widened. "Who are you, and what have you done with Ethan?"

He chuckles.

"I am happy," I say truthfully. "A little lonely at times, but I know it's not forever, and Samuel needs to do his required hours." I hand him the box. "I'll be your friend without substantiating it with a ring. And we both know my fiancé wouldn't appreciate me wearing it." He flips the lid open. "It's a beautiful ring."

Ethan pulls the ring out. "It's a friendship ring. Maybe it can be a sign of peace?" He holds up Amy's hand and slides the gold diamond ring on the middle finger of her right hand. "It held meaning when I bought it, but to be honest, it's a peace offering, and I have no use for it. I hope Amy sees it that way. It's too expensive to sit in a drawer."

"And too beautiful." I meet his gaze. "As a friend, I can tell you it's exquisite."

He smiles. "To friendship and getting the old gang back together again."

"Talking of, have you heard from Bree lately?"

He shakes his head. "I've received the odd message. At least we get to see her during the two-week holiday she's allowed."

"I understand how busy she is now after living with Samuel. God knows how the extra leave was granted for her to come on vacation with us."

Ethan leans over, places a hand on Amy's forehead, and then replaces the towel. "She's okay."

"If she were sober and you tried that, you'd better protect your balls."

Ethan chuckles. "You have a partner and a baby to care for tomorrow. Get some sleep."

Opening the Uber app on my phone, I tap on a car

only a few minutes away. I kiss Amy's cheek. "I'll call you in the morning because you're going to want answers." I glance at Ethan and wink while he walks me to the front door. Outside, the night air is still. The stars twinkle, and for once, it feels as though the universe is happy.

Ethan hugs me. "See you, Edes."

His words feel like closure, but in a good way, and a fresh start between old friends.

Depending on Amy's reaction in the morning…

25

SAMUEL

Samuel wakes around seven.

A sleep-in for him.

He was vaguely aware of Eden coming to bed last night yet too exhausted to wake and talk about the function. Guilt fills him knowing Eden was looking forward to a night out together. The gala awards was the last place he wanted to be, especially when time together is valuable. He'd have gone for her, though, until multiple motor vehicle accident cases arrived in the emergency room. Some were dead on arrival, but the children covered in blood sent him spiraling. He wasn't the only person who stayed back late to help. All he could think about was Rose and what he needed to do to save these children's lives.

He kisses Eden's shoulder and takes a moment to appreciate her beauty. She's an exquisite woman, and he's grateful she stumbled her way into his life. Eden changed his world, and everything he does is for her. He hopes she understands. Long work hours are a strain on all of them, especially him. He inhales a deep breath and forces himself to sit up in bed.

His body aches.

His head thumps with exhaustion.

Pushing up from the bed, he heads to the bathroom. His reflection in the arch mirror displeases him. His stomach clenches with disappointment and the onset of an anxiety attack. A heightened sense of mortality spikes fear. He tilts his head back and breathes slowly and deeply. The thought of food makes him nauseous. Yet he needs to regain weight to be healthy, at least visually because he's aware of her fingertips running gently over his ribs when she believes he sleeps.

Samuel gives himself a few minutes before showering. He avoids looking at his reflection until he's dressed. Running a hand over his hair, he likes the length, and growing it will deflect attention from his gaunt face.

Creeping around the room to allow Eden to sleep, he heads down the staircase and prepares a protein shake. He takes his healthy smoothy and sits on the balcony to admire the ocean view. Seagulls fly over calm waters while he inhales the salty, fresh air. He closes his eyes and listens to the waves gently breaking along the shoreline. Laughter comes from the beach, where children play in the sand. It's neither hot nor cold at this time of day and perfect T-shirt weather. It will be another story in a few weeks with packed beaches as they enter summer. His first Australian summer Christmas. Being here with Eden has ticked many firsts for him, and it brings back a youthful side in him. He wants a fresh start in life with Eden but forgetting some of the horror that traumatizes him will take time. He sips his drink and leaves the remaining third in the glass to finish later.

Locking the front door behind him, he strolls the esplanade path, smiling at walkers as they pass.

"Morning," he says to some familiar faces. He has spent many hours walking this path and recognizes the same people over the last couple of months. Many have dogs, and they congregate in groups discussing their breeds.

Samuel unlocks the front door of Monte Hotels and takes the stairs two at a time until he reaches the penthouse, where he uses another key to unlock the door.

"Here's Daddy," Grace sings when he closes the door behind him.

"Hello, princess." He scoops Rose from the floor playing with her toys, and showers her cheek with kisses. "Dad-da, missed you." Rose wraps her little arms around his neck, and it installs a calmness in him. He inhales her baby scent like he needs it more than air—the scent of *his* daughter.

"Is Eden still asleep?" Winston asks, not sounding surprised.

Samuel joins them at the kitchen table and places Rose on his lap. "Your mommy is sleeping like a baby." He kisses the top of Rose's head. "Thanks for looking after her. I could have taken her home, although I appreciated the extra time to rest."

"We know the hours you're working, so think nothing of it. We love having Rose." Grace places some chopped fruit on a plate and slides it toward Samuel. "Did Eden tell you anything about last night?"

"No. I was sleeping when she arrived home, and she was in a deep sleep when I left."

Winston frowns. "Do you know what time she got in?"

"No, sir."

"Hmm… I spoke with Anthony, and he said they left at a reasonable time. And Eden's friend was tipsy."

Winston is concerned about his company's image, and Eden didn't get home at a reasonable time. His gut clenches at the notion of Eden with Ethan.

He forces the thought out as he trusts Eden. Samuel has made ground the past week in dealing with the past. No better time than the present to discuss with Winston what he has waited to hear since Samuel arrived in Adelaide.

"Eden bought me a journal," he says, changing the topic. "I've been writing in it, and I believe it's helped somewhat."

Winston inclines his head in a deep gesture.

"Let me get us a cup of tea." Grace stands and fills the kettle.

Samuel looks Winston in the eye. "You might need something stronger than tea."

"It's too early for shiraz, son." He turns to Grace. "Do you mind making me a double shot of coffee?"

Samuel continues, discussing his time in Ulara working alongside the shaman and Kaikare. He tells them about Kaikare's personality and how she defied the chief and her father if she strongly believed what they were doing was wrong, even if no other Ularan had her back. He told them how Ivy lived in her. Grace and Winston smiled as they sipped their coffee.

He continued to describe Eden and her influence over the village. Seeing the pride in Winston's eyes reflected what Samuel felt every day.

He relived the death of the shaman with him. Tears fell from his eyes, and when he glanced down, he found Rose asleep in his arms.

Grace patted his arm. "She's been asleep for a while, but I didn't want to interrupt your story. The sound of your voice soothes her." She gives an understanding smile. "Rose loves you."

Samuel wipes his eyes. The next half of his story is what Winston needs to hear, yet Samuel can only manage pieces at a time without crumpling to the floor in the pain of his past.

26

EDEN

My hand ships to pat the space in the bed.

Samuel isn't beside me.

My eyes flutter open, and I moan with a thumping headache. Pressing fingertips to my forehead, I stagger to the bathroom and shower in record time. A few minutes later, I'm throwing ibuprofen down my throat and guzzling water before almost running out the door.

Stepping out into the sunshine, I squint and curse for forgetting my sunglasses. I don't get far before my phone vibrates in my pocket.

Amy.

"Hey, babe, how are you?"

"You abandoned me at Ethan's?"

I stop walking, hearing the exasperation in her tone. "Are you okay?"

"Yes," she says harshly. "Well, no. My head is full of semi-trucks colliding, and I can't stop puking. Mum's pissed because we arranged a family breakfast, but I can't move, and Ethan is being *sooo* nice I feel like I'm in another universal dimension. I mean, what the hell is going on? Why am I here and not with you? And why is

Ethan so freaking nice? I keep pinching myself like it's a dream. No… it's a freaking nightmare."

A giggle escapes me.

"Are you seriously laughing because I'm stressed and sick and ugh…"

"Do you need me to come over?"

"What are you doing?"

"Walking to Mum's. I assume Samuel is there with Rose. I woke up only minutes ago to an empty house."

There's a muffled sound. "Oh, thanks. You didn't have to."

I continue walking.

"Hey. Ethan has brought me breakfast in bed. I'll chat later."

"Be nice."

She's gone.

I'm grinning, and my body has a sense of weightlessness. She liked Ethan in the beginning, then toward the end of our relationship, something changed. She said something about him grating on her nerves, and she didn't trust him because he was a flirt. Amy has a good heart, and I feel bad for leaving her with him, and yet I hope it's a chance for my friends to make amends. They've known each other since school. The notion of them getting along gives me peace of mind. I have no animosity toward Ethan and need Amy to lay down her sword.

I open the penthouse door to Samuel speaking. He mentions Wayara. One word and I understand the seriousness of his tone.

"Morning," I say in a gentle tone to everyone. I lean to give Samuel a kiss and stroke Rose's cheek. She's peacefully sleeping in his arms. "Do you want me to hold her?"

Samuel shakes his head. By his anguished expression, she comforts him. "I'm telling your parents about my travels."

An unusual explanation, yet I say nothing. Mum and Dad are wearing the same shocked expression. "Can I make anyone a cup of tea?"

Everyone declines, and I sense the tension in the room.

Waiting for the kettle to boil seems like hours, not minutes.

"Excuse me." Samuel leaves the table and places Rose on the Disney Princess sofa bed. She doesn't stir at all.

"Did she sleep well for you last night?" I ask Mum.

"Yes, all night."

"Tell the truth, Grace," Dad quips. "She didn't go to bed until after nine when Faith and the kids left. She woke with me before dawn."

"Well, thank you again for letting her sleep over, but it sounds like both you and Rose need to have an early night."

"Same," Samuel says as he takes a seat.

"Can I get you something to eat?" I ask him.

"I already offered," Mum adds. She tilts her head at Samuel. "I can cook you eggs or anything you want."

"It's fine. I'm still full after my protein shake," he says convincingly.

I let it go and fail to mention I noticed some of it in the glass when I opened the refrigerator.

"I appreciate everything you have told us this morning." Dad's expression is genuinely grateful. "Eden told us stories of how they bonded together, and it warms my heart how Mum somehow brought my sister and my daughter together." He swipes a tear. "I only wish I got to know her and tell her how brave and wonderful our mother was in both of our worlds."

"Dad…" I choke up. I go stand behind him, wrapping my arms around him. "She knows."

"Is Dawn safe now?"

Samuel gives a subtle nod. His gaze lowers to the table.

"But?" I move around the table and sit beside him then place a hand on his shoulder. "Something is troubling you."

"When we stopped migrating, they set up a new camp. It wasn't until I sailed along the river a few miles that I found a remote Colombian community. We didn't make it to Peru. The risks outweighed the safety of stopping rather than crossing the border again." He glances at me. "We'd lost a few more men. At one stage, I ventured into a small town with a small amount of American cash on me and the gold nuggets Kaikare gave me. I bartered and purchased sneakers, medication, and food. It wasn't enough to sustain everyone. We'd traveled hundreds of miles by boat and just as many by foot."

"You had boats? It surprises me as I assumed you wanted to stay out of sight and deep in the jungle."

"We had no choice," he murmurs. "And I stole the motored curiaras."

Samuel could have murdered someone by his guilty expression. "I'm sure they understood." Resting my head on his shoulder, I then squeeze his hand.

"We'd already encountered thieves, and we handed over some other valuables Kaikare had hidden in her pack. She wisely grabbed them at the last minute. Rest assured…" he glances at Dad, "… Kaikare keeps Ivy's pearls hidden."

Dad lowers his gaze, and Samuel gives him a minute before continuing. Interrupting Samuel is the last thing any of us want, and we don't want him to stop talking.

"We eventually abandoned the boats to trek through the jungle to avoid larger towns and any attention on us. Most of the river journey happened at night and the jungle trek on foot during the day. When we discovered the remote community, we set up a new camp, a new home, and the warriors built a makeshift raft only to get me to the next river community. It was no secret I intended to leave and find you when the Ularans decided on a place to settle. I didn't realize the closest community was only ten miles away. A volunteer doctor was working when I arrived. He helped me to find my way out. I told him about the Ularans and how they'll keep to themselves. If any of them venture close, he can explain he knows me and ask if he could check on them. Like in other communities, I explained their lack of immunity and minimal interaction with the outside world. He promised to keep in contact, only I didn't have a phone number to give him except my father's number as I'd lost my satellite phone in the river months ago." He kisses the top of my head. "It's why I couldn't contact you."

Something doesn't sound right. "You're worried because…"

He closes his eyes slowly and opens them again. "Guerrillas infiltrating the area." He shakes his head. "I don't know. I don't have the answers." Samuel bows his head. "The location isn't ideal, although I have to have faith in Dr. Jacques."

"You're a remarkable man. Never doubt it, son. The lengths you went to keep my sister safe and help the community are honorable."

Samuel drifts into silence. His expression turns skeptical as he bows his head. "I feel I failed them."

He's struggling, and an audience isn't what he needs if he breaks down. I sense he's still hiding something, and it's why the cracks are showing.

"No, you saved them," I say firmly.

My parents agree.

Raising my phone from the table, I make a point of checking the time. "We talked about taking Rose on a picnic today." Pushing up from the table, I place my cup in the sink, giving Samuel an opening to leave.

Late afternoon, Samuel naps at the same time as Rose. I decide to check in on Amy, so I head out onto the balcony and sit on the recliner and stare at the boats fishing at sea for a few minutes before calling.

"Hey, Edes." She sounds chirpy.

"Hey. Just wanted to make sure you made it home safe?"

Amy chuckles. "If you thought Ethan was a serial killer, why did you leave me with him?"

"It was his idea. Admittedly, I enjoyed watching him fuss, and he wanted to take care of you. And a little bit of me hoped you'd see how he's changed. I want my friends… well, to be friends."

Amy is silent for a moment.

"I thought you plotted it because he was *sooo* nice it was sickening. But you're right. He's changed. Although you need to make it up to me after pulling that stunt."

I laugh. "Sure. Name the place, and it will be my shout."

"Or maybe you could come and visit me?"

"What a great idea. If Samuel and Rose came, they could enjoy some fresh country air while I hang out with you."

"Sam would enjoy the slower country life. Maybe working as a rural GP would interest him?"

The more I thought about his work, the more I realized his stress and inability to gain weight related to his choice to continue working as a doctor in modern city hospitals.

"I'm not sure working as a doctor is right for him anymore. Or at least in a busy hospital. I'm still worried about him."

"Plan to visit me sooner. Just saying, it could be the best thing for him."

"Hey." Samuel sits on the chair beside me. "Sorry, I didn't mean to sleep for as long as I did."

"Ames, I must go. I'll call you later in the week."

"Think about what I said."

"I will."

Samuel stares out at the ocean, where the sun shines a bright column of light over the water. Light sparkles over the surface like a dance of minuscule firecrackers.

"Is Amy okay?" he asks softly.

"Yeah." I rest a hand on his leg. "She invited us to visit her in Berri on your next free weekend."

His expression falters. "You realize my parents will be here soon?"

I take his hand in mine. "Then we should go next weekend after Dana's party."

27

SAMUEL

Samuel locks his bag in the locker and steps out of the staffroom into the hallway, almost colliding with Dr. Tolley.

"MVA in the emergency room," she says without looking at him.

Sliding his arms into a navy jacket as he walks, he falls into step alongside her. The distinct stench of hospital cleaning products assaults his nostrils. He begrudges taking the deep breath to prepare himself for the chaos awaiting them.

"Do we have numbers?"

"Eight." She checks the time on her wristwatch. "Two DOA. A provisional driver lost control on the freeway." She says it as if talking about what she ate for lunch. Her demeanor doesn't change. Motor vehicle accidents are part of their work life, and Dr. Tolley has seen her share of death.

He walks faster to keep up. Dr. Tolley is taller than him, and her long legs are used to walking at a faster pace.

"Two elderly patients are in radiology and being

prepped for theater. The driver is also in radiology for query rib fractures. There was mention of a middle-aged woman with a possible ruptured spleen. She was driving to the hospital to receive adjuvant chemo post a double mastectomy."

"Is she in radiology?"

Dr. Tolley hands Samuel the spare pager from her coat pocket. "The message wasn't clear. She is being prepped for surgery." She holds her card against the black box on the wall and the double doors swing open. Staff is passing before them like a busy intersection in downtown LA. They slide between bodies without colliding and head to the main desk. Three doctors who have not been introduced to Samuel are in a deep discussion.

"Morning, Dr. Tolley and Dr. McMahon," the clinical nurse, Margaret, acknowledges their presence although she only gives a fleeting glance. Her head is down, and she's moving patient files to create a clearing on her desk. Managing an emergency ward demands respect, and within minutes, she reminds him of a bear going about her duties. If antagonized, you know to back the hell away.

Margaret appears to be in her mid-forties with a gray regrowth around the crown of her head, and when she catches him staring at her, she grumbles, "This is no place to be just a pretty face." She waggles her finger to her right. "Bed sixteen is waiting to be assessed."

"We were expecting to see the oncology patient," Dr. Tolley interrupts.

Margaret continues clicking on her computer as though we had disappeared. "Still in radiology. Dr. Tolley, can you please assess room seven? I'll inform you both when the patient has returned."

Dr. Tolley shrugs at Samuel, and they head to the assigned rooms. When he locates bed sixteen, he slides the curtain aside before closing it again. He picks up the notes at the end of the bed.

"Morning, Megan. I'm Dr. McMahon."

"Morning, doctor."

He flicks over her chart. "I believe you have difficulty in breathing and a cough on exertion."

"Yes. I had x-rays, and now I'm back here awaiting the results." She pulls the blue blanket up and over her shoulders. "It's freezing in here."

Megan is shaking under the blanket even though the room temperature is steady and not at all cool.

"What time were your x-rays?" He watches her breathing, noting the rise and fall of her chest is labored.

"Half-hour ago, but I was rushed out as there was another emergency."

He takes the stethoscope from his neck and asks Megan to sit forward. Inserting the ear tips in his ears, he then places it on her back and listens. Crackles are evident along with a dead space void of sound.

"Can you take some deep breaths in and out?"

No change, and then she erupts into a coughing fit.

He rests a hand on her shoulder. "Can I get you some water?"

She points to her bag on the chair. Retrieving a water bottle, she takes a few mouthfuls and tries to catch her breath.

He then hands her the call button. "I'm going to see if they have sent your results. Press the button if you need anything."

With the emergency demanding attention, Megan's results may have been overlooked. He assumes the results to be double pneumonia. So he signs a form for the nurse to take blood cultures, arterial blood gases, and a sputum specimen. Then he arranges for her to be admitted for monitoring overnight, along with pulse oximetry and further blood tests to eliminate other diseases.

He accesses her results on the computer. Dark shadows indicate pneumonia, the right side more prevalent than the left.

He finishes his notes and calls the medical ward for Megan to be an inpatient and for an orderly to transport her to the ward.

"We're not made of beds," Margaret says from behind him.

"Then you better find one for my patient." Samuel stands and returns to Megan to tell her she'll be spending at least one night in the hospital.

He could have sent her home with standard antibiotic therapy for pneumonia and Ventolin if she needed it. With her breathing unstable, he's not comfortable risking any more lives.

His hands have enough blood on them.

At midday, Samuel seeks food.

He has little energy to continue working.

The last time he worked the wards he was in his twenties, and he's considerably thinner now. Before he makes it to the staff room, a queasy sensation overcomes him, and the hallway appears to move under his feet. He sways and then grabs the handrail for support, taking a moment to catch his breath.

A sharp pain stabs at his gut and his hand automatically presses for support.

"Dr. McMahon, are you okay?" He doesn't know who the nurse is but is grateful for her concern. He's about to brush her off and tell her he's fine, then he stumbles. Pulling the pager from his pocket, he hands it to her.

"Can you please call Dr. Tolley?" Samuel knows the warning signs for syncope.

"Sure, but let's get you to a bed first before you pass out."

Black dots join before his eyes.

She leads him to the side room of the medical staff quarters to rest if needed then assists him onto the bed, lifting his feet onto the covers.

"Do you want me to remove your shoes?"

Samuel holds an arm across his brow to block out the fluorescent light. "I'm fine. Thank you again," he says without opening his eyes. "I'll wait here for Dr. Tolley."

The door clicks closed.

Dang it. He should have asked her for food.

A short time passes before the door creaks as it opens.

"What happened?"

He opens his eyes at the sound of Dr. Tolley's voice.

"It's nothing. I just need food." He looks her in the eye, his expression solemn. "Can this please stay between us?"

28

EDEN

My hair is styled and makeup applied, ready for Dana's farewell.

A cab is booked for six o'clock to the city.

I've been anxious about today, and it's come too soon. Samuel promised he'd be home in time to go with me even though he hasn't arrived home before seven all week.

It's a family affair, and Faith's kids are sleeping the night at Jake's parents.

I booked Tiffany, Amy's cousin, to babysit, and I expect her to arrive within the hour. I'm also hoping to use Tiffany if I choose to follow the nursing pathway.

The decision needs to be mine without the influence or input of my family. I know Samuel will say to do it if it's what I want, though how can I when he's struggling mentally and physically?

I need to be here for him.

I *want* to be here for him.

Mum has told me I'd make a wonderful nurse like Gran.

My passion isn't as strong as hers. My dreams have already come true. Samuel is here with Rose and me.

Anything else is a bonus.

The thought of losing him makes me sick to my stomach. I'm not adding any stress to our lives until he shows signs of improvement. Only I feel like I'm not doing enough to help him. The contentment of him being by my side is now lost to constant nausea worrying about his well-being. His mindset has switched to survival mode. Slowly, his patience and strength are being stripped away.

It's time to step up and take control because I'm not losing him again.

The doorbell chimes and I check the camera at the front gate. "Hi, Tiffany." I press the button to release the gate. "Come in. I'll meet you at the door." Scooping Rose from the floor, I carry her on my hip down the stairs and then open our oversized, Italian wood front door. "Hey. This is Rose."

"Hi, Rose." She smiles at my daughter who plays coy and lays her head on my shoulder.

I stroke Rose's back. "She just needs a minute. Come upstairs, and I'll show you around."

"Wow," Tiffany exclaims as we ascend the staircase. "Your house is fabulous."

"It is, although I can't take any credit. We've only been here a few months, and I had no input on the architecture or interior design." We enter the kitchen, where Rose's dinner is on the stovetop. "She needs dinner, a bath, and then she might play awhile before bed. She goes down at seven. Just put her in the cot and walk out. I'm blessed she loves her sleep."

"Do you want me to do any cleaning?"

"Gosh, no. There's a spare bedroom for you in case

we're late, and you're more than welcome to spend the night if you're too tired to drive home."

"Thanks, Eden. I'll see how the night pans out." She pushes long blonde strands of hair behind her ears, so many of her features and mannerisms remind me of Amy.

"I'll give you the tour of the house, and then I'll leave you so I can change. I expect Samuel to be home soon."

🌴

An hour later, I walk into Dana's party alone. A server strolls past with a tray of champagne flutes, and I take one before mingling with the crowd.

Seeing my family, I join the circle.

"Hi, everyone." I step between Faith and Mum.

Mum places a hand on my arm. "Darling, jade green has always looked good on you." She glances over my shoulder. "Where's Samuel?"

Faith's forehead wrinkles, and I know what she's thinking.

"He's working late," I explain. "He wants to meet me here, but I told him to go home. Since he's on call this weekend, he should rest." I scan the room. "I haven't found Dana yet."

My phone dings with a message so I hand Faith my glass and open my clutch.

Finally a message from Samuel.

> Leaving now. I'll go home and shower
> and come immediately. I'm sorry xx

It's fine. Just stay home. Tell Tiffany to stay so you can get some rest. I was hoping you weren't on call this weekend as I wanted to take you to Berri for an overnight stay and see where Amy is living. Love you xx

...

Then the dots disappear.

...

Is he writing then deleting his comments?

I'll see you soon x

Does it mean he's coming, or he'll see me at home? Ugh. I drop my phone in my clutch.

Faith nudges my shoulder. "Everything okay?"

"For now." I force a smile then clink my glass with hers. "Bottoms up."

🌴

Three hours later, most of the guests have departed. Dana's husband is entertaining old work colleagues and close friends by the bar. Dana, Faith, and I are at a table with a fresh bottle of champagne and are in a 'deep and meaningful' meeting.

"I'm glad you're working at Monte in HR?" Dana says to Faith. "When I leave and your dad employs a random, I assumed he'll groom Ethan to take over Monte." Dana glances at me and flutters her long lashes. "I know he's changed…" she draws out, "… but he's not family." She points a finger at me, then Faith. "You're family," she stammers.

I stare at Faith. "This is true."

"And why did you leave again?" It's a rhetorical question, and Faith sits back and folds her arms. "I agreed, and then you both resigned. Feed me to the wolves, why don't you?"

"The wolves," I say and giggle. "It's not a courtroom. Besides, I haven't resigned. I'm working part-time and with you."

"When are you both coming to visit me?" Dana whines. She snakes her arms over Faith and my shoulders and pulls us close.

"Whoa." I balance my drink from spilling over our designer gowns.

"You know the Daintree Rainforest is right on our doorstep.

Dana looks fuzzy, and I have trouble focusing. "On your doorstep? How?"

"We bought a house in Cow Bay in the Daintree and can stay on weekends. During the week, the small apartment in Cairns is for the convenience of work. Selling our house covered both mortgages."

I lean my head on her shoulder. "It sounds dreamy."

"I'll visit, except if there's any sign of snakes or a freaking spider, I'm out of there," Faith warns.

"I imagine it agreeing with Samuel," Dana murmurs.

There are hidden messages in her words.

The three of us remain silent in the unspoken words of Samuel's health.

After a few minutes, I say, "Yeah."

29

SAMUEL

"One night," Samuel says when they're on the open road driving toward Berri. "Tomorrow we get up and drive back so I get the day with Rose."

Eden smiles at him as if he gave her a million dollars. Being together on a road trip and exploring a new place is more exciting to her than a wad of cash.

Eden intended to bring Rose and have a mini family getaway until her mother suggested Rose stay with them overnight to give Eden and Samuel time together. Samuel is desperate to have quality time with Eden, only partying with Amy isn't what he had in mind.

"Thank you for doing this for me." Eden places a hand on his thigh.

With one hand, he releases the steering wheel and squeezes her hand. "As long as *we* get alone time."

"We will, I promise." Eden leans over and kisses his cheek.

He recognizes the gleam in her eyes.

"We could pull over here. Tinted windows." He winks.

Eden giggles. "Keep driving, Dr. McMahon."

On the outskirts of town, orchard farms line the road and toward the horizon.

Eden stares out the window. "The Riverina is best known for its citrus and stone fruit, and personally, I believe the best apricots in the world."

"The world?" Samuel repeats and chuckles. On the side of the road is a little tin shed with a hand-painted sign reading *Fruit for Sale.*

Samuel slows to veer the Porsche off the road at a safe speed where no loose stones flick up and damage his car's paint.

They wander over to a variety of fruits on display, including figs and homemade jam.

"Someone could steal everything," he says, wide-eyed.

"It's the country, and no doubt someone's keeping check from a distance. There might be a camera to snap your registration plate, and they could call ahead to the locals to watch out for you."

Samuel spins, looking around. "For real?"

"No." She grins. "Now pick some fruit." She picks up an orange and peels a piece, then takes a bite. "Seriously, this is good. We should buy some."

"And if it wasn't tasty?"

She bumps his hip. "You're too easy today."

They pack oranges, lemons, apricots, and plums into bags and then select apricot and fig jam. The honesty box has a lock so Samuel leaves a hundred-dollar bill.

Eden shakes her head. "It wouldn't even cost fifty dollars."

"It will make up for any missing fruit."

Eden kisses his cheek. "You're very generous, and it's a reason why I love you."

He holds her gaze. "Yeah? What are the other reasons?"

She takes his hand as they stroll back to the car. "Your good looks and your smile. It can change my mood in a second."

He presses her against the car and kisses her hard. "I could change your mood right now," he whispers against her lips.

"You always do." Eden links her arms around his neck. He kisses her nose then opens the car door, closing it behind her. Dropping the fruit on the floor in the back, he starts the engine and veers the car onto the road. Inside the safety of the car has opened a part of him to chat easily with Eden. "You said I didn't smile enough when we first met."

"You didn't." She places a hand on his thigh. "You intrigued me beyond the pull of attraction, despite your grumpiness," she jokes. "So, tell me, what first appealed to you about me?"

Samuel grins. "You, in that bathing suit on the beach in Salvador." He gives her a sideways glance and winks before looking back to the road. "I've seen thousands of chicks in tiny bikinis, yet you stole the air out of my lungs. I had to get a closer look, and everything about you appealed to me. My brain was like tick, tick, tick."

"You had a type?" she asks incredulously.

"I didn't know I had a type, and if you recall, I was also backing away, trying to put space between us. I wanted you, yet I knew we couldn't be together."

"And here I am proving you wrong."

Samuel shakes his head and chuckles. "It's your superpower."

"Hey, it's okay. You did the same to me. I remember wading out of the water trying to find you."

The cabin of the car falls quiet.

Samuel is only half the size compared to when she met him. He taps the steering wheel with one finger as though it's a distraction. "I'm trying, Eden."

She gives him a few seconds before answering, "I know."

🌴

They arrive at Amy's quaint country rental in Berri. She gives them a quick tour before showing them to the spare bedroom.

"We'll head to the best bar in town tonight for dinner. You'll get to meet the locals."

"Great," Samuel says under his breath.

Eden gives a slight nudge with her elbow. "Sounds like fun, Ames."

"Get comfortable. I coached T-ball this morning and didn't get time to go to the shops, so I'll duck out now. I won't be long."

"I can come with you," Eden says quickly.

"No, it's fine. If you need to hang any clothes, there's free space in the closet. Besides, I want you to relax. It seriously will take me ten minutes." She flicks her ponytail over her shoulder as though shopping for groceries is exciting.

"Do you mind if I shower? I'm a little sweaty from the drive," Samuel asks with another motive.

"Yes, there are towels on your bed, and the bathroom is yours. I have an ensuite."

"It's a great little place."

"Thank you, I think so too."

She waves goodbye and almost skips out the door.

Eden places her small suitcase under the window and opens the lid. "I should hang my dress for tonight."

Samuel stands behind her and runs his hands over the rounded swell of her rear.

Eden freezes. "Samuel, it's—"

"Broad daylight and the window is obscured by grape vines. Can you stop yourself from screaming when I make you orgasm over and over?"

"Jee-sus, Amy said she'd be ten minutes."

"Exactly." He lifts her skirt and groans at the sight of her G-string panties revealing smooth skin. Sliding the thin material down her thighs, he bends to assist her in stepping out of them. He holds the satin strings in the air, and he smiles as she watches them fall to the floor. Samuel stands behind her, kissing her shoulders and neck. "Place your hands on the windowsill." His hands travel up her inner thigh and caress her slick creases. Eden sways her hips and moans with his touch. He adjusts her stance, pushing her feet wider with his and pulling her rear toward him. "You make me crazy."

She purrs at his words, moving her hips in a circular motion while his fingers bring her close to climax. Her reflection in the window is faint yet enough for him to catch the pleasure in her expression. Even better, he can't see his reflection except his face showing equal joy as Eden's. Before she comes, he slides his shorts down and finds her wet and ready for him. He pushes inside her, slowly, deeply. It's intimate, and she's all he feels. "I love you more than anything else in the world," he whispers.

"I love you too," Eden murmurs and then arches her back, seeking more.

Samuel leans back and lifts Eden's ass to perfect

alignment with his hips and thrusts until she's gasping out of breath and whispering his name.

Samuel's body shudders, and for a moment, he can't stand, slumping over her, enjoying the thrill of his orgasm.

"Wow," she whispers.

Slowly, he comes out of the sexual haze while he dots kisses along her spine. "Now *that* was worth the trip."

She giggles. "You better get in the shower, doc, before Amy comes home."

He coughs. "Doc?"

"You can heal me in minutes." She smiles at him as they adjust their clothing.

"For you…" he kisses her nose, "… anytime."

"It could be the country air invigorating you."

Samuel doesn't respond, unsure if she's referring to him being unhappy in her hometown. Or does she believe he's simply unhappy?

What does he have to do to prove he'd move the earth just to be with her?

He has done everything possible to be here.

Does she now doubt his love for her?

30

EDEN

Inside the tavern, a live band plays hits of the nineties, and the catchy beat has many patrons on the dance floor. In between songs, we talked quickly as we were almost shouting over the music. Amy secured a booth in the back near the bar, thinking we could have our own area, except it was a walkway, and she said hi to the locals almost every minute.

"You've made a lot of friends." My heart expands with pride.

She taps her glass several times before meeting my gaze. "Most say hello because I teach their kids or their friends' kids. You know how it is in a small town."

"Don't play it down. You're a magnet to people with your bubbly energy and beauty. And I noticed a couple of guys eyeing you off."

She waves a hand dismissing my words. "Oh, they're too young for me. A new face in the town has the appeal of a new toy." She winks. "I'm older and wiser not to fall for the hot guy with come-to-bed eyes and the smile to make you drop your panties."

Samuel chokes on his beer.

"I'm proud of you," I tell her, reaching out to squeeze her hand.

She squeezes mine back before releasing it. "Don't be too proud. I fucked a couple of hotties first before I realized small towns have a grapevine that's not only for wine."

I chuckle.

"Good for you," Samuel says. "As long as you're happy, Amy."

She smiles at him. "I am for now, but I'm a city girl, and I probably won't stay long."

We glance up at a guy staring at us.

"You know many a woman has said that *before* she falls in love with a hot country boy," a deep voice says.

"Rhett," Amy says and laughs before sliding across her seat. "You remember Eden, right?"

"No man would forget Eden." He takes my hand and kisses it. "How's your dad?"

"Rhett," I say affectionately. "Still the charmer, I see. Dad is good." I can't help but smile at Rhett as he always has a starry-eyed effect on girls. "This is my fiancé, Samuel McMahon."

Rhett stares at me, bewildered. "The doctor from the Amazon?"

I nod quickly as Samuel holds out his hand. "Good to meet you, Rhett. How do you two know each other?"

"Let me tell the story," Amy pipes up.

"You're quite the storyteller tonight," I joke.

Amy's gaze flicks between Rhett and Samuel. "Eden attended university for a short stint with Rhett when, what… you were around nineteen?"

"Yeah."

"And they remained friends although we barely saw

him as he played football and had superstar status until he got caught with drugs."

Rhett moans. "You had to mention it." His expression is serious when he addresses Samuel. "I was young and didn't handle fame well, especially being a country boy. My father died, and I had two younger brothers who also relied on me. Leaving Mum alone on the farm while I bathed in the pleasure of football stardom got to me." He glances at me and then Samuel. "I became an obnoxious prick."

"Wow," Amy says wide-eyed. "I wasn't going to say all that. Anyway, he went on a reality show to clean up his image on national TV, or he'd lose his contract."

Rhett stares up at the ceiling. "Not one of my finest moments." He meets Samuel's gaze. "Although I met my wife on the show."

"Hang on," Amy interrupts. She stares at Samuel. "She wasn't a contestant. In typical Rhett style, he fell for his mentor."

"Life puts us in extraordinary places so we can meet our soul mates." He nudges Amy. "I keep telling her she's going to fall for a local."

Amy rolls her eyes. "Hang on. You jumped ahead. Rhett was one of the surprise football guests at Eden's Dad's sixtieth. And Rhett knows Cleo, Yasmine's sister."

"Small world," Samuel comments.

"I have heard about you, mate. I know Eden was concerned for your safety, and I'm glad you made it safely to Australia." Rhett turns his focus to me. "Weren't you talking about a charity for the indigenous in the Amazon when you first came back?"

"I was." I'm smiling, as out of the corner of my eye, I can see Samuel's surprise. "I wanted to do something to help until life got busy."

Rhett leans his elbows on the table. Long, tanned arms protrude from his polo sleeve. His thick muscles twitch with the slightest movement. It's obvious he's remained fit working on the farm. "If you get it up and running, let me know. I'm looking to be part of a unique charity."

"Samuel's the one to talk to. He has all the knowledge."

Samuel stares at me. "We haven't discussed this, but it's definitely something I'm interested in investing in."

Rhett stands and shakes Samuel's hand. "It's good to finally meet you. We should set up a business meeting in the future. Amy has my number, so call me any time."

Rhett walks away, and Samuel kisses my cheek. "You're full of surprises." He drops his arm over my shoulder. "Have I told you how much I love you?"

"Stop," Amy says and groans. "Get a room. Wait, no… because it's in my house!"

Samuel elbows me.

Then he groans. I assume he's reacting to Amy's comment until his expression falters. "I don't feel good."

I freeze.

His hand is on his stomach, and even in the dim light, his face has paled.

"Would you mind if I leave?"

"I'm coming with you." I slide out of the seat, ready to take his hand. "I've only had one wine, so I'll drive."

Amy is beside us. "Can I do anything? Buy a bottle of water?"

"I need to get him home fast," I whisper.

Amy understands as I vented my concern to her, and she checks in on Samuel regularly.

Samuel limps out to the car as though his hip is painful. My stomach is in knots. How severe is his abdominal pain to make him hobble like an old man? The benefit of small towns is we arrive at Amy's house within minutes. After helping him inside, he almost falls on the bed and curls up on his side. He reaches for his phone in his pocket.

"Do you want me to call anyone?"

He shakes his head. "I underwent some tests during the week. I'm messaging a colleague to see if the results are in."

I sit beside him on the bed. "What tests?"

"A few different ones. We'll talk about it later."

His phone dings, and he groans.

"What is it?"

"Mum and Dad have arrived in Sydney. They're staying a few days to tour and adjust to the time difference."

"That's a good idea." Because I know Samuel would not want to be like this when they arrive in Adelaide.

"There's medication in my bag. Can you please grab it for me?"

His eyes are closed. I don't move for a moment as the truth hits me. He hasn't shared any of this with me. I then rush to retrieve his small suitcase. "There are two types. What are they for?"

"Spasms. It should help my gut. The ones in a bottle are antiparasitic. I need the small box."

"You have a parasite?"

"Not that I know of," he murmurs. "It's precautionary."

I have so many questions, yet I let them go. *For now.* I head into the kitchen, and Amy is warming a hot pack. "How is he?"

"Okay." I shrug. "I wish I knew what's going on with him." I fill a bottle of water and take it to Samuel.

"Thank you," he says, downing his tablets.

"Is it something you ate? The chicken? And you had a beer," I emphasize.

"Maybe." He screws up his face.

I glance up at Amy in the doorway holding a hot pack. I wave her in. Samuel opens his eyes and smiles at her. "Thanks, Ames. Please, Eden, I'm fine. Go and spend time with Amy. It's a chance to be with each other. And by the sounds of it, you still have much to talk about." He winks at Amy.

I run my hand over his forehead. His skin is cool with no sign of a fever. "Okay, but if you need anything, just call out."

Amy gets us bottles of water, and we head into the lounge room. It takes a while for us to fall into easy conversation.

"I almost forgot." She jumps up and heads to her room, and returns seconds later holding a small, wrapped box. She hands it to me. "I saw this in a local shop and thought of you."

It's a ring with turquoise cut into a heart shape. I slide it onto my finger. "Amy, it's exquisite. Thank you."

"The lady said turquoise is a calming stone and represents wisdom, love and tranquility, protection, good fortune, and hope. It's also the stone of communication." She shrugs. "It's pretty too, and the color matches your eyes, and I thought this has *Eden* written all over it."

I hug her tight. "You are so kind, babe."

"You deserve it."

Her kindness brings tears to my eyes.

On the coffee table, her phone makes a funny noise, and we jump apart. "It's Yasmine," Amy says excitedly and holds up the phone. "She knows you're here and wants to FaceTime."

Amy and I sit close together and wave when Yasmine's face appears on the screen.

"Hey, my girls," she sings.

"You look great," I tell her. Dark ringlets are pulled back into a small ponytail, and it's changed her face. Her cheekbones pop.

"Iquitos is steaming hot, and I need my hair off my neck. It's grown since being here. It also sticks straight out on the ends." She grins at us, and I want to hug her.

"We miss you," I tell her.

"You both look good. How's Berri?"

I grin at Amy. "Full of hot men."

Yasmine breaks into a hearty laugh. "Did she tell you about Chad?"

"No, she didn't."

"Oh, I can tell her later. I have another bone still to pick with her." Amy scowls at me.

Before we say it's Ethan, the image shakes, and Michael comes into view. "Hi, ladies, how are we?"

"Good, thanks."

"Has Yasmine told you tomorrow is the day?" He smiles at Yasmine, and the connection between them is obvious.

She drops her arm over his shoulder and pulls him closer. "We're doing Ayahuasca together." She kisses his cheek. "We've been on a strict diet and no alcohol, and we're prepared this time."

"I hope it's everything you're searching for," I tell her. "And I'll pass on to Samuel you have stuck to his diet."

She shoulder-bumps Michael as though coaxing him on.

"In a few days, we'll meet up with Deanne and… I'm coming to Australia with the girls."

Yasmine stares at us with a goofy expression.

"I'm so happy for you," I say louder than necessary, knowing this is what Yasmine wants.

"Is Samuel around?" Michael asks, leaning closer to the screen.

"He's asleep," I emphasize the disappointment. "He'll be excited to know you'll be here soon."

"We better go as we're catching the boat to the village where the shaman is located in about an hour." She smiles again, then she stares at Michael. "And you still haven't packed your case."

"It was great chatting with you," I say quickly.

"Talk in a couple of days, okay," Amy says more as a directive, still wary from the last time.

We end the call, stare at each other, and sigh.

"So. Michael is coming to Adelaide."

"Yeah. Not to change the subject… do you know Ethan has been messaging me every second day?"

I didn't, and I can't help the surprise creeping up my neck.

"And did you know he placed a certain ring on my finger?"

I place a hand on her shoulder. "I did. He emphasized it's about friendship."

"Hmm," she says and scowls at me. "Are you setting me up with him?"

I cough. "God, no. I wanted for peace and us all to be friends."

"Funny, it's what he said, except all this attention is weird."

I take a sip of water and consider my answer, "Don't think too much into it. And I'm glad he's trying."

Jumbled words and shouting come from the bedroom.

Then silence.

Amy stares at me wide-eyed before we both spring off the lounge and dash toward the room. The bedside lamp is on. Samuel is upright in the bed with his eyes closed. His fists swing at something, and then he falls back onto the pillow, mumbling and grunting. He flips from one side to the other.

Amy grabs hold of my forearm. A vicelike grip from concern. "What's happening?"

"Nightmares. They started a few weeks after he arrived. The first time scared the crap out of me. Now I simply wait them out. I observe and make sure he's safe. I used to hug him and tell him he's okay and he's with me. It didn't help."

She releases my arm and wraps her arms around her stomach. "He looks in pain and afraid."

"He's not the only one."

31

SAMUEL

After a week of solid traveling along the river at night and then sleeping during the day, they had finally set up camp. Exhausted, everyone needed sleep. For diseased feet, he treated them with antifungal medications and a balm for healing. Remaining on the boats at night and only walking a few miles during the day helped rest their wounds.

The small convoy of boats meant overcrowding to get all the Ularan men, women, and children on board. Samuel convinced them to wear the T-shirts he purchased, thinking they would attract less attention than if they were almost naked. He also distributed caps with either baseball, football, or basketball emblems embroidered on the front. None of it made sense to the Ularan people, yet they did what he asked. Some women and children giggled. The men only stared back with serious expressions, and he sensed they felt mocked for wearing the outside world's clothing.

As the light of dawn fell upon the earth, their silhouettes were now visible from the shore.

The river had widened. The hats and T-shirts helped to obscure their identity. Bare legs and feet were concealed by the side of the boat, along with arrows, darts, pots of poison, food, and tweed bags of belongings lining the curiaras' floor.

Another night passes, sailing the water without being questioned. When they find an uninhabited section of a sandy riverbed, he leads them ashore, pulling the canoes on land and into the trees to be out of sight. A simple chore leaves the warriors weak.

Besides the fish captured in nets hanging over the edge of the canoes, Samuel needs to arrange food to sustain their energy. The fish serves as food for breakfast, or is it dinner since they'll sleep during the day?

The women set up camp by starting a fire, then tying hammocks to the trees, and untangling mosquito nets. The men grab their blowpipes and wander deeper into the jungle. Samuel remains with Kaikare. They roam the nearby jungle, picking leaves and berries to use as medicine. His natural medical stock is low, and most detest taking Western world medication.

A twig snaps. And Kaikare spins to see what's behind them. After staring at nothing but tree trunks and palm leaves, they're satisfied no danger is present and finish collecting enough plant food to provide the community for at least the day.

After transporting the clay pots off the curiaras, they collect water from the plants and stems of bamboo. Water is poured into the pot over the fire. Kaikare grinds the leaves and drops the pulped mash into another pot of water. Samuel speaks to each woman about her health and the well-being of her husband and children. Being informed helps with his decision on how to treat and what his next move will be. Most want to remain here as they feel safe.

The men arrive home with several monkeys and two snakes, enough food to get them through the day. The fish is being served as he speaks. Kaikare has the medicine boiling in the water. The women will serve the snakes and monkeys soon.

Everything looks promising.

They manage around five hours of sleep before the camp comes to life, and the men decide to go out in search of more food. Something larger is necessary to feed the community.

Dusk falls upon the camp, and the men haven't returned, so Samuel distributes the fruit and berries he and Kaikare had scavenged. Originally, the stock was for the hours sailing the river, but with food scarce, he needs to focus on the present day.

With daylight diminishing, the atmosphere in the camp becomes restless, with the men and warriors not returning to camp.

With barely enough light to guide them, Samuel grows concerned and asks the elders to whistle and make animal sounds for the warriors to recognize so the sound guides them back to camp. A sequence of coos and whistles erupt every fifteen seconds. In the distance, a faint whistle echoes, and more men belt out whistles to lead their people in the right direction. In this strange land, trees surround them like twenty-story buildings, and the thick undergrowth hinders sight of anything beyond several yards away.

He understands the warriors are trained hunters and marked tree trunks, slashed palm leaves to guide them 'home,' yet they're in another country and, if caught trespassing, their poison arrows might be useless against powerful guns.

Another whistle sounds closer to the camp.

The men push through the palm leaves. Subtle cheering erupts when the warriors appear with three peccaries, inverted with legs tied to a bamboo branch. They tell stories about their hunt as the women prepare the meal and spear each pig to be smoked over the fire while they sleep. The excitement is a relief knowing how forlorn the people have become, yet in the back of Samuel's mind, he's alerted to the killing of protected animals in an unfamiliar location. The Ularans view pigs as food and part of the circle of life. Eat what they need and give back to Mother Earth. Rules beyond their community and the Western world's law about animal protection is foreign knowledge. Samuel struggles to find the words they understand when explaining how their behavior could be dangerous at every step of their journey.

The smoke wafts around Samuel, and it helps to mull the continual buzz of mosquitoes circling his head. He misses the days where fires in Ulara continually burned, giving a distinct aroma to jolt his memories.

Memories of good times comfort him to sleep, disguising the terror expanding in the back of his mind.

Deep sleep never lasts.

A bright light burns through his eyelids. Samuel rolls over and squeezes his eyes shut, hoping the tightness will block out the light. His thoughts confuse him as they're unaccustomed to experiencing sunrise in the thickest part of the jungle. Something sharp pokes his back. He twitches.

Another poke to his shoulder, only this time he senses aggression.

Samuel flings himself forward in the hammock, the gentle sway of the hammock offering split seconds of relief from the light shining directly in his eyes. He lifts an arm to shield the brightness until his eyes adjust.

A flashlight.

Spanish words.

Clothed men.

Another light shines from behind, and metal reflects in the light.

Guns.

Hurling himself forward to his feet, the light follows him, and standing with his arms raised in front of his eyes is a disadvantage. The Ularan men and women are already standing, unmoving and silent. He's thankful they understand danger and don't do anything to be shot.

"¿Cómo puedo ayudarle?" How can I help you?

A deep voice tells him they're trespassing and on private land. A threatening tone indicates they aren't getting away without a form of payment. He ponders his position to bargain, although his resources are scarce. Tiny pieces of gold are all that remain beside his American dollars. One of the flashlights shines over his hammock and lands on his backpack. A man dressed in a khaki shirt scavenges through his bag. He pulls out medication packets and his notes wrapped in plastic.

"Quién eres tú?" Who are you?

Samuel explains he's an American doctor caring for the people in the community, and they are traveling to find a new home.

The guy asks for their passports and visas, and it tricks Samuel into believing they're a sub-group of the government military.

Before he has time to explain, a gunshot fires, and a body falls with a thump. Wails sound before him.

"Por favor, colega, deje que le explique la situación." Please, colleague, let me explain the situation.

A grunt sounds from behind the intruder. The flashlights leave Samuel and shine on the limp body of an intruder gasping for his last breath. It gives Samuel a chance to flee behind a thick tree trunk. Flashlights scan the Ularan faces, all squinting their eyes from the light. Multiple beams of light scan the area like a prison yard searching for an escapee.

Another body falls, and a flashlight rolls out of his hand along the ground. It shines momentarily on a figure holding a blow dart.

Timenneng.

He disappears into the darkness, and the hostile men yell and flash the lights in search of him. Except one. The leader shouts a threat warning he'll shoot the women.

Before Samuel surrenders, he needs a plan. Only his thoughts scramble, and he has no weapon in defense other than his voice to reason with the criminals.

"Tengo oro," Samuel shouts. I have gold.

Lights shine in his direction.

Snickers of triumph and footsteps stomp closer.

Suddenly, an arm is around his throat, a blade pressed to his jugular. The intruder came from behind with a hand around his waist, holding Samuel like a vice. One slight slip could be fatal. The light is back burning his eyes. There are fewer men to fight thanks to Timenneng's swift skills, and Samuel knows he must act fast. The familiar thump of a body hitting the ground, and simultaneously, the light falls away from him, another flashlight rolling over the ground pointing at Samuel's feet. The attacker grunts and wails behind Samuel, and his hold loosens. Samuel flings his arm off his neck and turns to see him curled over, holding his testicles.

Kaikare stands behind, and he makes out her defiant stance.

He doesn't think, only acts and swings a brutal uppercut punch to the attacker's nose at an angle where the nasal bones, with enough force, penetrate the brain.

Samuel yells out with the pain of smashed knuckles and a loud moan of knowing he killed, not saved a life.

"Samuel, you're fine." The voice breaks through his pain.

He reaches for Kaikare to ensure she's safe, except her body shape is fading. He opens his eyes to nothing but black space.

A hand rests on his back.

"You're safe. You're with us, and everything will be okay."

Samuel scrunches his eyes closed with awareness of his surroundings. "I'm sorry," he murmurs. "It was just a dream."

"No, Samuel. You're experiencing nightmares, and it scares me," she whispers.

Nightmares are still dreams.

He wishes it was just that and not the truth of his dark past.

32

EDEN

On Monday morning, I awaken to a note from Samuel on my bedside table.

Morning Eden,
My parents have caught an earlier flight.
I'll pick them up from the hotel after work. Please don't worry yourself with my parents staying at our house.
Enjoy your day.
See you tonight.
Samuel x

For him to mention not to be concerned, I'm now thinking have I missed something, and should I be?

The house is clean.

There's plenty of food.

Are they fussy?

Do they have allergies?

Shit, we don't have fancy cutlery or crockery or—

Stop.

This is exactly what Samuel didn't want me to do.

Yesterday on the trip home, he didn't talk about his nightmare. Instead, he talked about his parents and the places they would like to see. When I brought up Rose's first birthday, he played it down, saying Rose won't remember anything and to keep the celebrations to family.

I intended to keep it to family, only I wanted to decorate the house.

And today I hoped to shop with Mum, but she has appointments all day. Faith is also busy with errands.

My friends are not here.

My thoughts go to Yasmine and how she's coping in the jungle.

Then I'm thinking about Gran and her journal.

Looking around the room, I find it on the coffee table stacked with other books. This isn't something I want on view when Samuel's parents arrive. I pick it up and start daydreaming about Gran.

And then I think of Brenda…

The white hallways of the care facility are empty.

I had called ahead to register my visit and confirm Brenda is up to visitors today. All the doors to the residents' rooms are closed, and something doesn't feel right.

A door swings open, and a nurse in a blue surgical gown appears. She stops with the door half ajar. "Can I help you?"

Flicking the brake latch on Rose's stroller, I stop in the hallway. "Have I come at an awkward time?"

She peels disposable gloves from her fingers and drops them in the waste. "And you are?"

"Eden Monteford. I've come to visit Brenda James."

She smiles at me. "Hi, Eden, I'm Lori. Come with me, and I'll show you where Brenda is having morning tea."

"If it's in the garden, then I know the way." I flick the brake latch off and rock Rose as she has fallen asleep. Hopefully, she'll stay asleep so I don't have to chase after her.

"She is. I'll follow you out as I need to lock the doors behind you for a few minutes."

I give her a blank look.

"One of our clients has passed. We need to wheel her out of the building, and we prefer all doors closed for privacy. It can upset the residents."

"Of course," I say quickly and hurry along because I'm not sure I'm ready to stumble across that scene.

The door clicks behind me when I step outside into the warm sunshine. Brenda is sitting in a wheelchair under the shade of her favorite tree.

It's the beginning of summer, yet a striped crocheted blanket drapes her knees. Closer, I recognize the nurse sitting beside her from my last visit. Still, I check her name badge to jolt my memory. "Hi, Sophie, I don't know if you remember me? I'm Eden."

"Hi. I do. And who do we have here?" She leans in to get a better view of Rose.

"This is my daughter, Rose. I hope she remains asleep so I can have time to chat with Brenda without her crying to get out of the stroller."

"For sure. Well, I'll leave you alone while I get Brenda her morning tea. Call out if you need anything. Enter through those doors, and it's the first room on your right." She points to another set of double doors on the other side of the lawn.

Positioning Rose's stroller under the shade, I sit beside Brenda. Her gaze is fixed across the grass, and I'm not sure it's on anything. "Hi, Brenda." I lightly pat her hand, hoping for some eye contact.

Brenda stares down at my hand and then looks at me. "Oh, you came back?"

"Yes, I promised I would." I'm relieved she remembers. "I have Gran's journal and would like to read some of it. Do you remember the good times with Ivy?"

"We shared some good times," she says in her husky voice as though she needs to cough.

"Are you unwell?"

She shakes her head.

I remove both journals from my handbag. I open to a section I marked when both ladies snuck out of the nursing home and met up with their boyfriends and soon-to-be husbands. When I finished reading the entry, I turned to Brenda. "You two were mischievous together."

Brenda blinks, and her brows crease. "I didn't know you wrote about us?"

"What? No, I didn't. I—" Her hand reaches for the other journal. The one Gran wrote while in the jungle.

"Tell me another one of your adventures." Her finger runs over the cover of the journal. Her swollen knuckles are twisted with arthritis. Her eyes are mere slits from the excess skin overhanging her lids. Yet there's a spark of life and excitement as her lips curl upward. "You had the best life, so don't feel bad. Stop beating yourself up about Dawn. You did what you needed to do… what was best for everyone. Albert will get over it one day. I mean, would he rather you be dead?"

She thinks I'm Gran. Her best friend, Ivy.

"Do you want me to read to you?"

She smiles. "Does the sun rise every morning?"

"Right." Good point.

I place Gran's first journal away and turn the page of the entry I last read.

33

IVY

March 10, 1963

*Last night Maria and I stayed up late after drinking a purifying
tea. We giggled by the fire and under a full moon, surmising they
gave us the wrong brew. Jennifer and Felix were in Canaima for
the night. A deserved break.*

*The moon's beauty didn't last in our thoughts as it encourages
creatures to hunt.*

Only the sounds we heard were not animals.

I'm still struggling to comprehend what happened.

*We heard the Spanish tones coming out of the darkness. My heart
is still racing as I relive the past night's happenings.*

*Maria sensed evil, she grabbed my hand, and we took off to our
hut. She insisted I pack my belongings. I told her not to panic, for
these men had threatened us before. In my mind, it had been
months since their last visit, and I assumed Dr. Leon could threaten
them enough to deter them.*

*An important factor I'd forgotten was Maria spoke Spanish and
understood the words yelled from a distance. She pushed my back,
urging me to hurry, almost forcing me out the door before I
managed to grab everything.*

"Leave it," she said. "If you don't need it to survive, then just go."
She yanked the netting from my hammock and rolled it into a ball
before tucking it under her arm.
I had my passport and papers. A little cash. Some toiletries and a
few clothes I stuffed in my bag. My suitcase needed to remain here.
I opened it and grabbed my pearls. I did not know why I even
packed them, but I wanted to keep them with me for luck. Then I
found my brush and mirror, not that I bothered brushing my hair
every day. It had become wilder with time, and now I was about to
hide out like an escapee from prison.
Maria stood in the open doorway, peering out into the darkness,
listening. She pressed a finger to her lips and then took my hand.
We crept around the furthest side of the camp and reached the river
as shouting broke out in the village. We ran, pushing past vines for
a few hundred yards. She stopped and listened. Pressing long grass
aside, she revealed a dugout canoe. Under the moonlight, I could
make out the weathered wood. It contained two rows of seats, not
large at all, and two wooden paddles.
"This is here for emergencies. Take it. Go."
Her words keep playing over in my head.
I couldn't help it.
I began to cry.
She helped push it into the water before throwing the netting
aboard. She then hugged me and said, "Look after yourself, Ivy." I
can still picture her bleak expression.
I asked her where I should go and when I should come back.
She told me to find my Ularan friend since I'd be safer there than
here.
The place where she emphasized I was lucky not to leave without
an arrow in my back.
She hugged me again then pushed my canoe away from the
embankment.
She told me to stay close to the river's edge, then she dashed into the
night toward the sound of gunfire.

I sailed throughout the night.

Part of me wanted to wake up from a horrible dream, the other part of my mind wanted to believe I was hallucinating from the tea.

This was no hallucination.

At night the river felt eerie, and I felt trapped, only to be catapulted onto the set of a horror movie.

Tree and vine shadows overhung close to the water's edge.

I stayed my distance in case something lurked near the shore. Yet close enough not to get caught up in the force of the current near the middle of the river.

I sailed through the fork leading me along the river toward Ulara.

Closer to where I ascertained the village to be, I found an embankment and went ashore to a small clearing beyond the sand.

Then I went back and lugged the front of the canoe ashore as best I could so at least it wouldn't get washed away.

Light was breaking above the treetops.

Dawn was almost upon me.

I didn't want to venture into the jungle.

I curled up into a ball, wrapped the netting around me, and tried to sleep. Only my eyes opened with every crack of a stick and every unusual howl from a monkey, a warning to its family of danger lurking nearby.

Sleep is impossible, so I'm writing this entry to capture my fear.

I don't know what will happen next.

There's barely enough light to check my writing, although enough for me to feel safer so I might get a few more hours of sleep.

With the intrusion of sunlight blaring down on top of me, I came to. Then a figure blocked the light, and my vision cleared.

He was one of them.

I wrestled with the netting and sat up. Though my sudden movement unnerved him, he jumped back.

He walked away and found a fallen log and sat on it. He looked awfully like the same man I saw a few months ago.

I said hello several times and pointed to myself. "Ivy."

He ignored me and continued to stare.

I was also busting to pee.

I climbed out of the canoe and headed downstream a little and away from the strange man. He began to follow until I held up my hand, insisting on privacy. He didn't understand my words, yet the hand signal worked. He stopped when he realized what I was about to do, only he didn't turn away. So, I peed in front of him on the edge of the river, and not at all ladylike. I zipped up my shorts and then washed my hands, along with my legs because I might be wild, but I want to keep my last shred of hygiene.

When I'm closer, I signaled to him for a drink. Then I rubbed my throat. After watching my charade, he then turned and assessed the bamboo behind him. He waved me over and cracked the bamboo, which I drank out of it like a long cup.

He yanked down an overhead branch full of dark purple berries. I ate one then I couldn't stop.

I asked him if he was taking me to his people. He merely sat down again as though he was about to watch a show.

At this point, I knew he wasn't a threat.

Maybe an assessment of whether I'm a threat, and he'd not take a risk for now. I also reminded myself how outsiders were not welcome in his village.

I walked back and gathered my bag then sat on another log in the shade and out of the sun.

With not much else to do, I'm writing this entry like a scientist.

I still don't know if I can go back or what happened to my friends. Did Maria know they were looking specifically for me? I wasn't worth anything for a ransom, although I guess they didn't know anything except I was from another country, and as I learned from their theft, they were desperate people.

Now I'm the desperate one.

I left my son and husband, who love me, believing I was doing something valuable in the world.
Now I'm in a world where I don't belong.
And every day will be a miracle from this time forward.
I'll keep writing in this journal for as long as my two blue pens last.
It might be my only link to maintaining any sanity.

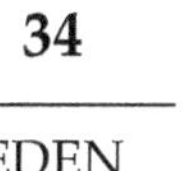

34

EDEN

Rose whimpers, and both Brenda and I glance up from the journal.

"It's him, isn't it," she says.

"I think so." I want to read more as I'm scared for Gran, only not now when Rose is awake. Dropping the journal in my bag, I unclip the safety belt and place Rose on my lap. She stares at Brenda in the way a one-year-old would to a stranger.

"This is Brenda," I say to Rose.

Brenda leans over and makes baby noises to Rose before I get the chance to add, "She's Gran's best friend." Rose wouldn't understand, only I wanted to say it for Brenda's sake.

"Oh, you're babysitting Eden again. Thank you for bringing her. You know how I love babies."

I'm stunned for a moment. Brenda still thinks I'm Gran.

Brenda's love of children hasn't waned, and I watch her connect with Rose in a special way for a few minutes. My thoughts drift back to the journal, but I can't become lost in Gran's world of the past when I must be organized in the present, and I'm already distracted by Samuel's parents' arrival.

Sophie interrupts us and says she needs to attend to Brenda and give her some meds with her morning tea.

I thank her for the wonderful care and promise to come back to visit soon. I kiss Brenda on her cheek and tell her I love her.

"I love you, too, dear," she says and smiles.

Before going home, I do some last-minute shopping to prepare for Samuel's parents' arrival. I also send messages to Faith and Mum asking for ideas for Rose's first birthday. Samuel didn't want a fuss, and although one minute he's indulging in extravagant gifts for me like the car, house, and engagement ring, the next he is playing down society's cultural ways like not making a deal out of one-year-old birthday parties. Wanting quality time with his family is understandable. Now we have all our families together, and I want to make a deal about it—confetti, balloons, cake, and poppers.

Walking into the party shop with Rose confirms her delight. She screams with excitement at the balloons on the ceiling. She kicks her legs, demanding to get out of the stroller. "Okay, okay." I unclip her safety belt and follow her through the store wheeling an empty stroller. "Which one do you like?"

She points randomly, then stops at the pink balloons and the silver ones with pink confetti. After ordering several for Thursday night, I pay and take one balloon away with us and tie the ribbon to Rose's wrist. We leave the store, and I sit to order online all the food for Thursday while my daughter is obsessed with the balloon floating from her wrist.

After clicking the delivery time for the food, my phone vibrates with an incoming call from Samuel.

"Hey."

"Hey, is everything okay?" Samuel rarely calls me from work.

"I'm sorry. I must stay back to work. I'll be there for dinner only it won't be until after seven. My parents can get a ride to the house. I'm checking you'll be home to greet them."

"Honey, I can pick them up from the hotel. Rose and I could go now as we're looking forward to seeing them."

"Please don't feel like they expect it, and they're happy to meet us at the house."

I shake my head. *Aren't they excited to be here, and why is he playing it low-key?*

"Send me their cell numbers and the hotel."

"Eden, it's unnecessary."

"It is necessary. It's an exciting time. I'll see you at home. I love you."

"I love you too. And thank you."

I end the call and can't help a weird sensation building in my gut that the truth of Samuel's relationship with his parents might be revealed during this visit.

A few hours later, I arrive at a busy city hotel. I veer into the concierge area, give him the details, and moments later, a fair-haired couple emerges through the revolving door. I step out of the car, and the closer I get, the more their appearances remind me of Samuel. I can't help it, I almost pounce on his mother.

"I'm so happy to finally meet you in person." I give her a tight hug. Turning to his father, I embrace him with equal warmth. "I'm Eden, if you haven't already guessed."

Caroline chuckles. "It's lovely to meet you." A few words and her American accent is noted.

"I'm sorry the traffic is crazy this time of day. Have you been waiting long? Please get in. Rose is in the car." My face is tight from smiling so hard. Although they seem pleased to see me, their expressions are almost professional, and I'm not overcome by their excitement.

Caroline moves to the rear door while Christopher takes the front seat. The concierge places their bags in the trunk, and after thanking him, I take the driver's seat and find the McMahon's already engaging with Rose. My daughter's eyes are wide, watching these strangers dote on her. Finally, she mutters some words, looks at me, and says, "Dad-da."

"Yes, we'll see Dad-da soon. This is Gran and Grandpa."

I glance at Christopher before pulling out into the traffic, and I'm met with the same blue eyes holding the seriousness I see in Samuel's eyes. I then turn to Caroline, and although her eyes are also blue, they are not as vivid as her husband's and son's eyes. Her hair is pure gray and cut into a stylish bob cut. She smiles at me, and the lines around her eyes deepen.

Along the Glenelg esplanade, I point out my family's hotel and explain how it's been in my family since the mid-1950s and we have transformed it to be a popular holiday accommodation. I can't help boasting as we have come a long way from struggling with finances for many years, and over the last seven years, we have slowly become financially comfortable.

"I understand the appeal of the location," Christopher says.

"And here's our place," I say with equal pride. "Samuel fell in love with our home the moment he saw it."

"It's exquisite," Carolyn murmurs.

Christopher seems to take it all in.

The garage door opens to the basement level, and I veer the car inside.

After turning off the alarm, I help Christopher lug their suitcases to the second level. I realize the stairs aren't ideal with their luggage and why they probably preferred a hotel with an elevator. Caroline requested time to unpack some of their belongings, so Rose and I wait in the family lounge until they are ready. I prepare refreshments since we're ordering takeout for the evening meal.

"It's a beautiful home," Caroline says after descending the staircase in the same stylish dress. She has kept her heels on, and although not a stiletto heel, the clicking sound on the floor reflects importance in the way she walks. She looks around the room while waiting for Christopher, only a few steps behind her. He remains in dress pants, white shirt, and black tie. They move toward the floor-to-ceiling windows and stare out at the ocean, the sun now lower in the sky and shining directly into the room.

"I can close the external blinds if you prefer."

"It's the first month of winter in LA, so we're happy

for the warmth. Although we can't complain about the California weather," Caroline states.

God, I hate small talk.

I bring out the refreshments and place the plate of cheeses and dips on the table. "Can I get you some wine or coffee or tea?"

"A green tea for me." Caroline stares at the plate. "Did Samuel mention I don't eat dairy?"

Shit. We won't be eating the quiche I bought for lunch tomorrow.

"He mentioned it, but since having Rose, my memory is terrible." I'm not throwing my husband under the bus to his parents when I know he's doing his utmost to impress them.

"Eden?"

My shoulder slumps at the sound of Samuel's voice coming from the lower level. "We're all up here, honey," I call back.

Samuel appears from the stairway wearing a white shirt, dark pants, and a navy tie.

"Samuel." His mother beams at him and almost falls into his arms, causing him to step backward.

"Mom," he says, stroking her hair. "I hope the trip was comfortable."

When she releases him for Christopher to shake his hand, her expression tells of the same concern as mine. When you hug Samuel, there's no hiding his thinning frame.

"Son." Christopher places a hand over Samuel's and then pulls him into a hug with three pats on the back. "You're looking mighty fine, son," he says, assessing his formal clothes.

I'm in a strappy top with a mid-length skirt and flip-flops. Only now do I realize how underdressed I am compared to the McMahon family.

"Dad-da," Rose calls out.

"Excuse me," Samuel says, his smile now for his daughter. He scoops her into his arms and places a loud kiss on her cheek. "Hello, beautiful girl. Have you met your grandparents?" He places Rose on his hip and returns to his parents while gushing over Rose.

I stand back and watch, a little bewildered as to why they didn't do this immediately when arriving home. I push the thought aside since they probably aren't thinking straight with time zones and probable exhaustion, then go about preparing glasses of cold water topped with ice along with Caroline's green tea.

There's more small talk, especially about their business-class flight and the sights of Sydney. Samuel also talks about the places he hopes to visit.

All news to me.

Samuel begins to boast about Rose. The conversation doesn't last before his father asks him about his work.

Our meal arrives, and we eat out on the balcony.

I carry Rose inside to bathe her and put her to bed.

By the time I return, Samuel is in the kitchen with his parents.

"Well, it's only Monday, and I have a big week ahead of me. I'll see you all tomorrow night." He smiles at me. "No doubt Eden has plans to show you around Adelaide."

"Is there anywhere in particular you wish to visit, or do you want me to take you on a mystery tour?"

"I recommend the mystery tour," Samuel jokes.

"We could discuss it in the morning," Caroline

suggests. "Perhaps have one day with Rose before we roam the countryside."

Adelaide is hardly countryside. And only one day?

Samuel explains they have their own living area off the bedroom so if they can't sleep, they're welcome to use it as they won't disturb us. He gives them the code to our keyless front door. His father mentions how they have adapted to the time zone, thanks to sleeping comfortably on their flight.

"I have also arranged for our cleaner to visit daily," Samuel adds.

What? Since when do we have a cleaner?

He doesn't look at me.

"She has a code to the door and will visit around ten every morning."

My jaw drops.

I glance around the room. The house is clean and tidy—I manage it fine.

Samuel kisses his mother's cheek then places a hand on his father's shoulder. "I hope you're comfortable here. I'll see you tomorrow night."

Why wouldn't they be comfortable? It's a freaking amazing house.

"We have a wine fridge in the kitchen if you need a little something to help you sleep," he says mainly to his father.

"Rose has me up early in the morning, so I'll head to bed as well. Have a think about where you would like to visit. I recommend the wineries… only a short drive from here."

"I'm interested in seeing the hospital where my son works." Christopher turns to Caroline, and she agrees with him.

"Sure. Just prepare a list."

I follow Samuel up the stairs and into the bathroom. He squeezes toothpaste on his brush and ignores me standing beside him.

"Since when has my cleaning been insufficient?" I fold my arms over my chest.

"It's something you don't have to worry about. You have enough with Rose, especially now my parents are here." His gaze remains on his reflection while cleaning his teeth.

Leaning forward, I force him to meet my gaze. "You invited a stranger into our home and gave her the code to our door, and what, the security alarm?" I ask, disappointed.

Samuel leans over, rinses then wipes his mouth with the hand towel. "Joan isn't a stranger. She works at the hospital and needs more work as she's a young single parent."

"So, you can account for her because of a few conversations. Jesus, Samuel, this is our home."

"I can assure you she's of no danger to us." He unbuttons the top few buttons, checks himself in the mirror, and leaves the room.

I follow him. "It's our personal space. Our belongings. I'm happy to do it."

"All material things that can be replaced."

My jaw drops for the second time tonight. "We don't need a cleaner every day."

He stops and turns to me with an exasperated expression. "My mother has OCD. For peace and to comfort her tendency, it's easier to have Joan come every day while they're here. Then I told her we can plan something permanent even once a fortnight after I discuss it with you." He turns to finish unbuttoning his shirt and drops it into the laundry chute.

He hangs his trousers and then climbs into bed, pulling the bedcovers up to his neck.

Inhaling a deep breath, I try a different angle. "I guess there's much for me to learn about your mother, although I sensed her concern for you."

Samuel rolls onto his side. "Eden, I didn't have a good day, and I don't have the energy to talk about it tonight. I'm thankful for all you're doing, and I'm happy to chat tomorrow. But please, not tonight."

35

SAMUEL

Thirty minutes of CPR and no sign of life.

Calling it never feels right.

When Dr. Tolley told Samuel to stop, he wanted to continue with compressions. The guilt of losing his friends never leaves him, and in a hospital with modern medicine, they still couldn't save the forty-year-old man, a father to three children.

Samuel squeezes his eyes tight and wills himself to get a decent night's sleep. *Please, no nightmares tonight*, he says in his head. The logical side of his brain kicks in, reminding him of the facts.

Death is inevitable. From the day we're born, we are destined to die. The preferable cause is aging after a quality life, yet the percentage of accidental deaths or lifestyle choices exacerbates premature death. Then he thinks of childhood diseases. Cancer. The very thing that drove him to search for a cure rather than treat the symptoms.

Samuel has done a full circle, and while he's not satisfied by his career choice, it's the only option to be here with Eden until he proves he'll not disappear and be reckless again.

Reckless.

If only his father knew the truth of how he came to stay in Ulara. And yet his journey to find a safer haven for the Ularan people was just that.

Reckless.

Many of them died in doing so with thoughtless consideration for his own health. Longevity is now in doubt after the stress he placed on his body. Modern medicine fails to find an explanation, yet in his heart, he knows it's a combination of physical and mental problems.

To make matters worse, the hospital has a shortage of staff and beds, and he understands why his employment got fast-tracked. He has committed to staying back and helping. What other choice does he have when he has taken a vow to heal? A vow where prevention is preferable to a cure.

Prevention must be a mindset in society.

He lets out a sigh.

He needs to get off the merry-go-round.

Set a plan and work toward it.

Ayahuasca can help him do this.

A place where he can clear his head and fight the demons threatening to undo him.

Visualizing the vivid colors of ayahuasca in his mind, he imagines the kaleidoscope of neon lights and changing patterns before fingers flick through the filing cabinet of thoughts and memories before dissecting each piece of emotion.

Hopefully, it's enough to lull him into sleep.

Every day is unchanging.

He wakes early and is out the door before his family rises. He returns after they have eaten dinner. His father chats to him briefly, asking about his day—standard conversation. Yesterday, his father's demeanor had changed. His eyes flicked with concern before he smoothed his expression to a trained poker face—a skill of their profession.

Samuel feels bad leaving Eden to entertain his parents without him. She told him not to worry as they are spending time with their granddaughter, and she's showing them all the sights. His heart warms, knowing she's trying. Eden is an amazing woman, and it's why he is here because he knows he can't lose her again.

He unlocks the door, relieved it's Friday night and walks the stairs to the living room and hears the low hum of conversation.

"We enjoyed Victor Harbor and considered staying a week," his mother says to Eden.

Interesting.

It's a small coastal town south of Adelaide, and he assumed it wouldn't appeal to his parents when they're used to the bustle of Los Angeles.

"Evening," he says as he enters the room.

Eden is the first to hug him, and it's tighter than usual.

"Are you okay?" he whispers.

She nods quickly. "I've missed you."

If something upset her, he trusts she'll tell him later when they're alone.

His mother also hugs him.

His dad comes in for a handshake. "How was your day, son?"

It's the same conversation as every night.

Tonight, he won't be in bed early.

🌴

After Samuel has eaten dinner and they have discussed their plans for the weekend, Eden heads to bed, leaving Samuel to have time with his parents. Alone.

After hearing about his parents' adventures over the past few days, his mother kisses his cheek and takes the stairs to the bedroom.

"Rose is exhausting her." His father's lips curl, hinting at a smile. "And she loves every minute." Christopher looks at the dark ocean as if he's enjoying a memory.

"Rose has that effect on you," Samuel replies. He lifts his feet onto the balcony's railing and leans back in his chair, crossing his fingers and placing them behind his head. Elbows wide, he relaxes into the deck chair and stares at the stars in the night sky. "By now, I assume you've grasped why I rushed to get here. I couldn't let another minute pass without seeing my two girls."

"Yes, it's clear you love your family, and they love you. Only I wished you remained in LA to have a few more tests, son. Eden would have waited. You might have found more answers." He stalls. "Am I correct in observing you have lost more weight?"

Samuel closes his eyes and opens them to focus on the moonlight dancing over the ocean. "I have it under control."

"You're pushing yourself too hard. I, for one, understand a sign of burnout."

Samuel looks at his father. His eyes hold an understanding he's never witnessed before. "I've only just started working, and it's not burnout," he replies, in case he's testing his commitment.

His father nods slowly. "Please keep me up to date with your treatment. I want to be here for you." Lines in his forehead deepen with a frown. "I mean it. We have all made mistakes in the past. You have a bright future with a beautiful family, and I don't want you taking the same path as me."

Whoa. Samuel sits in silence, taking in his father's words. During his brief trip back to LA, he witnessed a change in his father, yet he was firm in making Samuel promise to uphold his responsibility.

What has given him a change of heart?

Samuel heads to bed and slips under the covers, careful not to wake Eden. He tosses and turns, unable to sleep even though he's exhausted. He closes his eyes and visualizes the future, seeing himself as a happy, healthier man with enough energy to keep up with his daughter. Picturing his family together relaxes his mind into sleep until images of his other family creep into his thoughts and his dreams.

The dreams start the same…

Walking. Slashing vine leaves to make a path for those following behind him. Timenneng leads the way, ensuring no poisonous thorny vines are on the path, as a brush with certain plants can lead to death in minutes. He is astute, but he's tiring, and Kaikare takes over in her assessment of the potential danger ahead. The wails begin from behind, then a messenger trots up to him. It's time to rest. The crying lasts a few hours as he has pushed them beyond their capabilities.

The alternative isn't what he wants to consider.

They can't stay in guerrilla territory.

They have lost lives along the way, and the responsibility is on him. His antibiotic supply is low, and with another infection where it's not treated by the jungle garden, it may be fatal. Two more weeks of walking will place them in safer territory.

Two more weeks.

Some of them can barely walk for two more hours.

Timenneng and some of the younger warriors carry the weak in hammocks strung between them. It gives those who suffer time to rest. Every day, the warriors continue to amaze him with the strength of their minds to continue without complaint.

Night falls, and they sit around a fire.

Kaikare has taken her father's role and tells a story of their ancestors. The underlying message is bravery in the face of hardship and talks about those who have died for them. He compares it to war and fighting for freedom. Death for others to live a better life.

He wants no further death on his hands tonight.

A woman cries out.

Kaikare goes to her.

She's in premature labor.

A sob escapes him as he realizes this is his fault. He has pushed the women too far. In a foreign country and at night, danger lurks, so searching the forest for plants to slow the birth is out of the question.

The women beg to search for the plants they can use in a smoking ceremony. The wails begin as they pray to their gods. Kaikare nods at Samuel, and the women rush into the darkness, hoping to find something close to camp. Mari' Iwoi follows to guide them back.

Chirké and Itariru stay with the young girl, dancing and

singing around her. Arms folded, Kaikare watches Samuel, and when he waves her on, she goes to the group and takes charge. The decisions are out of his hands and into more capable ones.

The women return, and their ceremony begins. For hours, Samuel stares into the fire. The dry heat soothes his moist and swollen feet. The other men do the same, using the flames to heal their wounds.

Suddenly, the singing stops.

He can't see into the circle of women, especially with them away from the fire and closer to the jungle shadows. Kaikare emerges holding a bloodied baby, part of the umbilical cord dangling with the twine attached.

She asks him to give the baby a blessing, a blessing of the modern world as well as the Ularan world. They still believe his medicine holds magic, yet he can't save this tiny bundle. The baby girl doesn't cry. Watching her tiny chest, she's barely breathing, and he realizes she doesn't have long. Tears fall from his cheeks as he whispers to the baby. Dipping his finger in the ash from the fire, he marks the butterfly symbol on the baby's forehead.

Kaikare takes the baby from his hands and returns her to the mother. He stands and walks a few paces closer to the forest and looks into the dark shadows. The trees whispered their secrets to the shaman, telling him how to heal the people. Samuel doesn't have this power and only learns in the way of science and how the plants treat disease and save lives in the way he understands. If he could take ayahuasca, a light might direct them on their journey. For now, he needs to rely on a map he has inside his head and hope they find another river soon.

He snaps out of the daze when yellow eyes peer back at him. At first, he's caught in delirium wishing the eyes belonged to the shaman's spirit. The growl awakens him to the physical form. He doesn't have time to think before the jaguar has knocked him to the ground, its sharp claws tearing his skin. He rolls once, holding its head away from his face. In a second, his life flashes before him. In the moment, all he sees is Eden's beautiful face, her smile telling him she'll forever love him.

He yells a roar back to shock the jaguar, and then it rolls off him with the force of a blow. Dark hair catches his eye as the person rolls over the jaguar. Timenneng leaps and joins the wrestle until the jaguar's lifeless body is shoved off Kaikare. Samuel scrambles to her and pulls her to her feet. A bloodied knife in her hand. She may have stabbed its gut, but Timenneng slit its throat. Weapons from the intruders who tried to kill them. Blood trickles down his friends' faces and arms as he asks them if they're hurt.

They are more concerned for him.

Yet he can't stop thanking them over and over.

Kaikare told Samuel she could never live with herself if Eden lost both her grandmother and him. It's her duty to protect him as he's protecting everyone else.

Wrapping his arms around her, he allows the quiet sobs to erupt from his throat. A second longer and their fate may have taken a different path.

Behind them a chorus of cries begins. Fear of the jaguar among the people signifies they aren't safe here.

The mother carries into the circle the lifeless body of the baby. She drops to her knees at Samuel's feet.

What the hell has he done?

36

EDEN

Samuel moans, and it's loud enough to wake me from my sleep.

I force my eyes open and tap the bedside table several times, searching for my phone. The room is pitch black. I assume it's around two o'clock, the time he usually wakes me with his nightmares—2:20 a.m.

Sliding closer, I rest an arm on his chest and whisper, "You're safe."

Over the past few months, I have done this countless times while still half asleep.

I don't wake him. I'm sending a message to his subconscious to reassure he's with me and everything is going to be fine. Only tonight his moans were different.

And he's unusually cold.

Coming out of the daze, I palm his forehead. It's like he's been out in the snow. Reaching under the covers, I pat his inner thigh, a place of warmth only like the rest of him, there isn't enough flesh on his bones, and it raises a red flag.

I spring upright and switch on the bedside lamp.

Samuel is lying on his back, pale. Each breath comes with a low grunt.

The room tilts in a moment of panic, and I remind myself to breathe.

"Samuel," I say louder and press his shoulder.

No response.

"Samuel," I shout and shake him.

He groans yet doesn't wake.

I race out of the bedroom and bang on his parents' door.

"Christopher," I shout. "There's something wrong with Samuel. Please come and check on him."

I only make it a few steps before the door swings open to Christopher who's tying the cord of his robe around his waist. "I noticed he struggled with dinner." He runs a hand through his disheveled gray hair.

"It's not the food." I scurried toward our room, and he's right behind me.

He leans over Samuel and listens for a breath, then lays a finger on his neck pulse point.

"Call 911," he says in a low voice, even though I sense he's anything but calm.

"It's triple zero in Australia." I grab my phone.

"What emergency service are you requiring?" the operator asks.

"Ambulance," I blurt out.

It feels like an eternity before they connect. The medical operator asks me to describe his condition.

I emphasize how cold he is, and I can't wake him. I give my address and activate the speaker so Christopher can hear the directions.

Christopher arranges the bedding so more is covering Samuel.

"Does he have a pulse?"

"Yes. And he's breathing. Shallow breaths and moaning."

"A thready pulse," Christopher says, and I repeat it.

"An ambulance is on the way. Do you have stairs?"

"Yes, we do. Our bedroom is upstairs."

"Please switch on a front light and be ready to unlock the door. Do you want to stay on the phone in case he deteriorates?"

I glance at Christopher.

He shakes his head. "I can monitor him until an ambulance arrives."

Caroline appears and leans over Samuel. "What happened?" She touches his forehead. "Christopher, he's so cold."

Christopher looks up at me. "Does he have a stethoscope and blood pressure monitor?"

I turn toward the cupboard. "Yes, er—"

"Caroline, please bring mine." He looks at me. "I carry a wireless monitor and a stethoscope."

"Thank you," I say quickly.

I move to get out of the way and sit on my side of the bed, lost in how to help. My throat is dry. My thoughts are racing. I'll need to go to the hospital with Samuel. Only I don't want to leave Rose with Samuel's parents yet.

Caroline rushes into the room and hands Christopher the monitor. He places the strap around his arm and presses a button to inflate the bladder. A digital reading comes up. His silence speaks volumes. Placing the end of the stethoscope on Samuel's chest, Christopher closes his eyes and listens to Samuel's heart.

His eyes meet mine.

"Is he okay?" I croak.

"How has he been the past few months?"

I blow out air slowly as I consider my answer. "He is stressed. And he's lost more weight, not gained any. He has struggled with eating and…" I can feel my heart breaking knowing he never wanted to return to society, "… his nightmares are bad. I thought he was having one tonight when he made weird breathing noises. It happens a lot around this time."

"The nightmares? How long has he been having them?"

"Since he returned. I thought he was suffering from PTSD and suggested he seek help."

Christopher stares at his son as though he's seeing him in a different light.

"That damn jungle," he mutters.

In the distance, I hear a siren. I race down the stairs and call Mum while I wait at the door.

"Mum." I burst into tears.

"Is it Rose, dear?"

"No. It's Samuel. An ambulance is on the way. Could you please come and stay with Rose so I can go to the hospital?"

"Of course. I'll be there soon. Try to stay calm, honey. He'll be fine."

"His parents are here. I'm sorry. It's not the way I wanted you to meet them."

"Eden," she says gently. "Stay calm. We'll all manage. Focus on Samuel. I'll be there in a few minutes."

For weeks, I have been telling myself *he's not fine*, and Mum has watched me worry despite Samuel saying over and over he only needs time.

Fuck time.

I should have gone with my gut instinct and made him tell me about his ordeal so he could heal faster. This treading around like I'm on an icy lake thawing out is bullshit.

I take a deep breath and remind myself not to panic because my thoughts are mashing together, and it's pointless looking for blame.

The sirens stop when the van pulls into the driveway. I greet two male paramedics and lead them up the stairs. They assess Samuel, asking questions and discussing his condition with his father.

The sight of him like this crushes me. He's so pale he looks—I can't say the word.

Don't you dare leave me again.

Tears choke my throat.

Please, Samuel. Fight whatever it is because I need you.

They take his blood pressure, immediately place a mask over his face, and begin oxygen therapy.

One officer pulls out a silver foil blanket and wraps it over Samuel. The other inserts a cannula into his arm and sets up a fluid bag. They talk in medical terminology to Christopher, and although I can understand some, all I hear is my heartbeat thumping in my chest while watching them inject drugs into the cannula.

"Does Dr. McMahon suffer from anorexia nervosa?"

"No. His condition is unique," I say in a low voice because I've heard unconscious people can hear, and I don't want to talk about him as though he's not in the room. "My fiancé was lost in the South American jungle for some time." The paramedics and Christopher gape at me. "He was close to starvation and physically exhausted. He also suffers nightmares, and I assumed it was PTSD."

One officer makes a note while continuing to monitor his blood pressure.

"He'll require VPI," Christopher says quietly. "And more blood tests considering his environment over the past several years. I wanted him to undergo more testing on his brief visit to Los Angeles, our home, in early August, only he was determined to travel to Australia only a couple of weeks after emerging from the jungle."

The paramedics and Christopher continue talking in their own jargon. My vision blurs from tears. I never knew what happened when Samuel first arrived in LA and those vital few weeks after barely making it out alive.

Has he known all along he was unwell, and it's why he rushed here to see us instead of seeking medical treatment?

"He should wake," the taller paramedic tells me after administering drugs into the cannula.

Samuel moans and opens his eyes.

"Hey." I sit beside him and run my hand over his cheek.

He blinks several times and looks around the room as though trying to comprehend his whereabouts. "What happened?" he murmurs.

I shake my head. "I don't know." I swipe tears from my eyes.

"Did I pass out?"

I shake my head.

"Dr. McMahon," the tall officer begins. "You're hypotensive. We're unsure if it could be from an infection leading to sepsis. Although your temperature is dangerously low, so you may have suffered shock from a nightmare. Your partner informed us of your recent trip, and you may have suffered some trauma."

Samuel's gaze flicks to mine.

I'm not backing down this time.

Christopher speaks, and Samuel's gaze shoots to his father. He still looks disorientated. "You need the tests I suggested you undertake back home, son."

If I leave the room, he might talk to them.

I grab clothes and head to the bathroom to change. Leaning both hands on the basin, I inhale a few conscious breaths to clear my head. Then I quickly attend to my hair, wash my face, and spray under my arms. I change into a summer dress then go into Rose's bedroom to check on her. Thankfully, she hasn't woken and is curled up on her side. Tentatively, I place a hand on her head. She feels warm—normal warm. After creeping out, I return to our bedroom and gather a change of clothes for Samuel because he'll not want to remain in his boxer briefs and T-shirt.

The paramedic is talking. "We need to stabilize your temperature and blood pressure in the hospital, and you might need to remain in for a series of tests, especially on your heart. We have detected an arrhythmia. Possibly a response to what happened tonight."

His eyes find me from across the room. "I'm sorry," he mouths to me.

"Don't be." I shake my head, then go to him and squeeze his hand. "I'll follow the ambulance and be there soon. Everything will be fine."

"No rush. Hospital protocol and all." He forces a reassuring smile. "You'll be sitting around. Stay and rest and come up in the morning."

"It *is* morning, and I won't be able to rest." I turn to the paramedics. "Where are you taking him?

"To the Bedford Park hospital."

"Good. Samuel works there. I'll follow soon."

"We'll retrieve the ambulant chair so we can strap you in for the stairs," the tall medic says.

"I can manage the stairs." Samuel moves upright in the bed.

"Sir, we prefer you in the chair."

"Samuel, your blood pressure," his father reiterates sternly.

In perfect timing, Mum appears in the doorway. Her hair is unbrushed. I walk with her to Rose's room. "How is he?"

"Stable for now. They're concerned about his temperature and blood pressure." She wraps an arm around my waist and pulls me in close.

"He's in expert hands. He'll be okay."

"I'm sorry I panicked and called you. Rose is still asleep and will probably remain asleep until six. I didn't want to leave her because Samuel's parents are still strangers to her."

"It's fine. I'll chat with them, and when she wakes, they can call me. I'll come up and get her then rather than wake her now. It might be good for the three of them to have some alone time."

"What if Rose cries because she doesn't know them?"

Mum squeezes my hand. "I know you're worried, but you don't have to stress about this. Caroline is a mother." She smiles. "And if Rose doesn't settle, they can call me. You go in the ambulance, honey, and don't worry about Rose."

🌴

Samuel still feels cold, not the ice-cold sensation of when he was unconscious. I take his hand in mine, and his eyes flutter open.

"I'm sorry," he whispers for the hundredth time. It's

all he says before his eyes close again, as though he's completely exhausted.

"After you get some treatment," I whisper. "You're not coming home until you have an appointment to speak to a psychologist."

His eyes search mine. He doesn't argue with me or simply doesn't have the energy.

I kiss his fingers wrapped in mine. "You scared me. We can make small talk and dance around this, yet nothing will help you heal except professional help."

His eyes well up. "I'm sorry I let you down."

Seeing him like this breaks me. "You didn't," I croak while shaking my head in disbelief.

"I tried to be strong." He slowly closes his eyes and opens them again.

My heart shatters with him being ashamed, as though it's a weakness on his behalf. "You're the strongest person I know." I lean and kiss his cheek. "You have superpowers to survive what you did."

Silent tears stream down his cheeks. "Many didn't."

I place his hand over my heart, my hand covering his. "No, it's to be expected. You tried. You can't save everyone. The alternative was they *all* died if they remained in Ulara." His eyes lower to our hands. "My heart beats for you, and it hurts for you. And right now, I'm hurting too."

Samuel turns his head and closes his eyes as though something is destroying his demeanor. Today isn't the time for him to deal with the past. I need him to focus his energy on healing himself so he can come home to me.

A doctor walks around the curtain. "Hello, Dr. McMahon, I'm Dr. Weeks." He glances at his chart and notes the machine beeping in the corner. Then he looks at me.

"Hi. I'm Eden, Samuel's fiancée. I'll pop out while you speak to Samuel."

Samuel eyeballs me, and his expression softens as though he understands what I'm doing—giving him space to discuss his condition honestly. "There's a café on the second floor, Eden. Grab a bite to eat, and you might need some caffeine to stay awake."

I'll need more than caffeine.

By mid-morning, Samuel is falling in and out of sleep. After speaking to Caroline and Christopher, they decide to visit after lunch, so I head home so Samuel can rest. They have the keys to his Porsche so they can use his car until the hospital discharges Samuel. Then I call Mum, and she insists on keeping Rose for the day, and I'm relieved. As much as I want Samuel's parents to see Rose, there's only so much I can handle.

After a brief conversation about his condition, I tell his parents I need to rest. Once my body touches our luxurious mattress, I melt into it. Only my mind can't shut down. My thoughts tear at my heart, and my gut churns.

Gran's journal is on the bedside table.

"Gran," I whisper as though she can hear me. I close my eyes and imagine her presence. "Please, help Samuel. I know you have touched him spiritually. Please, please heal him."

I open my eyes and reach for her words to heal my aching heart.

37

IVY

March 11, 1963

I survived another night sleeping in the canoe.

God, my back hurts.

My friend has given me a clay bowl of water from which I drink.
No cup. I simply tip the bowl and drink from it. I'm clueless as to
how the water is clear and thankful it's not scooped straight from
the river. While sitting and watching me, which seems to be his
new hobby, he refills it from the bamboo. A flower and leaves float
on top. I sense it's not where it is sourced. Regardless, I'm grateful
he's taking care of me during the day.

Last night I was afraid to close my eyes yet also exhausted from
only a few hours' sleep the night before. Without seeing any of his
people, I knew I was being watched. I could feel it. Sense it. It's
hard to describe, but out here in the jungle, my senses are on high
alert, and it's a new awareness I've developed—my body's
adaptation to prevent death.

It's something I've thought about frequently, especially facing it
every day. Will it be today or tomorrow? A few months from now?
Will I make it back to Australia, to my family?

My friend is watching me cry. I can't help it. I'm extremely overwhelmed. If I'm to survive long enough to get back to Maria, I must make peace with these people hidden in the jungle and hopefully return without an arrow in my back.

There are more men standing beside my friend.

They speak, not Spanish, their own indigenous language.

One is walking toward me, and I keep my head down, writing.

March 18, 1963

A week has now passed since I arrived in Ulara.

My bag was confiscated and only returned to me today.

The women took my clothes and washed them, and although I have them back, they gave me a tweed skirt and beads to wear around my neck. I wear it to keep the peace, but it doesn't leave much to the imagination. My joggers are gone, replaced by my flat sandals. I'm not risking a parasite entering my feet, and yet I'm bathing in a stream with the ladies every morning. I'm also living in the village in my own hut, although everyone keeps a distance.

In the mornings after bathing in the stream with the other women, I walk down to the river's edge and listen for a sign that Maria has come looking for me. I check where I abandoned the canoe. Again, the area is absent of any sign of her presence. Footprints get washed away by the late afternoon rain, yet I hoped she'd call out for me or leave a note or something in the canoe.

The people in the village are gentle. Most of the women have shorter hair, except for the children. They have long hair, and some are plaited with beads. It appears the older women with gray hair may grow their hair as do the women with children. I'm not sure about hierarchy, although the hair signifies a rule within the village. The men's jet-black hair is cut around their faces in a bowl shape, except for my friend. His hair sits at his shoulders. Until this morning, I never knew why. Only minutes ago, the chief, and I assume a medicine man—the shaman—emerged from their respective huts and gathered in the circle, both with the same fashionable long hair with graying strands throughout. Only they wore a crown of feathers on their head and walked with sticks that jingled with beads and bones of dead animals.

It feels safer for me to keep my head down and keep writing than to stare at… I guess they're my new leaders. The bosses of Ulara.

April 1, 1963

Two weeks ago, my journal was taken from me. The chief and shaman perceived my writing, being the pen and paper, as some form of magic or a demon. I guess it's referred to as evil spirits here, and I was associated as one. When they held my journal over the fire, I screamed. I fell to my knees and begged for forgiveness, then crawled to them and held out my hands while sobbing like a baby. It wasn't my finest moment. Desperation controlled my emotions as my journal is a link to home or for my family to know what has happened to me if I don't make it out of this godforsaken country.

It all started when I took the shaman's hand and showed him how to use the pen, hoping to impress him. Only, he threw it aside in fear.

I shouldn't have touched him.

My friend collected my journal and took it away for safekeeping. Today, my friend returned it to me, and I'm not sure if my journal has undergone some ceremony to rid the evil spirit away.

This isn't an April Fool's joke.

Much has happened in the past two weeks, and yet most days are the same. I'm now permitted to work in the fields with the women to earn my keep, so to speak. At night, I have the job of cooking the most basic vegetables.

The men hunt and fish. The women work the fields, prepare the meals, and are solely responsible for the children. Even in the fields, babies are carried in baskets on a woman's back. It's not like the men hunt all day, every day. I have found them sitting in the village making baskets from twine or fishing nets or hammocks. It's fascinating to watch.

The people are self-sufficient, surviving off the land with no running water or electricity. I'm quite amazed by their society. There's still no sign of Maria, and until I receive something, I fear not to return and place myself or the other volunteers in the community at risk. Some nights I wonder if any of them are even alive.

The thought makes me nauseous.

How did volunteering come to this?

Life or death.

For now, I'm happy to stay here while I'm still welcome and until it's safe to return.

38

EDEN

With a sigh, I close the journal and set it aside. At this point, Gran focused on coming home. The reality of how she ended up in the village would have been traumatic, and I respect Gran's bravery even more. Before closing my eyes, I send a text to Samuel.

> I hope you're okay. I'll come back tonight to visit. I love you xx

> I'm like a pin cushion with the number of tests being conducted and out of every orifice. Please stay home with Rose and my parents today, and I'll see you in the morning. I love you x

I bring up his number on my phone to call, and it goes to his voicemail.

"I'm not waiting until tomorrow to see you," I say. "I'm worried about you. I'll put Rose to bed then come and see you tonight. I love you."

As soon as I finish my message, the phone vibrates with an incoming call.

"Hey. I'm sorry. The specialist was here. He just left."

"How are you?" My voice trembles with concern, hoping he doesn't push me away.

"I'm fine. A little embarrassed and sorry you had to see me go through this."

"Samuel, don't. I've been expecting something to happen only I assumed it was PTSD and not something sinister. I could've helped somehow."

"Edes, there was nothing you could do, and I'm sorry again I couldn't hide it better."

"The point is you shouldn't have to hide it," I murmur.

"It's something only I could deal with and believed time would help. Unfortunately, I ignored too many signs indicating I wasn't okay."

I inhale a sharp breath. "Please don't say that. You're going to be okay."

"I'll be doing everything I can to get out of here, bar for now, I need rest, so I'll see you in the morning?" His voice ends on a high note.

"I want to see you tonight."

"Babe. It was a rough night. Get some rest. Look after Rose. You could take my parents out to dinner."

"They're as concerned for you as I am."

"There's nothing you can do. I'm having never-ending tests. Fecal, urine, blood, nasal. Seriously, tomorrow will be a better day."

I let out an exasperated breath. "Okay, but please message me regularly so I know you're fine."

"I'm fine. There's a nurse in my room every ten minutes. I'm already wanting to come home for a rest because the monitors beep constantly throughout the night."

His reassuring words fail to ease my concern.

"Okay. I'll see you in the morning. I love you."

"I love you too."

I end the call.

I find Samuel's parents sitting on the balcony admiring the ocean view. If anywhere could alleviate worry, it's this vista.

"How is Samuel?" Christopher asks.

"He's okay, although he wants to rest tonight. We can see him tomorrow."

I notice Caroline wipe a tear. I go to her and lay a hand on her shoulder. "He promised me everything will be fine. You know your son never breaks a promise."

Caroline places her soft palm over my hand. "Thank you. For years I told myself he knew what he was doing and we shouldn't interfere in his life. He's an adult, and it's no longer our responsibility to guide him. Yet I can no longer pretend everything is okay. It's not, and I wish I did more to help him."

His parents have surprised the hell out of me.

"The three of us love him unconditionally, and together, we'll make sure he comes out of this with answers because he can't go on without treatment."

A single sob escapes Caroline's throat.

Christopher places a gentle hand on her back. "I promise you both I have colleagues I can ask a favor of and have them help with his case. This isn't a clear-cut diagnosis, so the more doctors to brainstorm, the quicker we'll get answers."

"Thank you, Christopher." Caroline lifts her chin and wipes her eyes.

"Do you mind if I leave you for a bit unless you want to come for a stroll to my parents' house so I can get Rose?"

"I'd love to join you," Caroline says quickly.

"We could head out to dinner in Glenelg. It's a short stroll, and Rose loves sitting outside at the restaurants."

Christopher glances at his wife's heels. "Best we change our shoes first. Maybe I could adapt to you Aussies wearing flip-flops all the time."

Samuel's parents' visit to Australia may be the best thing to bring their family together.

🌴

The following morning, we drive to the hospital to see Samuel. After kissing him and letting Rose crawl over him for a couple of minutes, I sit back and try to amuse her while his parents sit and chat. There are times when I see them making ground and showing concern for their son. No longer is there a stiff upper lip and the posh attitude I first witnessed. I don't want to let an opportunity pass, so I tell them I'm taking Rose out to the garden to buy her something from the café to allow them time to talk.

An hour later, I return to red eyes on all three of them. It's not a bad thing to cry, and it doesn't show any weakness if it's not in anger and they have worked out their problems.

"When we leave, would you like us to take Rose home?" Caroline asks.

I glance at Samuel, and he gives a subtle nod. "Sure. I'll let her cuddle her father one more time." I place Rose on the bed, and she sits on top of Samuel. He grunts and exaggerates her heaviness, and she giggles. He lifts her in the air and plants a smoochy kiss on her cheek.

"See you soon, princess."

"You know she's going to believe it's her name as you use it so often."

Samuel chuckles. "It's not a bad thing."

I roll my eyes and smile at Caroline. She stands and comes to hug me. "Thank you for giving us time to spend with Rose. We really appreciate it."

"It makes us happy you can spend time with Rose," I emphasize. I pack up her belongings and pluck a screaming Rose from Samuel and place her in the stroller. "I'll walk your parents down to the car," I tell him.

I slowly rock the stroller to calm Rose while his parents hug Samuel goodbye. We walk the long hallways of the hospital until we get to the parking lot. Rose is almost asleep by the time we get to my car.

"She'll only rest for an hour and then go down again after lunch."

Christopher lifts Rose and clips her into her car seat. "We'll let her sleep then take her down to the beach." He smiles at me as though he's excited to have time with Rose.

"If you have any trouble, let me know, and I'll come straight home. I can either uber it or Mum can come get me. I don't want you making another trip with Rose."

"We'll be fine. And thank you," Caroline chirps.

After waving goodbye, I use the time to mull over all the questions I want to ask Samuel, especially why he considered struggling through this alone.

After Samuel wakes, our conversation is trivial, starting with the details of our dinner last night and how his parents got on well with mine.

My questions start slowly and recount his dreams over the past few months.

"I didn't want to mention this," he says and looks warily at me. "And I know you'll object without consideration."

"What? Tell me, please."

"I've been contemplating returning to Peru and taking ayahuasca."

"Nooo," I whisper.

"It's a way for me to understand what's happening with my body. Find some answers."

"Have you forgotten what happened the last time? How a dark entity interfered, and it could have been disastrous."

"The circumstances were different. This will help me to find the answers within my body. Not to connect with another shaman as powerful as—" He stops and looks at me. His eyes turn sad, and then he looks up at the ceiling. "It's the only way."

"It's not the *only way*. You must have faith in modern medicine as much as you do the shaman. I know you miss him, but you must find the strength to get through this."

"Don't you think I've been trying?" he murmurs and not in anger, more in despair.

I stare at him. Until now, my gentle probes haven't worked so I cross my arms. "Then fucking try harder."

His eyes widen. "You don't know what I've been through."

"I have a fair idea by the details you have shared. You have a lot at stake here, and giving up isn't what we signed up for as a couple. So do what you must and stop trying to avoid the inevitable. I'll find another way… even find some herbalist here if we need to, but you aren't traveling back to Peru, so get that plan out of your goddamn head."

His nostrils flare. I sit on the edge of the bed and hold his hand, ignoring the stubborn anger rolling off him in waves.

"Get mad. Be sad. We're in this together, and we're not leaving Australia, at least not until you're a lot bloody stronger than you are now."

He shakes his head, and a tear rolls down his cheek. Then another. I want to weaken and hug him and let him do what he needs to do, only I can't. I need to be tough and help him get through this without ayahuasca because *I'll* never forget the last time.

"I thought I was going to die." He chokes up on the last word.

Oh god. I crawl up onto the bed and lie beside him. "I won't let it happen."

"In my mind, I had an out-of-body experience and sensed my soul with other souls. In the darkness, I was overwhelmed by the presence of others."

I wrap my arm around him and tighten my hold. "Yet you didn't die. There's a reason you're here. And I'm never allowing you to be alone like that again."

Samuel turns and kisses my cheek. "I thank the universe every day for sending you to me even though you're a pain in the ass."

I snuggle closer. "I'll be whatever it takes to never leave you again."

🌴

Come Thursday, Samuel is still in the hospital. I know it saddens him not to be home for Rose's birthday, especially with our families together to celebrate.

Helium balloons float over the family room ceiling. I can hear Faith, Caroline, and Mum chatting in one corner while Jake, Dad, and Christopher play noisily with the children. I FaceTime Samuel when we light the candles on the cake Mum made—a caterpillar topped with candy. He's smiling and chatting to Rose, telling her what a clever girl she is, although her efforts in blowing out the single candle resulted in her bangs receiving more air than anywhere else.

After everyone leaves, I take my tired one-year-old and read her a story in her crib. It's not long until her eyes flutter close. I creep out of her room and join Samuel's parents in the living room. The curtains remain open while the sun is near the ocean horizon, casting streaks of pink and orange color across the skies.

Christopher pours a whiskey on ice and stands at the glass admiring the view. Caroline is packing the last of the dishes into the dishwasher.

"Thank you." I place a hand on her back. "I appreciate your help."

She smiles up at me. "I'm glad to help. It's been many years since I've been able to help someone."

It's possible they have a housekeeper, and with only the two of them, I understand what she's saying. Yet I see satisfaction in her eyes and know we all can feel good about ourselves when we do the smallest of gestures to help someone else.

"Would you mind if I asked the cleaner not to come for the rest of the week?"

Caroline blinks at me as though she doesn't know what I'm implying.

"Our house doesn't need to be cleaned daily," I say gently. "And I enjoy cleaning. Once a week is adequate for a house cleaner. Is that okay with you?"

Caroline straightens. "Eden, it's none of my business how you manage your home."

I sit at the kitchen table and pour a glass of red wine from the bottle Faith brought over. "Would you like one?"

She comes to sit beside me. "I have taken a liking to Australian wine."

I chuckle lightly, pour a glass, and slide it to her. "I know we do things differently here, and I like things done my way. My home isn't dirty, and although it's large, it's a new home and easy to manage. I can keep it clean between a professional clean. The reason we have someone visiting daily is Samuel's concern about your OCD."

Caroline takes a sip then slowly her blue eyes meet mine. "I try hard not to let it affect me. Only when I'm somewhere foreign, for the first few days, I find it hard to control."

I place my hand on hers. "I understand. Our home is your home, too, and I want you to relax here."

She twirls the wine in her glass before taking a sip. "Thank you, and to be honest, I have relaxed considerably over the past few days. It's quite laid back here and surprisingly, I enjoy it."

Christopher comes and sits at the table, lightly shaking the ice in his glass to blend with the whiskey.

"I'm glad I have both of you here as I want to discuss Samuel. He's highly strung since leaving the jungle."

"Eden, we tried to make him stay with us in LA and receive all the tests when he first arrived. We were concerned and alerted the authorities to what happened, only our son is stubborn and refused to stay longer than necessary so he could come to you. It's why our last email omitted concern as he made us promise not to mention he was home."

I gasp. "Why would he do that?" He knew I'd go crazy worrying about him.

"He believed enough time had passed for you to have moved on. Or you assumed he wasn't returning to you and again moved on with your life. He intended to assess the situation, and if you chose to be with another man, then he'd understand, except he wanted to see with his own eyes rather than discuss it over the phone."

I shake my head in shock. *Did he really believe I could move on so quickly?*

"There's nothing I won't do for him," I blurt. "It's why I'm going to bring him home tomorrow regardless of what the hospital doctors say. They won't get answers. He's suffering from PTSD. You need to have a long chat with him about why he remained in the jungle for so many years. Some motive resulted from his relationship with you both. He also didn't cope after Inesa's suicide. But the main reason was his love of helping people without benefiting himself." I sip more wine. "He's the kindest and most unselfish man I know. Despite whatever it is destroying him inside, being with Rose and me is the one thing saving him. I need him home with us. I'll fight for him, do what's right for him regardless of who I offend."

Caroline smiles. "I'm so happy he found you, Eden."

Christopher's expression remains stoic. "Please allow me a little more time to talk to a colleague before you do. There might be one more thing I can do to help."

39

SAMUEL

On Friday morning, Dr. Tolley enters Samuel's private hospital room with a gentleman in a navy-striped suit and lemon-colored tie.

Samuel closes his eyes momentarily to prepare himself for the questions to follow. He's done repeating his answers to every specialist who has walked through the door. Every physician thinks they have missed something—a clue or a misdiagnosis—so questions are endless until they find a lead to his illness.

There are more viruses than stars in the universe.

A small percent invades our body to cause illness. Considering scientists have only discovered around one percent of the viruses that exist, Samuel's condition might be unknown and rare, considering the Amazon is one of the most biodiverse places on the planet. He had ventured deep into the jungle, barely survived, and watched those around him perish, despite bats flying overhead at night, their droppings landing on their food and belongings. Good hygiene was compromised while they trekked and hid away from civilization. In a perfect condition, viruses are waiting to leap from wild animals to humans. The characteristic of the microbes is a mystery. Another specialist probing into his life to seek answers is futile. Samuel knows the origin of his illness may never be known. The least information given about his journey and why he was 'lost' will help protect his Ularan family.

"Good morning, Samuel." Dr. Tolley comes to stand beside his bed. "We have received more blood results. While we have found nothing significant, your levels suggest there's an infection and not bacterial related." She lifts her chin toward her co-worker. "Professor Mundy is visiting from Sydney and has an interest in your case."

Samuel glances at the professor. "My case isn't that difficult. All fecal and blood results are absent occult blood and known micro-organisms including parasites." He shrugs nonchalantly. "I have an undiscovered virus so the fact we know very little about it means treatment is trickier until my body works out a means to fight it."

"This is true." The professor sits beside Samuel's bed and pushes his glasses up his nose to read Samuel's notes. "Although your weight loss and digestion lead us to believe your body has been trying to fight the micro-organism for many months now, and unfortunately, you're losing. Unless we intervene and try to identify and familiarize ourselves with its behavior, you might not produce the antibodies to win this battle. First, we need to commence nasogastric fluids and gain some weight, so your body has the energy to boost your immune system."

"My knowledge of T-cell production is adequate, and I don't need a lecture." Samuel reaches for his glass of water, already tired of where the conversation is headed. "I merely need time and will not consent to gastric feeds when it will not help."

"Dr. McMahon…" Dr. Tolley gently presses, "… your father has been in contact with the professor to help us find answers."

Samuel crosses his arms defiantly. "I'll tell you what I know. The deforestation of farms and the logging industry is affecting the biodiverse balance. Add climate change to the equation, and we're playing with disaster.

"The rivers are being poisoned, the indigenous tribes are forced further into the jungle, and the safety and food sources are compromised by the greed of these industries. What's the world doing about this? If it continues, the entire planet will suffer. Almost one-fifth of the Amazon has burned or been cleared for these purposes. Between fifteen and thirty years, if it continues and we reach twenty-five percent, then the effect could be irreversible. The reduction of the jungle along with climate change could lead to the jungle creating more carbon than it can absorb. Not enough rain will fall to sustain the jungle, and it could become a hothouse. Not a great outlook, Professor."

The professor peers over the rim of his glasses. His gray hair grew in patches over his balding head. The lines around his eyes depicted years of experience. "Dr. McMahon, I understand you're passionate about protecting the rainforest. This isn't the reason I have been called in to view your case—"

"My *case* has everything to do with what's currently happening in the rainforest as we're awfully close to anthropogenic change. The changing conditions are ideal for pathogens to pass from animal to human. Pathogens we have no prior knowledge of or how it will mutate."

Professor Mundy stares at Samuel before lowering his gaze and reading more of his notes. "Is it my understanding you believe this happened to you? That you were in an environment where you contracted an animal virus because of ideal conditions similar to high humidity and the trudging through mud and flooded terrain for months? Perhaps a mysterious virus survived in a natural balance until you appeared and somehow ingested it, or do you believe it to be mosquito-borne? Or inhaled like fungus or mold?"

Samuel glances at Dr. Tolley. "I presumed whatever I have is not contagious, and I'm doing all I can for my body to eradicate it."

Dr. Tolley places a hand on his shoulder. "Of course. I know of your love for your family, and you wouldn't place any of them or your work colleagues in jeopardy."

"Or my patients. I took my oath seriously. I keep thinking back to SARS and HIV and how we could have managed the disease better if we gained information prior to outbreaks." He turns to the professor. "I'm more than happy for blood tests to continue so you can observe how the pathogen behaves, and I'm happy to try certain medications. Although only for one month. If there's no notable change, then I'll manage the symptoms myself."

"I think it's a reasonable agreement." The professor stands. "Although, I highly recommend you cease work to take a month of leave, so you're available for certain tests and getting adequate rest."

"I'm not sure it's possible so early in my training." Samuel looks to Dr. Tolley for confirmation.

She shakes her head, and brown strands of hair move slightly across her forehead. "You need to focus on your health first, work second."

"Do you live far from the hospital?" the professor asks with his eyes lowered to his note-taking.

"Not far at all."

"And I understand you would like to be home with your family?"

"Yes, sir."

"Family support is important. I recommend twice weekly tests, and hopefully, we can identify what's making you sick." He stands and straightens his lemon-colored tie.

"Can I be frank with you?"

"Any advice is helpful, Dr. McMahon."

Samuel's lip twitches at the professor's ability to recognize most of Samuel's comments classify as advice or feedback, be it with sarcasm. "This is just the beginning. The indigenous lived harmoniously in the forests and didn't leave a footprint. Human greed is massacring the Amazon, opening the way for a killer virus to emerge. It will be our next pandemic, one difficult to control as the consequences could be worse than SARS, Ebola, and HIV all combined as we'll have little to zero warning or knowledge about it."

The professor listens astutely. "Similar to an RNA virus? Possibly SARS-related coronavirus."

Samuel shrugs. "Scientists have been studying novel coronaviruses since the seventies, so at least we have some knowledge about them. The Amazon has the potential to create something far more deadly. We both know how quickly disease spreads, yet flights carry a killer around the world. Viruses kill more than any war, and they're always one step ahead of us."

The professor removes his glasses and holds them in his hand. He moves to the end of the bed. "When you're better, I hope you can join our research team.

You'd fit in fine as something tells me you weren't in the jungle to simply admire Mother Nature."

Samuel's lips curl up slightly. "There's much to learn as there is to explore."

The professor gives a knowing, lopsided smile. "I can discharge you today. I'll be in contact next week after your first results are in. If you're feeling unwell or your symptoms change, please call, and we'll arrange for immediate admission."

"Of course, thank you." Samuel wants to spring out of bed and pack his bag immediately.

Before the doctors leave his room, his father enters and introduces himself. He is wearing trousers and a shirt and fits in with the other doctors on the ward. Even though he's on holiday, his father hasn't worn what Samuel considers casual clothing to relax in. Not even denim jeans.

"Dr. McMahon, I've heard quite a lot about you from Professor Roxby." They shake hands. "We are dining out tomorrow night. You should join us."

"Thanks for the invite, although we're flying out to Uluru, Kata Tjuta tonight. Perhaps on my return. How long is your visit?"

"I'd like to be involved in your son's case, so I'll have Professor Roxby's assistant get in contact with you."

The door closes, and Christopher takes a seat beside Samuel.

"Have we made any progress?"

Samuel is honest with his father. He tells him what he said to the professor and then goes into the gory detail of what happened during the months he almost died in the middle of the jungle, the very place he felt most alive.

After Samuel finishes retelling his story, his father

takes him in his arms and hugs him. "I know we've had our differences, son. I'm proud how you tried to make a difference to a community and to the planet, but nothing is worth your life."

"No. And…" he hesitates, "… I'm not happy like I was back then when the village was peaceful."

"I can see that, son. It's something you must work out with Eden. Whatever you choose, we'll support you."

Samuel stares at his father. "Who are you, and what have you done with my father?"

Christopher chuckles. "Last night, I engaged in a long conversation with Eden. You're a lucky man to have her. All we want is for you to provide for your family and be responsible. I misunderstood why you remained in the middle of a dang jungle, but you have clarified questions and thoughts of it as *wild* or meaningless work." He pats Samuel's hand. "Our focus is to help you heal and ascertain what is causing your illness."

"Am I to thank you for getting Professor Mundy on the team?"

Christopher smiles. "It's the least I can do for my son."

Samuel swipes each photograph on his phone. Eden sent through the pictures this morning with a text saying she'll be there to pick him up soon. She's waiting for his father to return as his mother wanted to take Rose to the beach and build sandcastles. The quality time his parents have spent with his family means a lot and a positive outcome from his hospital stay. He'd have bent to their every command. Eden would set them straight to what she expected as grandparents. It saddened him to miss his daughter's birthday last night, although he'll make it up to her. More importantly, his parents celebrated it with his Australian family. His father recommended he rest, and it was unlike him to promote rest over work. He promised to tell Samuel all about the adventure on Tuesday and, although disappointed, understood why it was best for Samuel not to travel to Uluru with them. At least it will give him time with Eden to discuss his future as he knows the current path isn't the right one.

He imagines her feistiness, ready to argue with him before telling her she's right. Eden always knew what was best for him.

Several months ago, there was a time he believed he wouldn't survive and thought he'd never see Eden or Rose again until he imagined her holding their baby, pictured Eden's beautiful smile, and her kind voice telling him he'll be okay. Her image motivated him to not give up.

And he certainly isn't giving up now.

"Good morning." Eden walks through the door wearing a summer floral dress, so radiant it's as though sunshine follows her. She checks the Apple watch on her wrist. "My bad, it's lunchtime."

He chuckles. "Do you choose not to mention the hour, or do you prefer to reference time like the Ularans?" He waggles his eyebrows. "Some habits stick."

"Oh, you mean noontime?" She leans in and kisses him. "Some habits should never be lost, especially those that bring you joy."

"You bring me joy." He pulls her hand so she lands

on the bed, and this time he gives her a long, lingering kiss, showing Eden how much he has missed her.

Eden breaks the kiss and places a hand on his cheek. "Are you ready to go home?"

He leans his forehead to hers. "Yes, please. I can't wait to get out of here."

"It's not fun being on the other side of your work, is it?" She squeezes his hand when he shakes his head. "To be honest, I was coming here to take you home regardless. You need to be with your family. So, they were going to have a fight on their hands today."

Samuel's body buzzes with pride at how Eden would fight his work colleagues to take him home. "Did you mention this to my father last night?"

"Oh, I mentioned quite a few things to your father. To my surprise, he listened, but I think he realized he'll inherit a stubborn daughter-in-law."

"Our wedding is something else I want to discuss. I hoped we could have a small wedding while my parents are still here."

"Samuel." She leans in and gives him another kiss. "All that matters is you focus on getting better. Our wedding can wait, and I'm sure your parents will return whenever we decide the time is right."

"The time is right. In fact, it's never been better."

40

EDEN

Convincing Samuel to rest is difficult.

All morning I'm reminding him to play with Rose and leave other things to me.

Caroline and Christopher arrived in Uluru and already sent through photographs. Samuel reads the comment under each like a documentary account of their experience.

My phone buzzes with a call from Dana.

"Hey."

"Hey, Edes. How are you? How is everyone?"

"All good." I glance at Samuel and decide not to mention his hospital stay right now. "Rose turned one during the week."

"I saw Faith's photos on Instagram. She's grown so much, I can't believe it."

"She has. I haven't forgotten to book a visit. I have a few things going on. How is Cairns?"

"Fabulous. I want to take you to the rainforest. It's so beautiful, and it reminds me of when you visited the Amazon."

"Right. I'm on my way," I joke, only I'm staring at Samuel thinking how he'd love it.

"There are homes set in the thick of it and a stone's throw to the beach."

"What?"

"Don't get too excited as you can't swim all year round because of the stingers and crocs."

I laugh.

"I thought it too good to be true. No, seriously, the Daintree is something you must experience because…" she pauses. "I noticed Samuel wasn't in the pictures on Instagram."

I lower my tone. "No, he was in the hospital having some tests. I'll tell you about it later. Could you please send me some links to the accommodations?"

"Sure, but please stay with us in Cairns, and I'll organize the accommodation in the Daintree. I'll send links so you can choose where you'd like to stay."

"I really appreciate it, Dana."

"Okay, we'll chat soon. I'm doing the rounds and now calling your mum and dad. Is it crazy that I miss his grumpiness in the mornings?"

"Not crazy. I miss those days with us all in the office. We've been so busy with other matters I rarely speak to Dad about work."

"Eden, we all understand you have a lot going on. Check out my photos on Instagram. If I were a gambling woman, I'd bet you'll be booking a flight soon," she says seriously. "I'll talk soon."

"I miss you," I say a little louder before she's gone.

I keep hold of my phone and open Instagram not only to see Dana's photographs but to view the pictures Faith shared.

The images of Rose's birthday have me smiling. The photographs of the kids with goofy expressions are cringeworthy, and I can't help giggling. Then I find Dana's profile, and my jaw drops. The house in the Daintree is on stilts and surrounded by beautiful rainforest gardens and an ocean view from the mountains. Inside the home are all comfort and modern furnishings.

It's better than I expected.

I keep scrolling and find images from Yasmine's trip. So many pictures in Peru, and it reminds me of what Samuel said and how he wants to return. Maybe there's someone who can help him in the Daintree rainforest?

I stop and read an inspirational post from Yasmine because her posts are always worth reading. There's an image of the stars, and it has a Milky Way feel so it hints at being thankful to the universe.

Remember our first love?

Do you ever look back and wonder what letter could I write to my younger self warning of the heartache and yet tell her to experience it all because it will shape you to being the best version of yourself? And you won't get there without the hurt and pain of a broken relationship to a douchebag you assumed you wanted to spend the rest of your life with.

I'd tell myself to be young, have fun, and don't worry about all the dumb mistakes because you're going to be okay. Despite the pain of lies, betrayal, and the emotional rollercoaster of getting through one day when your heart is shattered, it is worth knowing who you don't want as a partner and listening to your own heart, protect her first because you're worth it.

There will be mistakes.

And your forever partner will make them too.

Know the person who's your soul mate may not be rich, may not send you flowers, may not open car doors, and may not say yes to your every demand. But that person is here for you, especially in the tough times, and learns from mistakes. When they make a promise, they honor it.

Most of all, they treat you like you're the most important person in the world. When you stare into their eyes, you see a future together, and it feels so right. A balance of the sun rising and setting every day.

And you thank your younger version for being brave and riding the storm because the best is yet to come.

Yasmine is happy.

They have worked out their differences and are in a good place.

And now I miss my friend.

🌴

As I roll onto my side, I wrap my arm around Samuel. He's propped up on pillows while scrolling on his phone, his way of avoiding sleep.

"Dana wants us to visit her and make a trip to the Daintree Rainforest," I whisper.

He looks at me sideways. "When?"

"Whenever you want. I read some plants have medicinal properties and many other secrets known by the indigenous communities living in the area."

His eyes widen. "I feel like I'm being given hidden messages. Even Dad sent me some photos tonight and mentioned a conversation with an indigenous leader at Uluru and how some of their medicine might help."

"Your father said that?"

"Maybe, we could visit Dana after Christmas?" His eyes are wide and earnest. When he makes this expression, it highlights his gaunt face, and my stomach drops, knowing how he's struggling. Hurting for me.

"Check out Dana's Instagram," I gently prompt.

He opens his phone. "Wow, it's beautiful."

I peer over his shoulder, and he continues to search the area. "A wedding. Now that's an idea."

I rest my head on his shoulder as he peruses beach wedding images with the rich green rainforest as a backdrop.

Leaving him to get lost in his imagination, I open Gran's journal, ready to be transported back to Ulara with her.

41

IVY

May 20, 1963

It feels strange to put pen to paper.
It seems like months since I wrote my last entry. Yet it's only seven weeks.
I have marked the days on the bamboo posts in my hut and added the days to estimate the date.
Though I fear I'll soon lose track of the days. The rainy season is upon us, and I've been stuck inside alone for many days. With no protection from glass windows or doors, only a hammock, I sit and watch the never-ending waterfall flow from my thatched grass roof to the ground. When I need to eat, I trudge through the water at mid-calf to get to the central hut—Waipa—where the fires burn for our food. They string bananas and other fruits from the bamboo beams. Many of the huts are above water, built on a slope with trenches surrounding them so the runoff flows away, protecting the important huts. Others are on stilts. Mine is on low stilts at the front section of the village and close to the river. I have a great view, yet I'm still being observed and not trusted. It's why I stopped writing, as the disapproval in their expressions was clear. I

don't want to do anything to upset these people who are feeding me and giving me a safe haven for now.

I have given up hope of Maria coming for me until the rainy season is over. Jennifer and Felix were volunteering for six months, so I assume they have vacated the camp if they're alive.

I'm slowly learning some of the Ularan language. Previously, I didn't bother when sign language worked for most things, only I hoped to have been rescued by now.

Rescued because my canoe disappeared last month. I assume from the force of the river with the water gushing down from the tepui into other tributaries that feed into this part of the river.

My friend, Weju, comes and visits me daily to check on me. Lately, something has changed in his eyes, as though he knows a secret and can't share. I fear it has something to do with my fate.

Though some days, I feel it's easier to have died. Maybe then Albert would have been informed. They could have made it appear as an accident.

An unknown future scares me. I don't want to be stuck here forever. Yet how do I leave?

I can't simply walk out.

No trails. No canoe. I can't even follow the river as the rainforest consumes every space. I have no drinking container or anything to carry food. My sandals have frayed and are almost unwearable, although I still cover my feet when I walk around.

The stench. My skin. Sometimes I don't feel human.

But I'm alive, so I shouldn't complain. Right now, I wonder what I have to live for.

If there were a chance I could go home, I'd take it. If I could turn back time, I would, as my world was right in front of me in Adelaide, and I set off for an adventure and my selfish need to fulfill a dream.

A dream that has become a nightmare.

Writing this from the safety of my hut, it makes me think of home. At least the rain has eased, and I can see some of the village.

Weju is with the shaman.
They're discussing something.
I remember teaching him to pronounce Eden since our phonics are quite different.
Here, everyone's name holds meaning, so I told him my name was of the rainforest, as in a way, it's their paradise. In the Ularan language, Weju is the sun. He certainly has been my ray of sunshine through these tough days, even now when the sun barely shines at all.

This is an exciting entry. Weju came and led me to another hut. A younger girl went into labor and became distressed. I don't know how long she's been like this, as she was tired and running out of time to deliver safely. When I examined her, the baby was breach, and all I could think about was the young girl back at the camp. I'd not lose another life if I could help it.
It was too late to turn the baby, and it came out breach. A miracle she survived it and the tiny baby too. Due dates were irrelevant here. The baby comes when the baby comes. Three ladies assisted me. One sung, be it close to yelling, in a distinct language. Another wafted smoke, almost choking me, but I ignored their custom and focused on getting the baby boy out.
I'd never witnessed the cord being cut by a piranha tooth and twine to tie the umbilical cord. The women carried the placenta in the rain and into the forest. I'm curious about what they did and why, yet not enough to do anything to offend them.
By the look on the shaman's face, I had proved some worth and not just another mouth to feed.
I also have a name. They refer to me as Tamu'ne Pupö. When I asked Weju, I made out his explanation to be white woman. Not very exciting or warrior worthy, yet it's a name.

June 1963

I have stopped counting the days, and enough time has passed for me to know it's June.
I stopped writing because of what I'm about to confess.
So, I'll simply write it, and hopefully, it will explain matters so if my journal is ever found, it might be understood.
I slept with Weju.
It just happened.
Like most nights, I was crying. I feel like a prisoner in a hut, and I may as well be in the middle of the bloody ocean for the amount of water I wade through just to pee. I'm always nauseated. Hungry. Thirsty. Dirty. I am beyond feeling unclean. Sometimes I feel like a trapped animal.
It's hard to fathom this is my new life.
I keep telling myself to focus on staying alive. Hope is always in the stars.
And then he appeared at the doorway, his silhouette unmoving in the dim light. He approached me cautiously as though my sobs terrified him. When close enough, he climbed into the hammock and curled himself into me. I needed to feel human. I needed to be touched. I wanted someone to tell me I was going to be okay. Instead, Weju showed me. And I had a moment of happiness. Only he isn't allowed to have a partner as he's being groomed by the shaman to be the next medicine man. And they're like a priest with no partner and committed to healing the people and learning the secrets of the rainforest.
In his culture, I'm not sure if it's considered a sin for him to have sex, but it is for a married woman in my culture.
The guilt has overshadowed any happiness.
Not that I can be sent to a prison for my crime as I feel I'm already locked away.

September 1963

I now count the months by the full moon.

And it's three full moons since I menstruated.

It's no surprise.

Weju didn't stop coming to my hut. He came every night except when he left for brief hunting trips.

Some of the older women assume. Their eyes drift down to my belly and breasts.

They don't treat me any differently, I simply sense disappointment.

But I don't have the energy to deal with judgment as I must cope with surviving here not only for myself but for my unborn child.

How do I explain myself to Albert?

Will I ever see him again?

Will my baby and I survive the birth?

If I could leave, I'd have this child in Australia. However, I don't think walking out with the future shaman's baby is as simple as it sounds.

Lonely nights are part of my existence. My debilitating thoughts surface through the constant chatter of creatures are the only noise I hear. When my mind calms, the panic returns, hearing the squeals of animals in the distance. It squashes any ideas of running away. Weju comes for sex then sneaks back to the long hut he shares with the other men. Our relationship is dangerous as are my thoughts.

The moment he's gone, I'm back to silent tears.

I assume he knows I'm with child even though I have said nothing. The men here have little to do with their babies — it's all women's work. I have someone in my life, and I've never felt more alone.

It's like I'm reliving my post-natal depression with Winston.

November 1963

The second trimester has been kind to me.

I'm no longer nauseous.

I have also found a way to bring some happiness.

I taught Weju how to make love.

Instead of intercourse like animals with him behind me, I have showed him how to love in the missionary position, since our time is limited with my growing belly, or I straddle him. And by holding his hands, I have showed him how to caress and just hold me tight when I need him to make me feel human.

42

EDEN

I slam the journal closed and let out a long sigh.

I can't read anymore.

These are Gran's private times.

My heart is racing.

They called Gran Tamu'ne Pupö. *White woman.*

I recall how the shaman recognized me on the day he appeared from the rainforest like magic as if my spirit called to him. Not exactly my spirit but Gran's presence within me. In Ulara, my name was similar.

Tamu'ne Akare meaning white tortoise. At least they didn't consider Gran to be a slow learner like me. Still, my head is spinning, thinking about her time in the village as well as mine.

Samuel has fallen asleep, so I switch off my light and close my eyes ready to dream about Gran.

I wake before Samuel.

It's light enough for me to read, and I'm surprised Rose hasn't woken yet.

Last night my dreams were of Gran, and somehow, we were in the jungle together. In my subconscious, I wanted to help her. I'm scared for her as I know what happens in the end.

Placing another pillow behind my head, I open her journal and keep reading until my family stirs from their sleep.

43

IVY

December 1963

Last night when I ventured out of my hammock, there were stars above the trees, and I caught the light from the moon in the cloudless night sky. It was like seeing rolling green hills of endless countryside after spending months in a cave.
Again the rain has eased.
I'm beginning to feel half-human again.
The village has come to life.
Like ants, everyone is scurrying in the fields, reviving whatever they can and preparing the soil for more plants. It hasn't affected the banana palms. If anything, many of the plants here have thrived in the rain. The men and warriors have been gone for a week on a hunt. Weju has spent more time with me and stayed most nights. Today he moved his hammock into my hut.
I should be happy, only I know this has cemented my fate. I have observed a few of the younger couples. There's no wedding ceremony. The man moves his hammock into her family's hut. The guy becomes part of her family, and they all sleep in the one hut—the newly wedded couple, the in-laws, and all the sisters and brothers. Not quite the wedding night I imagined.

Permission is granted from the chief and shaman, and I have seen the father-in-law and the guy speak with the leaders.
So, I assume something has passed between Weju and the leaders. I'm surprised as I couldn't see the shaman giving up his young apprentice easily. The shaman and chief continue to keep their distance. I'm unsure what to do to prove I'm not a threat. Maybe the shaman can see through me and knows I'll leave at the first opportunity.
And flashes of new hope of getting out of the village have surfaced now the rain has eased.
At an estimate, I'm around seven months pregnant, give or take a few weeks. My stomach is smaller than when I had Winston, although it's to be expected with the change in lifestyle. With no doctor to check on me or the baby, I'm grateful to see my stomach swell and confirm we're doing okay. It's all I can assume for now. The idea of giving birth here isn't ideal, and it scares me. I've witnessed many complications and aware help is minimal even compared to the camp where I volunteered. The camp now has the appeal of a modern hospital with trained doctors and nurses compared to Ulara.
I must look beyond my white privilege and recognize how the people here have survived over time with their own natural medicine and how they rely on Mother Nature and the rainforest for disease prevention and treatment. In my mind, I need to plan ways to make peace with the shaman as he could be the one person who decides on what care I receive.

I know why Weju moved his hammock into my hut.
Nothing could have prepared me for last night.
I'm still crying while writing this entry.
Weju escorted me to the special round hut where they perform their

ceremonies or rituals. Until now, I haven't been allowed to be present or even observe.

The exception came when the ceremony was for me.

I was 'encouraged' to drink the tea despite my tears.

Awarö is a word for bad. I repeated it over and over through my sobs, afraid it would hurt my unborn child since I didn't know what was in the brew. All natural yet for medical sake, the leaves boiled in ayahuasca ceremonies cause the hallucinations. An effect similar to DMT and not ideal for a pregnant woman.

Weju very calmly told me Wakü, a word meaning good. His eyes pleaded with mine, and he kept looking back at the shaman. It wasn't until I realized it was a test or an initiation to be accepted. I can still feel the tingle of an alien intruder sifting through my thoughts.

And the images have remained with me. My thoughts connected to the shaman's beliefs, and I sensed his presence long after the effects left my body.

I was gifted a new warrior name. Itariru Enu Tykaraije, meaning blue-eyed jaguar.

When I finally stopped fighting the inevitable and allowed my body and mind to connect with the rainforest, I sprinted through the jungle and saw the forest through the eyes of a jaguar. I interpreted the vision as a dream or a hallucination which I expected from the tea. I felt no enlightenment, only a never-ending sprint. Not lost yet, no destination. Now I've learned it's my spirit and, I guess, a new identity.

I've never asked about Weju's other name. Yet I can't help feeling a sense of power by being connected to the jaguar.

Regardless, today I'm left exhausted and confused.

Angry yet relieved.

Scared.

Afraid of what the future holds for Weju and me.

What future will my baby have if the brew has harmed it? How *will a baby with physical abnormalities be perceived? As an evil spirit? Be an outcast?*

My thoughts are out of control, and I need to be optimistic for my own sanity, yet at the least, the effects of the tea could bring on birth and cause me to miscarry. Was it a test that my child was meant to be in this world?

The miscommunication and unknown will be my undoing.

How can they trust me if I don't trust them?

I guess time will tell how my story will end.

January 1964

Another full moon has passed.

At some point, Christmas and the new year have come and gone.

The second without my beloved Albert and Winston.

I'm holding back tears since this month Winston turns three. What a big boy he'll be. What I would do to hold him one more time. Will he even remember me?

Has Albert given up on me and met someone else?

I continue to pray for a future with my family. Yet I'm here, about to embark on a different life with a new family, and I'm worried my husband has found someone else. My selfishness sickens me, yet I must hold out for hope for this isn't my fate, and I have a life back in Australia because I can't imagine spending the rest of my life here.

Weju loves me in his own way. Only not the way I'm used to. I see infatuation in his eyes. Yet there's shame in giving up his time with the shaman and no longer special in rank yet considered a warrior like the other young men. The shaman still eyes me as though he senses an evil within me despite his intrusive thoughts in my mind during the ayahuasca ceremony.

I'm grateful for Weju's support.

And he seems proud to have Itariru Enu Tykaraije for a wife. It's going to take a while to adapt to my new names.

If only he knew how much I wanted to go home.

44

EDEN

Oh, Gran. I swipe a tear from my eye.

Her circumstances being in Ulara were vastly different than mine. I had a choice. Gran feared for her life. And the cheating on Pop which everyone believed stemmed from a survival aspect.

God, I want to read on, although right now, I'm not sure my heart can handle it with what's going on in my life.

"Are you okay," Samuel whispers and curls into me.

I shake my head. "Gran… I had no idea." I swipe tears from my cheek. "Did you know the shaman's name?"

Samuel shakes his head. "I knew him as the shaman or the Ularans called him Pyjai, meaning *medicine man.*"

"His name is Weju," I whisper.

"The sun," he says as though it makes sense. He stares up at the ceiling as though he remembers something. Or simply the man who was his friend and mentor.

"You miss him," I say with understanding.

He kisses my forehead. "Everyone and everything. I keep visualizing how they are and hope they're safe."

"You did your part. It's more than anyone could do." I kiss the tip of his shoulder. "I often think about Kaikare. I miss her too. And wonder if there's a chance Dad and her could meet." I stop myself and shake my head. "It's too complicated."

Samuel's Adam's apple bobs. "I have an idea where they're located, only the idea of returning so soon…" He closes his eyes slowly. He opens them, and he's overcome with sadness. "I'm not ready, and it could compromise everything."

"And too dangerous."

Rose stirs from the other bedroom, and I go to jump up.

"Eden." Samuel places a hand on my shoulder. "I'll get her."

"Bring her back to bed while I'll shower," I tell him because I want to prepare him a nutritious shake. Something easy to digest. I'm committed to helping my man get well.

By mid-morning, I've finished my chores. Samuel and Rose are playing quietly on the floor with blocks.

My phone dings with a message and my heart does a little dance seeing Yasmine's name.

Can we FaceTime?

I find my iPad then press the video button rather than wait. "Yasmine wants to FaceTime," I call out to Samuel.

Her face comes into view with a broad smile. Her black curls are tangled and unkept, yet she looks the happiest I've seen her in months.

"Honey, is everything okay?" Her smile falls away.

I nod quickly. "I miss you." I cough to clear my throat as emotion boils up inside me. I wish she was here so I could chat with her.

"I miss you too. We're flying out in a couple of days and home in time for Christmas." I laugh and sob together because I can't wait to see her.

"How is your trip? Is everything okay?" I know it is by the joy on her face, but knowing she intended to try ayahuasca, I needed to check on her.

"Oh, it was a fabulous experience and everything I hoped for. It opened my mind, and I now know how I want to live my life."

"Oh." I cough. "That's great. I'm truly happy for you. And there were no complications?"

"We did everything Samuel suggested and drank lots of bottled water after we came to. And tell him we took our trash out of the jungle with us."

I smile at her still doing good deeds. "Is Deanne still with you?"

"Yes, we met up with her last night, and she'll be back with our pizza soon. It feels like forever since I've eaten anything other than fresh fruit and nuts."

Samuel comes to sit next to me and positions Rose on his lap. "Look, it's Aunty Yasmine," he says. He smiles at her. "Hello, Yas."

"Hi, Samuel." She waves enthusiastically at him and then blows a kiss to Rose. "And you have grown, princess."

Rose stares at the screen. "As," she says and points.

"Yes, it's Yas," I say, understanding her.

"I'm glad you had an enjoyable experience," Samuel says, sounding interested. "Who was your shaman?"

"Santino. Michael said you'd remember his brother, Juan."

Samuel smiles at Yasmine. Then Michael comes to sit next to her. "Hey, hey," Michael says. "How are the Aussies?"

Samuel grins at Michael. "Really?" He shakes his head, amused. "How's Iquitos?"

"Like old times." Michael gives Samuel an understanding look as though they both share a memory. I'm watching Samuel's expression on the screen, our faces minimized compared to Michael and Yasmine's, yet I don't miss how his smile fades and his brow pulls together. It's slight, still I see it. It's like he's hit with a sense of missing out as he's reminded of a happy memory.

"I'm looking forward to hearing all about it," he says genuinely.

She turns and plants a kiss on Michael's cheek.

Michael drops an arm around her shoulder. "Thought you could use a friend Down Under," he says to Samuel and grins.

"Is that right?" Samuel remarks. He's smiling, and despite our history, I know Michael used to be a good friend to him.

"I think it's wonderful."

Samuel is still smiling, and I let out a sigh of relief as this might be exactly what he needs.

Rose is having her afternoon sleep, and I insist on Samuel taking a nap as well.

It allows me time to call Amy and catch up on her

news. The school term ends on Friday, and she's traveling back for the Christmas break. She mentioned she might not return to Berri even though she loves the country. Before I ask her what led her to the decision, she mentions Ethan has traveled on three occasions to visit her.

For a while, I'm gobsmacked. The last time we spoke, he was proving to her he was a decent guy and a good friend. I must have missed the signs he wanted more with Amy. I never considered them compatible and believed it would take a lot for Amy to forgive him. I never imagined either of them taking the next step toward a relationship.

I'm not sure what I feel, although a sense of relief is swirling in my gut. They are both my friends, and while I'll always bat for Amy as one of my besties, I'm happy if they're happy. I grin, imagining Amy keeping him on his toes. That girl won't hold back if something pisses her off.

The universe is finally aligning for my friends and me. I then send Bree a message.

Hi Bree, are you visiting Adelaide over the Christmas break? We all miss you, and it's time for a reunion.

Hey, Edes, I miss you all. Life has been hectic yet I do have time off over the holiday break. I'll be in Adelaide for a week and then on a cruise to Fiji with someone special. I can't wait for you to meet Benjamin.

I let out a little scream.

With a sense of contentment, I decide to rest on our bed beside Samuel.

Without waking him, I open Gran's journal.

45

IVY

February 1964

*My abdomen has grown considerably, and I'm close to full term.
Labor is on my mind, and I'm having nightmares of the worst
possible outcome. I have been observing other pregnant women and
noticed the younger women have the elder ladies to assist them.
From a distance, I've watched their smoke ceremonies during the
birth. The purpose of smoke isn't clear, although I don't see the
benefit of smoke inhalation for the lungs of a newborn.
Last week, a heavily pregnant woman worked in the field near to
me. I noticed her as she struggled with the work and would stop
and place a hand on her lower back. It was like a future image of
myself. After a few hours, she wandered off, so I followed her,
keeping a safe distance. I watched as she dug a hole.
She moaned quietly, almost singing words over and over in a
mumbled chant.
Another woman joined her, then she squatted and gave birth to a
child over the hole. I wanted to go to them and offer my assistance.
Only many don't see me as someone who cares for them. I still have
a shadow of doubt surrounding my aura, and I didn't want to
scare her.*

Yet it was the most simple and stress-free childbirth I have ever witnessed.

The next day, she was back working in the field with her newborn on her back.

As much as I wish the same labor for me, I'm afraid, after my last labor, it will last for days, being my experience with giving birth to Winston.

Special ceremonies followed by a feast happens approximately once a month. The people dress up for the occasion. Feathers secured by twine fan out like wings from their upper arms. Bodies are painted with a sequence of lines and V's and dots over their limbs and torso. The men also paint their faces. Some prepare with tattoos inked into their skin by paint and a piranha tooth. It's when I noticed Weju's new facial tattoos. Dots and lines and a star to his cheeks. The lines join those down his neck to his chest, reminding me of a diagram of the night sky. I know the people follow sun and moon cycles, yet the astrological artwork on their bodies is remarkable.

Like other feasts, last night began with song and dancing to celebrate a successful hunt of five wild boars. The men imitated other animals in their dance—birds, jaguars, caiman. The descriptive body movements are easy to decipher.

Smiles were big.

Stomachs were full.

The shaman told a story, and warriors were praised.

Then the mood changed.

Weju was standing beside the shaman. They called to me to join them. The circle of dancers surrounded me. The song started again, the dancing lifted a notch to hands waving at me, then up and down like the flapping of wings. The song was directed at me until the shaman's song rose above everyone else. He took my face in his and blew smoke into my face. I coughed and spluttered while he did the same action at my swollen stomach. Then I realized he was either purging the evil spirits out of me or protecting me from them.

Weju's eyes were closed, and his arms reached toward me. His expression was trance-like and being the center of a voodoo-like ceremony freaked me out. I wanted to run far away and ugly cry. Thankfully, the ceremony didn't last, and when the dance finished, I walked back to my place, sitting on the ground at the back of the circle.

Today everyone is back to their normal routine.

And barely noticing me, which is a good thing.

I feel safer living in an invisible bubble.

A few nights after my last entry I went into labor.

I'm overjoyed to be writing this while my daughter suckles my breast.

It seems the shaman took no chances once my water broke. Many of the elder ladies assisted in the labor and performed that damn smoke ceremony.

The details remain blurry.

I recall pushing with the contractions, coaxing myself through my own thoughts while imagining an out-of-body experience to assess my progress. As I pushed through the contractions, the women sang a harmonious chorus over and over as my daughter came into the world.

Daylight was breaking through the leaves, and the overwhelming relief deemed it appropriate to name her Dawn, especially with the meaning of her father's name being the sun.

I've monitored her vitals and checked her reflexes. So far, everything looks to be in order.

Dawn has stolen my heart and provided hope and happiness when I was struggling to find the strength to live another day.

Weju is smitten. He comes and stares at our daughter even while she sleeps. He's not like other men in the village, and I'm glad he has the love in his heart I hoped for our daughter.

He has given her another name.

Turùpo Kapu. He pointed to the sky then to our hearts. So her heart is as big as the sky. Or he loves her, I guess, for infinity. I'm not sure, nevertheless, I love the meaning. Yet this name is only between Dawn and us. A secret name. I'm yet to learn why it's a secret, but I assume it's one of honor.

Weju decided her name in the village is Kaikare. In few words, he likened our daughter to a tortoise and a black jaguar. Maybe the tortoise is a reference to me.

In my heart, she'll always be Dawn.

A new day full of hope.

46

EDEN

My mouth drops open, and I slam the journal closed to relish the beautiful feeling of love swirling inside me.

The noise startles Samuel from his sleep, and his eyes snap open with a fright.

"I'm sorry," I whisper and pat his shoulder. "Go back to sleep."

He's on the couch and rolls onto his side. "Are you okay?" he murmurs.

I'm sitting on the floor in front of him with my feet under the coffee table. I swivel to face him and bring my knees close to my chest. "Gran just gave birth to Kaikare."

He smiles, his eyes blink, trying to wake himself up.

"Go back to sleep," I coax. "I need a minute to feel all the feels. It's so beautiful. The shaman's name reflects the sun. Gran named Kaikare, Dawn, as she was born at daybreak, and she offers hope to Gran like the start of a new day." I shiver as tingles of happiness roll over me.

Samuel chuckles quietly, then rolls onto his back and closes his eyes. "You can tell me about it after."

I'm still smiling and want to continue reading her

296

beautiful story, especially about Kaikare-Dawn as a baby.

If only Samuel knew about this. He could have told Kaikare how Gran felt.

I pick up the journal and continue reading where I left off.

47

IVY

Approximately May 1964

For many months I didn't find the need to write.
Life was good.
We were happy.
Dawn brought joy to us in a special way, and my lonely days were
few. Dawn barely cried.
At first, I thought something could be wrong, especially since she
slept through the night. I was getting sleep. Dawn was feeding
well. I then considered the tea I drank and the smoke therapy
during birth and wondered if any of these calmed her. I only hope
the tea hasn't affected her brain. Around me, the children are fine,
and everyone is calm most of the time. Still, learning by way of
school and university is what concerns me, and if these natural
remedies have hindered her learning capability, I'll never forgive
myself. Because I do hold out hope of us leaving one day and
Dawn having a future as an academic.
I now have time to try and assess her.
Because the damn rains are back. Over an inch every day.
Sometimes more. Sometimes less. Either way, after several weeks,
the ground is saturated, and there's nowhere for it to drain so the

village becomes a swimming pool once more. The main huts are fine. My hut is surrounded by water. It makes bathing Dawn difficult, and the non-use of cloth nappies has been harder to manage. I'm not complaining as urine and feces has never bothered me if I can clean up the mess.

The musky stench surrounding the village is back. Food is scarce. At least I have plenty of fresh water to aid my breast milk. It's something I have focused on as it concerned me how to feed Dawn if I couldn't provide milk. It happens. I had problems breastfeeding Winston. Though I assume other mothers here would step up and feed her as the women all look out for each other. Once upon a time, I wouldn't have agreed to it. Now I understand and find the gesture rather beautiful. We must unite as the men have an authority here, which isn't surprising.

Except Weju. He's back learning from the shaman. And he comes to check on us every day.

Dawn is different.

Her hair is brown, not jet black like the other babies. And her eyes are almost a honey color, not the dark eyes of her father nor my blue eyes.

As expected, her skin is also lighter in color, although it's premature to determine what features will dominate.

I often imagine taking her home to Australia, except Albert's reaction scares me.

Would he welcome me home with open arms, welcome us both? Or would his honor be tattered by my infidelity? Would he want to raise another man's child? I see a vision of Winston and imagine how happy he'd be to have a sister. I often daydream of my children playing together, sharing a swing together or playing chase on the grass.

Grass.

I've forgotten what it feels like under my feet.

It's when I put pen to paper my mind wanders, and the tears flow, missing my old life.

It's why my entries are few.

More importantly, my pen is considered a form of bad magic, so I do it in private. The pen didn't come naturally from the forest, so if not sourced from there, they have trouble comprehending between good and bad. It's why I need to take photos on my camera without anyone noticing. Unfortunately, I don't have many clicks remaining on my film wind. And I want to save some for Dawn.

Tonoro, a young girl, is wading toward my hut. She loves to come and help me.

I'm signing off for probably some time unless the rains get to me again. Like Tonoro, there's much for me to be grateful for.

And I'm still alive.

Alive with a beautiful daughter.

Approximately August 1964

The rains have showed signs of easing. We have more sunny days, and it's a good sign.

Over the past couple of months, Weju has helped me to understand their language. I can comprehend the important things and talk with the other women.

I'm finally being accepted and considered equal.

Weju and I are closer than ever.

More surprising is his time with the shaman. I'm so proud of him and how the community respects him. He and the shaman work together most days, even their songs to the rainforest relax me. It's a beautiful harmonic tune with strange phonics. It doesn't always make sense. They repeat what the rainforest is telling them. Weju believes the trees whisper how to heal their people.

After my science training, I find it hard to comprehend, yet I wonder how they find the knowledge of what plants heal certain diseases and the process of using the plants for medicine. Boiled. Crushed. Drained and drank as tea. How did they know what to do when they have no contact with the outside world or with other indigenous communities? Their spiritual world is fascinating, and I'm beginning to understand and respect their values as long as it doesn't affect Dawn and me.

I must stop calling her Dawn in private. I can't allow her to answer to the name I gave her. I don't want to upset anyone here when I'm making progress on friendship and my own happiness.

I stopped writing as Weju returned from the forest, so I hid my journal. He was a man on a mission, and we made love twice and in the middle of the day! The man knows how to make me feel alive. He told me it's what the spirits want.
I'm not going to argue.

It's only been a few weeks since my last post, but I have to write what happened today. Weju saved my life.
After bathing in the stream, I almost reached the village before being bitten on the leg by a snake. I guessed by its striped markings it was poisonous. I screamed loud and hard and fell to the ground with Dawn rolling from my back.
In seconds, Weju was by my side. After seeing the bite marks, he pulled a piranha tooth from his pouch and sliced the puncture wounds on my skin. One warrior cared for Dawn while another gave him twine, and he wrapped it below my knee like a tourniquet. He then sucked and spat. Sucked and spat. He drained most of the poison from my blood in a quick response I believe saved me.
I almost passed out during it all. I have been vomiting. I'm not sure if it's from the special tea the women have prepared for me or the

poultice on the markings on my leg. I didn't have the energy to assess their treatment.

I only hope it works.

In hindsight, I needed to write this in case something happens and I don't make it.

If I do, it's because Weju saved my life.

Approximately October 1964

My life is good.

I had to write words of my contentment as I'm not sure how often I'll make new entries.

Weju and I are very happy. My old life now sits at the back of my mind because I need to think and behave like a Ularan.

My entries have been about remembering my old life and holding out hope to return home.

I can no longer visualize a life beyond the jungle walls.

I have accepted this is my future, and I'm now bonded to Weju for the rest of my days. We have a beautiful family, and considering how often we make love, I expect our family to grow very quickly. I could even be pregnant now.

If the gods want me to be, I will be. It's only a matter of time before my stomach will swell. Until then, I'll enjoy every minute practicing with my amazing lover.

Approximately November 1964

I didn't expect to be writing another entry so soon after my last one. Only I wanted to document that something is wrong with Dawn. She keeps crying and has endured a fever for days. Whatever medicine the shaman is providing isn't working, and I wish to hell I could take her to my practitioner because it could be any number of viruses or bacterial infections. I don't want her to be another statistic like many children in the jungle by lack of advanced medical help.

Weju said I need to drink the ayahuasca tea again so I can help her. Does he not realize I could be pregnant again?

For the first time in many, many months, I'm afraid.

48

SAMUEL

Samuel's eyes flutter open at the sharp inhalation of breath beside him. Eden's hand clutches her throat.

"Is everything okay?" He pushes up onto his elbow.

Her eyes are wide with concern.

"What is it?"

"I've reached a point in Gran's journal that's going to upset me."

"Do you want me to read it with you?" He hooks an arm around her shoulders.

"Not today." She closes the journal. "Until now, Gran was really happy. She and Weju were…" she hesitates, "… *in love* even though she never stopped loving my grandfather."

Samuel nods slowly. "What happened?"

"Dawn… Kaikare is sick, and Gran thinks she might be pregnant again. Until now, she believed she'd live out her life in Ulara, only her words in the last entry said she was afraid." Eden looks up at Samuel, her eyes saddened by what she has read. "I felt happy, and so I kept reading about Gran's happy times, but I don't have the emotional energy to deal with something as heartbreaking as losing her baby.”

“Are you sure she’s pregnant?”

“No, but I can’t read anymore today.”

Eden rubs her hand over Samuel’s stomach. “How are you feeling?”

He kisses the top of her head. “Don’t worry about me.” He taps the couch for her to lay beside him. Eden crawls up and stretches out alongside his body. His heartbeat shoots up in response. He kisses her neck and slips his hand under her tank top to find her breasts.

“You’re all the nutrition I need,” he says against her skin.

“I wish that were true.” She muffles a laugh.

“I can show you it is,” he murmurs and hooks his leg until he’s between her thighs.

“See,” he says in a deep voice. “A perfect fit.” His kiss is long, passionate, and full of the love that has always been inside him waiting to come out.

Monday morning, Samuel drives into the hospital for routine tests. While in the waiting room, he flicks through a geographical magazine. An article on deforestation in the Amazon rainforest triggers emotion and his chest to tighten. He recalls his memory of the rainforest and pictures it with clarity after living there for eight years. He focuses on remembering the early years and the adventure before him. He met challenges with an open mind and heart, and what he did never seemed like work.

Providing medical care in places of need was gratifying, and he never wanted to be rewarded. His work transformed to be more of a biologist, and his interest in medicinal plants overtook his life.

Back in society, he's struggling to adapt. Eden sees it more than anyone. Yet there's no other alternative because he wants to be with her and Rose. This is now his life and as much as he's trying to get the job done and move on, it's like his body or some deep-seated psychological problem is holding him back.

Watching the medical staff around him reminds him of a colony of insects all working hard in a robotic way within the sterile walls of a lifeless building. Cures for disease come in packaging, not picked fresh from the garden. It seems backward and yet it's referred to as modern medicine. He's not ignorant of the power and lifesaving breakthroughs of advanced medication he'd love to take back to the jungle to his friends. Yet, for basic health and well-being, society has it back to front. Prevention is the key, and yet fast food and a sedentary lifestyle contribute more to cardiovascular disease than if people were hunters and gatherers. There's so much humanity could learn from their indigenous ancestors by surviving on the food you can grow.

He lets out a long sigh.

Despite all his effort and knowledge, the root of his ongoing illness is unknown. If he could take ayahuasca, he knows he could find answers. He closes his eyes and imagines connecting with the shaman and Ivy. He knows they'll protect him if another entity attempts to control him.

Eden remains skeptical about the benefits. She still considers it to be a dangerous psychedelic drug. She's right. Although Samuel understands the importance of preparation and is trained, so his thoughts lead him to seek the answers he needs, as his soul has already been infiltrated and cleansed by ayahuasca's probing fingers over many years.

He opens his phone and messages Michael.

I'm jealous of your travels. I miss the jungle. There are many things I miss so I'm eager to hear about your experiences with Santino. Did he learn from Juan? It's been years since I've seen either of them. Remember our first holiday in our early twenties when we discovered Iquitos and the shamanic ceremonies? We were like kids in a candy store. Behaved like it too. Yet I'd never change a thing, and we learned from our mistakes. I'm looking forward to seeing you soon. I have many questions to ask and hope we can keep this between us. My health has declined, and after eliminating the obvious causes, I believe ayahuasca will help me to find the problem and heal. Unfortunately, Eden doesn't hold the same view as me and still considers it dangerous. Time isn't on my side, and if I suffer further weight loss, I may develop chronic issues and irreparable damage to some organs. I'm waiting on more tests, and I highly doubt anything will come from all the internal probing. So far, I have convinced Eden I'm doing all I can to find answers. The doctors here are querying an unknown virus which is the obvious answer, except the damage it's causing is concerning, and furthermore, how to eradicate it is anyone's guess. A long flight to Peru isn't ideal, but I'm lost for alternative answers, especially when one session could save me months of mistreatment. In your opinion, could Santino help me, or should I simply seek out Juan? Do you have a contact number? See you soon, Mick. Or should I say mate or matey? You'll be learning the lingo here with me.

Hey, Samuel, good to hear from you,
'mate.' I'm looking forward to coming to
Australia and catching up with you. It's
been a long time, and I know I must
rectify the crap decisions I made in the
past. Yasmine has forgiven me, and I see
her as the chick I want to be with.
Something about her makes me want to
be a better guy. Man, that sucks about
your health. I'm surprised they haven't
found answers after all these months. As
for Santino, we had a good experience
with him, and the brew was light, which I
insisted on for Yasmine's benefit. Maybe
it's best to seek out Juan. He's more
experienced and knows you. I have
Santino's contact number. As you know,
he only gets coverage on his cell when
he travels closer to Iquitos. His resort is
five hours by boat on a tributary river. We
fly to Argentina tomorrow and stay a
night before flying out to Australia the
following day. Sorry I can't be of any
more help.

Samuel contemplates his next reply.

Send me his cell details so I can contact
him before booking a flight. Safe travels.

A few moments later, Michael sends through the
information.

"Samuel McMahon."

Samuel looks up to a nurse. He follows the nurse
into a room where she has numerous vials ready to take
his blood. She reads the form, and when their eyes meet,
he senses the curiosity.

He prepares himself for a barrage of questions.

Later in the afternoon, Samuel is resting on the couch. Out of curiosity, he opens the browser window on his iPad and searches for flights to South America.

How quickly could he plan a return trip in the new year?

He checks Eden is still preoccupied with Rose.

She picks up the television remote. "Want to watch *The Wiggles*?" Rose nods her head, and the way she does it is slow and exaggerated as though it's a new thing and dang cute.

The Wiggles dancing and singing on the television could keep their daughter amused for hours.

"Okay. Mummy is going to rest now."

"Mommy," Samuel corrects and then receives an eye roll.

Eden turns on the lounge and places her feet on Samuel's lap before rearranging the pillows behind her head.

She opens Ivy's journal.

The last time she read, she closed it quickly before she became upset.

At least he knows and is prepared to comfort her if she needs it. Yet part of him would like to also understand Ivy's journey. He didn't know her, yet he feels connected to her. Not only through Eden but through their Ularan spirits.

He wonders if his next ayahuasca ceremony could bring her closer to him.

49

IVY

December 1964

I'm writing this entry while lying in a hospital bed.
Much has happened in the past few weeks.
After the last ceremony when I drank the tea, I became weaker, not
stronger.
The good news is Dawn came out of the fever, although it was a
close call as some days she was limp in my arms. I expected her to
get sick since she's now crawling in the dirt and often putting things
in her mouth before I stop her. It's what children her age do. Only
the thought of losing her scared me.
In a turn of events, I had been vomiting for days, sweating
profusely and extremely dehydrated. At first, I assumed I caught a
stomach bug. Only the pain was different, like a knife in my lower
gut, twisting and slicing. If it was an infection or a parasite
feeding inside me, in the back of my mind, I understood if it
turned to sepsis, I wouldn't survive.
Then I hallucinated, and in my dreams, I saw my death.
That morning, I strapped Dawn to my back, then grabbed my
journal. I stumbled to the river. Like I was possessed, I had to get

*to the water and get there any way I could. I collapsed before I
made it and crawled the rest of the way.*

*I questioned the thirst and why my body craved fluids. Drinking the
murky river water could be even more detrimental.*

*By the river's edge, I splashed water on my face, moistened my
mouth then spat it out. I sat back and ignored the soft grizzle
coming from Dawn on my back. She was safe, and I needed to
clear my thoughts as everything blurred around me.*

*Looking over my shoulder, I spotted my journal and pen in the
sand. I must have dropped them when I was close to fainting.*

I didn't know what to do.

There was a fallen palm frond beside me.

I scrambled to my journal then wrote:

*Help me.
From Ivy Monteford.*

*Sweat dripped off my chin and onto the page. Regardless, I tore out
the page and wrapped it in a palm leaf. I tied it with twine to a small
branch and was about to toss it into the river when I heard a motor.*

I managed a croaky, "Help."

*I waved the palm frond in the air to get attention. In a last effort, I
screamed at the top of my lungs. "Maria."*

*Then I collapsed by the water, the side of my face in the sand as I
struggled to keep my eyes open with the black dots joining before my
eyes.*

*Lying and simply breathing must have been enough to stop me from
passing out.*

*I could still hear the faint sound of a motor, and I wondered if I
was hallucinating or wishing it to be true.*

*As I blinked through my tears, I lifted a hand to wave and only
then heard the tears from my daughter still stuck on my back.*

Maria jumped out of the boat and helped me to my feet.

"You came back." I just managed to say the words.

"Many times, but you were never here," she said quickly.

She kept repeating something in Spanish to the others.

"You're going to be okay, Ivy."

I clung to those words.

Until Weju yelled, "Tamu'ne Pupö." White hair. The name I'm known by in the village. He glowered at Maria and her colleagues and yelled, "Awarö itoto." Bad strangers or it could mean the enemy.

I was already in the curiara. Along with his threat, spears were raised in our direction. A hazy curtain fell over my eyes, and I was close to passing out. Maria panicked, pleading with me to convince them not to kill us.

In my mind, it happened in slow motion.

I'd never witnessed Weju's intense expression. The shaman whispered in his ear. Even through my delusional haze, I knew it wasn't good.

I managed to speak and begged him to let me go or I would die. I told him I needed white persons' magic medicine to heal, and then I'd come back to him. I kept repeating I was dying and also told him I was pregnant and needed to save our child. I made a vocal promise to the spirits I would return.

He yelled for Kaikare with open arms, but the motor was already pushing us away from the embankment. She was in another woman's arms.

My promise must have been enough.

Still, he looked furious.

I called out, "I love you," before collapsing into Maria's arms.

I have whispered those words to him in our special times, and he understood the words to be a secret bond between us.

What happened after that is a blur.

Maria radioed ahead to organize a flight from Canaima to Ciudad, Bolivia.

I had emergency surgery for a ruptured ectopic pregnancy and a hysterectomy.

The weeks passed while in the hospital and allowed me time to heal and process the past and my future in a safe environment.

Dawn received antibiotics for an ear infection and has commenced her childhood vaccinations.

Maria has alerted the authorities, and word has reached Albert I am safe but not up to talking yet.

I'm not sure I can even write anymore.

I am confused.

My heart is torn.

I almost died.

Why am I still alive?

January 1965

I have been in the hospital for almost two months and have finished extensive antibiotic therapy.

I anticipated writing in February, not January. In December 1963, there were two full moons. So, my journal dates were incorrect. Dawn was, in fact, born premature, only by a few weeks. During my stay, I have felt foolish not knowing the happenings of the outside world. My daughter doesn't even have an exact date of birth.

Going by my hazy memory, we predicted the middle of January. Maria said, pick a date. So I went with the same day as Winston's birthday, January 23, 1964. I'm not sure why, as I'd prefer to celebrate my children's birthdates apart, yet in a panic, his special day came to mind, and possibly a sign of how much I missed him.

I also gave her Albert's surname.

Dawn Monteford.

Not her father's because who knows what that is.
It was the right thing to do because Dawn will be part of our family in Australia, and her birth certificate will have the same surname as ours with the father listed as unknown.
There's also a process for sending me home since I was listed as missing for so long.
In my heart, I know I must return to Ulara first.
I need to retrieve my bag, especially my passport, visas, and camera.
I also made a promise to Weju and will uphold it to the gods, even if it's for him to see us one more time.
And for me to say I'll always love him and will never forget him.
I can already imagine the pain in his eyes and almost don't want to go as there's a slight chance I'll stay for love.
Until I think about our future.
What will happen the next time I become seriously ill?
What will happen to Dawn?
I'm thankful she has received her childhood vaccinations and soon the measles vaccine. Something I am extremely grateful for.
And will Weju still love me if I can no longer bear more children?
This is also the miracle I'd wished for not so long ago—a chance to return home to the family I've missed.
Albert told Maria he's thankful and only wants me home safe.
I'm yet to tell him I have another child.
I only hope the husband I'll be returning to will love me as much as the one I'm leaving behind.

Tonight, I spoke to Albert over a very bad telephone line. The crackling made it difficult to hear, but still we managed to talk a little and confirm I was okay.
I told him a lot has happened, and we'll need to talk first.
He said his prayers had come true as he never gave up hope I was

*still alive. He knew my strength and how I'd fight to come home to
him and Winston.*
I broke down when I heard Winston's voice.
I couldn't tell him about Dawn. Not yet.
He reinforced he wanted me home safe again.
*I want to believe it to be true. I also know Albert is a proud man
and may not accept Dawn.*
If he loves me like he says, then I must believe him.
Our family deserves a second chance.

50

EDEN

Oh, Gran.

My throat burns from holding back tears.

I swallow hard, only my mouth is dry. I close my eyes and try to control the emotion and pain swirling inside me for my grandmother. I can't read anymore, partly because I already know the ending.

She returns to Australia alone.

Dawn, or should I say Kaikare, remains in Ulara.

What happened on her final visit?

Oh God, I can't help it, and the tears cascade down my cheeks. I want to ugly cry.

"Hey." Samuel's arm snakes around my waist.

I take a deep breath and shake my head. "Everything is making sense. Gran…" I shake my head again, trying to string my thoughts together. "Her trip wasn't an easy one. When she arrived home, people believed she was a little crazy, well, you know differently." A sob escapes my throat. "No one knows what she went through except for Brenda. Pop wasn't as forgiving as she'd hoped, yet she didn't simply cheat on him with another man because of physical attraction.

She did it to survive. She believed she might not make it home. It was so much harder in the sixties, and a gang, it's not what they're called, but you understand when I say they were after her. They wanted to kidnap her, so she hid in Ulara, and there was no way she could escape on foot. It's more complicated than I can describe, and my heart is breaking for her."

Samuel pulls me into his side. "You've always loved her."

"I have." I sniff. "I miss her so much."

"I understand."

Samuel wraps himself around me, and we simply lay together without speaking, holding each other until Rose demands our attention.

🌴

The Friday after my friends arrive back in Adelaide, we arrange to all meet out at The Shores cocktail bar for old-time's sake.

After leaving Rose with Mum for the night, Samuel and I take a stroll along the esplanade, inhaling the fresh sea air. We haven't spoken any more about him wanting to return to South America, and I'm wondering if he'll bring it up when he sees Michael. They haven't seen each other in over a year, although it's not unusual for them. When I first met Samuel, he mentioned how his friends would make him take a holiday once a year to vouch for his sanity and to ensure his safety. So, the time apart never made a difference in their friendship. Samuel has been friends with him since school and vouched for him. The blackmail stunt with Yasmine was out of character, and I still don't understand why he did

318

it. Yasmine has forgiven him, and Samuel is happy to see him, so I'll lower my guard for Yasmine.

Amy and Ethan have secured a booth by a window. It's weird to see them together, and strangely, it makes me happy. Ethan is not someone I'd pick for Amy, but if they're happy, so am I.

Ethan stands and adjusts his tie, then shakes Samuel's hand. "It's good to see you both." He leans and gives me a light hug. "Edes. I haven't seen you around the office for a while."

"No. We've quite a bit going on, especially with Samuel's parents being here. We're still recovering from playing tour hosts," I joke. After Samuel was admitted to the hospital, I only visited a few places with his parents. I made the remark as I don't want to focus on Samuel's health tonight.

"Amy," I say affectionately and step past Ethan to give her a tight hug. "I've missed you, girl."

"Me, too, babe. And I'm here to stay now. I've applied for teaching contracts in the city." She pats my back. "I have really, really missed you."

I take a seat and wait for Samuel to hug Amy before he sits beside me. "Have you ordered?" I ask and pick up the drinks menu.

"Waited for you," Amy says and winks. "Thought we'd start with a cocktail then get a bottle of wine."

The waitress arrives, and we place our order while waiting for our other friends to arrive.

"Ruby is an asset. I'm glad Dana recommended her before she left," Ethan begins with office talk.

"That's great," I say in a high voice. I should be interested in my family's business, only the happenings in the office are the furthest thing from my mind.

"Talking of Dana, we're going to visit her." Before I say any more, coughing interrupts us.

"Am I intruding?" Yasmine stands at the end of the table with a goofy smile on her face. "This is Michael," she says and giggles. "I mean, can you believe Michael is here? What the actual heck? She grabs his shoulders and pulls him in for a hug. "You know everyone except Ethan."

Ethan stands and shakes his hand, then Michael hugs Amy and then me. Finally, he shakes Samuel's hand before pulling him in for a hug with a standard three pats on the back. "It's good to see you, man," he says in a thick American accent. "We have a buttload to talk about."

Samuel is smiling, really smiling as he moves over for Michael to sit beside him. They begin their own conversation before Yasmine has even sat beside Amy.

"So, are we going to address the elephant in the room?" Yasmine begins. I look at Michael, then Samuel. Is she talking about what happened the last time we all saw Michael?

"What the actual hell, guys?" Her arms reach out for emphasis toward Amy and Ethan. "When the fuck did this happen? And how?" Her eyes widen. "You two hated each other."

"Did you consider secretly we didn't," Ethan says and winks at Amy. "He drops an arm over her shoulder and plants a kiss on her cheek.

Amy laughs and rests her head on Ethan's chest. "Life's full of surprises."

Yasmine smirks at her. "It is, girl. Well, I'm very happy for both of you."

Our drinks arrive, and Yasmine gives her order. Michael is drinking water, which is surprising.

"Before I forget." Reaching into her bag, Yasmine reveals two wrapped gifts and hands one to Amy and then one to me. "I got you both a little something from Peru."

Amy gives a strangled scream and tears at the gift wrapping. My gift is soft and seems delicate, so I unwrap it carefully. On top is the colored geometric-shaped Inca cross. "Oh, wow! You knew I wanted one of these." The cross holds deep meaning and importance and it's the same one Yasmine wears around her neck.

Her fingers go to her chest, and she strokes the cross. "Now all three of us have one." Her gaze lowers to my present while I continue to unfold a braided band with feathers attached.

"It's a headband." She gives me a warm smile. "Wear it when you're at your happy place, be it physical or spiritual. It's about feeling at peace wherever you are."

I gently run my fingers over the unique band as though it holds magic. "Thank you, I love it." I lean to hug Yasmine and give her a squeeze. Her gifts always have a special meaning.

"Just what I need." Amy pulls a colorful chullo hat over her head then tugs on the earflaps before tying it under her chin. "I love these hats."

"We know," Yasmine and I both say in tune then laugh.

We pack our gifts away and then Amy clinks our glasses. "To love and friendship."

"Any special occasion?" At the end of the table, a tall, dark-haired, beautiful woman smiles at us. It took a moment to process it's Bree, as the guy standing beside her looks a little out of place in a suit. Screams erupt from our table as we spring out of our seats to hug Bree. It's been too long since we were all together.

The four of us have finally moved on with our lives and found partners who complement every one of us.

It's the night before Christmas, and we're home surrounded by our families. The Christmas tree is decorated, and lights flash on and off. Presents are stacked under the tree. Caroline has made eggnog and pumpkin pie. She's in the kitchen because it's too loud in the family area with Rose and Faith's boys playing dramatically.

Jake, Samuel, Dad, and Christopher are on the balcony enjoying the sunset, each holding a crystal glass with their favorite alcoholic beverage on ice. Samuel, like his father, is drinking whiskey on the rocks. I doubt it's the best thing for Samuel's stomach, but it's the holidays.

Mum and Faith are sitting on the floor near the Christmas tree—the present police. Not one has been opened under their watch. My phone dings, and it's a message to unlock the door. I do so from the kitchen and wait for my brother to ascend the stairs.

Mum screams. Will is standing in the doorway wearing a black shirt and chino shorts, grinning because he loves making an entrance. Faith and I roll our eyes, and we joke about him being the favorite. Mum and Dad are the first by his side. They never admit it, but we know they miss Will terribly. Sometimes I wonder if he's a younger version of Dad with Gran's blonde hair and blue eyes like me.

If only our grandparents could see us now…

"Have you grown again?" Hands on hips, Faith chastises him like he's still our little brother. Younger brother, yes, only Will is far from little. He is now taller than Samuel.

"Hey, sis." He leans in and kisses Faith. "How are the rug rats?"

"Ha. If you babysit while you're here, you'll understand why I already have gray hairs." Faith tilts her head at him. "Come here, ya big teddy bear." She pulls him back for a hug and leans her head against his chest. "I've missed you."

"No one to boss around?" He pats her back. "Talking of being whipped, where's Jake?"

Jake emerges from the bathroom, and his face lights up when he sees Will. They shake hands. "Good to see you, Will."

For a few seconds, I watch Will chat while looking around, taking in my home and the people surrounding us. He rarely comes home these days, and my parents have made trips interstate to see him during university breaks. Making Melbourne his home, he rents a house with other friends and has part-time employment. He plays football for a local club and hopes to get drafted. With all his commitments, I understand why he can't come home whenever he wants. I should arrange to visit him with Samuel and take him to an Aussie football match at the Melbourne Cricket Ground. The atmosphere alone would be worth the trip.

Will turns his blue eyes on me and gives me a cheeky grin. "Here's my jungle girl. Where's Tarzan?"

I shake my head. "Your jokes are lame."

He leans down and squeezes me. "I do it to get a bite, but you're boring now you're a mum."

"Is that so? Then maybe I should tell you to get a

haircut since *you* look as though you've emerged from the wild and not brushed your hair for a month."

"It's because I don't own a brush." He runs a hand over his head. "It's a certain look, sis. Only you wouldn't know because… boring."

"Ha. You didn't see me when I was in the jungle." I bump him in the stomach in a playful way. "Come and meet Samuel's parents."

After all the introductions are made, the night passes quickly, and I constantly refill my champagne glass because this mum is *not* boring.

🌴

"How's the head?" Samuel asks as soon as I open my eyes.

"What time is it?" I lick my lips, only my mouth is dry.

"Almost eight. Rose is entertaining my parents."

"Oh shit. I better get up and get organized." I push up and cringe before flopping back and holding the side of my head. "It hurts."

Samuel chuckles. "So, it's a no to a champagne breakfast?"

The thought makes me want to heave. "Why do I do this to myself?"

"Hmm." He taps the side of his cheek as though he's thinking. "Word was someone called someone boring?"

"Ugh. Right."

Samuel chuckles. "Baby, you're far from boring and, at times, you were entertaining, although it's going to be a tough day."

I groan again.

"I'll get you some Tylenol and water. And perhaps something with electrolytes will help."

"Please do your magic." I moan again, then compel my ass out of bed and to the shower before attempting breakfast.

"Pesens," Rose screams as soon as she finishes her toast with vegemite. She claps her hands.

"Yes, honey, now we can open our presents."

Samuel gets on the floor with Rose. Pure joy sets in on her little face with every present she opens. "Bluey," she screams, pulls the soft toy to her chest, and hugs it.

Samuel whispers to Rose, and she pushes up and waddles over to Caroline and Christopher and hugs them

"You're welcome, beautiful girl," Caroline says.

She waddles back to Samuel, and he gives her a parcel to deliver to his parents. She carries it and helps them unwrap their gift. When they reveal a furry toy kangaroo, Rose claps her hands, then runs back to Samuel ready to deliver the next gift. "It's from Rose," he says and winks. "She chose it. Your real gift will be delivered when you return home. A dozen red wines from my favorite McLaren Vale winery."

His father beams a wide smile. "Thank you." He holds up the kangaroo. "We'll find a special place for this fellow."

Rose carries another present to Caroline. She pulls out a small furry koala. "Oh, I love it." Rose claps her hands again and giggles when Caroline rocks it like a baby.

"Okay, my turn." I hand a box to Rose. "Give this to Dad-da." I watch his face as he opens the lid and reads the card inside.

Samuel's lips part in a grin. "I have a good feeling about this."

I push up and go over to Samuel, lean in, and kiss him on the lips. "So do I."

He grabs my hand and holds me so he can keep kissing me. Until Rose taps our faces. "Pesen."

Samuel laughs against my lips. "Mommy is distracting Daddy."

"Ha." I go to rise, and his hand holds me still.

"I haven't given you my gift." He picks up a small box topped with a bow and places it in my hand. "Merry Christmas, Eden."

Inside the box is diamond-encrusted heart earrings to match the special necklace he gave me last Christmas in Georgetown after being discharged from the hospital. It was our first Christmas as a family, and it came close to being the last. As I placed it around my neck this morning, the happy memories came flooding back to me. I wrap my arms around him and kiss his lips. "Thank you."

I thread the earrings in my ears and move to our framed wall mirror to admire my gift. The earrings and necklace are stunning. "Oh wow, honey. They are beautiful." Only I don't have time to dwell as I hear the door downstairs with our guests arriving.

🌴

Presents are unwrapped, and food is consumed. Popped Christmas poppers and streamers cover the table and floor.

Mum is in the kitchen preparing the pudding and custard for dessert. Faith has positioned her pavlova in the center of the table.

I'm so full I have no room for sweets, but it's Christmas, and our tradition is to eat dessert. Samuel has eaten small helpings of food that won't upset his stomach. He's trying.

Will is entertaining the kids like the big kid he is.

"Tell me…" Faith says to him, "… is there a girl we should be meeting soon?"

Will dips his head back and stares at the ceiling while letting out a loud sigh. He looks back to Faith. "I knew you would ask me this. The answer is the same. No. If there were a chick, I wouldn't be introducing her to you because I don't want to scare her away." He turns and messes James' hair. In retaliation, James wrestles with Will at the table.

Faith shakes her head. "We'd kiss any girl's feet to tolerate you."

"Ha-ha," he says without looking at Faith. "I'll keep you to that."

"Sorry I haven't been around the office," I whisper to Dad, seated beside me.

"It's what happens when you resign." He winks at me.

"Yes, although I want to check in occasionally and offer to help out."

Dad rolls up his shirt sleeves. "You've a lot going on, my girl. We're not going anywhere. When you have time, come by and say hello to everyone."

I pat his forearm and lean closer to lower my voice.

"I wanted to let you know I almost finished Gran's journal." He stares at me, waiting, only I don't know what to say.

"You need to read it."

He runs a hand along his jawline. "I don't think I can."

"It's important. I wouldn't say it if I didn't believe you should. It will give you a better understanding as to what happened, and I can't express words for the respect I have for what she went through. My heart shatters into a million pieces with every page, which is why I can't tell you about it."

Dad stares at me for a few seconds. "Okay. I don't read much these days except the *Financial Times*, except I'll do it for you."

"Not for me, Dad. For Gran."

He nods politely and then turns away when Mum carries the pudding to the table.

🌴

It's after nine o'clock when everyone leaves, and I want to fall into bed. My feet ache, and I'm in pain from overeating. Caroline and Christopher thank us for an enjoyable day and head to bed.

I take Samuel's hand and lead him to the bedroom. "How are you feeling?"

He kisses my lips. "I'm fine. Everything is going to plan, and so far, there are no setbacks."

I nod, even though he isn't convincing. Minutes after I switch off the light, I hear the gentle sounds of Samuel sleeping.

I can't relax. Some nights I wait until after two-thirty in case he has another nightmare. Holding a pillow to my chest helps to calm me. Not tonight. I give up and reach for my iPad and open the E-book app. I'm not ready to read Gran's journal tonight.

🌴

A loud grunt jolts me awake.

I gather my bearings and realize it's labored breathing.

"Please not again," I murmur.

I check the time—4:23 a.m.

"No. No. No…" I groan.

I grab my phone, and with the light, I shine it so I can see his face and not directly on him to wake him.

His breaths are fast and shallow. I find myself counting, and the only thing I know about hyperventilation is I'll need to get a brown paper bag for him to breathe into.

Samuel's eyes remain closed, yet there's movement beneath his eyelids. His face is twitching as his head moves gently from side to side.

"*Run,*" he croaks.

I hate the dreams where I scream at the top of my lungs for help, yet only a squeaky voice comes out. I imagine him feeling like this.

"*Run.*" Jagged breath.

"*Run.*" Sharp inhales.

"*Jump.*" He flings himself forward, and his head flops.

I massage his shoulder to calm him. The last thing I should do is speak to him and spook him.

His eyes are closed.

"*Nooo,*" he wails. "*I'm sorry. So sorry. Awarö itoto.*" Bad stranger.

He falls on his back, and his head moves from side to side. He's mumbling, and it's difficult to comprehend until he cries out, *"I did this."*

"Samuel," I whisper. "You're safe."

It has no effect on him.

"I love you," he murmurs. *"Please forgive me."*

"Honey." I gently rub the length of his arm. Is he talking to me?

"You were like a father to me." He mumbles other words.

"This can't be happening. You were the best part of my life." Choking sounds in sobs erupt from him. I want to wake him. Only this could be his way of letting go of his pent-up emotion. The trauma of his past. Whether it's a new dream or he is reliving the nightmare that has haunted him for months, it must be progress, as he's never cried like this in his sleep.

"I'll always remember you." It comes out in a wail. *"Never forget you. I love you and promise to protect your people forever."*

Forever?

51

EDEN

Beautiful words not intended for me.

Lying beside Samuel, I stroke his shoulder. This wasn't like other nightmares. I assumed his dream included the shaman and maybe Kaikare. He could have been reliving the day the shaman was shot or…

I wrap my arms around his chest and wiggle closer to Samuel. His brow is heavy. His lips are moving like he's saying a silent prayer. A chant, maybe. Samuel has a wonderful, open mind, and there's a possibility he is connecting to the shaman in his dreams. Like he would after taking ayahuasca.

The idea of him taking the brew again scares me. I'm the one who helped save him the last time, and I never want to see that again. I understand certain plants can enhance the experience, and he promised it would be a light brew. Nevertheless, there must be another way. A safer way to help him heal. If it's spirituality he's seeking from a higher being, then he has many religions to pick from. He needs to choose one to facilitate his healing.

We have come too far as a couple, and I'm not

giving up without a fight. I won't lose him. I can't. Samuel is a part of me, and my life would never be the same.

The first day I saw him on the beach in Salvador, I knew there was something special about him. Out of the thousands of people on the beach, our eyes met, and a spark of hope and excitement shot through me. Then he was gone. He admitted he felt it too, and it spooked him enough to retreat to the hotel. Thinking about his reaction should have been a flag that he's no ordinary man, that his life differed from mine, and our meeting would impact his life to a degree none of us ever imagined. I was a willing victim and would have done anything for this man even after knowing him for a short time.

Was it a coincidence? I don't believe so.

Somehow, we were meant to be.

Maybe from the time I was born, my Gran saw something in me and knew something about my future no one else could possibly know.

Regardless of how and why we came to meet, we did, and all I know is we are meant to spend the rest of our lives together—long happy lives. And no way in hell am I going to allow Samuel to weaken and think the only way for him to heal is through a damn *magic* tea.

Because he's better than that.

He is stronger than he realizes.

And so am I.

We're not broken.

When I met him, I was emotionally ruined and had given up on love.

Samuel saved me and offered hope.

Showed me a new life and happiness.

It's my turn to help him.

Grabbing my phone from the bedside table, I send Dana a text.

> We're coming to visit you soon. Looking at accommodation and flights now!

Then I search for holiday homes in the Daintree Rainforest.

I'm lost to images in the rainforest when he stirs beside me.

"Morning," he whispers, then leans over and kisses me. "What time is it?"

"Almost six. Go back to sleep if you're still tired," I say gently.

"My parents fly out today. I should get up and spend time with them this morning." He glances at my phone. "What are you doing?"

"Looking for holiday homes in the Daintree." I give him a sideways glance to check his reaction.

There's a tell-tale dent between his brows. "For when?"

"As soon as possible. It will be good for you. Best you give me the dates between tests so I can arrange a private getaway."

He pushes up on his elbow. "Eden, I see what you're doing here, and as much as I appreciate it, I've made up my mind. I'm going to Peru for a couple of weeks. Then I'll be back. It's the only way for me to find answers."

"It's not the *only* way," I state. "You're not even considering new options or even another place where we could be happy."

He shakes his head as though I'm not making sense. "Another place?"

"Yes." I scramble to sit up and show him the houses

on stilts perched on the side of a mountain and surrounded by rainforest, some overlooking the ocean. "How beautiful are these? I could imagine us living there."

"Living there?" His forehead furrows. "How? What do we do for income? And do you want to sell this house?" he asks, exasperated.

"No, of course not. Maybe we could divide our time. Or even have a home for getaways when you need a break." I shrug. "We'd find work. Please trust me on this. You'd love it there."

"I..." He shakes his head again. "I can't keep up, Eden. I thought you wanted me to live here with you and be close to your family and friends. If none of it matters, why did you want me to come here?"

"If you remember correctly, *you* bloody sent me home without a choice," I snap. "I was happy as long as I was with you. You're the one who emphasized the jungle was too dangerous for me. You were right, but it was also too dangerous for you. And this place doesn't have as many risks. The homes are surrounded by the beautiful rainforest as well as creature comforts for modern living. It's perfect."

Samuel rolls onto his back and covers his eyes with an arm. "What about work? Do I continue my studies from there? Is a hospital even close?"

"Do you want to continue your training?" I murmur. "Are you enjoying it? Because from where I'm standing, the night you collapsed also stemmed from overworking."

He stares at me for a few seconds with a look I've seen through his charade.

"Please trust me on this." I lean over and kiss his lips.

He wraps an arm around my waist and guides me on top of him. "I do trust you. It's part of loving you. But if we spend a few days there, and it doesn't resonate with me in the way you hope for, then you must trust my instinct and allow me to go to Iquitos and see a shaman. Alone."

"Alone?"

"I need to focus on healing and not be distracted by anything else." He takes my face in his hands. "I want to be the best husband I can for you." He then kisses me, and our tongues tease with the passion capable of turning me into liquid lust. My heart beats so fast and, in a way, beats only for him.

"After the last time, it scared me. Why are you so desperate to return?"

"You know why, Eden. I need extra help beyond what modern medicine can offer."

"Maybe, yet you've only seen a psychologist twice. You m-must give it time." My voice cracks, and rather than look at me, he closes his eyes as though some other thought is controlling him. Then it dawns on me. "It's not the healing part, is it? You want to connect with the shaman's spirit. You want to—" my voice cuts out.

"See them." He finishes for me. Samuel opens his eyes, and this time when our eyes lock, I find determination and hope. "I need to know they're okay."

"Jesus," I murmur. "That's not a light brew. You need…" I stop myself and swallow any more words. Saying the truth out loud doesn't make it better. Samuel always intended on taking a strong tea, and the last time he took ayahuasca, I almost lost him. God knows what could've happened to his mind.

This changes the perspective of this holiday, and I'll

do everything to show him the Daintree is exactly what he needs because I can't risk losing him again.

🌴

Samuel and I spend the rest of the day with his parents. We head down to the beach for one last stroll before taking them to the airport.

The seagulls fly overhead, squawking in search of food scraps. The ocean breeze wraps around us like a silk blanket transporting us to her world where all we can see and smell is her. Nothing else matters when your feet touch the sand and salted air hits your senses. Like meditation, the unique sound of waves gently breaking along the shore caresses the mind. It's the best therapy and food for the soul, especially in summer. Children frolic in the water or ride the waves on boards. Parents sit under the shade, relaxing in their own way. Lovers are in the water, hugging, kissing, and being swept up by the ocean charm. We all lose ourselves in her.

"I don't want to leave," Caroline says to us. "It's been a wonderful seaside holiday, especially with you all."

"Well, you always have a place to come and stay for however long you wish," I tell her. "And if you want to retire here…" I wink. "I'm sure it can be arranged."

"Please don't give her ideas," Christopher says and chuckles. "I'll never get her to the airport."

"We'll miss you both." Samuel looks at his father then his mother. "You can visit anytime and see your granddaughter, or like Eden suggested, you could almost retire here. Return to LA when you need to for your visas."

"Talking about visas," his father adds. "I'm not sure

what you'll decide for your future regarding your medical training, but please be aware of the circumstances involving your work visa."

"I will. And I've already discussed a wedding with Eden. When we set a date, we'll let you know."

"Thank you, love." Caroline smiles at Christopher. "I'll need a mother-of-the-groom outfit."

"Mom." Samuel looks at his mother. "I'm considering a beach wedding."

"Oh." She ponders it for a minute. "Do you wear shoes?"

He chuckles. "I wouldn't recommend it on the sand for the ceremony. After, maybe."

Caroline nods slowly, taking it all in her classy stride.

The moment we arrive home after taking Samuel's parents to the airport, he retreats to the couch to take a nap. During Caroline and Christopher's time here, bridges were built and relationships mended. He wouldn't admit it after being independent for the past decade, but still, I think he's already missing them. Seeing him build a relationship with his parents warms my heart, and I hope he's finding some peace in his.

Rose curls up beside Samuel on the couch and, within five minutes, is also asleep.

I'm not one for daytime sleeps, so I head to the bedroom to find Gran's journal.

The last entry left me with an uneasy feeling in my stomach, so I want to be alone when I read what's to come.

52

IVY

February 11, 1965.

I'm beginning to feel human again.
I'm not sure I have enjoyed hearing the news of the world. It was certainly easier living in a bubble.
Maria witnessed my heart shattering into a million tiny pieces. Too many parts to heal. My heart will never be the same.
It's been weeks since my miscarriage, and I'm still grieving for my baby.
I was about to have two children with a man I loved, and now I'm returning to a man who misses me, only I'm not sure I'll ever receive the kind of love Weju gave me again.
Putting my emotions aside, I must decide in the next few days as the authorities said I need to return.
The cost of my health care is enough for me to leave the country.
I'm thankful Albert has met the government and insurance companies halfway.
Albert doesn't know where I have been living or my story. Only I survived by living amongst an indigenous community.
My mind reminds me of how close I came to death.
My heart misses Weju.

*Although after all these weeks of living in comfort, I know the
rainforest isn't the lifestyle I want.*

Maria warned me not to go back to Ulara.

*I made a promise, and I have to say goodbye to Weju. After all, he
saved my life. I remind her of my promise and that my passport
and belongings still remain there.*

*She waved her hand at me to forget those things as they can arrange
new ones. Only I don't want to wait weeks or months.*

*She told me I'd be stepping on dangerous ground and hoped I knew
what I was doing.*

Is a promise and saying goodbye to a man I have loved enough?

*After living with the Ularans and following their spirituality for
months, I know not to betray them now.*

March 12, 1965

Tomorrow, I board the ship for my long journey home.

*Last night I cried to Albert about how I can't wait to get home.
Only he didn't know the truth behind my tears.*

*I need to recount the past two weeks and address the pain I'm
suffering. I fear I'll never be the same woman again.*

*So this will be the last entry in this journal as it will forever be a
part of my life that has broken me.*

*The authorities and Maria escorted me back to Ulara. Maria told
them about the community and how they must never speak about it
again and never return.*

*The many hours we sailed along the river, she warned me of a bad
feeling.*

*I now wished I had listened and didn't act on the good faith of a
promise.*

*As though they were expecting us, the shaman, warriors, and Weju
were waiting on the riverbank. I had told him about the dangers of*

getting too close to outsiders and how they carry disease, so I was relieved when they were standing closer to the forest.

That alone made this visit problematic, and I knew I couldn't touch him even though my heart yearned to one more time.

When I disembarked the canoe, I held Dawn in my arms, and his face lit up. I told him he couldn't touch us as we were with the paranakyry, a word he understood as white people or Europeans.

Weju and the shaman's expressions hardened to anger.

Still, I didn't heed the warning.

I told him I'm still sick and need to leave but hope to return one day to see him.

The shaman then spoke with authority. He told Weju not to be angry. His wife—me— was always from another place. I never belonged in Ulara.

I sobbed and said it was untrue and how much I loved him.

The grief inside Weju surfaced, and I'll never forget the expression of my husband's tortured expression. A broken heart because he truly loved me.

And I had betrayed him.

My love wasn't enough to stay, and it was killing him in front of an audience.

His anger exploded, his eyes turned venomous. More warriors and the chief emerged from the trees. It was unusual behavior as I have rarely witnessed hostility among the Ularan people. His reaction shocked me into a panic.

I pleaded for my bag and belongings. To my surprise, Weju retreated to fetch them, except spears were raised, and Maria was begging me to leave. I asked her to wait until Weju returned.

Minutes seemed like hours.

On his return, his calmness fooled me.

He handed me my bag and then asked to hold Kaikare one last time.

My tears fall as I write this entry, and with every word I continue to write, I want to vomit, acknowledging my ignorance of the warnings Maria had shouted at me from the curiara. Warnings of offending their culture.

I was a fool for love.

I passed Kaikare to him so he could cuddle his daughter one last time, even though I knew of the infection risk. I couldn't deny him. He dropped the bag at my feet. When I bent to pick up the bag, Weju had taken his position beside the shaman. The shaman palmed Dawn's forehead and sang a song. Stupidly, I assumed it to be a blessing, and it gave me a minute to check inside my bag for my passport and other important belongings, including my camera. I was blind in understanding what the exchange meant.

Weju's expression hardened. He announced to all how Kaikare has medicine magic and can't leave the village. The shaman confirmed it. Her future was there, and she, too, will grow up to become a shaman.

Overwhelmed with hysteria, I begged for my baby.

Weju asked me again to stay.

Maria's voice was in the background telling me we must leave now as it's our last chance.

But I couldn't leave without Dawn, so I continued begging for my baby.

Weju held out his hand for me to come to him, and for a moment, I caught a glimpse of the love we shared, yet in those few seconds, he realized I wasn't going to change my mind, and the chief gave a command.

Spears lifted.

Maria shouted as the motor roared. I had one last chance to stay or go.

A warning arrow missed us. The next might not.

Leave without Dawn or stay.

I could get sick again. So could Dawn. I'm fresh out of surgery and can't bear more children.

Albert and Winston expect me to come home.

The authorities might not give me another chance if I stay.

Can I undo the damage I have already caused within the village?
My sobs were uncontrollable, and I couldn't hear myself think, yet
alone make a decision.
Until Maria yelled, "Ivy, now or never."
"Wait," I screamed.
Through my tears, I opened my bag and retrieved my decoupaged
mirror and pearls and held them out. No one made a move toward
me. So I placed them in the sand and backed away with my eyes
still on my daughter, knowing this was the last time I'll ever see
her. I climbed aboard the curiara, my heart shattering into a million
tiny pieces.
As the curiara reversed, the shaman strode to the river's edge. Like a
gatekeeper, he slammed his stick on the ground, and the beads and
bones attached at the top rattled in warning.
The ferocity in his eyes will stay with me forever. Then his
expression changed to fierce understanding. Not in pity, more that he
knew the ending of my story.
I'm reminding myself to breathe as I write this entry.
Even the months aboard the ship will not be enough to heal my
heart and wear a brave face for Albert.
I remind myself I have another family who's eagerly awaiting my
return.
Another family who loves me.
My broken heart can't be revealed as I could ruin a chance of
happiness with them.
Maria told me never to forget my daughter in my heart, but to my
family, I must never speak of her if I want to move on. Only
mention the hysterectomy and my baby died.
It's not a complete lie.
Only now, I mourn so much more.

March 23, 1965

I'm on the ship and in my quarters.

Out of the porthole, all I see is blue. For many months, green was the only color surrounding me.

Blue represents another chance at life.

Last night I dreamed about my two babies I have lost. Set in the future, Dawn was four and my baby, a boy I named Albert, Jr. was around two years of age, and they were playing in the rainforest. Then the rains came and along with it, sadness.

Did I have the mental or physical capacity to survive another rainy season with two children?

I'll never know.

Have I made the right choice leaving my husband and child for what many consider a better life?

What will my life become if Albert decides he no longer loves the woman I have become?

Will I ever forgive myself for the many bad decisions I have made to get me this far?

I should never have walked away from Albert and Winston to follow a stupid dream.

Because I'm no longer the same woman who left them all those years ago.

53

EDEN

Closing the journal, I curl up into a ball and allow the tears to flow down my cheeks. I keep swallowing the lump in the back of my throat, hoping to get control of the emotion soaring through me. My chest feels like it's been split open by an ax—a raw wound.

My dear grandmother…

I love her even more for what she went through, and respect explodes from my heart. Respect as she did live out her life the best way she could. I know Pops found out about her affair, and it led him to alcohol and eventually to become an alcoholic, but did he ever understand the position she was in and what she had to do to stay alive?

It's hard to imagine if you have never been deep in the heart of the Amazon rainforest. I'm still shocked by the hostility of the Ularans and wonder if it's why Weju exercised his right as a shaman with love, and if he promoted calmness in the people after the shellshock of Gran leaving him. He had Kaikare and eventually found peace and contentment in his life. He also connected with Gran's spirit during ayahuasca. Their spirits were reunited in another world, I know that now. I only hope she'd reconciled with Pop and found peace with the two men in her life.

Years ago, Mum mentioned how Gran had blessed me. It was a weird thing to say, and I can't help wondering if Gran possessed a sense of what my future held.

I take the journal and press it close to my heart, closing my eyes and visualizing Gran's smiling face. "I'll love you forever," I whisper.

The journal must remain in the family. Both journals do, and my family needs to read both. It will be hardest for Dad, as he remembers Gran's depression when he was a child and the arguments. He needs to know why, understand what Gran endured, and how his mother was a warrior.

Not crazy like people assumed.

"Are you okay?" Samuel sits on the bed. Rose is curled into his chest still half-asleep.

"I finished her journal," I murmur. "I'm still mulling over it all. Everything makes sense why Gran behaved the way she did when Dad was young and why Pop became an alcoholic. He was proud. I only wished he understood Gran better and shared some of that pride her way."

Samuel takes my hand and squeezes it. "Is it appropriate if I also read it?"

"I'd like you to as there are topics I need to discuss. And you can offer support when my family also reads it."

"Do you want me to read both before offering them to your family?"

"I think that's a good idea. And so you know, we're leaving for our holiday up north in a couple of weeks."

Samuel's expression softens as though he knows better than to argue with me.

He's not the only one desperate to reconnect with the rainforest. It's a place where I can feel closer to Gran.

🌴

Two days later, Samuel comes with me to say goodbye to Will. It feels strange ascending the stairs of our apartment complex when I used to do this several times a day.

"Do you mind if I stay for a bit, then leave?" Samuel asks before we enter the front door. "Michael messaged and wants to catch up since Yasmine is back at work."

"Sure. We're only going to hang out here for a few hours until it's time for Will to leave for the airport."

We open the door to cheering. Will runs to us, being chased by Faith's kids. "Look, it's Mowgli and Shanti." He points to Samuel and me. Faith's kids stop chasing him and stare at us.

"No, it's not. It's Aunty Eden and Sam," Sebastian corrects him. He continues to chase Will with James following and copying everything Seb does.

Rose squirms in Samuel's arms. "Did I hear him right?" he asks while lowering Rose to the floor so she can chase after them.

"Yep." I shake my head at Will.

"Stop." Will holds his arms out straight at Faith's boys. "We need to wait for King Louie." Rose tootles after them.

"Will," Samuel warns in a low deep voice.

"Just kidding, mate." Will chuckles, then jab steps

and sidesteps away from the kids as though he's on the football field.

Samuel and I sit with the family at the dining table. "Morning."

We join in the conversation about the upcoming Autralian Football League season. I don't add much, considering I haven't paid attention for years, and Samuel is clueless, still he listens attentively. "We need to go to a game," I whisper to him.

"We should all travel to Melbourne for a game," Dad adds. "And Will could come along."

Will pulls a seat up at the table.

"Enough," Faith says firmly when her boys jump on Will. "Excuse me. I'll amuse them for a bit so we can talk." Faith switches on the television, and the three kids sit in front of it, ready to watch *Pokémon*. Rose isn't familiar with it, yet she'll copy whatever her cousins do.

Faith takes her seat again. "When are you two heading to Cairns because I seriously want to come?"

Jake chuckles beside her. "With us or on your own?"

She rolls her eyes. "Do I need to answer that?"

I laugh at my sister. "In two weeks. I've booked the flights, and we're staying in a hotel for a few days, then with Dana in her holiday home near the rainforest." I glance at Samuel and smile. "It will be good for all of us."

"Exactly. It's why I want to come in your suitcase."

"We can go another time," Jake adds. "I know we haven't been on a family holiday for some time, so maybe it's something we could plan."

"We should all try and get up and see Dana," Dad says in a low voice. "Have to say I miss her bossing me around in the mornings."

Samuel's phone dings with a message. He reads it

and pops it back into his shorts pocket. "Excuse me. I'm meeting a friend." He stands and shakes Will's hand. "Have a good flight. I'm looking forward to seeing you in Melbourne and at a possible football game."

"Thanks, man. Look after my sis. And I'll deck you out in the right colors for the game." Will winks at him.

"Right colors are debatable," I quip. "Will and I don't root for the same team."

"Maybe I need to choose my own team," he jeers. I walk him to the door. "I'll see you at home. Say hello to Michael for me." I kiss him on the cheek and close the door behind him.

"I've mentioned to Dad about Gran's journal," I begin after I sit. "I know Will doesn't remember much about Gran." Will was only around eight years old when she died. "I've finished both journals and think you all should read them."

The air around the table changes with the silence except for squeaky kids' voices echoing from the television.

"It's important you all understand what she went through, as I don't believe Pop understood her trauma. If he'd read the journals, they may have experienced a better relationship. I'll let you be the judge." I stare at Mum and then Dad. "I have this heavy feeling in my heart that she suffered alone, and no one understood her except Brenda."

Dad nods his head slowly. "Frankly, I didn't want to relive any bad childhood memories or think of my father in a bad light. He did a great job caring for me."

"No one is arguing that, Dad. The point is Gran wasn't crazy."

Dad lowers his gaze to the table. There's anguish in his expression as though he's remembering his past. "If you believe it's something we need to understand, then I'll read them."

I let out a sigh. "I do. For everyone. We can chat about it after."

"I'm keen to read both journals." Faith smiles at me. "And I volunteer to go first."

"You should read them too," I say to Will. "I want you to know about our grandparents and how amazing they were."

"Honey, maybe you should find the box Gran left for you. It's been years since you opened it."

We're all staring at Mum. "What box?"

"Gran, gifted you all something." She smiles at Faith and Will. "You both received photographs and a few of her trinkets." I have stored them in my cupboard for when you're ready. You didn't want yours yet," she reminded Faith.

"How did I forget this?" Faith shakes her head. "Can I take it home today?"

"Of course." She smiles at Will. "I assumed you didn't want yours until you came home."

"What about Dad's box? What's in it?"

Mum glances at Dad, and she waits for him to answer my question.

Dad's thumb rubs at a spot on his opposite hand. He stares at his hands for a moment before looking at Mum. "I don't know," he admits. "The first time I opened it, some things brought back memories of my childhood. Mum rarely discussed my childhood because we all got on with life after I had you kids."

Mum gives him a nod to continue.

"After she passed, I received everything I needed, only the boxes included contents I'd never seen. She kept them hidden until after her death." His shoulders rise and fall as he takes some deep breaths. "It was like opening Pandora's box, and sad memories poured in. I stuck it in a cupboard until the right time."

"Dad," I murmur. "The time is right."

Dad gazes at Mum, his eyes begging for support. I've never witnessed this side of him. "It's okay, Winston. We can go through it when you're ready. Then you can share what you need to with everyone."

I swallow hard. Should I offer to go through it first and screen things for him? I need to know what's in the box and what he doesn't want to share with us.

"Please," I say gently. "No more secrets.

54

SAMUEL

The fresh sea air wafts around Samuel as he sits at an outside table near the Glenelg foreshore. It has a trendy vibe with its outdoor cafés. Many offer organic food, and yet he struggles to feel at home, even by the beach with the woman he loves. He'll stay and work and do everything he can to make his family work. Except the cost of his health has him second-guessing his decision. One trip to Peru could be life-changing for him.

Michael slides into a chair opposite him. "Sorry I'm late, mate."

They both chuckle at the way he says *mate*.

"Are you settling in okay?"

Michael grins. "I enjoy the laid-back lifestyle and how easily assessable everything is." He leans back in his chair and pushes some dark strands out of his eyes. "Yasmine is awesome, man. I'm not messing up this second chance."

"How long can you stay?"

"I'm still sorting visas and hope the accounting company I worked for can organize work for me here. Pass some regulations." He shrugs his shoulders. "If not,

I'll make the trips back and forth until I know Yas is in for the long haul, and we can make it official."

"Official?" Samuel chokes out. "I knew you wanted to give it a go, but are you seriously thinking of moving here?"

"We're not sure. Yas suggested she could spend some time in LA. She'll give anything a shot."

"I'm happy for you both, and it would be nice to have a friend here."

Michael taps the table as though he wants to say something. "You know you barely have time for your family yet alone our catchups."

Samuel eyes him carefully. "I hope it's not the case for the long term."

He juts out his chin. "You don't plan on staying in the medical field? Because we both know nothing will change in the future."

His friend knows him well. "I devised a two-year plan for Eden and Rose to have financial security if—"

"You're planning on leaving them?" he asks incredulously.

"If something happened to me," he finishes. "Or..." he shakes his head, not knowing how to answer Michael. To say it out loud sounds selfish. How does he explain if he can't live in society, if he's not cut out physically and mentally to cope, and he can't continue like this? It would leave him with no other choice than to leave Eden with family and return to nature. He doesn't plan on living like a recluse, yet short visits to see them he could cope with. He can't ask her to leave her family and friends to be with him. He's different, he acknowledges it, but how different is yet to be seen after his tests are completed. The investigations won't reveal anything he doesn't already know.

"It's a time thing."

"Right." Michael leans his elbows on the table and leans closer. "You're going to break her heart."

"Not as much as if I were dead."

Michael eyes him carefully. "So you'll work something out? You know she'll travel to the other side of the globe to be with you."

"I do, and it's why I won't ask it of her. She has the support of her family here… I'm not really a people fan."

Michael laughs. "Not people, man. You're not a fan of entitlement and arrogance in society. You're a great doctor, and it's because you care for people. You've got to give yourself more credit. And stop running away from the very thing that scares you." He reaches out and lightly pats Samuel's shoulder. "You have to give her the choice."

"If it comes to that, I would. It's why I need to go to Peru. It might be the answer to everything."

Michael opens his phone. "It might not be either. To be honest, I didn't gain much knowledge this time. I also wanted to be there for Yasmine and take care of her." He places his phone on the table. "I sent his number. If I can be frank, I'd be trying something else before rushing over there. If you don't get the answers you want, then what happens?"

Samuel hesitates because he doesn't want to consider his last option. *Leaving them.*

"What do you suggest?"

Michael raises both his hands defensively. "Hey, man, I'm not getting involved. But if it were me, I'd be seeking the advice of an indigenous healer. Ask around. Your doctor friends should know of someone."

"Funny, it's what my father suggested."

Michael grins. "Well, I'm starved. You want to get some food?"

🌴

Samuel walks the esplanade path and is surprised to see a message from Eden letting him know she's still at Monte apartments with her parents.

He takes the stairs and opens the door. Eden and her parents remain at the kitchen table and are deep in discussion.

"Is everything okay?"

Eden turns, wiping her red eyes. "Hey. We just got news."

His stomach tightens. "What happened?" He sits beside Eden and wraps an arm around her waist.

"Do you remember when I visited Brenda in the nursing home?" Samuel nods. "She passed away yesterday. Her brother-in-law called to let Mum know and to also tell her they found some photos in her belongings they suspected belonged to Gran."

Samuel looks to her father. His expression sags. Grace gives him a nod. "There are photos of a baby." Grace wipes a tear from her eyes. "We have so much history we never knew about, and it's hard to take it all in."

"Samuel," Eden says and touches his leg. "I told Dad about the baby Gran lost and how Kaikare ended up in Ulara. It's so sad to know how everything would have turned out if Gran didn't return to say goodbye to the shaman."

"What if..." Samuel murmurs, "... is one of the hardest things to accept in life."

He lives with speculation every day.

55

EDEN

Brenda's wake is small and intimate.

Mum is by my side under the shade of a gum tree near the door of a small service room in the same gardens where she's buried. Garden, I repeat, not cemetery—it's an ugly word in my head.

Gran and Pop were cremated and had asked for their remains to be released over the ocean near Monte Hotels, an ocean where they'd spent their lives pondering decisions and life choices. A place where we all connected as a family. Later, we celebrated Gran's life at the apartment with her close friends and our family.

I recall Brenda wearing red shoes when she attended Gran's funeral. It's the one thing that stuck in my mind. Another woman commented it was disrespectful and a sign of a festive vibe, not sadness. Brenda agreed and said to Mum it's how she remembered her friend and their good times together. She was celebrating Ivy's life.

I down the last of the champagne in my crystal flute.

"Would you like another?"

"I think I do."

"Come on," Mum urges. "We should go inside and give our condolences to the family."

"The last time I visited Brenda, she thought I was Gran. She said a few things to me as though she was reliving old times."

"Did she tell you anything believable?" Mum takes my flute, places it on the table, and grabs two more.

"Little things like Albert will come around. And I shouldn't feel guilty. I had a wonderful adventure. I'm not sure *almost dying* classifies as that, but she understood Gran and supported her one hundred percent."

"Here's to Brenda." Mum clinks my glass. She turns to a photograph propped on a stand of a younger Brenda as a nurse. "Their friendship was special."

"It's final, you know. A door for more information has closed."

"Oh, honey." Mum wraps an arm around my waist and pulls me closer. "Not closed. Brenda had Alzheimer's, and some of what she told you might not be true. Besides, your father is yet to open his box. He will. And Thomas is yet to give me the photos Brenda kept." Mum downs her champagne like a pro and takes my hand. "Let's speak to Thomas."

I wave at the staff I recognize from the nursing home before standing in the outer circle of Brenda's family. I assume some are children and grandchildren, and others might be related to her late husband.

Thomas comes to stand by Mum. "Thank you for coming," he says to both of us. He has aged since I last saw him. Maybe I didn't notice his gray hair until today.

"We're thankful for the invite." I let go of Mum's arm.

"I don't have the photos on me, although I can swing by your home and drop them off tomorrow."

Mum glances at me. "That would be great. Eden and I will be there." Mum gives Thomas a hug, and we say our goodbyes.

"You and I should both be there," she whispers. "Before your father has a breakdown if the photos are of Dawn."

🌴

Photos of Kaikare as a toddler fan out over the kitchen table.

There are patches of red where the images have faded, yet it doesn't take away from the enormity of seeing these for the first time. Gran captured moments of her crawling with the jungle as a backdrop and another of her sitting on the hammock, with her smile lighting up her little face framed by dark hair.

Ivy is written in cursive on the back of each image.

Mum places a picture of her as a baby, maybe a few months old, on the table, and she keeps staring at it.

"What is it?"

Mum glances up. "I can see features that remind me of you as a child."

"Really?"

She nods yet doesn't say anything.

I pick up the image of the shaman—Weju. He didn't know she was taking a shot. He was a handsome man—a sculpted jaw, high cheekbones, and dark hair to his shoulders, wearing a short, woven skirt hanging from his hips, his bare muscular chest and arms on display. He was looking up, which gave Gran time to take the picture from, I assume, her hut, yet I can see a gentleness in his eyes.

One image confused me as it was a group

photograph. Gran held Kaikare in her arms, the shaman beside her, and other Ularans stood next to them.

"They don't like objects from our world, yet someone took the group photo." I show Mum the image. "I guess they didn't know what it did, so it was like a hard box to them that made clicky sounds."

"Why do you say that?"

"Because they wanted to burn her journal and pen, believing the pen was bad magic."

"I see." She holds the photograph closer. "This is like the one she left for you."

In my beautiful engraved wooden box, the images included herself and a similar group one, only it was taken further back and hard to identify anyone. This picture is closer so she must have asked the person to come forward. Thankfully, whoever peered through the lens wasn't spooked.

I pick up another image. "We're lucky to have these."

"We are," Mum murmurs, still engrossed in the photograph she's holding.

"Do you think Pop found them? Or is it why Gran gave them to Brenda for safekeeping?"

"If Gran had lived longer, I believe she'd have told us about Dawn. Only at the time of her sudden death, your father wasn't ready."

"Is he ready now?"

"It's hard for him as he feels a sense of responsibility to help Dawn now he knows Samuel tried to keep them safe."

"He can't," I emphasize. "He'd never find her, and she's with the only family she knows."

"He said he regrets not meeting his sister, and if given a chance, he'd do it."

Wow.

"That's a beautiful thing," I say gently. "But it might never happen."

"No. I'll sit with him while he goes through the photos and then keep them somewhere safe."

"Has he had a chance to look at his box?"

"No, love. We can't force him. He wants to know more about his mother and Dawn, but it's affecting him more than he's saying. Your father is a strong man, and when he allows emotions to break him, he often falls sick for weeks. When I see the signs, I protect him by spacing out whatever is causing him stress. It's why I'm not pushing him. The photos are enough for now."

56

EDEN

Ten Days Later…

Samuel smiles as we sit at the base of a waterfall in the Daintree rainforest. He dives into the waterhole and surfaces, waving for Rose and me to join him. "It's too cold," I call out after dipping my toes in the freshwater.

Four days into our holiday, we have bathed in the cultural experience of North Queensland. While Dana works, we have snorkeled the Great Barrier Reef and traveled to Mossman Gorge, to fast-moving streams, and found organic cafés with tropical fruit that agrees with him. He's booked an Indigenous tour, a guided walk through the rainforest, and to learn about the medicinal plants. He can't contain his excitement.

"You know there could be crocs in the water," I call out to him.

He chuckles. Other people are swimming closer to the falls. It's unlikely crocs are in this part of the stream.

He wraps a towel around his waist then lifts Rose to his hip. He stops and points to a spider web. "Look, spider." I shudder at the sheer size—bigger than my palm—yet he's undeterred.

"Gross," I remark.

"They remain in the trees," he says as though spiders have never bothered him. They didn't in Ulara, but in the city, it's another matter. It doesn't make sense, yet I know this is where he thrives, so it's natural for his anxiety to subside.

By the time we arrive back at Dana's apartment, she has finished work for the day. We talk about our adventures, then head to bed, ready to do it all again tomorrow.

The following day, Samuel decides to do the indigenous tour alone. He borrows Dana's car, and it gives us time to catch up.

"Fishy pool. Fishy pool," Rose says in excitement.

"Yes, sweetie. We'll take you to the fishy pool." The kids swimming lagoon is on the Cairns esplanade. Large metal fish sculptures rise from the water and is something Rose identified with the pool.

Dana and I take a stroll with Rose to the esplanade lagoon. We sit with our feet in the shallow water while Rose splashes about to cool down.

I tell Dana about Gran's journal, how she came to be in Ulara, and why she was depressed at times. "I identify with Dawn as Kaikare. Mum and Dad like to call her Dawn, as it's the name Gran gave her. While in the village and knowing her personally, it's what I called her."

Dana adjusts a cap over her eyes. "And the photos?"

"We'll have the photos restored." I peer up at the fluffy white clouds in a blue sky. The humidity is extreme, and even Rose has adapted. She screams as she runs, falls in the ankle-deep water, then giggles to herself. I laugh at Rose's antics and imagine myself living here until my thoughts drift to my family and friends. My father...

"I worry about Dad. At first, he didn't want to know about the jungle. Then he accepted it all and wanted to know more, especially about Kaikare. Now he's guilt ridden about Gran. A complete misunderstanding and the secrets didn't help."

"Your Gran had a kind heart. She'd come into the office to say hi and see Winston. She'd take you girls out for the day when Grace cared for Will."

"It must have been when she took us to visit Brenda. At least she had a friend to confide in and not judge her."

"We all need friends like Brenda. I have one, only she lives in Bali. Thank God for FaceTime. Her photos are what inspired me to live in the tropics."

"Lucy?"

Dana nods. "She reminds me of Yasmine. All worldly and spiritual and looks at everything with positivity."

"I feel like I know her already," I joke.

"We should get this little one out of the sun." Dana scoops Rose from the water, and she kicks her legs in protest. She kisses her cheek. "You're like your mum. But Aunty Dana needs to go home and finish packing as we're taking you to the jungle."

I laugh. "It's not really the jungle."

"It's as close to it as I'm going to get."

Samuel is quiet when he arrives home.

"How was it?" I ask when we're alone.

"Incredible. I'm still processing everything he told me. I might need to document some points he suggested."

"Sure. We're packed and need to get our bags in the car."

"I'll tell you about it later." Samuel sits on the end of the bed with a notebook and writes frantically as though his pen can't keep up with his trail of thoughts. It's a déjà vu moment from Ulara. He still likes to use a notepad over the computer.

The drive to the Daintree was as picturesque as I imagined. We lined up to get the cars on a ferry to cross a river. Then we followed a narrow road lined with palm trees and thick shrubbery, and I knew we were close. We stopped to get biodynamic organic ice cream, and the flavors were amazing.

Dana and Samuel point out the window telling Rose to keep watch for a cassowary. We turn off a side road and drive up a long driveaway fenced in by the rainforest. All I can see is green with the occasional pop of color of heliconia flowers and pink-leafed plants. Kerry parks the car under the house.

"We're here," Dana announces.

My phone rings, and I almost don't answer it as I'm excited to explore the house. Only it's Amy.

"Hey, Amy."

"Edes."

Something is off with her tone and my thoughts race to Ethan, but I rein in any accusations.

"Is everything okay?"

"No. I've been in a car accident."

"What?" I gasp.

"I'm okay. A few broken bones, that's all. Ethan is fine apart from whiplash."

"Oh, honey. What do you mean a few broken bones?"

Samuel stares, waiting to see if she's okay. I mouth for him to go inside with Rose.

"A few cracked ribs and a broken collarbone."

"Not a fun way to spend your holiday break, babe."

"No." She bursts into tears. "The other driver died at the scene. It was awful."

"Oh, honey. I'm sorry."

"I keep seeing her face. Apparently, she suffered a heart attack and crashed into us. I can't stop seeing her bloodied face."

I peer toward the house. I want to be here with Samuel, only I hate hearing my friend sound distressed. "I can come home. If you need a friend, I'll be there."

"It's okay," she sobs. "Ethan is here with me, and Yasmine is checking in. I'll see you when you come home in a week."

"Are you sure, Amy? Because if you want me to come home, I will."

"No. I'm fine. I might need to call, okay? Because you're the one I talk to when life is hard."

My chest tightens. "Call anytime, Ames. I love you, and I'll be home soon to give you a hug."

I end the call.

For years, my tight circle of friends has supported each other.

Standing on the elevated driveway, I stare out at the ocean bordered by the rainforest. There is something magical about this place. There's an energy surrounding us, pulling us closer to the rainforest's heart. A similar sensation I felt in Ulara with Samuel.

Maybe it's calling to him.

To us.

Amy's phone call highlights the important people I'll be leaving. Can I leave my family and friends?

57

SAMUEL

After an extensive tour of the grounds, Kerry and Dana retreat to their room, leaving Samuel alone with Eden. Eden unpacks their case and smiles at him.

"It's certainly a beautiful place. Almost enchanting." She moves her case aside, and he senses her watching him.

"Enchanted, yes. I felt something similar on the indigenous tour… a magnetic energy drawing me to the forest."

Her eyes widen. "You enjoyed it?"

He takes a deep breath. "I resonated more than I thought possible. Even from the beginning, there was a smoking ceremony, and we focused on leaving bad thoughts outside the forest."

Eden sits on the bed and gazes at him. "Tell me about it."

"The poisonous plants appear the same as the non-poisonous varieties, including figs. And creeper vines… if you touch them, you can break out in blisters. I'll be educating you in your own country," he jokes.

"Now you're showing off." She pats the space beside

her on the bed. "Would you remember the plants if you saw them again?"

"Maybe some. The more I think about it, the more I'd like to learn the ways of the forest up here."

"What are you saying? Do you want to have a holiday house here?"

He's aware of how much Eden wants him to like this place as she sees it as the answer to him not taking ayahuasca. He's not convinced. Yet. "I'll let you know after a few days." Samuel takes her face in his hands and kisses her gently. "Thank you for bringing me here."

"It wasn't all for you." Eden winks at him. "I also wanted to come and visit Dana. Anyway, what was your favorite part of the tour?"

"The edible wild fruits and medicinal plants. Some of the kernels can be ground to a flour consistency to make bread." He shakes his head as though he's clearing his thoughts. "Even the sap of certain trees can be used to treat fever. I'd enjoy a night walk to observe the bioluminescence of the fungi growing on the plants. It might transport me to some happier times." He places a hand on my thigh and squeezes it. "Although I'd want to check out a path first to ensure there were no harmful plants in the area. The guide mentioned fine hairs on one of the heart-shaped leaves stinging plants having the effect of glass, and the pain can last from weeks to months." Hearing his own words, he has resonated with the Daintree rainforest more than he lets on.

"Oh." Eden averts her gaze. "I'd have to be watching Rose twenty-four-seven."

"Eden." He waits for her to meet his gaze. "If we were here, I'd do routine checks to ensure the forest around us was relatively safe."

She bites her lip. "Apart from the creatures because you can't control them."

He looks out the window to the sky-blue ocean. "Or Mother Nature, and we'd have a rainy season of different proportions here."

"Meaning?"

"Cyclones. There's no evading Mother Nature even in paradise."

A storm Samuel has weathered before.

He can't deny the energy swirling inside him, ready to meet his problems with new insight he has gained from the tour. Not only about the medicinal plants but how to use the strength of his mind when dreaming and to think about his memories in a different light before falling asleep.

To reset his brain and way of thinking through memories in his dreams.

The brain is powerful.

If his new friend is right, maybe he has the force to not only weather the storm but to become the storm.

58

EDEN

One Month Later…

My experience in the jungle has taught me how fate tests the balance of life and to never become complacent.

It's hard not to be when every morning I open my eyes, and I wish for nothing more than what I have in front of me.

With Rose and Samuel by my side, I flourish effortlessly. The three of us together is my ultimate happiness.

Eudaimonia.

After arriving home, I made Samuel a promise. A beach wedding. My only condition, we wait until he's *happy*.

He has to find a new job that agrees with his health and become physically and spiritually happy.

Money or material things don't buy happiness. It's why he loved Ulara. And I have faith he can find the same inner peace without traveling to Peru to take ayahuasca.

Already, the nightmares have subsided.

He's dreaming more about Kaikare and his friends. What they're doing in their new home. I suggested he could be connecting with Kaikaire in his dreams.

Because anything is possible.

Samuel walks into the room after receiving a phone call.

"You'll never guess who called."

"Who?" I ask impatiently.

"Dr. Mundy. He wants me to be part of a project in the rainforest finding medicinal properties in the unique plants of the Daintree."

I throw my arms around his neck and kiss him hard. "All you had to do was ask the universe. If it's meant to be, then it will happen."

"Like magic?" he mocks.

"No. Like fate." I kiss him again.

"Ah." He glances down at me and grins. "Like you coming into my life."

"You're right. No point fighting it. I'm destined to be with you forever."

"Forever isn't long enough," he whispers against my lips. "I have no intention of fighting fate."

"Your best decision yet, Dr. McMahon." He leans and pulls me close to his body, the warmth radiating from him surrounds me like a calming blanket. He kisses me slow and meaningful, passionate yet gentle.

"Thank you for fighting for me," he whispers against my lips.

I pull back and stare into those blue eyes filled with love and contentment, and hold his beautiful face in my hands. "Honey, I knew from that first moment we were destined to be together. Nothing and no one will take you away from me."

He leans his forehead against mine and closes his

eyes. "I'm ashamed to admit for a while, I thought I wasn't going to make it. Contemplated leaving and—"

I smother his words in a kiss.

Words I don't want to hear as I knew what Samuel was feeling.

He struggles to survive in society, and he didn't want to ask me to leave my family and friends when inside he was slowly dying.

I could see it.

I'm even more determined for a new life for both of us.

After all, I have the courage of my grandmother inside me.

For even fate has no idea what I would do or how far I would go for love.

EPILOGUE

EDEN

Ten Months Later…

Before I lock the door, I eye the huntsman spider in the corner of the kitchen ceiling.

"Keep the mosquitos and flies under control while we're gone, please, George."

"Bye, George," Rose says as though he's a pet. With a *Bluey* bag slung over her shoulder, she toddles out the door. Everything on our front deck is packed safely away in time for the wet season. I gaze out over the green forest canopy to the ocean meeting the horizon. I'm going to miss this view.

Disappointment dissipates in seconds with my body overheating in the extreme humidity. I take Rose's hand as we amble down the steps toward the car.

I head south along a road with walls of rainforest on either side until a queue of cars brings me to a stop.

After showing my pass, I press the car window button to shut out the heat. With the sun sitting directly above us, there's no shade from the towering trees.

Putting the car in drive, we crawl forward until we're on the ferry, ready to cross the river.

From the back car seat, Rose eyes the water eagerly, searching for a crocodile sunning on the muddy banks. It's a game we play—the first one to find a croc. We have only spotted a small crocodile twice over the past few months, unlike 'Mo,' the resident crocodile near Port Douglas that captures tourists' attention as they cross the Mowbray River Bridge on the outskirts of the town.

"There." Rose points to her left.

I follow her gaze. "No, honey, it's a log."

She sighs in disappointment.

"Maybe next time."

It's extraordinary how my daughter is excited to see a crocodile. Over the months, she has become accustomed to a place many consider has the most-deadliest creatures on the planet. We have learned what's dangerous and what not to do, like swimming in the ocean in the summer months. The deadly Irukandji and box jellyfish bloom from around November to May, so if you're not looking out for a crocodile, the smaller creatures are a threat.

Thankfully, we have a swimming pool in the house we bought a few doors down from Dana's holiday home. And as for snakes, thankfully, I've only witnessed pythons in the garden.

Many things here remind me of Gran and my time in Ulara.

"I'm hun-gy," Rose moans.

I meet her blue eyes in the review mirror. At two years of age, she's a mini version of Samuel, although her eyes are bluer and more like mine.

"Seriously? We have not long left, and your snacks are for the plane."

She huffs and folds her arms. "Yes, sewios-ly."

I can't wait for the sassy two-year-old stage to end.

"Mooksy might have some wild figs for you to eat."

"Yuck."

I hide a smirk at her expressing the distaste of bush food. I imagine, over time, it will change with her father's encouragement and passion.

I press the button for my Spotify list to play a song list, especially for Rose, and it distracts her long enough until we reach Mossman.

Driving through the parking lot past rows of four-wheel drives, vans, and motorhomes, I stop in the staff zone. The gateway to the Daintree Rainforest. People visit here to learn about the culture of the Australian indigenous people and come from all over the world to experience the Dreamtime Walks. Among the trees boasts the biggest conifers in the world, almost as large as the statue of liberty.

Rose and I meander through the center and wave to the staff before heading outside to the bus waiting area. A group of tourists circle a guide. They listen intently to the guide talk about the plants and how they can treat certain diseases. Questions are answered with respect to the indigenous way of life and include his extensive medical knowledge. The guide with messy blond hair isn't indigenous but has studied and learned from the leaders here, and I'm proud how he's passionate about their culture.

The rainforest has much to offer us all.

"If you have further questions, please see Mooksy inside the center," Samuel says to the group. The circle breaks apart. A smile lights up his face as he shares a joke with one of the tourists. Samuel's cheeks are fuller, his body more muscular. His energy has returned, and so has his zest for life.

My chest expands with pride.

My heart is full.

Samuel raises a tanned arm and comes to join Rose and me. He lifts Rose into the air and plants a kiss on her cheek before taking my hand and leaning in for a kiss. He pulls me close to his body, our tongues entwine, and my insides flutter as warmth fills me with his lingering kiss.

"I've missed you," he murmurs against my lips.

"Eww." Rose squirms to get down.

He lowers her to the ground and takes her hand. "Are you excited to visit Nanna and Pop?"

"Yes, and my c'usins. I want to play on the beach," Rose says in a higher pitch.

"We'll have months of beach fun," I add. I hand Samuel a bag with a change of clothes from his khaki shorts and shirt. "We'll wait in the car while you change."

"Before I forget, I received a call from Asoo. He wants to bring his family out for a visit. I told him I could help pay for flights, after all he did for me in Ulara."

"Oh honey, that's wonderful news." He leans and kisses me on the lips, slow and enticing. "Go, and change," I murmur, breaking the kiss. He gives me a quick peck on the cheek before striding toward the office.

"He's takin' for-eva," Rose complains.

"We have time before the plane departs. And we're saying goodbye to Aunty Dana first."

One Day Later…

We stayed up late last night celebrating our return with the family. Even Amy and Yasmine popped in to see me. Apart from our time at the beach, the day has been about relaxing in our home on the esplanade.

We have committed to living in the Daintree from May to early December. Samuel works at the cultural center, teaching about the benefits of the rainforest. From mid-December to early May, we return to Adelaide, to our beachside home, where we can enjoy the dry summer months by the ocean while avoiding North Queensland's wet season. Since summer is Monte Hotel's busiest months, I help in the office three days a week while Samuel takes care of Rose.

Mum and Dad arrive, and I pour us a glass of wine before dinner. We share the stories of our new life, and then they talk to us about Gran's journal.

"I want to feel closer to my mother," Dad confesses. "After reading her journal, I found the box she left for me. There was another journal where she documented notes about Dawn and her memories of being in Ulara. Most were sad entries, but it's triggered an enormous amount of guilt. I wish I knew before."

Mum lays a gentle hand on Dad's shoulder, and I sense there's more to say.

"If there is a chance to meet my sister, then I want to try."

Samuel stares wide-eyed at my father. "Sir, I-I…" he stutters.

"Samuel isn't sure where they are?" I interject. "And it might not be safe."

"I could get a message to the nearby missionaries." He shrugs.

We both know it's risky to go into the jungle after getting his health back to some normality.

I have fought for his happiness so we can be *free*.

"You know how we talked about setting up a fundraiser?" Samuel rubs my thigh, and I know it's to calm me.

"Yes, but…"

"The missionaries close to where I left the Ularans welcome volunteers. I'm sure they'd be grateful for monetary donations or unwanted pharmaceutical products." He smiles at me. "I can't promise anything, although it might be a way to find Kaikare. She'd want to see you again and meet her brother."

"Oh, honey, I'll do anything to help," Mum adds. "I could help with the administration and set up of the account while you focus on marketing. We'd like to contribute to Dawn's community."

"Your friend, Rhett, has already offered to sponsor." He kisses my cheek. "It might be the answer to uniting your family."

"It's your family too," I say warmly.

"We can only try." Pride oozes from Dad. "Because it's what families do. My mother was brave, and I want to honor her memory and show the same courage in finding my sister."

I take Samuel's hand and gently squeeze. "Only if there's no danger to anyone."

"I'll get correspondence to Dr. Jacques. It's all I can do for now."

My father once thought of Gran as *wild*.

Brave and wild, maybe.

And he wants to venture on the same path as Gran to find answers. Maybe it is our destiny.

I glance around the table at my family.

Then to the man who is my world.

The man I once thought to also be wild.

To me, he will always be *perfectly wild*.

~

Thank you for reading Eden and Samuel's story. I hope you enjoyed it as much as I did writing their love story.

For any news on spin off books connected to the Beautifully Wild Trilogy please sign up to my newsletter email.
If you would like to read more of my stories keep reading for details.

Thank you again for reading the Beautifully Wild series. After many years of writing, this story is close to my heart.

ALSO BY LEESA BOW

THE HENDRICKS BILLIONAIRES

The Wrong Proposal #1

The Wrong Move #2

The Wrong Promise #3

The Wrong Time #4

Beautifully Wild Series

Beautifully Wild

Hopelessly Wild

Perfectly Wild

WILD BOXSET

The Player Series

Winning the Player

Winning the Game

Playing for Time

Caught Out Series

Jardine

Caught Out

Standalones

Charming the Outback

www.leesabow.com

ACKNOWLEDGMENTS

Twelve years is a long time to write a story, and there are many people to thank during this time.

First and foremost, to my husband, Lynden. Thank you for your encouragement, love, and support of my writing journey.

To my four beautiful daughters, Jamie-Lee, Shauni, Ashleigh, and Demi, for providing constant inspiration. To my wonderful parents, Pam and Vic, and my sister, Vickie, and her family for believing in me and helping in any way possible. A big shout-out to my friends and biggest fans. Mum, Deanne, and Helen, Dayna, and Alison for believing in me from the day I decided to give authoring a shot. Your love for my story gave me the confidence to take a giant step forward.

To Marilyn, Juls and Tracey, and all my friends, including the basketball and football communities, Sacred Heart community, my nursing friends (the Mudgettes), and my Nestle crew, who have been by our sides from the beginning while I wrote this story from my heart. You have witnessed the story of Ulara evolve from a dream to a reality, and I'm thankful every day for your support and patience. Especially during one of the toughest times of our lives.

To Kaylene Osborn at Swish Design and Editing. Thank you for all your expertise, for answering endless questions, and for making my book shine. You are my rock! And a big thank you to Nicki!

To Letitia Hasser at RBA Designs, thank you for my beautiful cover.

My appreciation extends to my Facebook reader group, Leesa Bow's Lovelies, and all the blogging community for helping to get my book out to the world. You all make the book world a much better place. A special thank you to Ena at Enticing Journey Book Promotions and all the blogs and bookstagrammers for promoting Beautifully Wild.

To my author friends, who I've chatted with while writing this book. You have been with me from the day I decided I wanted to publish my story. I can't express enough gratitude for all your advice and inspiration. To Nina, Maggie, Jen, Beth, KE, and Jodi you always have my back, and I appreciate you all! To Yon author group, and all the authors whom I've met at retreats and at signings, you are my writing family.

To Carol, Kellie, Robyn, Jen, and Megan, thank you for beta reading my story and helping me refine it. You are all awesome. And to Adriana for helping me with the Brazilian terms. And to Carla for all the information about Venezuela.

To my doctor friends who answered my medical questions. Thank you to Professor Roxby, and Dr Tolley. You have characters named after you!

To my readers. Thank you for your endless support, and most of all, for loving my stories. Some of you have been with me from the start of my author journey, and to others, I'm a new author. What I love most is you all embrace my characters and stories and love them as much as I do. Thank you for reading, reviewing, and talking about my books to your families and friends in book clubs and blogs.

I appreciate everything you do for me!

My appreciation extends to my friends Donna and Geoff, for showing me the beauty of North Queensland, and the Daintree Rainforest.

Finally, to my daughter, Shauni, and the special teenagers and parents, we met at the Royal Adelaide Children's Hospital—Gina and Jenna, Michael and Sue, Will and Sherie, and Shauni's oncologist, Dr. Tapp. Thank you for your friendship and for showing me what it is to truly embrace fear. Your strength is admirable, and I'll never forget the bond, the support, and love when faced with the battle of cancer. To all the children in the oncology wards around the world, some of you now live in the stars, but you are never forgotten. You are forever the real heroes of the world.

ABOUT THE AUTHOR

Best selling Australian author, Leesa Bow writes alphas with a fierce determination to win, and the women who will push for them to fight harder. She is known for her steamy sports romance and her latest adventure romance.

Leesa lives in sunny Queensland, Australia. She spends her spare time with her family, and catching up with girlfriends for coffee or a wine.

Leesa loves to keep fit with pilates, and yoga, and keeping the fun with laughter in her life.

She loves nothing more than to curl up with a good book, and a glass of South Australian wine.

www.ingramcontent.com/pod-product-compliance
Lightning Source LLC
Chambersburg PA
CBHW060819120726
47909CB00006B/1993